Tales From the City of Bathos

Escape

from

Devil's Head

Joel Jenkins

Escape from Devil's Head

Dedicated to Damon Orrell whose enthusiasm
and artistic skill helped bring the City of Bathos to life.

Introduction:
The City in Darkness

You can cover a lot of miles in the darkness. And there are a hundred thousand directions to ride in, but they always lead to the city.

Whether it's called Lankhmar, Sanctuary, Tanelorn, Ambergris or New Crobuzon, all roads lead to the city in the darkness. In Joel Jenkins' stirring dark fantasy epic, Through the Groaning Earth, that city is Bathos. Bathos the savage. Bathos the corrupt. Bathos of the guilds.

It is a facet of a dark crystal, one of an infinite number of decadently beautiful iterations of the Ur-city. The remorseless urban sprawl that carries humanity into darker, deeper depths. Gods roam its streets, but like the Gods Of Lankhmar or the Graycaps of Ambergris, they are foul things, not in the least anthropomorphic. They are Lovecraft's Gods, crawling out of the secret bowers of Lost Leng and icy Kadath, dripping through convoluted streets like ichors in an alembic. Monsters from the stars, trapped beneath cramped streets.

But these nightmares are as babes before the wolves in human clothing that compete with them for territory within these pages. The tropes and archetypes jumble and intermingle, coming out wrong-footed and fittingly savage. There are no heroes in Bathos but there is heroism, though it's of a world-weary Chandleristic variety. Men and women forced into brute combat with a hostile world, trapped in the belly of a stone beast, fighting to not be digested by the City that at once shelters them and damns them.

That is the story of Bathos.

-Joshua Reynolds

Prologue:

The smoke of burning incense writhed thick into the air, gathering in the gloom over the glowing brass braziers that lit the chamber with a hellish glow. Thirteen men sat in assemblage around the polished table, each eyeing the others with well-founded suspicions and lurking hatred.

The ancient guild master rose at the head of the table. A fine white beard spilled down his silken tunic, almost obscuring the golden symbol that he wore on a chain around his wrinkled neck. For the hundredth time he consulted the parchment in front of him, then his voice boomed out, surprisingly strong and resilient.

"Twenty two of the Thieves Guild slain and seven wounded, forty six of the Warriors Guild slain and thirty three wounded, the third in command of the Warriors Guild nearly decapitated, and at the East Gate of Old Bathos seven dead guards." He paused and looked at each man around the table with piercing eyes. "These numbers might be acceptable if we were fighting a war, but against one renegade with a dual membership in the Warrior and Thieves Guild and one rogue assassin these are hardly acceptable figures. In point of fact, this incident is an embarrassment to our guilds."

The Guild Master halted his speech, and silence reigned in the shadow-spun spaces of the room. Only the crackle of the burning incense broke the quiet.

In one bony fist the guildmaster held up thirteen straws. "To save face, someone must be blamed for this horrible blotch upon our records. Someone will die- and it will be one of you. Who will draw the first straw?"

Part One:
Escape from Devil's Head

Cadryn Ironthew's mighty seven-foot tall frame tottered. He clutched at the axe protruding from his chest, and scarlet threads of blood rolled from his mouth as he crashed amid the splintered bones, and gnawed skulls that littered the cold stone floor of the shunned temple at Devil's Head Peak.

His killer dodged away, coal black cloak and hair flowing behind him as quick footsteps carried him between the altar and the ominous visage of Vlad the Dark, which was carved out of black living stone, and rose to the height of the cavernous temple chamber that existed within the very peaks of the Skeltor Mountains.

Sedrah drew back her thin stiletto blade, and slipped away from the edge of the altar behind which their foe had ducked. For a moment she was tempted to reach out and grab the Broach of Baal from among the rotting red velvet scraps of the tray that protruded from the altar, but she knew that to linger would mean death.

It was obvious, now, that Lothar was a man to be reckoned with. The Assassins Guild had maligned his abilities and told the four of them that he would be easy to kill. They called him a penny-ante thief and wastrel, but any assassin worth her salt knew that she should never underestimate her target. Sedrah had carefully set the trap, but some intuition had warned Lothar of the danger, and her strike to kill had been avoided.

Now Cadryn Ironthew was dead, and their numbers were whittled from four to three. Hawk-nosed and eyes gleaming ferally in the dim guttering of the red torchlight, Hastur Slingblade stood to her right, sword in hand, an imposing warrior that stood a head taller than she.

Standing ten feet to Sedrah's left was Adryl. He was a knife man, and a phalanx of throwing daggers were arrayed across his bandoliered chest. He was a foot shorter than Sedrah, and as he raised a knife to his ear, the bone and sinew jutted from his pole-skinny arm. Despite his unforbidding stature, his reputation steered all but the most foolhardy of men away from him. At one time a drunk sailor attempted to pick a fight, and Adryl had put a knife in the man's eye from twenty feet away.

Lothar shouted something from behind the altar, and Hastur made a snickering response, but Sedrah didn't hear what they were saying. Her keen ears began to pick up other, more sinister, sounds within the dark recesses of the vast hall; a strange hum that was at the edge of her hearing, accompanied by a clicking that was reminiscent of a dog's nails on the cobbles of a city street.

Suddenly Hastur's ears caught the sound, and he was jarred from his sneering conversation. "Did you hear that?" he asked, concern and fear growing on his face.

Sedrah surveyed the massive piles of bone that reared up about them on all sides. They extended as far as her eye could see into the dim tenebre that licked out its inky tendrils, held in abeyance only by the flickering of the smoky torches. She cried out as a mottled gray palm, clawed with five sharp talons reached up over the summit of the nearest bone pile. In a moment the creature hove into sight, its four furry arms spread out to balance on the precarious pile of skull and ribs while it leaned back on its haunches and examined the three intruders below with baleful eyes. The visage of the creature resembled that of a monkey, but long, yellowed incisors hinted at a beast that was far from docile, and a meat eater- not an herbivore.

Breaking her eyes away from the evil creature's gaze, Sedrah let her sight drift across the crests of the bone piles around them, and found that the beast was not alone. They came by the hundreds, licking their chops with pale gray tongues, and letting out fearful screeches that echoed impending doom to the intruders.

As if of one mind, they suddenly charged. Leaping from their vantage points, or streaming through the narrow paths between heaps of human remains. One creature leaped upon Adryl's back, howling and clawing at the knife thrower's chest. As flesh tore away, Adryl frantically struck back with his upraised knife.

Hastur and Sedrah quickly moved so that they stood back to back as the beasts encircled them, bringing a charnel house scent that swept with them like a wave. Hastur cut down any beast that charged within range of his sword. He slashed with lightening movements that split the screaming monsters asunder, or he speared them upon the scarlet tip of his blade, and hurled them back in the yowling faces of their brothers.

Sedrah reached into the pouch at her gold-entwined belt and slipped an iron gauntlet on to her left hand, and then she pulled a dagger, just a bit shorter than the one she bore in her right hand, loose from her thigh high boots. Her blonde hair whipped behind her as she moved with sudden speed, skewering one of the beasts through the heart while she fended off another with the blade in her right hand.

Black ichor gushed over her hand and splattered the filigreed bodice, which barely contained her voluptuous figure. It wasn't exactly practical attire, she thought as she cast aside the still-quivering carcass of the beast, but it had been part of the plan to distract Lothar. Unfortunately, she had not distracted him quite well enough.

Seeing his opportunity, Lothar leaped over the altar and snatched the throbbing Broach of Baal from its tray. With battle-axe whirling about him, he sprinted through the piles of bone, splitting the skull of any beasts that ventured within striking distance. In a moment he was lost in the darkness, two score beasts scrabbling over gleaming bone, and cascading after the warrior lest he escape.

Sedrah had no time to worry about the loss of the broach now. Yes, the guild would be furious that the party had failed to bring the broach back, but it wasn't necessary to worry about that unless the three of them were able to survive and make the return trip to the City of Bathos.

Adryl finally managed to dislodge the beast that had been riding his back. He fell upon the creature, plunging his dagger into the wretched thing over and over, black droplets of ichor flinging into the air. Much of his own blood mingled with that of the beast's, and, streaked in crimson, Adryl turned to fight off yet another of the stinking creatures that had grabbed hold of his foot, and viciously worried at it with scissor-like teeth.

The circle around Hastur and Sedrah grew tighter, and every few seconds a beast would lunge forward to test the defenses of their two inmates. Each time they came either Hastur or Sedrah would beat them back with their blades, but the creatures were sly and they were not content to die upon the blades of their prey. As one side would feint an attack the opposite side would actually leap in, and only the quick blades of the two humans kept the foul things at bay. Even now Sedrah could feel the fetid breath of the creatures as they hovered only a few feet away, hungrily eyeing their intended dinner.

Hastur had seen Lothar break off into the darkness, and realized that if they stayed much longer they would all die. They could only hope to keep the beasts at a distance for a few minutes, or until the creatures got bold, and hungry enough to overrun them. "We've got to make a break for the entrance," he growled to Sedrah.

"There's no chance," she answered. "They'll pull us down before we get half way there."

"What's the difference?" snapped Hastur. "We're going to die here anyhow."

"I thought I saw a door in the temple wall when we came in." She motioned with her head into the darkness. "Maybe we can make it there."

"I'd give anything for a doorway," said Hastur. "I could kill these things all day, if only I could face them one on one."

Adryl screamed as the beast tore off his foot and retreated into the darkness with his grisly repast. "Help me!" he cried.

Sedrah steeled herself against the horrible cries, but the desperate pleas seemed to have no effect on Hastur.

"We've got to help him," she said.

Hastur shrugged. "He'd only be a burden to us now. I wouldn't help him if I could- and we can't."

As he finished speaking a dozen hungry beasts leaped upon the knife thrower and began ripping at the unfortunate man with gory crimson muzzles. In moments, the painful cries were cut mercifully short.

A few of the beasts, which had surrounded the two survivors, slipped away to take part in the fight that was developing over the grim meal. This slightly thinned the ranks of the surrounding creatures, and Sedrah could see that this would be their best opportunity.

"Now!" she said.

On her word, Hastur began a steady stride toward the temple wall. Sedrah followed behind, moving backward, defending their rear against the snapping attacks of the drooling beasts. She realized that at any time the beasts might make a concerted effort, and overwhelm she and Hastur, but the fear of their blades kept the creatures from launching a simultaneous attack.

Still, the creatures mustered enough bravery for one or two of them to lunge forward, gnashing their yellow incisors at the sword or dagger tip that blocked their path. Often they were driven back by the pain inflicted from a mere nick, but others came on more boldly- and Hastur and Sedrah cut them down, their horrible screams echoing in the cavernous temple halls.

Each danger fraught moment dragged as if an eternity, and it seemed that they merely inched their way across the terrain of splintered bones and split skulls, but finally they reached the wrought iron doors that were set in the porous black walls arching upward into the gloom. The doors were engraved with wicked tableaus illustrating the blood-drenched coming of the many-tentacled Mahmackrah, but neither of the harried warriors had any inclination to examine them, beset from all sides as they were.

Sedrah thrust aside the attack of a monkey-beast with the point of her ichor-stained blade while Hastur fumbled with the latch, and opened the door. The portal hissed as it slid open, air gushing into the room and dust swirling from within. Hastur leaped into the pitch night beyond its threshold, with Sedrah slipping in behind. The beasts, realizing that their prey was slipping away, renewed their attack.

Bone broke and black blood gushed as Sedrah slammed the heavy door on the outstretched paw of one of the beasts. The others hurled themselves against the metal door in screaming rage and insatiable hunger, the sound of their bodies a heavy thumping that reverberated in the darkness. Sedrah heard the door latch, but wondered if the beasts might have enough intelligence to open the door. She hoped that there might be some further locking mechanism, but couldn't see a thing.

There was a spark in the darkness as Hastur struck a flint. After several tries he managed to ignite a tar-soaked torch of bound rushes, and the ruddy light illuminated his hawk-like features. He cursed as he examined the bite marks on his left forearm. There wasn't much blood, and he had slain the beast before the thing could do some serious damage, but it was painful nonetheless.

"I hope this doesn't become infected," he said. "Did the little demons get you?"

Sedrah found a metal bar and laid it through several ornate brackets. Feeling a little more comfortable about the security of the door, she answered. "No. They slashed my boots to pieces, but they're tanned from elk hide, and nothing broke the skin."

"Good thing," answered Hastur. "It would be a waste if they were to make a meal of a pretty thing like you."

The full meaning of his words were evident in Hastur's gaze. Sedrah had seen the same meaning in the eyes of many men before. Her father had sold her into slavery at a young age because he couldn't meet his debts, and the Courtesan Guild had seen potential in her voluptuous beauty. It had been a horrible initiation into the degrading realities of the city of Bathos, but she had hardened her soul- and learned to survive. Her experiences had shown her that there were few within in the city that she could trust, and those who were trustworthy were often singled out to be made an example. Even as she had left the city she had been informed that a sister courtesan, whom she had grown to be trusted friends with, had been kidnapped off the city streets, and no one seemed to know of her whereabouts. The City of Bathos was a dangerous place, and the only way to gain any sort of safety was to become more hardened and more dangerous than the rest of the predators that roamed the street. This is why she had learned the skills of an assassin- in the hopes of shedding the debasing grip of the guild that had enslaved her, and many others like her.

Sedrah shook the black blood from her blades, and examined their surroundings. The licking fingers of torchlight revealed an antechamber containing a divan carved from black oak. It was still draped with rotting red velvet, and deep purple silks hung from cold gray walls. A cobweb-draped bookstand stood near the divan, with a leather bound tome resting open, a dark ribbon of blue protruding from between the brittle parchments. At the left wall stood an ornate fountain with a stone demon's head dripping hardened calcite. The water had long ceased flowing, and the marble bowl was empty except for the stain of mineral deposits.

The silk came easily from the wall, and Sedrah wiped her blades clean before slipping them into their sheaths, which were hidden in the now-torn confines of her thigh-length boots.

"Give me a piece of that," demanded Hastur.

Sedrah ripped away a section of the decaying material and tossed its dusty, billowing folds to the warrior, who followed her lead, and cleaned the curving sweep of his sword. Besides the door through which they had entered, there was one other egress from the chamber, a narrow hall of uniform brick that extended further into the mountainside.

"I guess we're stuck here until daylight," said Hastur as he resheathed his sword. He came up alongside Sedrah and grabbed hold of her right arm, and nodded toward the divan. "What do you say we make good use of our time?"

Sedrah coolly raised the metal gantlet up to Hastur's neck. "This gauntlet isn't merely a fashion statement," she hissed as two sharp needles slipped from the tip of the last two fingers, venom dripping from their points. "Quick-bane is an intense stimulant. It speeds up the heart until it explodes within the chest of the victim. Take your hands off of me or you'll be dead inside of thirty seconds."

Hastur scowled and released his grip, taking several steps back in case Sedrah should decide to use the poison anyway. "What's wrong? My coin not good enough for you?"

"I'm done with that line of work," said Sedrah.

"Does the Courtesan Guild know this?"

"They've named their price for my freedom. I was going to pay them off after completing this job."

"Well I've got some news for you. We didn't make the kill, and we didn't recover the broach. We're not getting paid a lead crown for our work here tonight- and I've got debts of my own to pay."

Hastur was a notorious gambler, so it didn't take a leap of logic for Sedrah to figure out what the warrior was talking about. "You bet on the wrong gladiator in the Blood Ring?"

"I got a bad tip," he mumbled as he turned away. "Now the Collections Guild is riding my back. If I don't come up with at least a token payment they're going to have my head on a platter."

Sedrah slid the bookstand around and blew away the dust from the yellowing pages. "If you mess with me again they may not have the chance. We're strictly business partners here, nothing else."

Hastur responded with a sullen stare. The pounding on the door had ceased, and been replaced with a scratching noise that carried through the walls of the room. "The stinking monkey-beasts may get us both before then."

"We could stay here and hope to hold of the beasts until morning," said Sedrah as she examined the cramped handwriting within the book. "These creatures are probably nocturnal, but I'm not so sure that means that they won't be lurking about after daylight hits. They seem awfully hungry…"

She let her words trail off as a few of the lines within the book caught her attention.

> *Though Mahmackrah, the great destroyer, will come and lay waste to this world, there are many other darknesses which lurk beneath our own earth- and I have plumbed those dreadful depths and discovered the horrors beneath the Temple of the Skull.*

"What does the book say?" asked Hastur. "Hopefully it tells a way out of here?"

Sedrah shook her head. She knew that Hastur didn't read, and that she could tell him anything that she desired, but didn't see the point of deceiving him. "Looks like the journal of one of the priests of Mahmackrah."

Hastur shrugged. "Why waste your time? I think we've already seen it all. Any warning he can give us comes far too late."

The assassin shrugged her bare shoulders and turned the page; it collapsing under its own weight as she did. She pieced together the broken parchment.

> *Now I know of the horrors beneath. They have made me one of their own, and I hold court over their heinous feasts, but my power is a prison of my own making. Forever, am I to be shunned by my own kind, for one does not eat the flesh of thy brother within the city walls of Bathos, and still hold court with the noble men and finely dressed women of lofty repute.*

Sedrah broke off from her examination of the moldering pages as she heard a scratching behind the very walls of the room.

"They're in the walls!" spat Hastur.

Listening carefully, Sedrah tracked the noise as it proceeded down the length of the wall. The scratching halted behind the fountain, and the fanged demon spout trembled as some force rocked it from behind.

"The things are crawling through the dry aqueducts," spoke Sedrah.

"They're looking for another way in."

As the words left her lips, the ancient spout rattled in its fitting, and the heavy block of stone from which it was carved began to inch forward- slowly pushed from the wall in which it was imbedded, old mortar sifting into the marble bowl.

Hastur bit back the sharp fear that worked its way into his throat, and analyzed their predicament. "We can hold them off," he decided. "Even if they work the fitting loose, it's a narrow opening and we can slaughter them as they come." He jumped forward and pressed his hands against the snout of the demon, lending his weight to that of the stone to provide increased resistance against the efforts of the beast within the aqueduct.

Sedrah wrenched loose Hastur's torch from a crack in the divan where he had thrust it. Holding it aloft she searched the room for any other possible entrances, from which the beasts might emerge and take them unaware. Amber torchlight flickered across the bare east wall, and as it became illuminated a massive brick scraped loose, and thundered as it struck the floor, splitting into halves. Immediately a mottled gray arm reached from the newly formed gap in the wall, groping along the wall for a handhold.

Sedrah leaped for the wall, her stiletto blade flashing from her boot. She thrust it into the dark gap, and a horrible screech emitted as her sword plunged through spongy flesh and lodged in bone. She wrenched the long knife free, wretched black ichor spattering from the razor tip as she withdrew. Before the first beast could finish its shuddering death throes, it was snatched away by glinting claws and another of the creatures climbed into its place, its monkey-like maw bursting through the opening. The creatures' fears of death were now forgotten, and their hunger and bloodlust drove them on, regardless of the consequence.

Before the beast could leap free and into the room, Sedrah forced her blade down the craw of the creature, and as it gurgled, choking on its own black blood, she looked to the portal- and there she saw a dozen furry paws reaching through the gap between the door and the threshold. The soft iron bar she had put into place across the door was bending beneath the weight of hundreds of the beasts as they hurled themselves against the portal with reckless abandon, their dark blood seeping into the room.

With the assault renewed with in such horrible fury, Sedrah knew that the door wouldn't stand for long, and that they soon would be swept under a wave of howling four-armed demons. "Forget the spout!" shouted Sedrah. "Make a run for it. The door won't hold for much longer."

Hastur turned his gaze to the door and swallowed hard. Without asking of Sedrah's safety, he let go of the carved demon head, and sparked up a second torch. In a moment it blazed, the red flame licking through a blue haze of tar smoke. Once Hastur was sure that the torch would stay lit, he turned and fled down the stygian corridor, which delved more deeply into the mountain peak.

Blood squelched and hissed as Sedrah jammed her torch into the gap, and the creatures screamed and scrambled back down the aqueduct, away from the burning flare. Sedrah used this brief respite, and followed the receding light of Hastur's torch as fast as her legs could carry her. Behind her the howl of the beasts was deafening, and she hoped that they would not, too soon, take up pursuit.

In his haste Hastur rushed by rococo walls, dark intersections, and randomly chose which splitting corridor to travel. No longer with a light of her own, Sedrah was forced to follow without questioning his decisions. Their path descended deeper into the bowels of the mountain, and it spiraled downward into dank catacombs, the bodies of which had long since been devoured for any last vestige of nutrition that they might contain.

Finally Hastur paused as he came to a dead end grotto that contained three stone doors set side by side. Each massive slab was balanced perfectly on heavy hinges, which could be viewed through the jamb of the door. It was here that Sedrah finally caught up to the warrior, and for a moment they said nothing, the sound of their panting breath resonating from the low, rounded ceiling above their heads.

"The doors are locked," said Hastur, indicating the massive mechanisms wrought from brass. "We're at a dead end."

"You forget," said Sedrah, as she withdrew a set of steel lock picks from the pouch at her golden-threaded belt. "I'm a member of the Assassins Guild. One thing that we are trained for is breaking and entering. It's often part of the job."

Hastur looked at Sedrah doubtfully. Even though he had seen Sedrah in action, it was difficult for him to view her as anything more than an object of desire, but he kept his tongue quiet and watched her supple form as she crouched, and began working at the lock.

Sedrah glanced back and saw Hastur's voracious eyes. "Watch the corridor. Not me!" she snapped.

Snorting, Hastur turned and watched the corridor for the encroachment of the four-armed beasts. The hall was narrow here, and if he had to, he reasoned, he might be able to hold them off for a while. Still, he realized that his earlier estimations of the beasts had been low. Fighting the strange creatures was not like fighting a human being. They were incredibly agile, and small enough that several of them could leap at you at a time. Shieldless it would be difficult to defend against them for long. His torch sucked at the soot-stained ceiling, and he listened for the howl of the beasts, and waited to hear the skittering of their claws on the cold stone. It didn't seem possible that they had lost the creatures, not if their sense of smell was similar to a dog's. Still, there was no saying what manner of beings these demon-bred things were. For all he knew they might not have a sense of smell at all.

Sedrah used one pick to exert a constant turning pressure upon the lock, and with the other she quested about until she managed to depress all five pins of the lock. The lock turned, and she pushed lightly on the stone slab. With an ease that belied its great weight, the door pivoted open.

"I've got it," called Sedrah.

The click of claws against stone filtered down the long corridors, and Hastur hissed a sigh of relief at Sedrah's words. In a few moments he joined the blonde assassin in the chamber beyond, his torch sputtering briefly- then lighting up the small room.

The flaring light revealed a profusion of gold and silver that spilled from two oaken chests, their mold-grown lids thrown back. Among these coins of various mints sparkled an occasional ruby, or emerald. A body lay between the chests, and unlike the other bodies that they had encountered, this one had not been stripped of its flesh. Where the dark and rotting robes of the former priest of Mahmackrah had rotted away, the withered gray skin lay hollowly against the desiccated muscle. The face was contorted in waxen agony, pale hair falling over the grim visage.

Sedrah briefly examined the body, the scent of jasmine rising to meet her as she bent over the dead initiate. "No signs of violence. He might have locked himself in here and died of starvation. Probably he couldn't leave without those monkey things eating him."

Hastur cast his eyes about the chamber and found a burlap bag that contained a few pearl necklaces. He immediately began to shovel coins into the bag. "I don't care how he died," grunted the hawk-nosed warrior. "There is enough gold and silver here to pay my gambling debts ten times."

"You'd better care," warned Sedrah. "There's only one way out of here and those beasts are coming after us. We'll die just like this priest did- trapped in a treasure vault."

"What are you waiting for then? Go pick the lock on another of the doors before they're upon us."

Sedrah headed toward the door, but she wasn't immune to the temptations of the gold either. In it she saw the opportunity to pay off the Courtesan's Guild and gain her freedom. She paused only long enough to scoop several handfuls from the nearest chest, coming away with a pouch full of one-ounce rilled-edge gold coins bearing a vulture's head, and two glowing sapphires. She knew that it would suffice to pay the guild's blood-price, and might even leave her with a coin or two to rub together.

"Give me the torch!" she said.

Hastur paused from filling his bag long enough to withdraw an unlit torch from his belt and thrust it into the flame of the other. It burst into smoky life, and he tossed the flaming brand to Sedrah, who snatched it from midair.

Her pouch weighing heavily at her side, she left the chamber and jammed the torch into the jamb of the door upon which she would work. Crouched at the base of the second door, she once again plied the trade that she had learned at the behest of the Assassins Guild. Behind her the clatter of nails against stone grew louder. Her hair cast a golden halo about her as she glanced fearfully backward, but the creatures had not yet burst into sight.

The position of her torch was less than ideal, and the flickering flame cast little light on the keyhole over which she worked. She cursed Hastur. "Get out here and hold the torch for me!" she called.

There came no response but the clink of coin on coin. Despite the lack of quality illumination, the lock finally yielded to Sedrah's persistence, and the door ground open, Sedrah's torch falling to the stone floor. She snatched it up and raised it aloft to better view the long hall down which they had fled. The sound of a hundreds clawed feet was almost overwhelming now, a cacophonous echo in the grotto's enclosure.

Sedrah stepped beyond the door she had opened, and found that it contained an arched hallway that disappeared into the darkness beyond the meager reach of her torchlight. "They're coming," she called again, and this time Hastur grunted a response and came around the corner with a bulging sack that held at least forty pounds of gold and silver. Hastur laughed. "I'm going to be living in luxury. Maybe I'll buy myself a couple of slave gir…"

At that moment a wave of the monkey beasts leaped into view, screeching as they sighted their prey. Sedrah began to pull the door shut. "Get in here!" she shouted.

Hastur leaped toward the door. He was a strong man and the added forty pounds hindered him only a little, but the forward lurch strained the seams of the old bag and it burst open, spilling a confusion of gold, silver, and gems out across the floor.

Swearing at his misfortune, Hastur knew that any further delay would cost him his life, and he slipped through the door, which Sedrah closed and locked behind them. The beasts yowled and scratched at the heavy stone portal, but Sedrah felt confident that there was no way in which it could be breached.

Hastur mournfully slipped into a crouch against the wall, and examined the collapsed burlap bag that he still held in his fist. Rooting through the folds he found a few gold coins and several small diamonds that still clung to the seams. He grudgingly transferred these to his pouch, where he felt they might more safely survive the rest of the journey. "What's left won't even be enough for a decent payment on my debt," he said.

"At least you're still alive," Sedrah replied.

"Not when the Collections Guild gets a hold of me," he opined, and he mumbled it again underneath his breath. His complaining stopped when he spied the pouch, hanging heavy on Sedrah's shapely hip, and he rose to his full height.

"Let's find a way out of this cess hole. I've had enough for one evening and I could use a few flagons of ale."

"We've only got one way to go," answered Sedrah as she turned and led the way.

The hall sank deeper into the guts of the mountain, winding around its core until it emerged in a grand hall, the ceiling of which was supported by thick basalt pillars carved from the living stone of the mountain. The walls were thick with rotting tapestries that hung askew, their once brilliant colors concealed beneath the gray mold that grew on their face. The scent within the hall was thick and momentarily inspired nausea, but Sedrah fought it back and as she and Hastur spent the next few minutes exploring the vast chamber, she became somewhat inured to the smell.

At one end of the hall, they discovered a stone dais upon which was set an iron throne. The silken pillows had long since rotted away, and the dark metal was flecked with oxidation.

"I was hoping for more treasure," said Hastur, "not an empty throne room."

"I was hoping for a way out," Sedrah answered. "It seems as though we've descended far enough to be at the base of the mountain, but there weren't any side passages during our entire descent."

"This room appears to have a few passages branching off from it," said Hastur, motioning to the dark wells of a half-dozen arched doorways.

"Perhaps we'd best get started on the first of them," Sedrah suggested.

Before they could make a move to explore the first passage a voice came to them, as raspy as a withered reed flapping in the wind. "What? Leaving so soon? I must insist that you stay for awhile and enjoy my hospitality."

The two of them whirled as a spectral light began to fill the room, and where the light fell it transformed. The slimy pillars became brightly polished, and the rotting tapestries regained the brilliant hues of their former glory. The decaying carpet that lay beneath their feet became dry, and their feet sank into the bright vermilion hue of its plush surface.

The wrought iron of the throne became black and solid, no hint of decay upon its gold inlaid surface. Velvet drapes lay across the silk-cushioned seat, and a handsome young man wearing the dark robes of the worshippers of Mahmackrah descended to greet them. He stood and descended from the throne, motioning to the carpet on which they stood. "Sit with me," he said. "Eat and drink. You arrive just in time for the feasting."

Both Hastur and Sedrah were bewildered by this sudden change in their surroundings, and by the arrival of the square-jawed man with the glinting black eyes.

Sedrah ripped her blade from her boot sheath and pointed it toward the man's chest. "Don't come any closer," she warned.

Likewise, Hastur's curved blade leaped from his sheath, and he warily eyed the gorgeous trappings of the temple, which, moments before had appeared to be in a state of irreversible decay. "What kind of sorcery is this?" he hissed.

"It is sorcery of the best kind," answered the stranger, who seemed unperturbed by their hostile reaction. "But until I could be assured that you were not emissaries of Nahmtokep, I could not remove the illusion of decay."

"And what makes you so sure that we're not emissaries of this Nahmtokep?" asked Sedrah, still holding her sword at the ready.

"Obviously the two of you are lost and seeking egress from the mountain, not seeking to do me harm. Dine with me. I will fill your bellies, and give you instructions on how you can find your way from beneath the lofty peaks of this mountain."

The priest snapped his fingers and servants dressed in gold embroidered vests, with red silk entwined about their loins, streamed from brightly lit corridors, bearing silver platters of fragrant fruit, dishes of meat, and gourds of wine. The men were uniformly muscular, their wide backs tapering to narrow waists, and their narrow brown eyes seemed to laugh beneath the solemn expression they wore on their handsome faces. Sedrah couldn't help but compare their unmarred skin to the rugged and scarred exterior of Hastur, who had obviously lived a rough and dangerous life- and bore the marks of his travails on his body. By contrast, the servants appeared to have been cloistered away from all harm or accident, yet their physiques were somehow powerful and commanding.

The women were dark-skinned and their features exotic. Deep-bosomed, with willowy waists and impossibly smooth skin, they placed the steaming platters before Hastur and Sedrah, the appetizing, but unrecognizable, scent wafting upward. Entranced by the dark-haired beauties that surrounded him, Hastur sank into a cross-legged position, and let the servant girls begin to feed him grapes.

Seeing that no one within the hall bore a weapon, Sedrah reluctantly sank to her knees at the edge of a dining mat, which had been laid out before them, and heaped with an amazing variety of foods. She was hesitant to partake of this stranger's hospitality or even trust that he had good intentions. Still, if he truly did possess the knowledge that could lead the two of them from beneath the mountain, it might be best to humor him.

Hastur, it appeared, had rapidly discarded any reservations that he might have felt. Surrounded by fawning women with foamy black hair, he reveled in the attention of their soft caresses. Their masculine counterparts attempted to lavish their courtesies upon Sedrah, but she politely rebuffed their attempts to feed her.

"We appreciate your hospitality," said Sedrah, "but in truth, it has been a long night, and the sooner you could point our way from beneath this mountain, the better we can use the cover of night to return to the city."

The priest smiled. "I take it that the Emperor still has a moratorium on visits to Devil's Head?"

"Yes," answered Sedrah, "and now that I've been here I can understand the reasoning behind his edict."

"Well, I would never want anyone to say that I, Pathan, former priest of Mahmackrah, was a poor host. I will certainly describe the path you must take to return to the outer world. Perhaps you can at least take in some refreshment while I do."

"I have heard of splinter groups of the worshippers of Mahmackrah, who dwell in Bathos," said Hastur as he lifted a haunch of meat to his mouth.

"Yes," agreed Sedrah. As she spoke, one of the manservants leaned over and filled a golden goblet with wine. "How is it, Pathan, that you find yourself here dwelling beneath the mountains. Don't the beasts above harass you?"

The woman who stood behind Pathan looked sharply at Sedrah as she finished pouring the priest his drink, but Pathan seemed unalarmed by the question, his brow furrowing but slightly. "A darker and more malevolent creature I have never come across," he agreed, "but they personally offer us no harm."

"We can't say the same," said Hastur as he gulped down a mouthful of food, and lifted a full goblet of drink to his thin lips. "The demon spawn nearly made a meal of us."

Sedrah tentatively lifted her goblet, but a peculiar odor kept her from assuaging the thirst she had acquired while fighting off the mottled gray creatures in the temple above. She noticed the priest's gaze fixed upon her, and feigned at sipping the drink, setting the goblet closely in front of her after each false swallow, so that neither Pathan nor his attendants could see that the level of the liquid had not dropped.

Thinking to warn Hastur not to drink, she attempted to catch his eye, but as she looked toward him he finished swigging his alcohol, and his female companions quickly poured another cup from a convenient gourd.

"I have to admit," said Hastur, his tone becoming more jovial as the alcohol rushed into his system, "your illusion had me fooled. I never would have suspected that all this opulence lay beneath the grimy hall that we saw."

"Sometimes illusion is merely a different way of looking at reality," said Pathan, his black eyes laughing.

"You spoke of a way out," Sedrah reminded him, returning to the subject that most interested her. She was curious, to be sure, of why this man might choose to live so near to a pack of ravening beasts, but those questions could wait for later.

"Certainly," responded Pathan, no longer reticent to share this information now that he saw his guests had partaken of food, wine, or both. "If you look to the south wall of this chamber, you will see an undecorated portal. If you take that path, and keep always to the left- do not deviate- then you will eventually emerge in the foothills at the base of the Skeltor Mountains."

"What happens if we do not stay to the left?" asked Hastur.

"Then probably you will become lost in the maze of tunnels and mines that honeycomb these ancient mountains."

Happy to have received some directions, Sedrah let her curiosity take over now. "Tell me why it is you choose to live here so near to the beasts of Devil's Head?"

"That's simple," said Pathan, "and now that you have both indulged in drink, I can share my story with you, but please do not scoff, for no living man or woman has heard this tale."

Hastur finished his second goblet, and wiped away the glistening drops with the back of his forearm. "Tell us your story," he grinned. "Nothing goes with ale better than a tall tale." He paused and glanced at the gorgeous women around him, who hungrily devoured him with their eyes. "Or almost nothing," he revised, supposing that their stares indicated lust.

"Oh, this is the tallest of tales," Pathan answered amiably. "Once, centuries ago, I was a lowly priest that served in the temple of Mahmackrah. We yearned for the day that the great destroyer would come and lay waste to the land, and place us beneath only him as the rightful rulers of all that we might survey. But waiting sometimes leads to boredom, and boredom sometimes urges a man to seek out other, more immediate gods. Some turn to earthly pleasures, or vices, like wine or women, but I turned my efforts to the occult studies, that which was forbidden even to a worshipper of a dark demon like Mahmackrah."

"You expect us to believe that you are centuries old?" asked Hastur, the wine loosening his tongue. "Why you don't look any older than I."

Pathan suddenly took on a stern and even menacing tone as he responded to the warrior. "Did I not ask you to refrain from scoffing at my tale? I tell you nothing, now, that is not the unadulterated truth."

For a moment anger sparked in Hastur's eyes, and Sedrah thought that he would rise up and skewer Pathan where he sat, but instead the anger faded, replaced by a dull, and sleepy expression. "Then go on," waved Hastur. "I shall not interrupt again. I have plenty here to keep my mouth busy." He gestured at the great platter of food that was set before him.

Pathan fell back into the somber cadence of his story. "I found that the forbidden gateways of Nenmohtep lay within a hall in the very caverns below the temple of Mahmackrah, discovered by miners a hundred years earlier, and sealed up so that none might disturb the evil therein. Foolishly, I stole forth at night, and began to break down the wall. Armed with spells of dominance I opened up the doors, and let the horrible beasts loose, and I cast a spell that would bind them to my will."

Sedrah shifted uncomfortably, disturbed at where this story was heading. She curled her toes beneath her, so, that if need be she could rise quickly from her kneeling position.

"With my beasts I over ran the mines, slaughtered the miners, and drove out the priests of Mahmackrah from their own temple. Alongside the demonic beasts that I released, I fed on the raw flesh of the men we had killed-drinking their warm blood as though I, myself, had been born of a demon father and mother."

As Pathan spoke, his black eyes moving voraciously from Sedrah to Hastur, the sorcerous guise that he had cast began to falter, and for one brief moment Sedrah could see all as it truly was.

The handsome priest's face became waxen and withered. Snowy hair dropped in unkempt mats that fell to his waist, as did the bristling beard, which sucked at the hollows of sunken cheeks. The black eyes were glazed and dull, but a malevolent hunger still lurked behind the pupils that had seen two hundred years of these dark caverns.

Sputtering beside her was Sedrah's torch, lying on the filthy floor. The mat that lay before them held rusty platters and cankered goblets. Instead of the delicious feast that their senses had told them existed, dung was lumped in steaming piles. The servants that had borne these trays of feculent for their consumption were hideous half-human beasts. They bore the monkey-like visage of the demons that she and Hastur had encountered in the temple above, but they approached five foot tall, and they stood on two misshapen legs. Patches of gray fur grew irregularly from their skin, as though it were some sort of infection. Each of the beasts owned two functional arms, but an additional two protruded from their torso, and hung shriveled and useless.

A trio of the things stood slavering over Hastur, and Sedrah could see another three of the servants hovering nearby her, as if waiting...but for what?

Then Sedrah's malign vision passed, and once again her eyes beheld the luxurious surroundings that would rival a king's palace for all its glorious tapestries, and she once again saw the handsome priest, surrounded by the feminine and masculine pulchritude of his servants.

Hastur looked up blearily from his cup, and then he slumped over, falling onto his side, the contents of his goblet streaming out onto the dining mat. Pathan looked singularly unsurprised by this development. He glanced at Sedrah, as if puzzled to see that she was still sitting upright.

"Why haven't you partaken of my wine?" he asked.

"Why do you think?" snarled Sedrah as she leaped to her feet, upsetting her, still full, goblet. Three quick steps carried her to Hastur's side, and the courtiers who crouched around him, licking their lips, scattered away.

Sedrah's Assassins Guild training had included the handling and administration of poisons. Without resorting to decapitation, which was a less than discreet way to kill a man, there were several methods of ensuring that a victim had passed on. Sedrah put two fingers beneath Hastur's limp neck and felt for the beat of his pulse. After a few frantic moments she found a weak and molasses pulse.

"He's nearly dead," said Sedrah. "What did you do to him?"

"Why poisoned him of course," answered Pathan. "I believe the alchemists refer to it as a depressant. It slows down the body's functions until they cease altogether. I shouldn't imagine that he has more than a minute or two to live. As should have you, if you would have more readily accepted our hospitality. It would have been so much neater, and a much more pleasant way to go. Look at your friend! He falls into blissful sleep, unaware, even, that he is dying."

With her left thumb, Sedrah triggered a button on her metal gauntlet. A dripping needle sprang from the tip of the glove's littlest finger. She thrust this into the artery along Hastur's exposed neck, and pressed on the reservoir inside the glove. Quickbane slipped into his bloodstream. The dosage that she gave him would normally be enough to kill three men his size, but Sedrah's aim was not to kill, but to revive.

Though Sedrah was no expert, her assassin's training had given her a basic understanding of how different poison's work. Pathan told her he had administered a depressant to Hastur through his wine. Quickbane was a deadly stimulant. Perhaps, if she could pump enough of it into the warrior's bloodstream, before its flow ceased completely, it might be enough to counteract the affects of the other poison, and revitalize the unconscious warrior.

Sedrah certainly had no fondness for the man whose life she was attempting to save, but she realized that she was in a predicament. At any moment, Pathan might order his demon-spawn to attack and kill her. Hastur was more than a capable warrior, and she could use his skills. As she worked over Hastur, she turned her back to Pathan so that he could not see what she was doing.

"There is nothing you can do now," said Pathan, his tone even and beguiling. "There is no escape for you either. Make it easy on yourself and drink. I promise, you won't feel a thing." He lifted his hand, and motioned one of the male servants forward with a gourd of wine.

Sedrah leaped to her feet, her blade flashing from her boot. "Get back! I'll skewer the first of these demon-spawn that steps within five feet of me."

"Back children!" ordered Pathan to the beautiful men and women that stood closely by, awaiting his command.

Pathan turned his black gaze on the blonde assassin. "So, you have seen through the illusion that I have created for your eyes. Your mind must be particularly strong to have resisted my sorceries."

"I'm not in the mood to be flattered," snapped Sedrah. "Keep your children away from me."

"Ah, but they are my children," said Pathan. "Don't you see? The bitter fruit of unholy union between demon and man. I am the whore of the earth and these are the six that sprang from me. We send our minions forth from our haven beneath the earth and feed upon the abundance of the land, taking offerings; unwary shepherds, or lone wanderers, sometimes a babe from its crib. None has impunity, and we demand what is ours."

"You're a sick man," hissed Sedrah.

Pathan smiled as though he took her words as a compliment. "And hungry, he added. It has been a long time since a meal has come directly to me."

Sedrah felt Hastur spasm at his feet, and she glanced down to find his eyes wide open, and his face strung taut like the strings of a lute. The blonde-haired assassin gave Hastur a kick. "Get up and fight, curse you!"

Still bewildered, Hastur leaped to his feet, his curved blade leaping from its sheath as his open eyes once again took in the illusion of the spell around him. "What's going on?"

"They poisoned, and planned to make a meal of you."

Inside Hastur the two drugs battled for superiority, his heart straining as the chemicals ate through his system. Finally the meaning of Sedrah's words sank into his hazy consciousness.

"Dogs!" shouted Hastur. He leaped recklessly toward the nearest manservant. As the blade bit through the muscular torso of Pathan's eldest son, the illusion was wiped away, the sputtering torchlight revealing the grim aspect of the beast, which he had just killed. Dark fluid spattered the air as the beast's bowels slipped to the ground.

Hastur smelled the stench, and took in the sight of the sickening repast in which he had been indulging. Then his eyes wandered up to the gibbering half-humans that had been his female companionship during the meal. He blanched in horrified realization, as they launched toward him, their screams echoing in the vast subterranean chamber, and their claws slicing through the smoky air.

In one moment, Sedrah realized, Hastur would be overwhelmed by the half-humans. Four of the demon-beasts moved to encompass him, and those were poor odds, even for someone of Hastur's incredible speed. She smoothly moved forward, and cut across the abdomen of the first leaping creature. Her razor sharp blade passed through the muscle and entrails without lodging in bone, and the howling creature fell at her feet in a gory heap.

Pathan cried out in anguish as he saw the second of his children fall. "Go!" he cried. "Be gone, and I give you my word that you shall not be harmed."

Before the words finished leaving his mouth, however, two more of his unholy spawn had fallen beneath the deadly blades of Sedrah and Hastur.

One of the remaining beasts fled before Sedrah, and the blonde assassin turned, stalking toward the former priest of Mahmackrah. "What? Leave you be? So that you can continue to prey upon defenseless babes in their cribs? I think not."

Pathan put his hands together, and raised them in front of himself as though he could push away Sedrah's attack, but the assassin's slim blade drove right through the crossed palms, and lodged in his throat.

Sedrah wrenched the blade free, and let the gurgling body of the priest fall to the befouled stonework of the chamber's floor.

"Two of them got away," said Hastur. "They fled into a doorway behind the throne."

Sedrah noticed that the hawk-faced warrior was visibly shaking, and she knew that it was not due to nervousness. It was the wicked cocktail of drugs that was wreaking havoc with his body.

"I'll get them," said Sedrah, bringing the bloody tip of her blade up into the air.

Hastur shook his head. "This place is maze of tunnels, and those beasts were born here. If they want to hide, we could look for months and not find them. I say we get clear of this wretched place."

Sedrah reigned in her impetuous urge to plunge into the dark depths of the tunnels and hunt down the surviving spawn of the priest. "Let's only hope that Pathan told us the truth when he gave us the directions out of here."

With shaky steps, Hastur followed Sedrah toward the south wall of the chamber, the blue smoke of their torches trailing behind them as they entered the undecorated portal, and traversed its rough and barren halls. A multitude of intersecting halls and forks presented themselves, but the two explorers stayed always to the left, sometimes ducking to slide through low-ceilinged passages.

"What exactly happened to me back there?" asked Hastur.

"Pathan put a poison in the wine that nearly brought your heart to a halt."

"Was there no poison in your goblet?"

"Oh, there was poison alright, but I only pretended to drink."

"It must have been a weak poison," snorted Hastur. "I snapped out of it when you kicked me into consciousness."

"I injected you with Quickbane."

"What? You could have killed me!"

Sedrah shrugged. "I couldn't be sure that it would work, but you were a dead man anyway. I needed your sword arm to fight my way free of those demon-beasts."

Hastur lapsed into silence for a few minutes as they traveled along the dank corridors. "I guess I owe you my life," he said finally.

Sedrah caught the scent of fresh pine wafting down the corridor, and as she turned to the ragged orifice of yet another tunnel on her left, she felt a whisper of chill breeze that disturbed the stagnant air they had been taking into their lungs.

"Maybe you'll get a chance to return the favor sometime," Sedrah answered. "But in the meantime, don't worry about it. You've got enough on your plate with the Collections Guild."

"The Collections Guild..." muttered Hastur, letting his words trail off into unspoken thought.

In a few moments they broke from the upward shaft, tossing aside a screen of pine boughs. Sedrah breathed in the crisp air as she hauled herself out into the stand of towering conifers that spread their needled branches overhead, blocking out the face of the moon, which shed its wan light on the bouldered terrain of the foothills around them.

They left the stand of trees and a short downhill hike led them into the grassy hills that rolled toward the grim bulk of the city of Bathos. Hastur's gait steadied as they cut the distance between them and the blight of Bathos, which rose up before them, its vast walls jutting and curling over the hilly landscape, sprawling, twisted city streets, and dark alleys spreading in a sinister maze. Strangely, Sedrah felt no comfort as she neared the gate of the Undercity. Within the city awaited deceit and treachery, and there were few in which she felt she could actually put her trust. The stench of death hung over the disease-ridden metropolis, smoke from the over-taxed crematoriums hanging in a thick pall over Bathos.

Adding to the fear of the quick leper death, was the prospect of traveling the crumbling streets of the Undercity after dark. The Undercity was the oldest part of Bathos, even more ancient than Old Bathos, and its decaying buildings hid bands of cutthroats and thieves that came out at night to play.

Hastur continued to lag behind as the east gate of the Undercity came into view. Sedrah assumed that this was because of the poisons that had ravaged his system. Just the fact that he had been able to make the journey on his own two feet, illustrated the warrior's incredible stamina.

They turned past a crook in the road, and the foot of a hill momentarily obscured their vision of the city. The rasp of metal being withdrawn from a sheath alerted Sedrah, and she responded with cat-like quickness, going into a crouch as she whirled, her narrow blade licking out to parry the downward swing of Hastur's curved blade.

The swords clanged then leaped apart as if of their own volition, and then they each hovered warily. The two enemies circled each other, waiting and watching for the opening that would prove fatal to their opponent.

Hastur sternly took stock of his opponent's stance. He was renowned for his lightening speed, and he was confident that he could easily slay a woman; even one as accomplished as Sedrah.

"You traitorous cur!" snarled Sedrah. "Have you already forgotten that I saved your life not more than three hours ago?"

Hastur's response was sullen. "There's little point in saving the life of a man who is already doomed to death. To truly save my life I need the contents of the pouch at your side. Throw it down and I'll spare your life. That will be repayment for the debt I owe you."

"You try to stab me in the back, and then talk of repaying your debt to me? Perhaps you think I'm some craven coward who dare not pit her steel against yours?"

"Many a fool has said the same to me, and then died beneath my blade," said Hastur. "But you are the only one who I have given the opportunity to live."

"Let me show you what you can do with your opportunity." Sedrah withdrew her second, shorter, blade, and slid forward, the tip of her long knife nicking Hastur's wrist, before he could parry her cut.

Immediately Hastur launched a dazzling attack that demonstrated his formidable speed. The sword strokes came in a flurry, from the left and the right. It was all Sedrah could do to fend of the attacks. Steel rang against steel, shrieking as the sliding blades parted, and several times the tip of Hastur's blade slipped through Sedrah's defenses and cut through the leather of her boot, or sliced the cloth of her bodice. It was solely her skill and speed that kept Hastur at bay.

Hastur's sword snapped out at her again and again in a bewildering web of swordplay that rivaled any that she had seen. Using both of her blades she fought off Hastur's advances, and as the long minutes passed, she could see that the warrior's exertions were taking a toll on him. Sweat poured down his face, and his chest heaved. His system was already taxed from the Quickbane that Sedrah had injected, and now his heart was racing with the added exertion of prolonged combat. The battle beneath Devil's Head, when they had fought Pathan's demon-spawn, had been bloody and quick. It had lasted only a few moments, but this battle was not over so soon, and the Quickbane in Hastur's body was still battling the effects of the recently administered depressant.

Sedrah could see that Hastur was faltering, and now that he was, she became the aggressor, pressing the attack, and taking the fight to the hawk-faced warrior. The tables had been turned and Hastur found himself desperately attempting to parry the silky attacks that Sedrah slid beyond his defenses. They came without respite, and each one was narrowly turned away, pinpoints of blood that flecked his arms and chest witnessing to the fact that Sedrah's blade had been there.

Though the battle had progressed in earnest for some fifteen minutes, it was over as quick as it had begun. Hastur's heart ruptured within his chest, and at that moment his sword dipped, and Sedrah drove the tip of her blade through his gullet. Hastur dropped dead to the ground, the weight of his body roiling the dust on the trail.

Now Sedrah crouched down, sucking in the chill air as she attempted to regain her wind. When she felt fully recovered, she turned her steps back toward the City of Bathos. Traders would find Hastur's body in the morning as they left the city, for all it mattered to her, the ungrateful wretch could rot at the side of the highway.

The gargoyle fiends that arched outward over the east gate glowered ominously as Sedrah walked beneath their shadow. The grim black iron gate was open wide enough only to allow entry to one person at a time, and four city guardsmen stood watch.

The guards leeringly appraised her disheveled, but beautiful form. "What's a woman like you doing alone outside the city walls at night?" asked the sergeant.

"Guild business," answered Sedrah, knowing that she was unlikely to be questioned further. The guilds held powerful sway in the city of Bathos, and to hinder somebody who was actually on guild business was to invite the offended guild to crush you.

"Very well, you're free to enter the city, but watch yourself. A pretty woman like yourself might find herself a victim if she wanders the streets of the Undercity without escort."

"I appreciate your concern," answered Sedrah, "but I assure you that I can take care of myself."

"I'm sure you can," smiled the sergeant as he took in the weapons that she wore, and noted the blood that still flecked their pommels. "But they come in bands. Sometimes they are even brave enough to attack a pair of soldiers on patrol."

"I'm not going far," answered Sedrah.

"You know, it's kind of odd. You're the second one through here tonight on guild business. Normally we don't get anybody through here after dark. The travelers who do get caught outside the city after dark, generally prefer to enter through one of the safer, more traveled gates."

"Was this other person a tall dark-haired warrior, who carried a brace of axes beneath his cloak?"

"That he was. He must have been on the same business as you then?"

The blonde assassin pursed her full crimson lips as she considered the fact that her prey was not far ahead of her. "He was," she said, "which way did he head?"

The sergeant pointed a gloved finger down a crooked street that cut southwest across a jumbled maze of intersecting streets. Crumbling facades carved with ancient figures overhung the street, blocking the moonlight and casting pitch shadows along the cracking foundations. Windows were shuttered and doors were barred, somewhere a street mongrel howled.

"He headed down Blister Street not more than fifteen minutes ago."

Sedrah favored the sergeant with a smile and put a hand on the cold chain links that protected his chest. "Thank you for your help."

The soldier couldn't help but grin back, and then Sedrah left the gate, striding boldly into the creeping tendrils of darkness that enshrouded Blister Street. Decaying stone eyes, granite demons and devils stared down sinisterly upon her confident stride as if they knew what lurked ahead in the night-veiled alleys, and were laughing at her brazen posture.

Sedrah walked at the street center, knowing that it would be unwise to step too near to the tumbling stone pillars and statued-daises that lined the street- things that might provide ample cover for lurking cutthroats. Though she knew little of Lothar, she had been informed that he had obtained dual membership into the Thieves and Warriors Guilds. She knew that the Thieves Guild maintained a safe house on Serpent Street, which intersected with Blister Street about twelve blocks down. It seemed likely to her that Lothar might hole up in the safe house until daylight, at which time he would deliver the stolen Broach of Baal to the merchant Biglun, who had commissioned its theft from the temple at Devil's Head.

The broach was reputed to have mystical powers that lent its possessor invulnerability to blade, spear, and fire- or so she had been informed by the Assassins Guild when she had been hired to intercept Lothar and kill him. Sedrah had seen wizards work strange and impressive magicks, but she doubted that the thing she had seen in the tray of the altar at Devil's Head possessed any such properties. If she could track down Lothar, and kill him, she reasoned, she still might successfully complete the job for which she had been hired.

With a fifteen-minute head start, she doubted that she would be able to catch Lothar before he reached the haven of the thieves safe house, but she might be able to position herself outside the building and wait for him to emerge. It would be foolhardy to try and enter the well-guarded house unless she was intimately familiar with the layout of the building, and had an entry and escape route meticulously planned; and she hadn't done much of that sort of assassin work before. Mostly she was hired as a pretty face that could easily slip some poison into a goblet, or slip a dagger into a man's back while he was otherwise distracted. A woman was often less likely to arouse a man's suspicion, and the Assassins Guild used her as such, not yet exploiting her full potential, she realized, and a bit perturbed at the notion.

The sound of a pebble bouncing across the crooked cobblestones, alerted Sedrah. With a sudden burst of speed, she went from mid-stride to a sprint, which carried her toward the deep shadows that cloaked the cracked statue of one of the city's elder patrons. She leaped over fissured masonry, and crouched behind the dais in the pitch black that encompassed her. Listening carefully, she heard voices out on the street.

"Did you hear somebody coming?" grunted an inebriated male.

A high-pitched laugh followed. "Have another drink. Eventually someone will happen by, and we can slit their throat for enough coin to buy some more."

Sedrah heard several laughs and grunts of assent, which led her to believe that at least a half dozen of the cutthroats lurked in the darkness. Fortunately, they appeared to be too inebriated to effectively spring an ambush, but even if all six of the men were completely drunk, which wasn't likely, it would be a foolhardy endeavor to try to pass in the open.

A voice suddenly whispered in the blackness next to her, startling Sedrah. She whipped her short blade out and found it blocked by the haft of a hand-axe.

"Sshhh," whispered the voice again. "I'm not going to hurt you. I just wanted to let you know I was here, so that you didn't try and run me through."

Though she couldn't see more than the hand that bore the axe, the voice was obviously of male origin. Sedrah was a bit reassured. She figured that if the stranger had meant her harm, he wouldn't have spoken at all and would have already killed her. Still, she didn't put her knife back in its sheath, yet.

"What are you doing back here?"

"The same thing you are. Hiding from those throat-slitters out there. I've had enough trouble for one night."

"Likewise," muttered Sedrah. "But I've got a guild contract to fulfill. I can't let a few drunkards delay me."

"Have you got any weapons longer than that?" asked the voice.

"Yes. Why?"

"I've got business to conduct tonight, also. I've got a horse nearby and I need to get to it. I've been listening for the last ten minutes, and I think I can tell where the cutthroats are hiding. If you follow me, I suspect we can sneak past them. But if it doesn't work, we may have to fight our way free."

This sounded like a practical suggestion to Sedrah. She briefly considered the possibility that the man might lead her into a trap, but she quickly rejected this theory. If the stranger wanted her dead, he would have already struck while she crouched next to him unawares.

"Okay," answered Sedrah finally.

"Hold on to the edge of my cloak, so you don't get lost in the darkness." The stranger handed her the tail end of his cloak, and Sedrah noticed that it was stained with black ichor.

Her first impulse was to reach for her blade and strike the man down, for she instantly realized that this was Lothar who had escaped her attack at Devil's Head, and whom she must slay to satisfy her guild contract. But something stayed her hand. Not only was Lothar the only other survivor of tonight's foray to Devil's Head, but he had just offered to help her escape the thugs who were laying in wait for them. Of course, Sedrah doubted that Lothar realized she was the same woman who had nearly gut-stabbed him a few hours earlier. Once he realized that, Lothar might not be so kindly disposed toward her.

They crept crumbling monument to fallen pillar, and Sedrah matched the man's silent footfalls, creeping along behind rows of broken and shattered statues, the shards of which no one had bothered to clean from the streets. They passed a few feet behind one of the cutthroats, a greasy-haired ruffian who took a swig from a clay bottle while he leaned against a cracking pedestal and stared up through the pall that overhung the city, trying to ascertain the starlit sky beyond.

Sedrah realized that she could easily step up to the man and slit his throat, but she had confidence in her stealth, and they moved into deeper shadows without the thug ever knowing that they had passed. Finally they slipped several blocks beyond the danger, and they ducked into a boxed alley a short way from Serpent Street. As they stepped around the jutting corner of an ancient building they passed into a pool of light, and Sedrah realized that someone had hung an oil lamp outside their third story window- probably to discourage ruffians from hanging about in the alley as they waited for passer-bys to mug.

Suddenly their identities were revealed to each other, and Sedrah's hand went warily to the hilt of her long blade.

Lothar narrowed his eyes beneath the dark brow and flowing mane. "So, it is the assassin who nearly gutted me tonight. I thought that you and your companions were certainly dead."

"The rest are," answered Sedrah. "I barely managed to escape that hellish place."

"Are you still bent on fulfilling your guild contract? If you are let's get on with it. If you aren't, then I've got things I need to do, and I'll even give you a horse ride out of the Undercity."

"What other things do you have to do?" she asked skeptically.

"My woman has been kidnapped and subjected to the quick leper death. The merchant who kidnapped her holds the cure, but only in exchange for the Broach of Baal."

"Sheesa?" exclaimed the assassin. "That's why you are working for Big-lun?"

"You know of her?"

Sedrah nodded. "She's one of the few people who I would trust not to sell me out for few copper coins from the guild. If she is the reason you want the broach, you can take it without my interference."

"The guild won't be pleased."

Sedrah nodded, her hair flaring in a sudden push of wind that swept from the skies, carrying away the stench of the crematories. "I know it, but even an item reputed to be as powerful as the Broach of Baal, can't be considered of much worth when the city is ravaged by the quick leper death."

Lothar raised an eyebrow. "I think you may be right. Come, I have a horse waiting for me at a safe house on Serpent Street. I'll take you to the Upper City, and we can part as friends and not enemies."

"Friends," repeated Sedrah skeptically. "I have few enough of those."

They followed the tortured roads of Serpent Street, and retrieved a black mare that was stomping in his basement corral beneath the gray stones of the crenellated safe house. Sedrah pulled herself onto the horse's back, and grabbed hold of Lothar's waist as the horse leaped out onto the cobbles, his iron shod hooves ringing as he galloped toward Hilltown, and cut through the tower-flanked streets toward the Upper City. A new wind blew in from the Black Sea, pushing down the Tiber River that wound, a gleaming ribbon, below.

Part Two:
The Demon Gate

The blistering sun of the day had departed leaving a fetid, festering stink that smothered the city of Bathos. Above the metropolitan maze of crooked stairwells, jumbled alleys and twisted streets the pale moon shone in a black crystal sky.

Milos crept carefully up the cracked and vine-grown steps above Piper Street, avoiding the loose chunks of mortar that the ravages of many winters had broken away from the once seamless stair winding up the back of Mortuary Hill. Once impeccably maintained, the way had long since fallen into disrepair. The crumbling buildings constructed on the hillside had been abandoned, their foundations weakened by crevices and slowly slipping toward the rubble heap at the rear of Piper Street.

The climb was a long and an arduous one for someone out of shape, but Milos had been off his Father's farm for only a few weeks and his sturdy frame was hardened against the rigors of labors far more taxing than this climb. He was dressed simply in buckskin sandals and pants. A dark cotton tunic was cinched at his waist with a hemp belt that supported a sheathed knife about a forearm in length.

At the hilltop Milos met a black, wrought iron fence that circled the hill's vast graveyard. Beyond, the cemetery was studded with the rounded shadows of a thousand tombstones and above these rose the threatening forms of strange gods and beasts, carven to stand guard at rich men's tombs in an eternity of stony watchfulness.

Though there was no breeze, but Milos couldn't help but to shudder. He glanced around, as though to check if anyone had noticed his moment of weakness, but he had taken pains to come this far unobserved. Sucking in a deep breath, he grasped the black bars with callused hands and began to haul himself to the top of the twenty foot barrier. With great care, he negotiated the jagged iron spear tips at the fence's top, and then dropped to the spongy earth of the graveyard.

Gargoyle-headed stones leered at him and grim skull-faced angels wrapped in grimy stone cloaks looked over him with empty sockets as he strode toward the center of the yard. An artisan might have spent months appreciating the grim handiwork of generations of stone cutters and sculptors, but Milos had no time to waste appreciating art. As fresh meat to the streets of Bathos, he had best make a name for himself soon. Those who didn't were quickly chewed up and spit out, dead or useless.

Though he had moderate lock picking skill that he had learned while tinkering with the locks on his father's farm, he had been unable to find a sponsor to help him gain admission into the Thieves Guild. Those he had approached laughed and put him off, whispering jokes of derision to their drinking companions. Finally, finding no other recourse, he had decided upon a bold course of action. He would accomplish something so daring that they would have no choice to admit him. He would rob the Tomb of the Kings.

Midway to his goal, the clink of sword on chain sent him diving behind a grave stone. Milos pressed himself against the welcome coolness of its slate surface, attempting to hide his thick frame in the shadow that it offered. The scent of decay was strong, here, close to the ground. It reminded Milos what would become of him if he were caught trespassing in the graveyard.

From his concealment, he watched as a group of six men emerged from the darkness and into the wan light of the moon. In the lead was a hollow-eyed bruiser, long thick arms hanging to his knees. Behind stood a taller, more artistically esthetic man, wiry and svelte. His eyes roved back and forth as if he were piercing the shadows with each glance. They all wore the uniform of the city guard, but the first two men, obviously higher ranking, wore chain mail shirts instead of the standard issue hard leather cuirass.

As the group wandered by Milos' hiding place, the guard with the ape-like build cracked a crude joke at the expense of some female acquaintance. Milos listened to their footsteps recede across the dank sward then continued his stealthy progress toward the crypt that lay at the center of the graveyard.

Broad steps descended to ornately carved doors of granite. The entrance to these steps were flanked by twenty-foot statues of the elder horseman. Male and female, the bodies were human, yet, they possessed the head of a horse- manes whipping violently in an imagined wind. Gingerly, Milos crossed between the sacred statues and down the ancient steps to the rune-inscribed doors. Heavy handles of brass, green from canker, were wrapped in thick chains and bound with a strong padlock.

Milos could see immediately that this lock had been constructed with a craftsmanship far beyond anything that he had ever seen before, let alone was comfortable picking. Yet the same boldness that had served him thus far, moved him to attempt the task that was likely to be far removed from his level of skill. He reached into a small pouch and removed some specially bent lengths of wire and began to probe the keyhole.

In moments he had the lock open. This surprised Milos. He had been expecting a struggle, but it was almost as if the arm of the lock had been barely pressed into place; for appearance only. Not one to question this turn of fortune, he quickly unwrapped the chains and pulled open the door. His muscles strained and cracked as the prodigious stone door moaned reluctantly open. Once he had the portal opened wide enough, he slipped through the crack and into the musty interior of the tomb. Moonlight seeped in through the askew double doors shedding enough illumination for Milos to see that he was in a mortared chamber. Kneeling, he drew a torch of interlaced brush from his belt. It had been soaked with a thick tar substance to keep it burning over a long period of time. Several strokes of his flint stone sparked the torch and he held its sputtering flame aloft, throwing light on the long and very empty antechamber.

This, figured Milos, was likely just an entrance chamber. He couldn't believe that he had actually gained entrance to the Tomb of the Kings. For centuries the Kings of Bathos had been interred here and many of the riches taxed and wrested from their minions were buried by their side. Now, Milos hoped, he could reclaim some of those riches and put them to some practical use. All they were doing here was moldering in the graves of the dead.

His torch cast guttering shadows along walls etched with fantastic scenes of demon-haunted chasms and depicting deals with incarnate devils reaching out from the Nine Hells. Milos couldn't read the ancient cyphers scrawled along the lower wall, but the images painted the stories vividly. Still, he had no time to waste and found a narrow tunnel at the back of the chamber. The ceiling closed to within a few inches of his head, so he held his torch out in front of him- its flickering glow licking feebly at the darkness.

The tunnel twisted and turned for some space and Milos felt a touch of fear gnawing at his gut. He had expected vast chambers to be laid out in an orderly array- with treasures ripe for the picking. The mortared path he followed slowly descended and suddenly widened to a three pronged intersection. Milos thrust out his torch to probe each of his three choices. The left tunnel curved off so that he could only see a few feet down the corridor. The other two passages contained narrow staircases that spiraled unevenly down perspiring shafts, boring into the bowels of the earth.

As Milos contemplated which path to take, he felt a sharp blade go to his throat. A hand firmly grasped his left shoulder. Though spoken quietly, a firm voice reverberated against the walls of the chamber. "I think the tunnel furthest to the right is the one you're looking for."

Instinctively, Milos' hand reached for the dagger at his side, but he found his sheath empty. "If you're looking for your blade, you'll find it at your throat," said his ambusher. He gave Milos a shove and stepped from the shadows of a recess where he had concealed himself. He was a hand's breadth taller than Milos and, though leaner than the stocky farm boy, his chest and arms rippled with wiry muscle. A brace of throwing axes glinted on his breast and he carried a double-bladed axe at his side. Wild, charcoal hair was pushed away from his features and fell down his back, over the midnight black cloak that was pinned at his throat. Hazel eyes studied Milos fiercely. Scarred fingers toyed with the dagger that had once been in Milos' sheath.

"You're an amateur thief," he said, finally. "You thought that you'd take a crack at the Tomb of the Kings."

Milos nodded slowly. He wasn't a practiced liar. The truth was the only thing that came to him. "Yes, that's right," he said cautiously.

"Do you know who I am?" asked the cloaked stranger.

"One of the King's guards?" ventured Milos.

The stranger laughed. "You are new at this, aren't you?" He tossed the long dagger and it stuck in the dusty mortar at Milos' feet. "Pick it up," he said. "You've nothing to fear from me so long as you don't try to do anything foolish."

Keeping his eyes on the man, Milos crouched down and retrieved his blade. "You aren't going to kill me?" he asked.

"The Guild frowns on killing fellow thieves. Besides, If we manage to live through this venture, I figure there will be plenty enough treasure for the both of us." He retrieved a small oil lantern that he had concealed in the shadows and lit it with a flint lock that was mounted to the side.

"You don't look much like a thief," Milos said skeptically.

"Call me Lothar," answered the stranger. "I also do a little fighting when the need presents itself. You don't exactly look like a thief, yourself- too burly. You look more like a farm hand and by the way you were blundering down the corridor, I'd say you haven't been off the farm for long. To whom are you apprenticed?"

Milos shook his head. "No one. I couldn't find any takers."

"You've got guts. I'll give you that. However, the King's guards catch and kill people like us everyday. You need some skill to go with your bravery or you won't be long for this life. How did you enter the graveyard?"

"I climbed the outer fence above Piper Street and jumped in."

"Piper Street was a good choice. It's little used and probably no one saw you enter. You should have lowered yourself in. No doubt, you've left footprints in the loam where you landed. A sharp-eyed guard might catch that. I'd already picked the lock to the tomb. Did you close it up after you entered?"

Milos shook his head. "I left it ajar so that I might slip out easily. I didn't think I would be long in the tombs."

"That was a mistake," Lothar considered. "It won't be long before the guards notice. They will either come in after us or wait in ambush. We have no time to waste." He hoisted the lantern aloft. "Come on, farm boy, take this and lead the way. The right passage is the one we need to take. Evidently the Kings liked to be buried deep."

Milos extinguished his torch and replaced the charred remainder in his belt. With lantern held high he began to descend the spiraling staircase. Behind, Lothar retrieved a mechanism of interconnected and hinged rods, which he threw over one shoulder. The gloom seemed to crowd around the lantern light as they sank further and further into the dank depths. The air grew colder and, glancing back, Milos noticed that Lothar had gathered his cloak around him.

He wasn't sure what to think of this stranger he had encountered in the tombs, nor the bizarre contraption he carried. As the ancient saying went, there was no honor among thieves. Though Lothar had appeared lacking in all deception, maybe it was just a clever ruse. Did Lothar plan to lure him further into the tomb to stab him in the back or was he really willing to combine efforts with a novice thief, just because circumstance had thrown them together? Maybe it was his naivete, but Milos preferred to believe the latter.

Still, a nagging suspicion kept pushing its way into his brain.

They descended, only the sound of their footsteps echoing softly in the well. Water dripped down the stones and cascaded into a pool somewhere in the darkness far below, creating an erratic and unnerving rhythm.

Finally, Lothar broke the unspoken vow of silence. "I'm curious. What brings a farm boy into the big city to break into the business of thieving? Farming's an honest labor that a man can feel proud of. Why abandon it for something so likely to get you dead or rotting in the King's dungeons?"

"Aye," answered Milos. "Farming is in my family's blood, but we are taxed near to starvation. Four tenths of our increase is sheared away from us by King Vlad's tax collectors and we are forced to turn to the usurer for money to survive. When the money changer is done with us it is only a matter of time before the farmer can no longer stave off the wolf at the door."

"I understand," answered Lothar. "Many are forced into desperate situations by King Vlad's heavy hand, but even the thief is subject to taxation. The tax on ill gotten gains is one half and the guild charges another tenth for membership. For the petty thief it is a starveling existence."

"And that is why you attempt to pilfer the Tomb of the Kings instead of resorting to picking pockets on the street corner?"

"Yes, and you, farm boy? Why do you, a novice thief by any account, start your career by attempting to loot the Tomb of Kings when, I'm sure you know, it is has never been successfully done? There is a pile of thieves' skulls to attest to that."

"I search for the Wheat Stone."

"Eh? I can't say that I've heard of that."

"It's a large ruby stone that my great, great grandfather found while tilling the wheat fields. He thought that it was a dream come true, but it turned out to be a nightmare. When the Emperor heard of my great grandfather's find, he came with armed men and burned the fields, threatening to put my ancestors to the sword unless the gem was handed over. It is said to be buried here with that same King that wrested it away."

"I've heard of it," muttered Lothar. "Although, called by another name."

Their descent ended, the black waters of the cistern lapping over slime-coated cobblestones that arched around the edge of pool. The two thieves circled the water's edge until reaching a doorway and plunged through into its soot black interior. The oil light seemed dampened here; the aura of illumination shrinking so that they could see only a few steps ahead of themselves at any given time.

"How do you know that this is the way?" asked Milos.

"If you had been accepted as an apprentice, you would know that the first thing a thief is taught is preparation. I've been here before. The tomb door and the statues that guard it are merely a façade. Old timers will swear to you that they have seen dead kings carried into the tomb resting in silver-gilded sarcophagi, their treasures borne behind them by a hundred naked slaves. Their words ring true, but those treasures are carried right back to the royal coffers beneath the palace."

This seemed far fetched to Milos, but his new companion spoke with conviction. "You've seen this?" he asked.

"Through these very tunnels I have been to, what I believe are, the underground gates of the palace. For a time I believed that I was the only one living who had seen those gates, but I managed to track down an old, former slave who had also been through those gates and seen what lay beyond. He had been one of the hundred that bore the King's riches into the tomb. They were all slaughtered when they reached their final destination. He was left for dead and he alone lived to tell me about it."

The tunnel twisted tortuously, sometimes cutting through solid rock, other times the ceiling supported by pitch-soaked timbers that warped beneath the weight they were called on to bear. One moment they were travelling in the claustrophobic confinement of the narrow shaft and the next it opened into a large cavern, lit with an eerie phosphorescent glow. In the opposite wall, set between jutting stalagmites, a massive bronze door twice the height of a man rose incongruously.

Milos approached the portal and ran his hands across the green, rivet-studded surface- searching for a keyhole.

"It wasn't meant to be opened from the outside," said Lothar. "I spent hours looking for a secret catch of some sort. When I found the surviving slave he informed me that the door was barred from the inside."

Unlimbering the mechanism from his shoulder, Lothar inserted the thin rod through a narrow seam between the door and the rock wall that formed its frame. Though Milos had never before seen anything like this, the function was now apparent to him. It was built with thin but very strong rods that could be slid between a door and its frame. By putting upward pressure on the rod and its hinged handle a bar could, in theory, be removed from the brackets that held it in place.

Milos watched as Lothar moved the device into position. He saw perspiration forming on Lothar's forehead. The muscles in his forearms and shoulders began to writhe as he pushed, the incredible pressure he exerted bowing the rods as he worked them. Finally, with an upward push from straining legs, Lothar heaved and the retaining bar echoed hollowly beyond the great door as it fell from its perch.

Lothar leaned against the cavern wall for a moment and regained his breath. Putting his raw strength to work, Milos leaned against the door and began to push it slowly inward. A musty draft of charnel house odor swept over them.

Lifting the lantern, Lothar saw the bent remains of the rod mechanism and the massive iron bar, as thick as a man's forearm, that he had moved aside.

"That was an expensive toy," mourned Lothar as he examined the ruined remains of his device.

"Finding the royal treasury should lift your spirits."

"Aye. That it should."

The two looters crept down reeking, tiled corridors that were hung with twisting chandeliers, wax encrusted arms projecting spider-like, as if preparing to leap down upon the two intruders who had dared breach their ancient sanctum. As they progressed a lurid crimson flicker overcame the feeble light of the lantern. In the cavern ahead red flame licked greedily from the abyss; a deep chasm that split the room, spanned only by an arched bridge of scorched metal.

On the nearer side of the chasm the rock floor was jumbled in skulls and bones with only the occasional stalagmite protruding above the grisly tableau. On the far side of bridge the floor was strewn knee deep in glittering riches. Statues created by the finest artisans of the centuries dotted the landscape of gold and silver. Caskets encrusted with sparkling jewels as white as arctic snow and as crimson as blood protruded from the sea of coins as if struggling to escape submersion. Strings of pearls, lustrous black and white, cascaded from chests of rare spices hailing from exotic lands. The two robbers could scarcely believe their eyes.

Perched on two promontories of stone that flanked the highest point of the bridge were two gray-skinned beasts, each of almost thirty feet in height. Jagged horns topped misshapen skulls stretched taut with ashen skin. Though their thick eyelids were shut, cavernous chests of ridged bone rose and fell in a steady pattern. They crouched on all fours as they slept, their gigantic paws tipped with curving scythes that fastened into the rock where they sat.

Lothar extinguished the lamp and they sat in the flickering shadows of the tunnel.

"Truly, King Vlad the Dark must be in league with Beelzebub himself to have such creatures guarding his treasures," hissed out Milos in a hushed awe.

"It appears as though they sleep," examined Lothar calmly.

"Perhaps we could sneak by them," suggested Milos, uncertainty tinge-ing his voice.

"Can you read the inscription at the mouth of the bridge?"

Milos could see the inscription chiseled into the stone plinth that marked the entrance to the gate. However, he had never learned to read. "What does it say?"

Lothar squinted as he read. "Fear not the Demon Gate, those who pass by once- for the demon claw lies still. Destroy the singular fruit of the sweat of the working man's brow, crush the bane that would silence the sickle and plow and pass twice in peace. Heed not and be sweet meat for the demon's palate, like slave, thief and soldier that have come before, and join, molder-ing, their bones and know no more."

Milos shrugged. He wasn't one for riddles. Give him some craft or handiwork that he could see or feel and he would feel more confident. Ask-ing him to decipher a riddle was like asking a smithy the recipe for a pastry. "What kind of nonsense is that?"

"The bane," puzzled Lothar. "That sounds vaguely familiar."

The echo of tramping feet filtered down to them from the passage be-hind. The two thieves could hear voices, but neither one of them could make out distinct words; just the tone and phrasing that was undeniably human. They looked at each other.

"The guards picked up your trail," Lothar said. "The dust was thick at the intersection. It would have been a small matter for them to choose the right path and follow us here."

"I spotted a squad of six guards in the graveyard."

"Maybe in an ambush we would have a chance," judged Lothar. "Without knowing the men, it is difficult to say. If we stay here we don't stand much chance."

Milos had already caught the meaning in Lothar's words. He stood and crossed the cavern floor to the bridge that the inscription had referred to as the Demon Gate. Side by side, the two of them crept out over the chasm, blistering heat funneling up past them so that Lothar's black cloak whipped wildly above him.

Glancing down between the metal slats of the bridge, Milos could see nothing but roiling flame. Above him rose the twin specters of the demons, so close now that he could see the rough texture of their hide-like skin and the black veins that traced like innumerable spider webs through vast folded wings. One talon of their massive paws, Milos figured, was half as tall as the average man. If the beasts should wake death would be certain.

Crossing the bridge, they found themselves wading through coinage of ancient realms gone by. The unimaginable wealth spread before them was blinding to the eye. As Lothar and Milos attempted to conceal themselves behind an exquisite block of jade statuary a cry went up from across the chasm.

"There's two of them!" pointed the short, stocky guardsmen.

Lothar turned and saw the guards. The first he recognized as Blackjack Pax, best known for hauling city residents into alleys on obscure charges, then hitting them over the head and taking their belongings. The dapper man behind him was the highest ranking officer of the group of guards. Trebor of the Stiletto, he was called; a jealous man who once cut off the fingers of a romantic rival to handicap his ability to play the harp. Needless to say, the woman who was the target of their affections lost all enamorment with Trebor. She died shortly thereafter in an apparent suicide. Some said that she jumped from the tower; others said that she was thrown. Having come into contact with Trebor before, and understanding his disposition, Lothar suspected that the death was nothing less than a murder.

"Scoop up some treasure and put it in your pouch," suggested Lothar, quietly to Milos who stood by his side. "We're not going to have time to pick and choose the most valuable items."

Milos frowned. "I came for the Wheat Stone. I've come this far and I'm not going back without it."

"Don't be a fool," growled Lothar. "Assuming the stone is even here, it could take days to find it. As it is, we'll be lucky to get out of here alive."

For a brief moment Milos considered Lothar's words, then in a crooked flash of insight, the time honored credo of no honor among thieves came again to his mind. "You want it for yourself, don't you?" accused Milos incredulously. "I saw you scooping up some gems a moment ago. You've already found the Wheat Stone, haven't you!"

"Don't be a fool." Lothar watched as the guardsmen cautiously moved toward the Demon Gate. Apparently, none of them could read, because they did little more than glance at the inscription on the stanchion. They passed onto the bridge all eyes fixed on the demons that, to the unperceptive, might appear to be merely fantastic statues created from the dark recesses of some insane sculptor's mind.

"Let me see you pouch," Milos demanded.

"Don't touch my pouch. Draw your blade, farm boy, we've got some fighting to do if we ever want to see day light again."

The guardsmen's booted feet clinked on the wash of gold coins as they exited the bridge. They spread out in a loose semi-circle guarding the mouth of the Demon Gate. Trebor twisted the waxed end of his thin mustache, balancing his stiletto in the other hand. "I had always assumed that the tomb was nearer to the surface," he said. "Thanks to you two I may be astoundingly rich in the near future."

A lanky guard standing next to Trebor cast a sidelong glance at him. "You're crazy," he said, perspiration pouring down his forehead. "This is the Tomb of the Kings. If we take as much as a copper coin our lives are forfeit."

With no warning, Trebor stepped behind the guard who had spoken to him, drew back his head with a handful of hair, and cut the man's throat. With a choking gurgle and a gout of crimson the unfortunate man sank onto a pile of gold.

"We're no longer impeded by this fool's sense of morality, now are we?"

Blackjack Pax erupted in a hearty guffaw, showing his usual sensitivity to other's misfortune. The three other guardsmen shifted nervously. None would dare object to pilfering the Tomb now.

"Now we just need to rid ourselves of a couple of pesky thieves," said Blackjack. "Isn't that right, Trebor?"

"That's exactly right," agreed Trebor. He motioned his men to advance toward the two thieves, as he himself began to close the distance over the glittering trove.

Outnumbered five to two, Milos glanced over at Lothar. "So, as a part time member of the Warriors Guild, what advice do you have for me?" he asked through gritted teeth.

Lothar snatched a throwing axe from his chest harness. "Don't get killed." He aimed for the outside guard, the one who would be the first to outflank the two of them and attack from behind. The axe tumbled toward the guard who slipped as he desperately tried to dodge. The axe head buried itself deep in his shoulder and with a howl he went to the ground. Lothar doubted that the man would be in any shape to get up and do any further fighting.

There had only been enough time for one throw and now Lothar unlimbered his double-bladed battleaxe. Trebor hung back and sent up two guardsmen to engage the thief. Quickly, Lothar found himself in a desperate melee of attack and counter attack. He feinted and parried, using all his skill to fend off the two attackers while he groped for footing among the treacherous slopes and piles of treasure. If he committed himself to a foolish attack he would open himself up to his second opponent so, for the nonce, he tried to outmaneuver his opponents so that he might be able to, if just for a split second, face one of them alone.

As Milos raised his blade, Blackjack Pax charged like a bull into the fray. Reaching up, he was able to catch Milos' wrist as the dagger descended. A quick wrench from Blackjack's massive hand sent pain searing down Milos' arm, numbing his fingers. The knife spun away. Blackjack pummeled the farm boy with his right fist until even Milos' sturdy frame was aching from the punishment. Milos tried to break free. The guard's grip was breaking; only a moment more and Milos figured he would be loose and could pay Blackjack back some of the pain he was feeling. Then, Blackjack dealt Milos a vicious head butt that sent him reeling to the floor where he lay, head bleeding and a rock-like protuberance jabbing into his back.

Rolling onto one side, Milos tried, with the sleeve of his tunic, to wipe away the blood that was obscuring his vision. With his other hand he reached around and grabbed the fist-sized object that lay beneath him.

Blackjack leaned over him, swarthy face sneering in contempt. "I bet you used to think you were pretty tough."

Milos chose this moment to strike. He hit Blackjack a vicious blow in the side of his head that sent the man to his hands and knees. Clearing the blood from his vision, Milos glanced at the object in his hand that had served as an effective bludgeon. Shocked, he realized that he held a giant ruby in his grip. Exquisitely cut, the facets gleamed, reflecting a hundred miniature images of his battered face. "The Wheat Stone," he muttered in awe.

He began to stagger to his feet when a guard pounded him across the skull with a metal tipped mace. The Wheat Stone fell from his hand and, slipping in and out of unconsciousness, Milos lay half buried in a cascade of silver coins.

Trebor leaped forward and snatched up the gem. "Come on, let's get out this accursed crypt," he said. "We'll seal the tomb and trap the thieves inside."

Hastily he began to beat a retreat across the flaming chasm. Trebor hadn't lived this long by risking his life when unnecessary. He held in his hand enough wealth to last five lifetimes and even though the odds weighed heavily in his favor, he didn't feel compelled to take the risk of sticking around any longer.

Blackjack Pax struggled dazedly to a standing position while two of the guardsmen held off Lothar. They slowly began to back away and Lothar let them. The few minutes of fighting had been intense and he was thankful for the respite.

Barely conscious, Milos' grasping hand fell upon the poniard of his dagger. Grasping it firmly, he gave a mighty roar and surged to his feet, silver coins cascading from his body. Through blurred vision he saw Blackjack Pax staggering toward the bridge. Leaping behind him, Milos drove his dagger, with every bit of strength he could muster, punching it through chain mail links and deep into Blackjack's side. Bile gushed over Milos' fist and Blackjack went down with a horrible, ear-rending cry.

Only one thought remained clearly in Milos' foggy mind- the Wheat Stone. He must have the Wheat Stone.

At the center of the bridge Trebor turned, a fanatic light in his eyes as he held the ruby aloft. "I have the Farmer's Bane!" he shouted. "You fools can try eating gold while you're locked starving to death in Vlad's treasure tomb."

Farmer's Bane, the words struck a chord in Lothar's mind. That was what he had heard the Wheat Stone called. A line from the inscription at the head of the bridge came back to him; Destroy the singular fruit of the sweat of the working man's brow, crush the bane that would silence the sickle and plow and pass twice in peace. Was it possible that the bane the passage referred to was the Wheat Stone?

As he looked on, he saw one of the guards push by Trebor and rush past the gray haunch of the squatting demon. The other two guards weren't far behind and just after them Milos charged like a wounded bull. "Give me the gem!" he roared.

The demon's head rotated almost imperceptibly, and Lothar saw the great eyelids flicker. It may have been just his imagination, but Lothar thought the corners of the creature's mouth turned up, momentarily, in a smile. The beast knew that his time had come to feast.

With speed so incredible it was hard to follow with the eye, a great claw reached out and sliced the first guard into gory ribbons. Lothar lifted a throwing axe. If he was ever to leave this place alive, he knew what he had to do. The distance was long for an axe throw, but Lothar figured he didn't have much choice. Harnessing every muscle in his body, he launched the weapon, spinning, through the smoky air.

Distracted by the death gurgle of the guard who had just gone by him, Trebor turned slightly to see what was the matter. A moment later the axe cut into him, fingers jumping from his hand at the point of impact. The Farmer's Bane fell to the bridge and hopped along its edge. Milos saw it fall and made a desperate dive, snatching it just as it teetered on the brink of falling into the blasting inferno below.

Lothar sprinted out onto the bridge. Ahead of him the demon guardians had woken and they wreaked bloody destruction among the guardsmen. Men howled and crimson sprayed the bridge. Trebor cursed wildly as he was lifted into the air. His ranting was futile and as Lothar reached Milos, Trebor was shoved into a hungry maw, where he died screaming.

"The stone," urged Lothar. "Give me the stone!"

Milos' faced him, eyes blazing insanely. "Rot in hell."

Lothar dove and knocked Milos down to the bridge deck just as a claw swept through the space they had been standing moments before. Bringing his axe down, Lothar's blade crushed the blazing ruby.

Pulling his fingers away from the broken gem, Milos moved them numbly- surprised to find that they were still intact. The insanity had left his eyes. "That was the best strike I've ever seen anyone make."

"You were just lucky," muttered Lothar grimly. "I was merely trying to hit the gem."

Scant feet above them a scabrous demon's claw was extended, frozen into place as the beast fell back to sleep under whatever enchantment was holding it there, and had held it there for ages previous.

"The Wheat Stone possessed me," said Milos. "I would have rushed down the throat of the demon trying to get that gem."

"You weren't the only one," said Lothar, standing up. "Trebor was so obsessed with the stone that he was oblivious to the demon killing one of his men a few feet away."

"Why just he and I?"

Lothar shrugged. "I can only guess, but you were the only two who touched it."

"So, it was a trick. In order to pass the Demon Gate twice one needed to crush the Wheat Stone, but to crush the gem would probably involve touching it. If you touched it you were under its spell and there was no way that you would ever give it up, let alone crush it."

Lothar smiled. "See, there is hope for you yet, farmer boy. You're beginning to understand how the city works."

He gingerly probed his swollen and bloody face. "And I've had enough. I think it might be time for me to head back to the farm."

"What will you do with your share of the treasure?"

Milos raised his eyebrows. "Treasure? I didn't come away with any-thing…and, since we stand at the center of the Demon Gate, we dare not go back and try to pass a third time. Surely, it would not be safe."

Lothar reached into the pouch at his side and withdrew a handful of gems that sparkled like the colors of the rainbow. "Fortunately, I was able to come away with something. What's in my hand will serve as your share."

Carefully rolling the gems into his own pouch, Milos tied the mouth securely closed. "In that case," he answered. "I understand that in Greenshire there is plentiful land and a King that lays only a light tax burden on his citizens. Though I hear it is a long and perilous journey, as you say, there is honor in honest labor and I know the farming trade. I'm too simple to understand the sophistications of the city."

They retrieved the lantern and began retracing their steps back to the surface. "You're not too simple to understand that the city is not the place to find peace for your soul," said Lothar after a time.

"Perhaps you'd like to be my partner. A farm can always use another set of strong hands."

Lothar shook his head. "I have obligations here. I would not be allowed to leave if I tried. Get out while you still can, but set a place for me at your table. There may come a day when I take you up on your offer."

"Consider it done," answered Milos.

As they sealed the Tomb of the Kings behind them, the bony fingers of dawn crept over the horizon.

Part Three:
Up from the Worms

With unnaturally stubby fingers, Adolphus the Sorcerer beckoned one of the silk-swathed attendants that swarmed about him beneath the blue velvet drapes of his private box. With lithe steps her bare feet moved across the cold stones of the sorcerer's mezzanine loge, and with carefully-manicured hands she held back her thick brown hair, while she bent, proffering a silver tray of delicacies.

Coal black eyes darted across the offerings, and he scooped up a handful of brine-soaked ox eyes. The crowds of the Blood Ring let out a great cheer, and as Adolphus moved his prodigious bulk forward to see the action below, dusky skin the texture of burlap folded across his wrinkled face, his sinister features splitting into a broad white smile that few suspected might lurk beneath. His attendants, however, knew the smile well, and it didn't signal joy or happiness, it signaled amusement at the misfortunes of others.

At the center of the arena rested a pattern of stonework that rose twenty feet above the spike-studded floor. From a central hub six spokes radiated outward, and intersecting these spokes were three concentric circles ringing the hub. In the hub, at the mouth of each spoke, stood six champions attired in black plate mail, and on a dais at the center stood the Grand Champion of the Blood Ring with platinum embossed shield, crimson plate armour, and golden-crested helm.

To oppose these champions six slaves hand-picked from the pens for their hardiness and ferocity started on the outer edge of the spokes and worked their way in; each naked except for a loincloth and sword.

This was, however, more than just a clash of brawn and steel. It was also an intellectual exercise developed by the ancients of Bathos. At opposite sides, ensconced in boxes at the lowest levels of seats that encircled the Blood Ring, the masterminds perched. These two men pitted their intellect against each other, moving their team of men across the playing board of the Blood Ring. Marked squares that were alternately painted blue and red covered the stone surface of the raised playing area.

While an armoured champion would be heavily favored in any combat that matched them against an unarmoured slave, it was the goal of the slave team's mastermind, to maneuver one or more of his men past the phalanx of champions, so that they might slip into the central hub unchallenged and face the Grand Master of the Blood Ring.

The rules allowed that the six members of the slave team could move both forward and backward, but the team of champions was allowed to move only outward from the hub where they commenced the game. For the slave team to win the game they must slay the Grand Master who stood at the center of the hub. For the champion team to win they must kill all six of their opponents.

If a slave slew a champion he was pulled from the slave team after the match to replace the lost warrior of the champion team. If the slave team won, their entire team would take the place of the champions for the next Blood Ring match, and the champions would be recycled into the slave pool to be used on future slave teams. Only a champion team winning thirteen consecutive matches was allowed to retire, and they were released from their slavery- but on some occasions these victors were lured back by the promise of gold, wine, and women, for a popular champion brought his owner much wealth and prestige.

But for all its strategies and intricacies, it was not this that brought most to the Blood Ring. It was the savage spectacle and sanguinary feats that left the playing board drenched with gore, and the spikes below littered with the impaled bodies of the defeated. This was what brought Adolphus to the Blood Ring. He could appreciate the strategies, after all, he had spent his life in searching out and studying arcane knowledge- but it was the carnage for which he came. Often he had a hand in picking the slaves who fought, and by selling these slaves to participate in the Blood Ring matches, he made a handsome profit.

An oddsmaker dressed in the finest clothing of the realm, stepped into Adolphus's box, and came to the sorcerer's side. He rubbed at his hairless pate as if shining a mirror. "The slave team has taken the ring," he said. "If you've had the opportunity to examine them, perhaps you'd like to place your bets."

"I would indeed," answered Adolphus as he dropped a pouch of gold into the oddsmaker's hands. "I'll wager that two of the slaves get through to the center hub, but that neither of them survive their encounter with the Grand Champion."

The oddsmaker slipped the pouch of gold beneath his voluminous robes, and marked the bet on a piece of slate board that he carried. "Good luck," he said, and then he disappeared through the cordon of beautiful brown-haired, green-eyed slave girls that Adolphus kept around him, and slipped past the two burly guards that stood with folded arms at the entrance to the box.

Adolphus scooted forward in his cushioned chair, several gold-tasseled pillows falling to the ground as he anxiously awaited for the spectacle to start. Each of the masterminds would take turns moving the man of their choice, each timed by the turning of a sand glass that drained in one minute intervals. Only for combat would the flow of sand be halted.

As Adolphus waited for the game to begin, he was distracted by a sudden cry that came from the mouth of his private box. He turned in time to see a wiry man dressed in a dirt-colored tunic and leather pants lift a glittering blade and cut down his two guardsmen before they had a chance to even draw their weapons. Moving as if he stood on a greased surface, the assassin slipped between the two guards before they had scarcely begun bleeding from their fatal wounds. He switched his falchion to his left hand, and with his right he hurled a dagger, the blade turning twice as it spun toward Adolphus' throat.

The dagger strike surely would have proved fatal, but Adolphus lifted his stubby fingers and waved the blade away so that it curved from its trajectory before it reached its target. The diverted knife struck one of his concubines and she went down with a scream.

Never faltering, the assassin continued forward, leaping into the air with his falchion raised high in the air, poised for a blow that would split the sorcerer's skull wide open. He never finished his leap.

Adolphus' sorceries gripped the man in mid-air, taking hold of the iron in the man's blood, and the steel in the man's blade, and he hurled the attacker backward against a pillar. Stunned, but still alive, the assassin slipped down the pillar to the floor. He dazedly reached out for his sword and regained his feet, but Adolphus was not going to give the man a second chance at killing him.

Mumbling a mantra that focused the power at his control, he once again seized at the trace ferrous elements that ran through the assassin's blood, and with a pulling gesture, he wrenched them out through the man's veins and flesh. Instantly the assassin began to bleed from a score of spontaneous wounds. Blood gushed out in scarlet trails, and the assassin dropped to the stone floor in mid-step, his heart rupturing.

Adolphus searched the surrounding aisles and crowds to see if other assassins might be lurking. He found none, so he turned his attention back to the game below, callously ignoring the cries of his slaves as they attempted to stanch the flow of blood from his dying concubine; she who had taken the knife intended for him.

Stagnant and still, the air lay thick and noxious over the city of Bathos. No breeze whispered or disturbed the rank atmosphere of decay that enveloped Wharf Town and its environs. Decaying clusters of huts extended past the ramshackle fringes of the river side taverns and brothels, up to the edge of the dense brambles that rolled over the jagged brown hills, which clawed to the very base of the Skeltor Mountains.

A half league out from the city at the further end of a worn trail that wound through the umbrous hills, a vast graveyard lay hidden by thickets that lifted their thorny tendrils toward the overcast sky. Few gravestones stood to mark the final resting place of the dead. This was where the impoverished and undistinguished were buried, many in mass graves with only the sunken earth to commemorate their passing.

As the light slowly leaked from the slate sky, a band of eleven men found a grave site marked only by a red-painted iron spike. Two of the burlier members of the group unlimbered picks and spades, and began to shovel away the clotted earth as the others lit torches to offset the fading light of the sun, which lay ever hidden behind the oppressive clouds that cloaked the sky.

"A nameless dead man to champion our cause," muttered a scrawny fop wearing a crimson silk blouse. He rubbed at a scraggly pointed goatee that accentuated his hollow and pocked features. "Our desperation knows no bounds."

Equally short, but polar opposite in bulk, the bloated Blevin responded. "It's not desperation, Tevol. Wizard killers are rare creatures, and if we have to bring one back from the dead to accomplish our aims, then we do it. Extreme times call for extreme measures."

"Perhaps," answered Tevol dubiously. "Perhaps."

Taller than his two compatriots, Dastolius stretched his lean physique and yawned as he watched their cadre of guards toil to open the grave. His young face was not unhandsome and his physique not unmanly, but his hands were soft, untouched by the taint of physical labor. Like his fellows, he was attired in the finest raiment that money could buy, and to further flaunt his status and inherited wealth his pale fingers were adorned with gem-studded rings of gold and silver. "The slave trade is a competitive business," he drawled, "or so my father would impress upon me time and time again. If bringing back the dead will preserve our wealth and status, then I will raise an entire graveyard if need be."

Three of their companions stood by in silence, unspeaking to this point. Each bore a remarkable similarity to each other; the pointed jaw, sloping forehead, and brass-colored eyes. Attired uniformly in gray cloaks, they wore pedestrian clothes beneath them; clothing that would be unlikely to distinguish them from any of the other thousands of peasant class workers that swarmed the city streets of Bathos. At their waists, however, they wore a string of pouches and bags of various colors and shapes, some of which emitted a foul smell that hung in a cloud about the trio of necromancers. These cloth and leather bags were stuffed with a variety of mystical concoctions that had been carefully compiled only beneath the waning moon, and derived from a number of unspeakable sources of which only the three brothers knew.

Afflick spoke first. He could be distinguished from his brothers by the deep widows peak of jet black hair that was slicked back with tallow. With narrow hands that bulged abnormally large at the knuckles, he made a swift motion in the air, and closed his eyes as if meditating upon some thing. Finally his eyelids fluttered open. "This is the grave we seek," he said. "You were properly informed."

"How can you say for sure?" asked Tevol, always the voice of skepticism.

"The spirits of the dead gather thick about this place," answered Afflick, unperturbed by the fact that Tevol obviously doubted him. "They have spoken to me."

"Ah…I see," said Tevol, still unimpressed, but choosing not to pursue the matter further at the moment.

As darkness gathered, spreading its shadowy fingers from the high brambles that surrounded them, Afflick's mystical brothers, Huard and Phalthos began to circle the gravesite, chanting multi-syllabic dirges and casting a fine powder into the air. It settled sylph-like, floating with unnatural grace to settle, sparkling, to the ground. Huard chanted, his over-sized skull moving in time, swiveling as if it were independent of his neck.

Phalthos raised a hideously scarred hand into the air and words broke forth from his tongue; unnatural and evil, in a voice that was not his own, they called to the demonic spirits that lurked in the cold ground beneath.

Though perspiring from the work at hand, the two burly shovelers shuddered at the sound of the words, and they glanced at each other as if to say that each of them had other places they would much rather be. Both were strong and brave men, employed by Dastolius because of those very reasons, but despite their broad leather-cuirassed shoulders, and the heavy short swords that they wore girded at their side, they felt no safety in their strength.

Bromur's spade struck something that cracked beneath the blow. He hissed beneath his breath, and carefully, he and Enstet began to clear away the dirt with gloved hands, revealing an urn from which spilled a fine, gray dust.

Lifting it up, Bromur showed it to Dastolius. "Nothing but a piece of pottery. Was this wizard slayer cremated?"

"In a manner of speaking, yes," answered Dastolius. "As Kolthos' last living act he turned his slayer into ash."

"Or so goes the story," added Tevol, his black goatee jutting.

Afflick came forward and took the broken piece of pottery while Huard scuttled forward and went to his knees in the shallow grave, carefully gathering up every bit of ash, and scraping it into a pouch.

Phalthos ceased his chant and stepped forward. A sliver of moonlight vainly tried to slip through the thick clouds above, but did little to illuminate the now dark graveyard. Six flickering torches guttered despite the complete absence of wind, throwing sparks that trailed across the grim mounds of the landscape.

"It is time," pronounced Phalthos. "The spirits have come to aid us in our task."

At Dastolius' instructions Bromur and Enstet laid out a thin lair of dirt from the grave beside the trench they had dug. Carefully Huard spread out the recovered ash in the shape of a man. During this time his brothers groaned out sinister phrases, and the darkness outside the circle of torchlight seemed to bulge and writhe as the horrible words were spoken.

Bromur and Enstet uneasily peered into the roiling shadows, their hands sweating on the hilts of their swords. Meanwhile, the three merchants stared in awe as the trio of sorcerers worked their foul magics, and even as the last words of their chants died upon the necromancers' lips, Phalthos raised a scarred fist above his head and the ashes began to stir. Barely noticeable at first, the gray particles became increasingly agitated until they sprung up into the air, sucking nutrition from the earth below. Blood vessels knit and intertwined, flesh compounding around charred bone that rebuilt itself from the ash.

Then an entire body lay where only ashes had whispered. The flesh was charred and black, the hair on the man's head growing in uneven patches, where it grew at all. Still, the body showed no signs of life. It lay in repose as if it were a corpse burning on a funeral pyre.

Tevol glanced sideways at his two business partners, wondering if the gold they had paid the trio of sorcerers had bought them only the assemblage of a previously scattered corpse. Impressive as this feat of magic was, a dead wizard slayer was of no use to them- whether he was scattered in minute particles, or whether he was a burnt body.

Phalthos strode forward, his fist full of some evil concoction. He knelt and smote the body on the chest as he cried some ancient word in a tongue that was not his own. Immediately the blackened body stirred. First a finger spasmed, and then a hand clenched, until suddenly the thing sat upright, and charred eyelids flicked wide open.

"What do you want with me?" croaked the dead man.

"Oh Kelvin, great wizard slayer, we summon you forth to once more ply your trade."

"My trade?" the question came through cracked swollen lips.

"You will slay the wizard Adolphus for us, or you will forever be relegated to your burnt prison of flesh."

"Wonderful," croaked Kelvin.

With this word from Kelvin, Dastolius spoke, and cast a foul smelling mixture of ingredients across the scorched back of the recently revived wizard-slayer. "You are bound!" he said.

* * * *

The sun blazed high in the sky, and the brightness hurt Kelvin's eyes. He skulked in the shadows at the corner of Brazen and Haven Streets beneath the overhanging eaves of the Silver Fan Brothel. All along Brazen Street jewelry clad women with coiffed hair, and smelling of strong perfumes sat in arched windows, preening, and passing beguiling smiles at the potential customers who trod the cobbled street below.

Among such other distractions, few took notice of the figure cloaked in clothing of dark green tones. If they had taken time to peer beneath the hood, they would have seen a horrifying visage- one that had permanently been scarred by the wizardry of Kolthos. The last thing that Kelvin could remember is casting his darts at the wizard, and then an excruciating pain that had been mercifully short.

He hadn't been sure if his darts had struck their target. Evidently they had, or the slaver fools and their sorcerous lackeys wouldn't have bothered to summon him forth from the grave. Kelvin vainly tried to remember what had passed from the time of death to his unwelcome resurrection. Vague shapes moved at the back of his memory, but it was though a veil had been cast over them and he could not recall them to consciousness.

Kelvin examined his cracked and burned hands. His new body left something to be desired. It was sluggish and slow compared to the nimble body that he had possessed before his death. Though he wore the same framework now, it was not the same body. That much had been obvious from the moment that he had awoken in the graveyard.

From his shaded alcove, Kelvin looked out across the squat buildings on Haven Street and found the copper-roofed, triple-pronged towers that rose far above them all. A glass-smooth wall that reached three times Kelvin's height encircled the towers. Razor wire coiled across the wall top, which was periodically studded with outward-pointing spikes.

Adolphus was obviously serious about his security. In the center of this smooth wall was an arched gateway that was filled with a wrought iron gate. Even from this distance Kelvin could estimate that there was not more than two inches of space between the pointed spears atop the gate and the keystone of the arch. The draft below the gate showed even less clearance, and the bars were set with less than six inches of space between them. Only an emaciated child or midget might slide between those bars. The Thieves Guild did employ such as these, but to discourage such trickery two guards outfitted in black scale mail, and wearing golden-hilted blades stood a constant vigilance within the courtyard beyond.

Marking time with a great stone sundial that stood in the square between Brazen and Haven Streets, Kelvin watched the guardsmen and noted when they changed watch. The afternoon guard seemed a bit more lax in their attitude, their attention occasionally wandering to a pretty servant girl that passed by on an errand, or to a scantily clad courtesan who wandered out onto Haven Street to purchase a loaf of bread from the bakery a few blocks to the west. Kelvin could smell the scent of fresh-baked bread but, for some reason, since his resurrection he had been able to muster little interest in eating. He did so in a perfunctory and obligatory manner, but even the finest delicacy tasted bland to his palate, and though he hadn't eaten since daybreak, the aroma of the bread did not arouse hunger within him.

In his new incarnation, Kelvin seemed unable to enjoy any of the pleasures that life had previously offered. Setting his scabrous jaw, Kelvin realized that he was not truly alive. He was existing in some pale and joyless imitation of life, where only his intellect had truly survived. He had been cursed to go another round in the city of Bathos, and this horribly disfigured body was the vessel that had been chosen for him.

He had no compunctions about killing Adolphus. The sorcerer was a slaver who profited from the misery and bondage of others. He took their freedom away and broke their will beneath the yoke and whip, then sold them to the highest bidder. The world would be a better place without Adolphus. Unfortunately, Kelvin's erstwhile employers: Tevol, Blevin, and Dastolius, were also heavily in the slave trade. Adolphus was their competitor, and they wanted him out of the way so that they might conveniently fill the vacuum that his death would create.

There was no righteous position in this little business war. Kelvin had been forced to one side solely because of the geas laid upon him by the three sorceress brothers who had brought him back from the land of the dead. Unless he killed Adolphus he would be forced to ever exist in this shell of a body. Even death would not release him, the sorcerers had reminded him. He could lie dismembered and rotting at the bottom of the ocean for centuries, and still his consciousness would remain within his corpse, or even his bones. It was a grim thought, and Kelvin was not entranced by the idea.

Though his employers had assured him of his success in slaying Kolthos, Kelvin couldn't consider the endeavor wholly a success. He had been slain, after all. He couldn't afford to let that happen again when he went after Adolphus. He needed to be able to return to his employers and have the curse lifted from him so that he could sink back into the blissful existence of his now forgotten afterlife. Whatever that afterlife was, Kelvin thought, it was sure to be better than this pale existence.

Kelvin stayed late into the night, still marking the changes of watch, and at what time the guards retired from their shift and left the premises. Despite the lateness of the hour, Kelvin had yet to feel fatigue or need for sleep. Perhaps, he wondered, this was another of the differences between his new and former body.

The gate of Adolphus' fortress opened narrowly and two men left the courtyard, the remaining guards shutting and locking the gate tightly behind. Slipping from the alcove where he had been posted, Kelvin crept the dark streets, following the two men who left the moon cast shadows of the triple-pronged towers.

Right away Kelvin could see that these two were not the same guards who had stood watch at the gate. This pair was dressed in finery that would be out of reach for even an extremely well paid watchmen. That they were guards Kelvin didn't doubt. Each wore a soft leather hauberk, bossed with metal studs. A tulwar swung from the waist of the giant on the right, and at each movement his broad back and thick shoulders threatened to tear asunder the leather that contained them.

Atop this mountain of muscle sat a bald head, and as he turned his face toward his companion, Kelvin caught sight of the giant's pug-nose, and the beady eyes that peered from beneath an overhanging brow. The face looked remarkably child-like and innocent, but Kelvin recognized the man now. He was known as Bester Backbreaker, a former slave who had made a name for himself in the gladiatorial pits by snapping the spines of his victims with his bare hands. Evidently Adolphus had recognized the man's talents and hired him on as a personal bodyguard.

"What are your plans for this evening, Costas?" Bester asked the man who strode beside him.

Costas, though larger than Kelvin, appeared miniscule in comparison to Bester. He looked up at his massive companion and smiled crookedly. "I found a nice little den in the mid-city. Some of the most beautiful girls you've ever seen, and some of the best opium dust in the city."

"Bathos grown?" snorted Bester derisively.

"So they claim, but I don't believe it. This stuff comes from Cathay, or

I've never slit a man's throat."

Bester guffawed at this jest. "Did you remember to bring the key to the central tower?"

Costas patted the leather belt at his waist. "Got it here. Adolphus is paranoid that while we are gone one of the slave girls will get vengeance on her mind, find a key to the central tower, and slay him while he's sleeping."

"I couldn't blame them for wanting to stick a knife in his gut," said Bester.

In the still of the night the conversation carried to Kelvin's ears, and he was able to listen as he quietly tracked them beneath the ornate, overhanging eaves of Slither Street. The two companions passed through an arched gateway at the end of the road that was scarcely large enough for Bester to squeeze through. This narrow archway cut through the wall between the Upper and Mid-City of Bathos. Few people knew of this small gateway, because it was hidden behind a large granite statue of a serpent, and those who knew of its existence often preferred not to use it, since this street had been used in centuries past as a haven for the cult of the snake. The horrifying tales of disappearing women and children echoed down through the generations, and still many of the citizens of Bathos shunned this once evil place.

As Kelvin passed, he laid one burned hand on the cold carved scales of the monstrous statue, and gazed up toward the crumbling fangs and narrow eyes. Maybe once he would have been perturbed, looking into the same merciless eyes that had presided over the murders of thousands, but now death held little fear for him. It was eternal life trapped within this obscene travesty of a body that he feared the most.

Kelvin pushed through the stygian gloom of the corridor beneath the wall, and emerged into a crumbling back alley that emptied into Stuck Street. Here he watched the uneven pavings and potholes that rutted the roadway, and followed its upward sweep along abandoned stone tenements, that now served as a home to beggars and panhandlers.

The decaying facades loomed above him as Kelvin once again caught sight of the two guards. Following a maze of streets and back alleys they emerged into wells of brilliant light on Peacock Street. Kelvin paused in the shadows of the alley, and surveyed the decadent grandeur of the street. Oil lamps hung at regular intervals, lighting the gleaming marble streets. At any hour of the night these thoroughfares were alive with action. Carriages and chariots lined the streets, with bored drivers standing idly while muscular men stood watch at a score of velvet-swathed doors, admitting only the beautiful and the wealthy to their establishments.

Music filtered out onto the roadway and two women painted entirely in gold, and wearing gold-threaded shifts, cavorted on daises that flanked the gated doorway to the Golden Eel gaming establishment. Without hesitation Bester turned his feet toward this door, and the burly man at the door recognized and admitted him.

Costas headed south and turned up Fennel Street, and Kelvin remembered that, before his death, he had heard of an opium den opening in a closed smelting house in that area. Confident that he could find the den, if necessary, Kelvin decided to glean a bit more information about the giant Bester.

Leaving the seclusion of his hiding place, he wandered up the street, past drunken fools who emerged dazedly from the gaming houses, their gold gone and their self-respect robbed. Kelvin had been an expert dartsman in his past life, and had laid many a wager on his skill. Even then, things had not always gone according to plan, and Kelvin didn't see the point of betting money on dice or cards; something that involved a high degree of luck, and something over which one had so little control.

Kelvin stepped between the daises and strode toward the door as if he expected to be admitted, but the doormen stepped between he and the velvet-draped portal.

"The gaming parlors are full," he said, crossing his arms.

With a quick snap of his wrist, Kelvin pulled a heavy pouch from beneath his cloak. He loosened it with charred fingers, and showed the doorman the profusion of gold coins that filled the leather bag.

"My apologies," said the doormen as he moved aside. "It appears that I was mistaken."

Without saying a word, Kelvin passed through the crimson drapes and into the dimly lit casino beyond. Nobleman and rogue crowded around cloth-draped tables, shoulder to shoulder as they cast their dice. Card players gathered about rum-stained tables heaped with silver and gold, and golden-skinned serving wenches passed among the crowd selling steins of ale and whiskey from brass-leaf trays. Drums and harp entwined in a lascivious combination to which a troupe of male and female dancers moved suggestively.

Eyes searching through the decadent chaos, Kelvin found Bester's massive form ensconced on a small wooden chair near the wrought iron rail of the balcony that encircled the gaming room. He sat at a small table in earnest conversation with a gaunt-faced individual wearing a silken chemise, and red leather pants.

Kelvin's new boots tread the finely-knit fibers of the crimson carpet that graced the stair. He still wore his dark green cloak with the hood pulled up over his hideous face. To allow people a full view of his resurrected visage would attract much unwelcome attention, but his current disguise wasn't much better. The concealment of his features made people curious, and curious people paid far too much attention for him to be inconspicuous.

Mid-stair he stopped a gold-skinned serving wench who was ascending to the balcony. She bore a full tray of meat and drink.

"Do you see those men on the balcony?" he asked.

She turned her dark sloe eyes to the place where Bester and his gaunt drinking companion sat. "Yes," she said, turning her eyes back to Kelvin.

He kept his head low so that she could not peer beneath the hood, but still she couldn't help but notice the charred fingertips that emerged from beneath his sleeves, and Kelvin could see her edging uncomfortably away. Before she could go too far, he dropped two octagonal gold crowns on her serving plate. "You listen in on what they are saying and I'll reward you with three more of those. Do you think you can find an excuse to hover about them?"

Her eyes glinted with avarice, and her teeth gleamed whitely as she smiled. "That's all you want?"

"That's all," answered Kelvin.

"I'll be back for the rest," she answered, scooping up the coins and slipping them in a secret pouch beneath the silk skirt wrapped about her waist.

"I'll be waiting down there," answered Kelvin, motioning to an empty table in the corner of the busy chamber below.

She nodded and continued climbing the stairs while Kelvin descended and took a seat at a small table in a shadowed nook of the gaming room. From here he leaned back against an outcropping in the brick wall, and he could gaze up at Bester on the balcony.

The serving wench shortly visited their table and placed several frothing mugs of ale in front of them. She smiled at Bester and touched him on the shoulder before departing to serve several other tables. As Kelvin watched she swung by many times, always casting a seductive smile at the giant man with the child-like face. For a while she made a pretense of setting down her tray nearby and rearranging a jumble of empty mugs into organized rows. Finally she returned to find Kelvin sitting in the niche below.

"I'm not so sure that this will be of interest to you," she said, "but I did as you asked."

"Then I'll pay you as promised," croaked Kelvin, his vocal cords still thick with disuse.

"They were talking about preparing a signal from a tower. I don't know why."

"Any idea where this tower might be?"

"On Seven Street, next to the Blood Ring. Does that mean anything to you?"

Kelvin considered this for a moment as he placed three more gold coins on the woman's tray. "It just might," he answered. "It just might."

* * * *

As dawn crept over the distant Skeltor Mountains, and the sun slowly spread cold fingers of light down its craggy face, reaching toward the still-shadowed walls of Bathos, Kelvin left the luxurious room that he had rented in the Mid-City, and turned his feet toward Wharftown.

Wharftown was still in its morning throes, and the drunks were climbing from the gutter along the string of taverns that lined Ship Street. To Kelvin's right lay the wooden spires of many a ship, their masts still furled, and their flags hanging limply in the still air. The river gurgled as it gushed through the piles that supported the vast network of wharves that reached from the cove toward the center of the Tiber's deep waters

Fisherman emerged from back alleys, deeply inhaling the scent of salt air that drifted sluggishly inland from the Black Sea. Unlike the sailors in the gutters that reeled to their feet with their heads pounding, they started the day fresh and unhindered by the excesses of the previous night.

The last wharf inland, Kelvin knew, was the docking port for the slaver ships. They came from distant lands bearing a cargo of human merchandise. Any land or people were fair game, so long as they were unable to put up a strong enough resistance to make their capture unprofitable. Towns along the shore were often raided and their human contents hauled aboard filthy ships to endure the voyage to Bathos. Sometimes even other sailing ships were raided, and their sailors put into chains to be sold as slaves upon reaching the decadent shores of the world's largest and most corrupt city.

Kelvin had spent a few gold coins plying the locals with drink, and he had learned a few things about Adolphus, and even his own employers-Blevin, Tevol, and Dastolius. It turned out that Adolphus was known to have a weakness for brown-haired women with green eyes. Now the women of Zeilan were known to often have such features, and Adolphus would often go to the slave ships before their merchandise was unloaded, and choose the most beautiful of these to be his personal slaves.

A high-beaked ship with the name Corrigan Raider, inscribed in black paint upon its hull, caught Kelvin's attention. This was the ship he was looking for. Recently returned from a foray into distant seas, it came bearing a hold full of slaves. A sailor on this ship had, after three flagons of ale, personally informed Kelvin that they brought female slaves from the island of Zeilan.

Kelvin stepped along the splintered timbers of the wharf, avoiding the piles of weather-blackened rope, and the guy lines, which secured the ship to the dock. He put his foot to the boarding plank, and soon found himself aboard the Corrigan Raider, face to face with a wiry sailor who appeared to be approximately Kelvin's size.

The sailor fingered the worn hilt of his dagger. "Where do you think you're going? This ship is off limits until the cargo is unloaded."

"I need to see the captain of the Corrigan. We have business to conduct."

"Over my dead b…"

The sailors words were suddenly choked off as Kelvin lunged forward. In his past life, Kelvin would have made the move before the sailor was able to react, but his new form was not as quick as the old, and the sailor nearly avoided Kelvin's blackened hand as it reached out and grabbed hold of his neck. With strength he had never before experienced, Kelvin closed off the man's windpipe and hoisted the sailor, flailing and choking, into the air.

The sailor's struggles succeeded in knocking the cowl away from Kelvin's head, revealing the twisted and burned visage that lay beneath. Horror flashed in the man's bulging eyes as he saw the hideous beast that held him captive.

The sailor renewed his struggles, but his strength flagged as his breath was depleted.

Kelvin eased his hold slightly so that man wouldn't pass out. "This is how it's going to be," insisted Kelvin calmly. "You're going to take me to the captain. If you don't, I'm going to decorate the deck of this ship with your corpse."

The sailor nodded weakly, realizing that the burnt man could easily make good on his threat. Unlocking his fingers from the man's throat, Kelvin let the sailor drop heavily to the storm-weathered deck of the ship. For a moment Kelvin let the man lay as he coughed and gasped, then he hauled the sailor to his feet. Kelvin was amazed at the incredible strength he now possessed. He marveled at how easily he lifted the man with only one hand.

A few minutes later Kelvin stood before the captain, his hideous face once again concealed by the cowl of his cloak. The captain was a rangy man with a weather beaten complexion that was creased by a hundred lines. Thick stubble covered the captain's face, and he scowled as he saw the two men at his cabin door.

"I ordered that no one was to be allowed aboard."

"I insisted," answered Kelvin. "I have a very lucrative proposition for you."

The captain narrowed his eyes. "Come in."

The interior of the cabin smelled of creosote. Light filtered in through warped shards of glass, which were fitted into a mosaic window that was more utilitarian than artistic. The thick shards were less likely to break in high winds and rough weather than if a full flat pane were fit into the captain's cabin, and the mosaic served its purpose and allowed a dusty light to eke through. Several yellowing marine maps lay on a scarred wooden desk, their edges curling up around the captain's log that held them in place. A tallowed overcoat hung from a brass hook near a carefully maintained sextant, and a narrow bed filled the corner of the chamber.

The captain pushed a heavy chair in Kelvin's direction, and took the other himself. He leaned back and took a short swig from a small metal flask that had been resting on his desk. He proffered the flask to Kelvin, who politely waved it away.

The captain took another pull at the flask, and returned the stopper. "I don't mean to be abrupt," he said gruffly, "but I'll soon need to begin offloading the slave cargo. They'll be auctioned at Slave Plaza this afternoon."

"Indeed," answered Kelvin. "Then I've come just in time. I'd like to purchase a slave without the hassle of the auction."

The captain began to stand up. "I'm afraid you've wasted your time then. No one gets first pick on the slaves. Even Adolphus, the owner of the auction house, bids like everyone else."

Kelvin ignored the captain's less than subtle suggestion that he should leave, and remained seated. "I'm looking for a green-eyed, brown-haired female slave."

The captain shook his head. "Adolphus pays much coin for such slaves. I'd be a fool to sell you such a slave, when I stand to gain a handsome profit by letting her go to the auction block."

"How much does Adolphus pay for such a slave?"

"Twenty, even as much as fifty gold pieces for a fine specimen."

"And I imagine that you only make a percentage of that money," said Kelvin.

The captain nodded. "I earn a third of the auction price, the rest goes to the owner of the auction block, which in this case is Adolphus. Any time Adolphus buys a slave from his own block he earns back the majority of his bid."

"I see," said Kelvin. "What would you say if I told you that I'm willing to pay up to a hundred pieces of gold, and that you won't have to split that amount with anyone?"

"I'd say, let's do business."

Dastolius and his two cronies were funding his efforts to take Adolphus down, and Kelvin was more than happy to bleed the slave merchants dry of their coin. He hadn't asked to be brought back from the grave, and didn't feel any particular need to be frugal with their gold. Dastolius and his companions ran a slave block that competed with Adolphus, and any money they provided him was blood money earned by the enslavement of others.

Kelvin smiled wryly. They were all in for a rude awakening.

It only took Kelvin a few moments to pick Ishay from among the other slaves. Her radiant beauty transcended her disheveled mane of hair, and the torn rags in which she was attired. Her green eyes sparkled fear as Kelvin escorted her from the wharf, her hands still bound in front of her. As they left sight of the ship, Kelvin halted beneath the bronze legs of a statue constructed in homage to one of the long line of Emperor Vlads that had ruled Bathos.

Ishay looked at Kelvin fearfully. Already she had divined the horrible visage that lurked beneath the covering hood, and seen the blistered and charred hands.

"I know I'm rather hideous to look upon," said Kelvin, "but I promise that you've nothing to be afraid of." She was of nearly the same height as Kelvin and he looked right into her eyes, not hiding the horrors of his visage.

The lower lip of her wide mouth quivered and she stuttered out a response. "Yes, Master."

"It's not going to be like that," said Kelvin. "I need your help, and if you'll agree to help me out, I can provide passage for you back to your homeland of Zeilan."

Ishay's round eyes opened wide. "Is this some kind of cruel trick?"

"Not at all," answered Kelvin as he produced a knife blade and severed the girl's bonds. "Now if you'll agree to help me, we have some purchases to make. You are going to need to look the parts that you are going to play."

* * * *

Once Kelvin produced a ring bearing the seal of Dastolius, the shop keeper, Shoz, was more than happy to run up a debt against Dastolius' line of credit. Ishay quickly got over her apprehension and enjoyed the attention that the fussy shopkeeper was paying her as he combed her hair, and fitted her with various outfits and ornamentation.

Kelvin could see Ishay's eyes wander to a golden bracelet that lay in a velvet case atop of Shoz's polished oaken shop counter. Lifting it from the velvet lining, Kelvin fitted the bracelet on Ishay's slim wrist.

Ishay's green eyes glittered as she admired it. "In my country, only the richest of women can afford such ornamentation."

"It is much the same here," agreed Shoz, tugging at his waxed mustachio.

"You're in luck," said Kelvin to Ishay. "Because today you're one of the richest women in Bathos."

"I can't accept something so expensive," said Ishay.

"Put it on Dastolius' account," Kelvin directed the shopkeeper. "Today, I'm feeling very generous with his money."

As Shoz wrapped up several outfits for Ishay, Kelvin found two white cloaks of the same size, and added them to the pile of items to be purchased. Then, using Ishay's glossy brown locks as a reference, he selected a wig woven from similarly colored hair.

The shopkeeper inscribed a writ of purchase and dripped hot wax upon it, which Kelvin impressed with the signatory ring that Dastolius had lent him. Kelvin hoisted the package from the counter. "It's been a pleasure doing business with you."

"Likewise," grinned Shoz as he considered closing up shop early. "Do come again."

Ishay shook her head as they left the shop. "I don't understand," she said. "One minute I'm doomed to a life of slavery, and the next you're buying me the finest clothing in Bathos. I've never even seen fabrics such as these in my own land."

"You'll be playing several parts," said Kelvin.

"What do you mean by that?"

"I mean you'll be pretending to be things you are not."

"And you?" she asked.

"The very fact that I am alive walking the streets of Bathos, means I pretend to be something I am not."

"Are you also an outlander?" asked the brown-haired girl.

"More than you'll ever know," agreed Kelvin.

Ishay accepted this at face value, and surveyed the narrow defile of Tailor Street that cut through high-walled buildings, the lower levels of which were filled with the shops of clothiers, and cobblers. Their signs protruded from the walls, swinging from polished brass rods. Richly dressed men and women haughtily strode the streets surrounded by fawning courtiers and accompanied by at least one man at arms to discourage thieves.

"Where do we go now?" asked Ishay, pushing a stray strand of her glossy mane back from her face.

"We visit a bowyer, a fletcher, and an armourer. Even in a war of wits, it is best to be prepared for violence. The people that we will be deceiving are not accustomed to being toyed with, and they might have the tendency to react violently."

"Will I be in any danger?" asked Ishay warily.

Kelvin turned his face toward the smooth-skinned countenance of the girl, and for a moment he regretted the scorched visage that he wore, wondering if he might have been able to find favor with this beautiful creature, had he still possessed the face with which he had been born. "I won't deceive you," he answered. "It is very possible that you will be in real danger."

He suddenly took pity upon the girl that had been snatched away from her native land and thrust into slavery. "I need your help," he said. "But if you choose so, I will give you money for passage back to Zeilan right now. If you stay, I will be depending upon you. I won't force you to help me."

For a moment Ishay considered this offer, and then firm resolution crossed her countenance. "Danger is nothing new to me. In Zeilan we are constantly exposed to the dangers of marauding tribes or wild beasts. If need be, the women fight alongside the men as fiercely and as bravely as they. I owe you much for rescuing me from the slave ship, and I will help you- before I accept passage back to my homeland."

* * * *

Though Kelvin might have spent much time admiring the weapons available in the shops of the bowyer, and the armourer, he had little time to waste, and after examining the craftsmanship and quality of the weapons, he quickly chose the ones he would need for the tasks at hand.

Immediately thereafter, he and Ishay crossed through the claustrophobic intersections of the Mid-City, and into the jumbled confines of Low Bathos. The streets teamed with cargo-laden carts hauling grains from the ships along the wharves. The surly drivers whipped at the loitering crowds of ruffians who waited to upset the carts of unwary teamsters and run off with the fallen grains and foodstuffs. This had become an all too common occurrence, and now the drivers hired men-at-arms to accompany each cart. This discouraged the ruffians, but their numbers were large, and their boldness grew as their hunger increased.

As Ishay and Kelvin crossed onto Spike Street, a crowd of ruffians surged at a passing cart. Their numbers were so thick that they caught up the edge of the cart and heaved it over, throwing the driver to the street. Ponies screamed, and barrels of grain rolled free, some dashing open upon the cobblestones.

A guard dressed in a studded leather cuirass, leaped free of the tangle of reins and tipping cart and lashed out to the left and the right with his short blade. The crowds scattered before him, but not before they had carried off most of the barrels, and not before the guard had slain one of their number. They fled carrying their booty, leaving behind their dead companion.

Kelvin and Ishay stepped aside, letting the fleeing horde pass.

"The city is no less dangerous than the jungle," commented Ishay.

"No less dangerous, but infinitely more treacherous," said Kelvin.

Wading through the river of spilled grain that still lay on the cobbles, Kelvin noticed the rats peering out from beneath the grated gutters, and knew that it wouldn't be long before they scuttled out to harvest the misfortune of the teamster who had been overturned.

They turned off Spike Street and proceeded down the jagged, uneven road from which Cloister Alley extended. Here they found a small church that occupied the basement of a tenement. Few realized that it even existed. Since this particular sect offered neither power, prestige, nor personal aggrandizement to its parishioners it was little frequented, its wall hangings threadbare, and the damp interior sparsely furnished. The small chapel lay in stark contrast to the grand temples that rose toward the slate skies along Cult Street. There, marble pillars supported grand facades, and the priests wore fine silk robes, their fingers adorned with sparkling gems the hues of the rainbow. They preached fire and death, and of dark powers below which might be grasped and exploited for personal gain- and sometimes, when the moon was nearly extinguished in the night sky, human blood was shed upon their dark altars.

In this small chapel, the bishop taught of kindness to one's fellow man.

Hence, it was of little popularity. A man with dark sandy hair, and of unassuming size and clothing approached them across the threadbare carpets.

"May I help you both?" he asked.

"Yes, Bishop," croaked Kelvin. "I need some advice on defending myself from the blackest of magics."

"Very well," said the priest as he motioned to the carpet. "Sit down for a moment and we'll discuss the matter. Your life is not at this moment in danger?"

"My life is long gone," said Kelvin as he threw back his hood and revealed his horrible visage.

* * * *

Slave Plaza was alive with activity. From the granite columns that encircled the plaza, Kelvin and Ishay watched as Adolphus arrived. The iron shod hooves of the horses that drew his chariot clattered on the cobblestones, and his gold-embossed coach hurtled through the thick crowds, which scattered at his coming so they would not be torn beneath hoof and wheel.

Adolphus lowered his bulk from the chariot, followed by Bester and Costas, who pushed their way through the crowd, creating a pathway for the deadly wizard to follow. Not that the crowd needed much incentive to move out of the way once they saw who followed the two roughnecks. Adolphus' reputation was well known in the slave markets, and many dared not even bid against him if he expressed interest in purchasing a slave that was being auctioned. Only the powerful and politically connected dared do so, and the competition was assumed to be sporting and good-natured, though rarely did Adolphus let a green-eyed, brown-haired slave girl slip through his stubby fingers.

The sorcerer settled his prodigious body into a broad wooden seat, and Costas and Bester took up post slightly behind the chair, one on either side. Since the assassination attempt at the Blood Ring, Adolphus had become increasingly nervous about exposing himself in public places. Now, at his order, Costas and Bester stood with their blades bared, so that if an attack was made they would not have to waste a moment of their time unsheathing their weapons.

The crowds pressed forward as the auctioneer, dressed in a gaudy red chemise, and delicate fingers dripping with begemmed rings, presented himself. He began his long-winded harangue, which promised the finest, strongest, and the most beautiful slaves. The wealthy slaveholders of Bathos stood at the forefront of the crowd. These were the ones that would actually be bidding on the slaves. Behind them and their retainers, gawkers filled the plaza.

Still concealed at the far edges of the courtyard among the high pillars ringing the area, Kelvin and Ishay watched as the first slave was brought forward in chains, his head proudly raised, despite the jeers of the crowd.

A pained expression crossed Ishay's face.

"Do you know him?"

She shook her head, her tawny mane flowing across her smooth shoulders. Now she was dressed in the attire of a slave; a simple linen skirt wrapped about the gentle swells of her hips, and another band of linen binding her breasts. On her neck she bore the collar of a slave, which was inscribed with the name of her owner, and set with a sturdy iron ring. "He is from another tribe than mine, and probably we were deadly enemies; but even so, I cannot bear seeing the people of my land sold like chattel. We should live free and unencumbered in the wild, living off the goodness of the land."

"So it should be," agreed Kelvin. "Are you ready?"

She nodded, nervously licking her rouge-darkened lips, and without saying another word she strode into the crowds, winding her way between thick-necked ruffians, crippled beggars, and other curious citizenry of Bathos. Kelvin watched her disappear into the crowd, and waited impatiently for her return.

As the fourth slave came upon the block, Adolphus scribbled a notation on a scrap of parchment with a piece of lead. It was his habit to keep careful track of the bidding, so as to calculate his profit from the day. As always he kept an eye out for green-eyed, brown-haired slave girls of which he might add to his growing harem. His appetites were insatiable in every respect.

He examined the sleek arms and narrow waist of the female on the stone dais, but noting her blonde hair chose not to place a bid. Suddenly Costas leaped forward into his line of sight, his blade flashing outward and halting near the collared throat of the most beautiful creature that Adolphus had ever seen.

Her tawny hair wreathed about her, fanning out above her waist, her green eyes flashing defiance as the blade hovered at her collared neck. Instantly Adolphus decided that he must have this girl. He waved Costas away, and as the guard stepped back Ishay took time to notice the cruel features, and the crooked, leering smile. She examined the wide belt that he wore. It was studded with iron rivets, and supported the sheath of his sword, but protruding from beneath, nearly obscured by the worn leather tunic, she noticed the glint of a brass key.

"She bears no weapons, let her approach," snapped Adolphus when Costas didn't move aside quickly enough for his tastes.

Costas lowered his sword and backed away, leaving the brunette space to approach Adolphus.

"What is your name, girl? And what brings you here?"

She knelt in front of him, noting the unsavory stench of his body, but not allowing her face to register any such expression. "My name is Ishay, and I come bearing a message from my master," she said.

"Indeed? And who is your master?" But even as he asked the question Adolphus read the inscription upon her collar.

"Baron Glavold, your lordship. She put her face down and proffered a scroll, holding it forward with both hands, in the same fashion that Kelvin had taught her.

Adolphus plucked the parchment away, taking care to simultaneously caress her strong hands. He methodically unrolled the scroll, and read the message inscribed.

To his Lordship Adolphus:

With most respect I propose a business alliance between the two of us. If you are familiar with my name you will recognize that we are in a unique position to benefit from this joining of forces. Reply with your terms, and we will strike a mutually beneficial pact.

Sincerely,

Lord Glavold

Seeing that Adolphus had finished reading the missive, Ishay carefully addressed the sorcerer. "I respectfully await your reply, master."

Adolphus appreciatively eyed Ishay's nubile form, but realized that the auction was progressing without his fullest attention. "Return to your master and tell him that I will envoy a reply tomorrow." He waved the supposed slave girl away and watched her retreat into the crowd.

Kelvin was relieved to see Ishay safely return. "Did it go as planned?" he asked.

"He did not offer an immediate response. He said he would send message on the morrow."

Kelvin bit his mutilated lip as he considered this unexpected kink in his plans. "The problem is that he will be delivering the message to Lord Glavold. Did Adolphus take an interest in you?"

She nodded grimly. "He fondled my hands as I gave him the message."

Kelvin nodded. "Your beauty offers far too much temptation for even a steel-willed man, let alone one that is accustomed to indulging his vices."

"You flatter me," said Ishay.

"It's not flattery. It's the truth, and it is vital to our plan."

* * * *

The duties of his long day finished, Costas wandered through stinking alleys toward Fennel Street. His body and mind were craving the sweet lull and abyss of the opium seed, and he paid little attention to his surroundings; a mistake which can often prove fatal on the streets of Bathos. As it was, though, he passed through the festering streets unmolested, and entered a squat building, constructed of gray river slate, through a small side entrance.

The scent of opium hung heavy in the air, and Costas wandered through the thick haze drifting in the air, sucking in the aroma. Olive-skinned women swathed in diaphanous veils and wrapped in red silk greeted him, the surly swordsman who stood by the door paying little attention to the newcomer. Costas Cutthroat frequently visited this establishment, and he always paid well for the services he received. He would be welcome in this den of iniquity for as long as his purse contained coin.

A dark-eyed beauty led Costas to a cushioned antechamber, which walls consisted of velvet hangings sewn with lurid scenes. In a moment the woman returned with an elaborate pipe made from blown glass, and she laid it before him. Costas quickly put the stem to his mouth and inhaled the drug, sighing as the narcotic took him deeper and deeper into a reverie of sublime and unreal dreams.

As he dreamed a woman dressed in the gossamer veil and red silks of the opium den, slipped into the tapestried chamber. She knelt down beside Costas, her dark brown hair falling across his chest as she slipped a brass key from his belt. From within the silks at her waist, the woman pulled a small wooden case, slightly longer than the length of the key. She opened up the case, and within lay two flat strips of clay. The woman placed the brass key inside of the box, and pressed the lid down, making an impression of the key. Then, green eyes darting from the key to the man who mumbled incoherent words in his dream-state, she quickly removed any residual clay from the key, and carefully slipped it back into the man's belt.

This accomplished, Ishay slipped from the small chamber, and drifted through the hazy halls. A similarly clad woman approached her, bearing a water pipe in her hands.

"When was it that Jostra hired you?" she asked.

"This is my first day working for him," answered Ishay.

Apparently satisfied, the woman slipped by her with a polite half-smile, and continued on her chore. Ishay took a turn and found her way out a back door into the reeking alley beyond. Kelvin met her there, emerging from the inky darkness that clung to the slate walls. "Any problems?"

"It went smoothly," she answered.

"Beautiful and talented," said Kelvin. "If only I weren't so hideous."

"And so dead," added Ishay. "I still have trouble believing your tale of death and resurrection."

"You still don't have qualms about working with a dead man?"

"You are more likely a liar, than a dead man," answered Ishay, and through the gloom Kelvin could see a quizzical expression form on her face. "The only thing that I cannot understand is why you would tell me such a story. I may be only an ignorant savage, and I have seen strange magics worked by the shaman of my tribe, but this I cannot believe."

"Believe what you must," answered Kelvin. He flexed his charred hand and the flesh split open, but strangely he felt little pain.

They crept through the darkness, leaving Fennel Street where it intersected with the nether reaches of Peacock Street. Even from this distance they could see the aurora of light cast up from the mass of lanterns that hung at the hub of the intersection where the taverns and gambling houses lay thickest. As they approached, the distant sound of a lute carried to their ears, and then the cries of bitter drunks who had carelessly thrown away their money at the gaming tables and now hadn't even a copper crown to line their purse. The unfortunates were now unwelcome in the gambling establishments and they were hurled out into the streets to lay besotted in the gutters.

Kelvin and Ishay emerged from the gloom into the brightly lit corridors that were lined by agitated horses harnessed to golden-hubbed chariots. The drivers patted their horses on the head whispering soothing words to them, but Kelvin's very presence seemed to disturb them. Perhaps, thought Kelvin, they could smell that he wasn't truly alive- sense the taint of death upon him. Because of their discomfort, he didn't venture too near the distraught equines.

Ishay was now attired as a high-born baroness. She had shed the diaphanous clothing of the opium den's servants, and now she wore the gold bracelet that Kelvin had purchased for her, and a low cut silk blouse of vivid red, which was embroidered with silver and gold thread. Her skirt was a dark blue silk, and her shoes constructed of calf-skin by the finest cobbler in town. She wore her brown hair piled high on her head, a few glossy rivulets cascading loose to frame her rouged cheeks and lips. She carried herself with a haughty confidence that belied the fact that she was a slave.

Kelvin stayed cloaked, his hideous face obscured. Perhaps, he thought, Ishay's beauty would distract others from him and allow him to pass less-noticed. Or perhaps, they would be drawn to her beauty, and be curious who the cloaked man that accompanied her might possibly be.

The doorman of the Golden Eel recognized Kelvin and let him pass with Ishay, who he probably would have allowed to enter just on the basis of her mien alone.

Gold-painted serving girls whisked past them and the establishment was alive with boisterous laughter and the ring of gold as it hit the table. Dice were cast and cards were laid down, and the two unlikely companions searched the chaos for a sign of Bester's broad back and child-like visage.

"Do you see him?" asked Ishay.

Kelvin's keen eyes pierced the hazy air as they roved back and forth among the press of flesh. "In the back left hand corner," he answered without pointing. "He's at one of the dice tables."

Near to the dice table was a thick desk, behind which hung a heavy piece of slate. Occasionally, a greasy looking oddsmaker would speak to a runner that entered the establishment and came directly to his desk. The runner would relay some information, and based on this the sweating oddsmaker would rise and scratch new odds on the Blood Ring match that was taking place at that very moment over near Seven Street.

Bester paid very close attention to these odds, and very little to his dice game and lost heavy amounts of coin. Kelvin and Ishay took a seat and ordered several drinks. To Kelvin the ale tasted flat and stale, just like everything else had since he had been resurrected. Ishay drank only lightly, lowering the level of the beverage in her flagon only slightly over the next thirty minutes during which they sat and observed.

Kelvin noted that the runner reporting on the status of the Blood Ring match came only every ten minutes. This ten minutes allowed ample time for the momentum of the match to change and shift drastically, and so, consequently, the odds shifted little- being based primarily on the past track records of the warriors and the masterminds that directed their movement.

Finally Kelvin pushed a heavy bag of gold toward Ishay. The match will be coming to a close soon. I'm going to see if we can make our move tonight."

"Tonight?" asked Ishay in shock.

"You remember what to do?"

Ishay nodded, but he could see the uncertainty in her eyes. "I just wasn't expecting to place a bet tonight..."

"There's nothing to it," answered Kelvin. "Just go to the man at the slate board."

Saying this, he slipped out the front door of the Golden Eel and took off at a brisk stride down Peacock Street. Several blocks down he cut into an alley, and increased his speed to a sprint. His reassembled body did not run as smoothly as his previous, and his steps were often jarring and uneven, but he still made excellent speed. He cut through night-shrouded alleys that he knew the Golden Eel's runners, who shuttled between the gaming room and the Blood Ring, would not dare to take for fear of an unsavory demise.

This shortcut would shave the distance to about half, but even as Kelvin was congratulating himself, three men dressed in threadbare burlap tunics stepped in front of him, their knives glinting in the moonlight. They said nothing, but Kelvin could read their deadly intent. They would knife him, and rob him for whatever few coppers he might be carrying, his cloak, and the boots that he wore.

Kelvin was in a hurry to reach Seven Street, so he did not slacken his pace. As he neared the trio of cutthroats that closed in around him, he reached beneath his cloak. The first of his assailants leaped in with his knife blade held high, bringing it down as if to plunge it into Kelvin's unguarded chest. His reckless attack assumed that his target was defenseless, but Kelvin's curved blade whispered from its sheath and glittered in the moonlight. The blade shivered as it cut through bone, and a crimson haze spattered through the air as Kelvin sliced through the man's wrist, completely severing the hand from the arm.

As the knife clattered to the pavement, Kelvin shifted his blade and pushed it out in front of him, the razor tip sweeping across the abdomen of his remaining two foes. His weapon was longer and they had foolishly rushed in upon him without ascertaining whether or not he was armed. They both fell back, dark blood seeping from a slit in one mugger's tunic as he went to the ground, and the other relieved to find that he had escaped with only a slash in his shirt.

By this time Kelvin had run between them and was well down the alley, disappearing into the wretched black corridors that twisted toward Seven Street. He momentarily slowed his pace to shake the blood from his sword, and slip it back into his oiled leather scabbard. He mentally congratulated the blacksmith who had forged the excellent weapon that he bore. There were many hallmarks of a fine blade that a warrior would search for when choosing a weapon, but until that sword had undergone the test of actual combat, it was difficult to be sure of the quality of a blade.

As he rounded a dark corner the torch lit arches of the Blood Ring coliseum appeared before him. The stacked arches encircled the building that rose six stories high, and in each curve a torch flickered brightly, casting a bloody red luminescence in the hallways, which led to the stone-benched interior of the magnificent building.

Seven Street ran along the nearest side of the coliseum, and without difficulty Kelvin located the tall tower, which he had remembered seeing aforetimes. It rose above all the buildings along the street, but that was its only distinguishing characteristic. It was a rather plain structure, built from gray river stone and mortar. No name plate adorned the stone beside the thick planks of the oak door that was blackened with age. No windows broke the rough surface of rounded stone until the tower reached its eighth and highest level.

The coliseum was actually set in a depression in the floor of Bathos, so it was obscured from the view of much of the city. Legend had it that the architects who had designed the grand building had been executed for their folly. During monsoons, the floor of the arena often became flooded with water. This was problematic until the emperors began staging boat battles, where the crews of several boats would engage each other in deadly combat. Eventually the problem was solved, altogether, by adapting the noblemen's board game past time, blood ring, into a life-size spectacle. The stone structure of rings was built high above the floor level of the arena, and when the coliseum flooded, it did little more than obscure the spikes, which were set in the bottom of the pits.

As Kelvin had suspected, this tower provided a much more commanding view than the coliseum itself, but if his theory were to prove correct he needed to test it. Inserting barely feeling fingers into the cracks between mortared stone, which had been smoothed by thousands of years in the raging torrents of the Tiber, the very numbness of his extremities hindered his climb, and he doubted that, had it been a smoother surface, he would have been able to successfully ascend the tower.

Reaching a small ledge beneath the southward facing window, Kelvin heard a great cheer go up from the Blood Ring coliseum, and he knew that the game had finished its course. He must work quickly now.

A murky pane of glass was set into a thick wooden frame, and it was latched from within. Hoisting his chest onto the flat ledge, he clung to the face of the tower with one hand, while he found the flat-thin blade that he wore at his waist. He slipped this knife between the sill's threshold and the wooden frame of the window. He moved the blade along until it halted against the metal latch that was pushed down into a small catch carved into the stone of the ledge. Kelvin pressed against it until it rotated out of the catch, and then he pushed the window open, and rolled into the dusty interior of the tower's highest chamber.

Only thin shafts of moonlight distilled through the turbid glass, and it took long moments for Kelvin's eyes to accustom themselves to his new surroundings. The room was sparsely furnished with an ancient ash table at the center of the room that was caked with thick dust. A lantern and a small wooden flask of oil lay on the table, with an extra wick nearby. The remains of a few broken chairs were jumbled in the corner, as well as the broken spokes of a chariot wheel, which iron band had come unstrung and lay in a loose coil.

From the window he could see the glowing lanterns of Peacock Street, and there were footprints among the gray powder that lay thick upon the floor. These clues, and the lantern suggested to Kelvin that his surmise had been correct. He carefully shut and latched the window. He would know for certainty in a few moments whether he was right or not.

With quiet steps he sank back into the molasses shadows near the door, and he waited in silence, his charred thumb toying with the pommel of his flat-bladed dagger. He didn't have to wait for long before he heard the creak of the ancient door far below, and heard quick footsteps up the spiral steps.

Breathing heavily, a man entered the chamber and moved directly to the lamp on the table. He flicked the flint built into the lantern, and sparked the wick to life within the still shuttered lamp. As he was about to lift it into the air, an arm pulled his chin back and he felt cold metal prick his throat.

"If you want to live, you are going to do as I say," rasped Kelvin.

The man nodded and choked out an affirmative reply.

"Is this a Thieves Guild set up?"

"Yes," answered the man. "I didn't know the Gambler's Guild was onto our game."

"I'm not with the Gambler's Guild," answered Kelvin. "Now tell me quickly. Who won the match tonight?"

"Xiberius won the match."

"And what is the signal should his opponent win?"

"Two long flashes of light from the lamp."

"I want you to give that signal now. If you do not do as I say, I will kill you."

Still holding the knife to the man's throat, Kelvin allowed him to pick up the lantern and move to the window. He moved the shutter aside for one long moment and let the light be seen by whomever watched for the signal.

"Very good," said Kelvin. "Now again."

Instead of opening the shutter of the lamp, the man kicked backward at Kelvin's knee. Kelvin felt something snap, but the pain was remarkably dull, and barely registered on his faulty nervous system. Still, his leg gave out and he staggered backward, crashing against the table. From beneath his leather vest, the signal man whipped out two wave-edged flame daggers and leaped toward Kelvin. Though he was off balance and his reflexes blunted, Kelvin was not so slow as to give his opponent the advantage. He withdrew a cluster of three darts from his harness, and cast them.

The darts scattered, not grouping as Kelvin had intended them, but the effects were still as desired. One dart struck his attacker in the forehead, another in the throat, and another in the chest. It was the dart in the throat that proved effective, and the signal man went to his knees, gurgling and clutching at the dart which had sunk deep into his windpipe. As Kelvin rolled to his feet he lashed out with his blade, and cut above the man's clutching hands, slitting the Thief's throat, so that he pitched forward and spasmed- his final agonized moments being played out on the tower's dusty floor.

Quickly, Kelvin lifted the fallen lantern to the window and once more opened the shutter, broken glass cascading outward as he did, and flame licking from the upset reservoir of oil within the lantern. He waited the same long moment, as had the thief, then he dropped the lantern below the level of the window and extinguished it with the cloak of the dead man.

His boots crunched on the shards as he once again stood. Rooting among the pouch at his side, Kelvin found the signet ring of Dastolius and dropped it on the floor next to the leaking corpse of the dead man. He took several steps, testing his knee, and found that the joint produced a crunching sound with each step. Something was definitely amiss, probably broken, but the pain barely registered, and by ignoring it he could walk with only a slight limp. He left the room, and descended the circling stairs to the door below. Revelers were now departing the coliseum, and he joined the departing throngs, losing himself among them.

* * * *

Ishay nursed her drink at the Golden Eel. Even so, combined with the prospect of the adventures that this night was sure to bring, the alcohol made her feel almost giddy. Several times she brushed off would be suitors who approached her poorly lit table with amorous objectives on their mind. One had been most insistent, and she finally rid herself of him by giving the large doormen a piece of gold to bounce him out the door.

Now she spotted Bester's massive form moving to the door, and she left her seat and slipped after him. The doorman grinned broadly at her as she emerged, and she smiled back at him, sharing their private joke. Glancing around, she found Bester crossing into a side alley. She pursued him and found him climbing the sagging stair of an old tenement building with an extended loft that peered above the level of the surrounding structures.

Ishay smiled slyly to herself. Kelvin had been correct then. Bester was watching for a signal from Seven Street, which would indicate the winner of the Blood Ring match. This would inform him before the runner could arrive from the Blood Bowl and the results could be posted. There would be a several minute window of opportunity in which he could place a final bet on the winner, and rake in huge winnings.

She waited in the shadows for Bester to emerge. There was no point in her following Bester up the stairs. She would wait for him to return to the Golden Eel and place his bet. It would be easy enough for her to stand close behind and hear on whom he put his money.

She returned to the interior of the Golden Eel and waited near the dice table. Eventually Bester returned, and he made his way directly to the odds-maker who stood in front of the slate board.

"Last call for bets on the Blood Ring," shouted the greasy man.

Bester threw a heavy bag of gold on the counter. "This goes on Stinch to win the ring. I'll take your five to one odds."

The oddsmaker viewed Bester through narrowed eyes. "You've been winning awfully big on the Blood Ring matches lately. What's your secret?"

"The gods of chance love me," he answered, a grin splitting his child-like face.

"We'll see about that," answered the oddsmaker, reluctantly deciding to accept the bet. He hoisted the bag and set it beneath his counter.

Ishay stood close by and she lifted her sack of gold coin to the counter.

"Let me guess," said the oddsmaker. "You're going to bet on Stinch, too."

"Stinch has good warriors," said Ishay, "but Xiberius has the ability to out think brawn. I'm placing this gold on Xiberius."

"That's a lot of gold," said the man, wiping at his knobby nose, but he accepted it all the same. He was happy to counterbalance the heavy bet that Bester had placed on Stinch. Bester's luck had been uncanny when it came to betting on the Blood Ring, and he was nervous that the Golden Eel would take yet another huge loss.

Three minutes later the runner came into the Eel. The odds maker smiled broadly when he realized that he wouldn't have to be paying out on the five to one odds. He posted the results of the match on his slate board, and Ishay watched as Bester's jaw dropped wide in dismay. He sat his enormous bulk down on the nearest stool, and put his head in his hands, his eyes glazing over in numb horror.

Ishay walked to the counter, and spoke to the odds maker over the clamor of the other bettors who were anxious to collect their winnings. "I'll come by later with some men by to collect my winnings," she said. "You can remember my face?"

The oddsmaker nodded. Part of his job was to remember the face of every bettor he came across so he could weed out the cheaters, the gamblers, and the overly lucky who were bad risks for the Golden Eel. "It would be hard to forget a face like yours," he answered.

"I hope that was meant as a compliment," she said.

"It was," the odds maker assured her. "But here is a marker. The bearer of this can collect your winnings, so you need not return yourself, if you prefer to send your servants."

He handed her a rectangular marker of brass that bore the stamping of a writhing eel.

"Thank you," said Ishay, and she turned and left the Golden Eel.

Ten minutes later, Kelvin came in and sat down beside the distraught Bester, who was doing his best to drown his misery in his fifth flagon of ale.

"What do you want?" snarled Bester. "This is my table, and I suggest you leave it before I snap your spine."

"I want to help you," answered Kelvin from amidst the dark shrouds of his cowling.

This response took Bester momentarily aback, and Kelvin continued before the big man could spew another threat.

"I know that you lost a considerable amount betting on the Blood Ring match tonight. I also know that money didn't belong to you. It belonged to the Thieves Guild."

Bester trained his bloodshot and beady eyes upon the newcomer. "How is it that you know so much about me?"

"How is not important. What is important is that I can extract you from your current predicament."

"I lost a thousand crowns of Thieves Guild money tonight. They should have doubled that money tonight, and they're going to come after me for it. I don't have it, so they're going to take it out of my hide."

"It so happens," said Kelvin, "that this very casino owes me a similar amount of gold. What if I promise you that gold will be yours by the end of this week?"

Bester looked at the stranger suspiciously. "And what do I have to do for it?"

"Nothing," answered Kelvin. "Absolutely nothing."

* * * *

The purple blossoms that grew thick along Manor Street waved in the whispering breeze; a breeze that did little to ease the overbearing heat of the afternoon. From a thick copse of verdant garden Kelvin watched the spiraling streets that wound upward to meet the mansion-lined marble street near which he hid himself.

His body seemed no longer capable of sweating, so instead he baked in his thick cowling. Only the shadows of the overhanging palm provided respite. Since the cooler early morning hours, he had watched the street waiting for a messenger to arrive from Adolphus. He had nearly given up hope when he saw a chariot, pulled by double steeds, began to mount the steep hill toward Manor Street. Through the straining limbs of the horses he could see the golden crest of Adolphus upon the forefront of the chariot car.

Stiff limbs rebelled as he slipped from his concealment and quickly made his way toward the other end of the street. He found Ishay, once again dressed in servant's garb, sitting on a stone bench beneath the gnarled fingers of an acacia tree. She saw him slipping along the wrought iron fences that lined the various palatial estates, and she stood awaiting him. Together they turned through a silver-hinged gate and traversed a graveled walkway flanked by exquisitely sculptured shrubs, and life-size statuary of incredible artisanship.

Climbing the broad white stairs to the pillared doorstep, Kelvin glanced behind, and found that Adolphus' chariot had still not hove into sight. He lifted the lion-headed knocker and let it fall upon the thick front door. The knocker boomed in the inner halls of the mansion, and shortly the door was opened by a timid looking man-servant.

"May I be of service?"

Kelvin leaped inside the mansion, and whipped behind the servant as he put a knife to his throat. "Cooperate and you will be unharmed."

The servant's lower lip quivered, and for a moment Ishay thought that the man would burst out crying. "We won't harm you," reiterated Ishay.

Somehow the man seemed reassured, and he allowed Kelvin to pull him off behind a turquoise wall hanging without a fuss. Ishay slipped the door closed and nervously waited beside it, hoping that no other servant would pass through the entry hall, and question her presence there.

Her luck held, and a moment later the boom of the knocker falling upon the door, echoed through the vast chamber. Ishay immediately answered the door.

"May I be of service?" she asked.

Before her stood Costas Cutthroat, and he let his cruel eyes devour her figure. "I have a message for Baron Glavold," he said with a crooked smile. He held out a sealed envelope, and Ishay plucked it from his grip.

"I will see that he receives it." Without further delay, Ishay closed the door, and listened to the sound of Costas' retreating footsteps. She heard the crack of the whip, the creak of the chariot, and the clip of hooves as it departed.

"He's gone," called Ishay.

Immediately Kelvin swept aside the tapestry, and released the shaking servant. "I would appreciate it," said Kelvin, "if you keep silent about this incident."

He holstered his knife, then reached out with a gold coin, which he pressed into the servant's gyrating palm. "If you can keep your silence for a week's time, I'll send you five more of these. Do you understand?"

The servant nodded, and Kelvin and Ishay slipped from the mansion. Ishay handed Kelvin the envelope, and he ripped the message open and read the contents.

"He's taken the bait. He's agreed to an alliance with Glavold, but only if you are offered as a gift to him."

"And that is a good thing?" asked Ishay.

"It's like a Blood Ring match," said Kelvin. "We've got to out think our opponent."

* * * *

Kelvin inscribed a message of acceptance, and forged the seal of Glavold. He hired a courier to take the message, and the next morning found he and Ishay in an enclosed coach at the gates of Adolphus' towers. The armoured guards were expecting them, and they unlocked the iron gate, and swung them inward.

The coachmen Kelvin had hired guided the horses through the archway and into the small stone courtyard beyond. Kelvin lay concealed beneath a rug at the bottom of the coach, while Ishay sat bolt upright, wearing a white robe that signified the purity of the gift that Glavold was giving. Her dark hair and pale green eyes could be seen through the window of the carriage, and she looked out in awe at the forked towers that rose above them.

At the sound of the horses' hooves in the courtyard Adolphus, studying ancient tomes in the lower levels of the central tower, moved his bulk to the window. He peered down from his vantage point and saw the sun gleaming from Ishay's brown hair, and caught a glimpse of her perfect features as she glanced up along the lengths of the triple spires.

Often Adolphus viewed prospective visitors from his drawing room, and

the senior gate guard glanced to the window to see if the sorcerer was surveying his current callers. Adolphus motioned inward, indicating to the guard
that he should send the woman up. The guardsmen spoke several words to
Ishay, who threw the hood over her head, and closed the blind of the carriage.

A moment later a white-robed figure stepped down from the carriage,
the coachmen reaching up to take hold of one gloved hand. The junior guard
escorted his charge to the lower door of the central tower, and produced a key
that unlocked the iron bound door. As the portal swung open, Costas Cutthroat bounded down a flight of stairs to meet Adolphus' newest slave girl.
He was used to the constant influx of brown-haired women, so it was nothing
unusual, or out of the ordinary, for him to escort them to their new chambers.

Traditionally, he received them garbed in robes, colored to indicate the
woman's status. Often they struggled, and Costas was forced to subdue them
before taking them to their chambers. More often, they were resigned to their
miserable fate, and they came with their heads hung low, as this woman did
now.

"Follow me," said Costas, making his first mistake.

Following the cutthroat, the white-clad figure glided up a stairway that
led into the left tower, scuffed leather boots occasionally slipping incongruously from beneath the hem of the pristine robe. Costas' back was turned
and he did not see this, leading the slave up four levels, through an arched
portal and down a narrow hallway lined with small chambers, each door bearing a specific marking to indicate the occupant. Finally, Costas paused at an
unmarked door on his right.

"Here's your new home, wench. And a word of advice; obey Adolphus'
every request as if your life depends upon it- because it does. Stubborn or
willful slaves do not last very long in these towers."

"I don't plan on being here long," answered Kelvin as he threw aside the
white robe, and plunged his sword through Costas' abdomen. He gave the
blade a twist, and wrenched out the crimson length.

Costas emitted a great groan as he staggered backward, clutching his
belly, eyes still wide with shock and surprise. Kelvin slipped forward, and
aimed a downward stroke at the cutthroat. To his surprise, the blade cut completely through the neck, beheading Costas. Previous to his resurrection that
same stroke would have been enough to kill his foe, but not dismember him.

His strength had increased in proportion to his loss of speed and agility.

Crimson pooled on the stones as Kelvin leaned over the corpse and checked the man's belt for his key. Kelvin had not expected to run into Costas so early into his excursion, and so it had been necessary to seek him out at the opium den he frequented and take an impression of the key. A locksmith had constructed a replica from the clay markings that Ishay had made, and Kelvin carried that key now, but if he could find the original, it would be better than having the replica.

A short search revealed no key, and, puzzled, Kelvin stood to full height, his charred face turning to the left and right to determine the direction he would take. Perhaps the door to the upper chambers of the central tower was currently unlocked, and there was no need to carry a key. Perhaps Adolphus was not worried about a vengeful slave girl getting a hold of the key during the day, when he was fully awake and could easily marshal his powerful magics to defend himself.

Kelvin turned his steps back down the stairs whence he had come. Any delay might prove fatal to the element of surprise that he had so carefully cultivated. Even pausing to hide Costas' body might be too much of a postponement.

It was only the work of a few moments to return to the velvet-swathed walls of the entry chamber, and fortunately he met no other living soul as he retraced his steps. Now he mounted the broad steps, which led to the central tower. The stairs narrowed quickly and began to circle around the inner edge of the tower in an ascending spiral that cut through several open floors thick with collected curios from the far corners of the known lands.

Intrigued as Kelvin was by the tribal masks, carved totems, and golden-threaded chalices that he spotted among the jumble of artifacts, he could not afford to pause his upward momentum. Moments later the stairs abruptly ended in heavy door, which was slanted toward him at a forty-five degree angle. An exquisitely fashioned brass lock, one that would be extremely difficult to defeat by known lock picking methods, was fitted to the door handle, and staying momentarily clear of the keyhole, lest it be some sort of trap waiting to be sprung, he pressed down the lever.

No poisoned dart spat from the keyhole, but the lever stayed firm, and Kelvin confirmed that the door was locked. His left hand went to his waist and he bypassed the first pouch that was heavily weighted with a stone, and found the second pouch. He removed his duplicate key, and sucking in his breath, slipped it into the keyhole. Gently, he turned the key and smiled grimly as a subtle click was heard emanating from the lock.

Kelvin eased the door open and slipped into the dim room beyond. The windows were now shuttered, but one hundred and seven candles flickered in the draft that pushed through the open portal. Amidst the occult pattern that Adolphus had created with flame, the grotesque sorcerer perched on a velvet cushion that was stitched with vermilion-dyed horsehair tassels.

The breath hissed from his lungs as Kelvin noticed the huge bulk that stood quietly on the right of the doorway, his massive forearms folded calmly even as he watched Kelvin pass by him. Kelvin was glad now that he had purchased Bester's inaction. If he hadn't, Bester might have already crushed him in the brawny, back-breaking embrace that so many gladiators had experienced in the pits.

Still, Adolphus was not unaware of Kelvin's entrance, and he broke off his meditations, opening his eyes and fixing his baleful black orbs on the assassin. He saw the inaction of his most trusted bodyguard, and scowled viciously.

"So, intruder! You have bought the loyalty of my own men, and you come skulking into the lion's lair- hoping that luck will win you victory."

Kelvin shook his charcoal-colored head. "Last time I went after a sorcerer I depended upon luck, and didn't come away from the contest so well off. This time I come prepared."

"Indeed?" mocked Adolphus. "Are you prepared for this?"

He waved his fingers, intending to rip the trace minerals from the very veins of the would-be assassin. Kelvin felt his body tremor as strange forces twisted and pulled at it, invisible fingers jerking his limbs, and plucking at his scarred face. But despite the strange sensation, no harm came to him.

Adolphus opened his eyes wide in disbelief. One word formed on his lips. "How?" He continued to exert his magics against Kelvin, but the intruder strode forward, his sword and dagger trailing out behind him, as if he were wading through the fast currents of a stream. Of all the items that he carried, these were metallic, and the objects that Adolphus could most easily exercise his powers upon. But where, normally, Adolphus could easily pluck one of these weapons from its sheath and plunge it into the very heart of its owner, it took the utmost strength just to slow the progress of Kelvin as he moved forward.

"What magics do you possess to resist my powers so?" sputtered Adolphus.

Kelvin pulled a sharpened stake from his belt, as he struggled forward. "The laws of alchemy are not immutable- even by magic. You have the power to control metal…"

Strange forces pulled at him, desperately trying to restrain his forward progress, but Kelvin forcefully put one foot in front of the other until he stood near Adolphus' quivering bulk; the sorcerer shaking with the mental effort of his exertions.

"But I carry with me a rare lodestone. A stone that tampers with very magnetic forces from which you gather your powers."

Fear pooled in Adolphus' black eyes. "By the elder gods, Bester. Save me!"

Bester stood beyond the broken ring of candles. Pooling wax flamed on the floor, and crumbled candles marked the lumbering path that Kelvin had forged through the outer circle to come face to face with the sorcerer. Bester made no move, standing impassively in the stygian gloom that gathered near the doorway.

Even as Kelvin lifted his wooden stake, his leather sheaths tore from his sides and the blades contained therein tumbled away, scattering candle and flame before their twirling lengths. Relieved of the metal objects that had impeded his progress, Kelvin lifted his first stake and plunged it, with both hands, down between Adolphus' left clavicle. The flame hardened point plunged deep through flesh and sinew, and the sorcerer bellowed in horrible agony, pitching backward in writhing death throes that finally decreased and halted as his life was extinguished.

Kelvin turned and retrieved his sword from the feet of Bester, where it had come to rest. Bester's child-like face still remained expressionless, and his limbs motionless. Kelvin turned and beheaded the wizard, so he could provide proof to the trio who had commissioned this killing.

His lodestone still hung heavily at his side, but Kelvin was quite happy that he had carried its extra weight. The bishop at the small chapel he and Ishay had visited, had proved not only to be a student of religion, but a student of the cryptic sciences- and upon his advice Kelvin had sought out a lodestone to help combat the powers of Adolphus.

"I believe you promised me some money for doing absolutely nothing," said Bester, finally stirring from his position at the door.

Kelvin produced a brass marker from his pouch that was stamped with a writhing eel. "Take this to the Golden Eel. They are holding your money for you. I will leave word that they are to expect you."

"Good," said Bester, surveying the headless corpse of his former master. "The Thieves Guild has already been hounding me about the money, but they are asking only for the capital they invested. It seems that some slave merchant by the name of Dastolius slew the signal man and sent me the wrong message. The majority of their attention is focused on him."

Kelvin nodded. "That will leave some extra coin for you to use at your own discretion."

Bester grinned, his small teeth glinting in the candlelight. "I think maybe you have something to do with this turn of events, but since this arrangement is proving very profitable for me, I'll let you live."

"I appreciate that," said Kelvin. He hoisted the sealed leather sack that held the head of the sorcerer. "May our paths not cross again."

Bester let out a high pitched laugh as Kelvin slipped through the doorway.

Several minutes later, Kelvin tossed a grappling hook up to the edge of the courtyard wall and it hooked on the outward jutting spikes. He had only several minutes with which to work before the courtyard guard made his rounds. He scrambled up the rope, Adolphus' head slapping heavily at his side.

At the top he carefully stood, shrouded in the three-pronged shadow of the sorcerer's towers. The shadows the towers cast was the only cover that he possessed. It was broad daylight and the streets were alive with people. Kelvin removed a pair of clippers from the waist at his belt, and quickly cut the strands of razor wire that were strung tight across the walltop. The stuff cut through flesh as if it were butter fresh from the churn, and Kelvin was glad to see it snap away without whipping him.

With little time to waste, he reversed the prongs of the grappling hook, and lowered himself to the top of the carriage that waited below. As soon as his feet touched the burnished top of the coach he called to the driver who sat a few feet away. The driver responded by lifting his whip and spanking the flank of the right hand horse. The horses leaped forward, and Kelvin snapped the grappling line that he still held. The grapple swung loose from its moorings and it hit the cobblestones, clanging along behind the coach as it sped through the city streets.

Kelvin reeled in the rope and grapple, then slid in through the window to the interior of the carriage where Ishay waited for him, her knuckles white as they gripped leather straps that hung from the ceiling of the coach.

"Did you slay the sorcerer?"

Kelvin nodded and tapped the bag, which held his grim trophy. "The sorcerers must return me to my grave now."

"Will Dastolius order it done?"

"I doubt that Dastolius will be ordering anything. The Thieves Guild found their signal man dead in the tower on Seven Street."

"They'll be coming after you, then!"

Kelvin shook his head. "I dropped Dastolius' signet ring in the tower. They think that he committed the killing."

Ishay quickly assembled the pieces. "You dropped it on purpose."

"Dastolius and his cronies brought me back into this miserable existence." Kelvin stretched out his scarred hands, scraps of flesh hanging loose from the bones. "My body is disintegrating, and if the appropriate spells aren't soon worked, I will forever inhabit an immobile husk- never to pass on to the next life. Blevin, Tevol, Dastolius; they are of the same ilk as Adolphus. They are slavers prospering from the misery of others."

"I can't say that I understand the ways of the city," said Ishay, " but it seems more treacherous than the adder-haunted paths of my own jungle. No man can truly trust another."

"I'll be leaving it soon," said Kelvin, " and so will you." He took a folded parchment from the pouch that contained the lodestone. "Show this to the captain of the Confluence. He will honor this paper, and give you passage back to Xeilan."

Ishay embraced Kelvin and took the paper. "I'd kiss you if you weren't so hideous," she said.

Kelvin laughed. "I'd kiss you if I weren't so hideous. But I'm afraid that's not to be."

The coach pulled to a stop beneath a shaded archway on Breaker Street. This street was cut so low into the earth that it served as a canal when the waters of the Tiber overflowed, and the overhead arches acted as bridges. Now it was dry, and above the current-smoothed stone walls of Breaker Street, were finely built residences, short brick walls separating the small courtyards that overflowed with blossoms and vines. Ancient fountains tapped artesian springs that bubbled crystal waters into their lichen-grown bowls. Here, Dastolius kept his ancestral residence and Kelvin was determined to pay him a visit.

Kelvin began to climb from the coach.

"Will I see you again?" asked Ishay.

Kelvin shook his head. "Have the coachman take you to the Confluence, they'll be setting sail early tomorrow morning." He looked at Ishay for a moment, a wistful expression crossing his malformed visage, then the door closed and he was gone.

As the rattle of the carriage, and the clip of the horses' hooves faded down the street, Kelvin turned and climbed the rusted metal ladder that was bolted into the stone aqueduct that helped confine the Tiber when it overflowed.

Dastolius' estate was surrounded by a six-foot wall set with rusted iron spikes. Most of these barbs were lost in the lush foliage that spilled over the stones; thick-leafed branches and sprawling ivy that blossomed with purple flowers. The gate was set in a small stone archway imbedded with a brass plaque bearing the family name.

Kelvin found it odd that the lock had been smashed, and it lay in pieces on the granite stepping stones that wound their way through the garden and to the pillared terrace. Here, Kelvin saw that the door was ajar. He slowly pushed it inward, and stepped into the richly decorated halls beyond. The air was scented with perfume, but somewhere beyond, masked by the overwhelming sweetness, was a sick stench.

As Kelvin crept along he could hear no sound from within the old ancestral mansion. Around a bend in the hall he found Enstet, one of Dastolius' bodyguards who had helped exhume Kelvin from the grave, pinned to a wood totem by a javelin. The bodyguard hung lifeless on the wooden shaft, and by the consistency of the blood pooled at his feet, Kelvin could tell that the man had been dead for several hours.

Kelvin slipped around a corner, passing a niche containing an old suit of armour that had been passed down from generation to generation, and descended several steps into a den that was thick with gold and silver knick knacks. Sprawled near an armless divan, Kelvin found Dastolius; his lean frame twisted in an impossibly awkward position, and blood dripping from the corner of his mouth. Thrown on his corpse was the signet ring that Kelvin had purposely dropped in the tower at Seven Street.

To Kelvin's right, a side table had been upset, and Blevin and Tevol lay sprawled in pools of their own blood. Each of them bore the marks of at least a half dozen dagger wounds. Kelvin wondered that he did not feel a pang of regret. He had been the instrument of their demise. The Thieves Guild had reacted exactly as he had expected, and moved swiftly to make an example of the three men who they thought had meddled in their plans to bilk the Golden Eel.

Ultimately these three men had been no better than Adolphus. Their sole reason for bringing Kelvin back from death was to slay their business competitor. And their business was slavery. A grim smile touched Kelvin's peeling lips.

Now he just needed to convince at least one of the sorcerers, who had worked the magicks to bring him back to life, to return him to the grave where he belonged. Bone ground in Kelvin's knee each step that he took. Flesh hung loosely from his hands, and even the flesh on his face was beginning to tear loose. If he waited much longer, his new body would disintegrate and his consciousness would be forced to inhabit its lifeless shell for eternity. It was a ghastly fate that Kelvin did not want to experience.

Kelvin quickly left the estate grounds. Many valuable items lay within the walls of the mansion, and he had been surprised that they had not yet been removed. Perhaps the Thieves Guild had employed assassins to do the job, or maybe a specialized arm of their own guild, and they would later send in thieves that were expert at despoiling estates of their valuables. Whatever the case, Kelvin doubted that it would be safe to tarry with the dead.

He envied the merchants. At least they had gone on to the next life. He was still here, stuck in a body that was a mocking travesty of life.

Kelvin still had some gold coin, which he had not given to Ishay, and he rented a room and tried to sleep, but sleep escaped him as it had since he had been brought forth for a second go round in the city of Bathos. Finally darkness fell and he slipped forth onto the nighted streets, and turned his path toward Somber Alley. A collection of ancient buildings rose up before him as Kelvin stumbled from the darkness, their dilapidated gable roofs darker shades of pitch that thrust against the star-imbedded sky.

His heart pumped sluggishly in his chest, and black ichor oozed from his flapping flesh. Never in his worst nightmare had Kelvin dreamed that he might endure such an existence. At the back of the alley he found a small green door, which was marked with several cryptic symbols. Glyphs, guessed Kelvin, to ward away unwanted intruders. Kelvin surmised that those symbols were effective in warding off the living, unfortunately for the three wizard brothers that inhabited this den of dark magics, Kelvin didn't fall under that category.

He tried the door and found it unlocked. The wizards had been so confident in their spells that they hadn't bothered to use something so simple as a bolt. Ducking his head, Kelvin entered the incense-tainted air of the hall beyond. No magical spell resisted his entry, and he stepped into the dimness. The gloom gathered thickest at the edges of the hall, and Kelvin slipped into it as he lumbered down the corridor, using every skill that he had learned in life to control the limbs that were losing their dexterity.

Strange sounds worked their way through the blackness, deadened by the very thickness of the air. Kelvin did not know their origin, nor did he dare guess. Finally his feet brought him to the inner sanctum. Foul smells seeped from beneath the double doors of cherry wood, and yet more glyphs were painted on the portal. Without hesitation, Kelvin pushed the doors wide open, and strode assertively into the chamber beyond.

"I'm here," he announced. "Send me back!"

Afflick's tallowed hair gleamed in the spectral light that hovered above the chamber's blood-stained floor. He lifted his head and pointed a narrow hand at Kelvin.

"How did you get in here, assassin?" he hissed.

"I walked," answered Kelvin. He lifted a leather bag from his belt and dumped it on the floor, the severed head of Adolphus rolling free. "I've completed my part of the bargain. Now you complete yours."

Huard glanced up from the strange concoction of herbs that he was grinding with a bone pestle. He swiveled his over-size head and glanced furtively at Adolphus. Phalthos halted his incantation, his eyes narrowing, and a web of crow's feet forming at the corners of his eyes.

"Where is Dastolius?" questioned Afflick.

Kelvin shrugged. He felt a tendon tear in his shoulder. "He was happy to see that Adolphus was dead, but he wasn't too interested in witnessing me return to the grave. I guess that once you've seen someone brought back to life, the reverse doesn't thrill as much as it used to." He shoved his hands inside of his cloak.

Phalthos took tottering steps forward, and thrust a scarred hand in the air as he spoke. "I think that we've got a problem, Kelvin."

Kelvin raised what used to be an eyebrow. "And what might that be?"

"Last time I spoke with Dastolius he thought that you might be worth more to him alive, than returned to the grave. He was planning to keep you around for future needs."

"Really?" bluffed Kelvin. "Well that is news to me. He told me to come here, and that you would take care of returning me to the grave."

Afflick frowned. "The spirits tell me otherwise. They say that you are lying. There is more…" He furrowed his brow as he attempted to commune with the dead and gather further information.

Kelvin had heard enough. From beneath his cloak he produced two small crossbows, and he clutched one in each hand, charcoaled finger upon the trigger. "Let me explain this more clearly. Send me back or you will die!"

Huard let out a mocking peel of laughter. "Do you even have an inkling of what powers we command? With one thought I can have the spirits of the dead turn aside that crossbow bolt, and send it plunging back into your heart."

"Let's try it," said Kelvin. He pulled the trigger on the right hand crossbow, and the bolt sluiced through the air, its blade plunging into Huard's chest.

Huard grasped at the protruding shaft, incomprehension on his broad face. "How?"

"I had an idea of what I might be up against, and took the liberty of having a certain bishop bless these shafts." Kelvin swung the tip of the second crossbow bolt between Phalthos and Afflick. "Who's next?"

Huard sank to the ground amidst a jumble of geometrical markings upon the stone floor. He let out a series of racking coughs that wretched crimson splatters across his protective glyphs, and he fell into dying spasms.

Rage burned in the eyes of Phalthos and Afflick, and they turned their venomous gazes upon the crumbling man in the dark green cloak.

"All I want is for you to return me to the dust," said Kelvin. "If you refuse, I've got nothing to lose by killing you both."

He had more blessed bolts in a small quiver beneath his cloak, but he realized he only possessed one loaded crossbow at the moment. If they both decided to gang up on him, he would be forced to reload, and that delay might prove his undoing. Still, the two sorcerers didn't seem to be in any hurry to join their brother in the kingdom of the dead.

"We'll do as you say," said Afflick. "We should have known better than to help Dastolius renege on an agreement."

"My thinking, exactly," said Kelvin. "Now I suggest that you commence your preparations, and don't try to pull the wool over my eyes. I took the time to do a bit of research before I came for a visit. I think your brother can attest to that."

"Very well," said Afflick. His brow furrowed, bringing the point of his widows peak down toward his eyes. "Dastolius is dead, isn't he?"

"And Blevin and Tevol. They should have let me rest in peace."

"We see that now," said Afflick.

Phalthos collected several vials from a rack that was bolted to the smoke-stained bricks of the wall. The spectral light continued to throb, its hazy illumination playing across Huard's draining corpse, and strobing across the actions of the two living wizards as they chalked fresh lines upon the floor.

In truth, Kelvin had no idea whether they were preparing for the proper ritual. For all he knew, they might be sealing his soul into the decaying body that he wore. He hoped that his bluff would be sufficient. Certainly, he had given them reason enough to want to be rid of him forever.

Now that he knew Dastolius had never intended to release him from his resurrection, Kelvin felt even fewer qualms about the deaths of the three slavers, the murders of whom he had so subtly brought to pass.

"Step into the middle of the diagram," ordered Phalthos.

Kelvin stepped over the criss-crossing glyphs and overlapping circles. As he walked he held his crossbow trained on Phalthos, ready to bury a shaft in his torso if he should make a hostile movement, or act overly suspicious.

The phantasmal light played over head, miasmic cinders dropping down around Kelvin and smoking on his already burned skin. Kelvin scarcely felt a prick of pain through the dead flesh his soul inhabited. Phalthos and Afflick chanted a monotone litany from some ancient book, which brittle pages turned as if stirred by a wind blowing off the Black Sea.

Disembodied voices hovered in the air calling out to him, and strange forces shifted through the black room, howling to be released from some eternal agony of the damned. But Kelvin, he welcomed the embrace of death. He had been there before.

Phalthos and Afflick raised their hands in unison, and like a hammer stroke reverberating on a gong, an undeniable force shivered through Kelvin's body. Before his eyes his limbs returned to dust. The crossbow dropped to the floor, loosing its shaft, but Kelvin never saw where that bolt struck. His body had returned to dust, and it lay shifting on the brown-stained stones as his soul fled to the crystal skies of nirvana.

Part Four:
Devil's Head

Devil's Head reared, a forbidding black rock jutting skyward, some five leagues from the city walls of Bathos, the City of Corruption. From the winding, maze-like streets sprawling across the hilly terrain the entire city was built upon, Lothar Shadow could see the evil looking rock formation that had, eons before, been carved by unknown hands into the shape of a demon's face. Massive pointed boulders lined the bottom of the skull- jagged teeth across a terrifying maw. Above the flared nostrils the eyes were dark, gaping holes receding into the depths of the cliff side from which the face was cut.

Legend told that it had been the haunt of bestial monsters that, crawling up from the slime-coated recesses of the earth, had worshipped Mahmackrah there. For centuries no one had dared set foot on the narrow stone ledges that led to that desolate promontory. Or, more accurately, thought Lothar, no one had dared that wicked place and lived to tell the tale.

Soon Lothar would brave those peaks. It was not of his own design, but if he did not, his beloved Sheesa and their unborn child would surely die.

In his younger years, he had been bold beyond comprehension; daring to rob the most heavily guarded merchant houses, and even foraying into the Dark King Vlad's own treasure house. He had known no fear. Now, past thirty years, his unreasoning bravery and unassailable assuredness were tempered by wisdom and experience. Still, he was not afraid for himself- for what would it matter should he die? He was afraid for Sheesa and the child within her womb. If he failed their fate would be sealed.

Hatred for the man whose machinations had done this burned in his heart. He longed for revenge, but that must come secondary to the safety of Sheesa. He turned, strutting boldly down the cobbled alleys of Bathos. Gargoyled facades loomed up on either side of him as he left the high street upon which he had been standing.

If a man walked unassured down these streets he invited robbery, rape, or murder- and during certain days of the year far worse from cults that stalked the streets, snatching victims for sacrifice to their heinous gods in torturous ritual.

A thick smoke settled over the city, dense and gray. With it came a nauseating stench. Any long time resident of the city of corruption recognized the scent. It meant that a plague had overtaken the city. The crematories were working long into the nights, and the Gravedigger's Guild would have extra dues in their coffers.

Like the smoke that lay thick over the streets in swirling eddies, so had this disease settled over Bathos. Leeches and necromancers, alike, claimed bafflement. It resembled no ailment that they had ever seen. In all stages it appeared as leprosy; the difference being the speed with which it acted. From when the first snowy white splotch appears the victim has ten days, and on the tenth day his body disintegrates into a pile of loose flapping flesh.

Even now, as Lothar walked the nighted streets he could see signs of the disease; the beggar leaning against the wall, his spotted hand clutching his tin cup; the scag that approached him under the oil lamp with the crimson shades, telltale spots of white appearing on her face.

"My services for only a tin. I must have food to eat."

Lothar shrank back. Only a fool would take the risk of catching the deadly disease to sate his appetites. The quick leper death could be contracted by merely making contact with the infection and the effects were almost immediate. Still, where formerly his heart had been hardened to feel no compassion or pain, he felt a twinge of sadness for the woman. He reached into his pouch, and by the distinct starred edge, found a silver coin stamped with the shadowed visage of Vlad the Dark. He tossed it to the woman. "Go eat a good meal, and don't tell the Guild of your windfall."

"Oh thank you, kind sir." She snatched the coin from the ground where her slow reflexes had allowed it to fall. "I am beholden to you. If I can ever repay you somehow…" Her words trailed off into silence.

Lothar nodded sadly. It was unlikely that this woman would live out the week. His hand went to the brace of throwing axes across his chest. There was no defense against the Quick Leper Death. Not even his skill with the axe could save him if the disease should find a home in his body.

After traversing a variety of back alley roads, Lothar came to the street of the Chanteuse along which gated mansions rested in marble-pillared magnificence. He found one of the larger of these and came to the gate. Two armour clad men of the Warriors Guild stood guard.

"I'm here to see Biglun the merchant, at his request."

"He is expecting you." The larger of the warriors took a key from his belt and opened up the massive lock, allowing the gate to swing back on well-oiled hinges. Hastur Slingblade, for Lothar recognized the hawk-like nose and feral eyes as they came into the light, escorted him up the bricked path between sculptured shrubs. Hastur had a reputation for lightening speed and incredible sword skill. But just because both he and Lothar were members of the Warriors Guild didn't mean they wouldn't cross paths or swords at some time.

Hastur escorted him through vaulted archways, through slab oak doors and down brightly lit corridors strewn with rich tapestries. Biglun was not above flaunting his immense wealth. Finally, Hastur brought him to the merchant himself, a man of considerable girth who, hunched over a polished marble dining table, attended to the work of enlarging his waistline even further. The appetizing scent of spiced roast fowl was thick in the air, intermingled with a variety of other pleasant smells- quite a change from the stench that hung in the sky outside the mansion.

Looking up briefly from his meal, Biglun wiped a greasy gobbet of food from his jowl and motioned for Lothar to sit. "Help yourself," he said, the epitome of generosity.

"I wouldn't break bread with you if I were starving to death," growled Lothar. "Where is Sheesa?"

"Not one for pleasantries, eh?" Biglun fixed his eyes on Lothar's cloaked frame. "Fine. I can get to the point. As you know I have exposed your scag to the Quick Leper Death. She, and the baby in her womb- which despite the laws of the Courtesan Guild she refuses to destroy- are currently residing in one of the chambers below, comfortable except for the disease that will kill her in nine days."

Lothar's eyes blazed. "I knew you were low enough to threaten the life of a woman, but I didn't know you were despicable enough to threaten the life of an unborn child."

Biglun shrugged. "By the laws of the Courtesan's Guild she must destroy it or be destroyed herself. I'm not doing anything that they wouldn't."

"She's no longer a member of the Guild."

Now the merchant laughed, his jowls shaking. "You know, as well as I, that she can't just leave the Guild. Sheesa was a moneymaker for them until you planted the idea of a better life in her head."

"I'm not in the mood to argue politics. You mentioned a cure to me. If you hadn't you'd already be dead"

"Ah, yes." The merchant motioned to a servant who returned momentarily, holding a small cherry wood rack that held a vial of bluish liquid. "This is the antidote to the Quick Leper Death. It is the only existing dose. I obtained it from an alchemist who told me that he had been retained by a certain guild that would profit from the deaths of numerous people. This guild hired him to create a virulent strain of disease and set it loose on the city. Naturally, he created an antidote in the case that he might catch the plague himself."

"How do I know that this is actually an antidote and not a bottle of dyed water?"

"Earlier today I had my servants perform an experiment. They dripped a small quantity on one of Sheesa's sores. I am told that it healed quite nicely. You will be welcome to confirm this fact with her."

"And what is to keep me from killing you now and going to this alchemist for another dose of the cure?"

Biglun looked down the bridge of his stubby nose condescendingly. "Do you take me for a complete fool? I hired an assassin. The alchemist is dead. I have the only dose."

He lowered the leg bone he had been chewing on and gave his entire attention to Lothar. "You fail to understand. Money is power...and I have a lot of money. I can buy life and death. Now, I offer you life for your woman in exchange for bringing me back a small item that you shall find at Devil's Head. And just so you don't attempt anything so foolish as revenge, I have left word with several parties that in the event of my untimely demise that they are to pass a message on to the Courtesan's Guild. This message will inform them of Sheesa's pregnancy and her refusal to do away with the child."

* * * *

A chill wind whipped at Lothar's black cloak as he scaled the cliff at

Devil's Head. Sheesa had confirmed Biglun's story of the cure's efficacy. Even now, as he hung perilously from a scant handhold of pitted rock, he could envision her pale skin framed by foamy black hair. Her formerly ruby red lips paling with her ailment, and the parchment white sores that that had begun to blister her body. Never in his life had so much ridden on such a desperate gambit.

The small item that Lothar was to find at Devil's Head was the fabled Broach of Baal that was legended to be buried at the foot of Mahmackrah's altar. Set in filigreed gold and platinum, a black diamond was centered in its face. The eons old tales, whispered from parent to child around crackling campfires, told that before Baal had been thrown down from the heavens and had gone into hiding, he had worn this broach over his heart. It had lent him invincibility against blade, flame, and missile.

Biglun had not told Lothar why he wanted this broach but Lothar could guess. The merchant had stepped on many toes climbing to the top of the dung heap in Bathos, the City of Corruption. There were powerful merchants who would gladly unite forces to kill Biglun. The merchant wanted some protection. Too late, he had realized the cost of rising to the top of the dross. One could only survive there for so long before being destroyed by some one else equally hungry for power and riches.

Lothar pulled himself onto the ledge that wound upward to the plateau of the Devil's Head. For a moment he crouched in the shelter of the leaning cliffside, taking respite from the wind, and warming his hands with his breath. By climbing the cliffs he had avoided King Vlad the Dark's guards, which kept a constant vigil at the bottom of the trail. King Vlad had declared the cliffs off limits to all- not that many would venture here, even without the penalty of death hanging over their heads.

Fingers rested and his wind recovered, Lothar set out at a brisk pace towards the plateau. The moon shone palely through dark clouds that scudded across the ebon skies. It shed enough light so that he made good time, and before two hours had passed he reached the broad black slate of the cliff top. Here, details impossible to see from a distance became apparent to him. This had truly been the site of some ancient temple. Crumbled pillars littered the plateau, breaking over decaying walls and scarred steps like frozen waves.

Mounting a broad stair lined with broken bones and the cracked skulls of many a human being, Lothar wondered what horrible rituals had been performed here before the altar of Mahmackrah. As the mouth of the Devil's

Head yawned before him Lothar reached into his pack and with a flint sparked a torch into flame. Pushing aside a strong sense of foreboding that swept through him, Lothar steeled himself and stepped into the blackness. The torch flickered, its light playing across grisly tableaus of ages past that had been immortalized in the stonework of the temple walls.

Despite himself, Lothar shuddered. Here he was, utterly alone in the bowels of hell. The place seemed alive with evil energy and he imagined that he heard a slight hum at a tone somewhere near the outer reaches of his hearing.

The entrance tunnel opened, yawning into a vast cavern within the head of the devil. Bones, split and shattered, were mounded like heaps of refuse on Scatter Street. The floors were stained in crimson rivulets. Stench hit him in the face; worse than any charnel house that had ever existed. Above this scene rose a massive head carved in black marble- forty feet high and a thousand tons in weight. Lothar stood in paralyzed recognition, for he had seen the visage of Mahmackrah stamped on every coin of Bathos.

A cry startled him from his reverie, and he cast his eyes lower. There, upon the massive, ornamented altar directly below Mahmackrah, a feminine figure writhed in fear.

"Please help me," she cried imploringly.

This had been the last thing that Lothar had expected to find. Casting aside caution he ran through the treacherous, bone-scattered paths until he reached the altar where the girl was bound. As he came toward her he was immediately struck by her beauty. Her full lips parted slightly, blue eyes recognizing him as her only source of hope. Thick blonde hair cascaded across sun-darkened skin.

As he drew his dagger to sever the thick hemp ropes with which she was bound, she leaned closer to him and he felt the warmth of her body against his. She was dressed in a filigreed corset, which left little to the imagination. Red silk fell at her loins, bound with gold entwined belting. Her thigh length boots were constructed from tanned elk hide. Whoever she was, she came from money. A peasant girl would not be dressed like this.

The bonds fell away from her and she briskly rubbed her chafed wrists.

"What's your name girl, and how did you come to be here?"

As she answered, Lothar withdrew an ivory key from his pouch and closely examined the intricately carved altar upon which the girl had been bound. There! Just as Biglun had described. Lothar slid the key smoothly into the waiting slot. The key turned easily, as if the lock had been oiled daily during the long centuries since the broach had been placed in its resting place.

"I'm Sedrah," answered the girl. "I'm a member of the Courtesan's guild."

Lothar pulled the key towards him, and a stone tray emerged from the side of the altar. Throbbing evilly in its velvet cloaking, the Broach of Baal glinted back the torchlight. Lothar reached tentatively forward, prying away the rotting crimson velvet that fell from his touch as though it were cobwebs.

He glanced back at Sedrah as a sudden suspicion crossed his mind, and discovered that it was well founded. With practiced precision she was drawing a thin stilletto blade that had been expertly concealed in her boot.

As she thrust it at him, Lothar twisted aside and the blade meant for his heart struck against the altar.

Swearing loudly, Sedrah back-pedaled and Lothar became aware of the full extent of the trap that had been set for him. Hastur Slingblade stepped from behind a pile of bone, flanked by Cadryn Ironthew of the Warriors Guild and Adryl Knife Thrower of the Assassins Guild. Lothar had traveled in many of Bathos' social circles and was familiar with these men. He himself held a rare dual membership of the Thieves Guild and of the Warriors Guild.

Cadryn Ironthew was one of the biggest and baddest of the Warriors Guild. He was three hundred pounds and seven feet of sheer power. Lothar had been on assignment with him before and watched him crush skulls to splinters through iron helms.

Adryl Knife Thrower was deadly with the blade. He wouldn't do his work close in. He preferred to do it from a safe distance. In a bar fight, Lothar had watched him put a dagger in a man's eye socket from twenty feet away. If Lothar wasn't careful he would end up another long distance victim.

Even as this thought flashed through his mind Adryl drew back his arm, a knife blade flashing in his hand. Lothar moved quickly, putting Cadryn Ironthew between himself and Adryl. The seven-foot warrior, he hoped, would serve as a shield of sorts- keeping Adryl from getting a clear throw.

Cadryn hadn't considered Adryl's throw and saw only an opportunity for a quick kill. He leaped forward to the attack. At the same instant Adryl decided that he could make the throw. A moment later Cadryn Ironthew bellowed in pain as Adryl's blade severed his spine. Lothar snatched a hand axe from his harness and finished the job by burying it deep in the giant's chest. Gurgling blood the big warrior sank to the ground.

Leaving the broach still in its tray, Lothar dived behind the altar.

"You're a dead man, Lothar," shouted Hastur. "You can only hide for so long."

"Why are you attacking me?" Lothar shouted back, his mind whirling. "I'm working for your boss."

Hastur Slingblade snickered. "Let's just say that I'm now working for a higher bidder. Biglun has many enemies with deep pockets and they don't particularly like the idea of Biglun owning the Broach of Baal."

"But they want it for themselves. That's why you waited for me to use the key."

"Exactly," answered Hastur. "You are a bright boy."

"Hey, bright boy," hissed Adryl. " Why don't you stick your head out from behind that altar for a second."

"I can't believe that I didn't kill that snake," spat Sedrah.

Lothar grabbed a throwing axe in each hand. After these were spent he had no more weapons except for his battle-axe, which was quite unsuitable as a throwing weapon. He would have to make a desperate gamble and attack around one side of the altar or another. He hoped he could pick the side for which Adryl wasn't prepared to throw. If he couldn't he would be skewered before he took three steps.

Just as he was about to make a break to the left side, Lothar heard the hum again. This time it was louder, more pronounced, and accompanied by a clicking noise. The clicking sounded similar to that of a dog's nails as he ran across a cobbled street. The sound echoed in the chamber. It was all around them.

"Do you hear that?" whispered Hastur

Sedrah cried out.

Hoping this outburst would serve as a distraction, Lothar took this opportunity to make his attack. He whirled around the corner of the altar, an axe in each fist. The scene that faced him was incredible. The entire situation had been reversed in a matter of moments, but before his throw could be halted, instinct took over and one axe whirled from his right hand. Hundreds of four armed creatures, scampered monkey-like over the bone piles. One had leaped on Adryl's back and was raking him viciously across the chest with sharp claws. It screamed demonically as the axe meant for Adryl struck it in the head, handle first, and punched through its brain.

Mottle-furred beasts attacked left and right in a maelstrom of claws and fangs. Gibbering wildly, their lean muscles propelled them through the air as they leaped in for their attacks. Hastur, Sedrah, and Adryl were surrounded by the beasts, barely keeping them at bay. Lothar took this opportunity and snatched the Broach of Baal from its tray. Then he dashed through the mounds of bone, following the meandering trail that led to mouth of the Devil's Head where he had entered.

As he fled Lothar struck out with his battle-axe, severing an outstretched claw here, or crushing a fanged snout there. By the time that he reached the broad steps to the temple, he was splattered in gore. Gathering all the speed that he could muster he sprinted away, the monkey beasts spilling from the maw of the Devil's Head after him.

Once he reached the narrow ledge that led downward toward the base of the mountain, he turned and faced them one by one. His battle-axe lashed out again and again, warding off the attacks of the beasts. The length of his axe enabled him to keep his distance as they scrambled over one another in a gibbering frenzy to feed upon his flesh. He drove them back, spilling their black blood on the edge of his axe, and sending them screaming over the edge- falling into the darkness that lay like a blanket across the foothills below. Finally, they tired of being slaughtered and the survivors slunk away, hoping for easier pickings within the temple.

Weary and wounded, Lothar turned and stumbled toward Bathos.

* * * *

The dark-cloaked warrior strode into Biglun's dining room, bleeding from a half dozen bites and cuts inflicted by the razor talons of the beasts he had fought. Biglun looked up in shock and surprise from his early morning meal as Lothar entered.

"I have the broach," said Lothar. With thick leather gloves he unstrung his pouch and gingerly removed the ancient artifact. It gleamed with unnatural light as the warrior displayed it to Biglun. He set it on the marble table and placed the haft of his axe six-inches above the gold wrought sigil of Baal. "If you want it in one piece bring Sheesa to me and let her drink the cure for the Quick Leper Death."

Frantically Biglun called for his guards to bring Sheesa. "There's no need for these antics," he said fumblingly. "You have what I want. I no longer have need for deception."

"All the same," growled Lothar. "I prefer to do this my way."

Sickly and spotted with the parchment sores of the Quick Leper Death, Sheesa stumbled into the room supported by the two guards wearing thick leather gloves, which would later be burned, to handle the diseased woman. Biglun motioned to his retainer and he came forth with the vial of sparkling blue liquid in one slim hand. Holding it to Sheesa's lips she drank, then sank into a cushioned chair where, moments later, Lothar could see the miraculous return of color to her cheeks, and watched in awe as her decaying flesh began to mend before his astonished eyes.

Lifting the haft of his axe, Lothar slid the Broach of Baal across the table to Biglun, where the merchant snatched it up barehanded and incanted the ancient words that would bring him complete invulnerability against all blades, flame, and missiles.

Carefully, Lothar let his gloves slide from his hands and drop onto the table. He had called in a favor before visiting Biglun tonight. When explained the situation, the scag he had earlier given money for food had willingly exposed the broach of Baal to her disease.

Lothar brought Sheesa up to his side. All traces of the plague had disappeared, the only sign that she had ever been infected was the pink of her newly healed flesh. As he and Sheesa turned to leave, Lothar glanced back at the merchant and smiled grimly as he noticed the telltale white of the Quick Leper Death; a sore was forming on Biglun's cheek.

Part Five:
The Guildsman of Kolthos

On screeching brass hinges, tar-blackened double doors of oak opened onto the cobblestones of Necromancer's Alley. Narrow and maundering, the alley's refuse-spattered walls rose precipitously above the canyon-like path.

Kolthos the Lean stepped from a pool of dim lantern light and onto the street. Raindrops spattered from his withered face as he watched the angry clouds hurtling across the night skies far above the spire of his windowless tower. At his feet the storm swept debris from the stones and carried it along a newly formed stream that would eventually empty in the cesspools of lower Bathos.

Around him, Kolthos' black clad bodyguards locked the doors open with timber braces and in the pelting rain watched for the shipment to come. Patiently, Kolthos waited, claw-like hands wrapped in the silk sash of his scarlet robe. He listened to the howl of elemental fury that the gods were unleashing on the city of Bathos and, eventually, he heard the tramp of feet intermingled with the gusting of the wind.

Carrying hooded lanterns and with cloaks thrown over their heads, they emerged from the darkness- a squad of his bill collectors come home to give the master his due. Kolthos' investments were far reaching. He had used his wealth to gain power. By design, he had lent money to many people and when they couldn't pay him back he would dictate his unsavory terms. If they did not like his terms they were welcome to spend the rest of their miserable lives in debtors prison.

But, by nature, Kolthos was not a businessman. He was a sorcerer, and his driving desire was to revel in the obscene power of the dark arts and wield that power indiscriminately. Flanked by his bill collectors, six terrified peasant girls stumbled forward in their rain-soaked rags- flaxen, auburn, and raven hair hanging in bedraggled locks. Their eyes widened with fear when they saw Kolthos and once they had seen his terrible gaze, they knew their doom was at hand.

These were daughters of struggling farmers and tradesman who had been unable to pay their debts. For the nonce their debt was paid in full. The blood of their daughters would be mingled in unholy rites to raise elder demons from the darkest depths of the nine hells. The bill collectors ushered the women into the tower's basement and with unfeeling eye, Kolthos coldly appraised them.

"They'll do," he said, his voice rasping like the strings of an untuned violin. "Lock them in the pen and feed them some gruel. It looks like they haven't eaten for days. I can't have my sacrifices starving to death before I can put them to use."

One of the girls shrieked and fell to the floor in terror. Kolthos turned and began ascending the stairs to his sanctum above. "Be sure to lock the gates well," he said to his bodyguards. "Tonight is the kind of night that assassins will be afoot."

"Yes, my Lord," replied the guards. The gates creaked shut and the restraining bar clanked into place.

Entering through a blue cherry wood door at the highest level of the tower, Kolthos returned to his sanctum. His sandals crossed marble tiles that were warmed by the crackling flames of an open fireplace. Kolthos' laboratories and libraries rested on the levels beneath. Here, he relaxed among the silken cushions, embroidered tapestries and the scent of sandalwood that wafted from the incense burning braziers hanging on golden chains.

Pausing momentarily at a waist high chessboard constructed of marble, Kolthos furrowed the parchment skin of his brow. The board had been a gift from Antoni the bloated, a rival sorcerer. The Mage's Guild required that rival sorcerers give each other notice of an impending sorcerous attack or assassination attempt; a professional courtesy of sorts. This was Antoni's method of keeping him warned. It was an ongoing game of moves and countermoves. The goal of the chess match was to take the opponent's mage piece. If that happened, the real sorcerer would be removed from the land of the living.

There had been no movement on the board for a long period of time but, as Kolthos watched, a white marble guildsman piece began to tremble, then slowly it began scraping across the board until it rested next to his black mage. A guildsman piece was the weakest piece on the board. Each player had eight of them to fill the front ranks.

This piece's movement meant that he should expect an attack soon by an employee of one of Bathos' many guilds. Kolthos' mage piece rested securely nestled among the ranks of his own pieces. Antoni the bloated must be growing desperate, decided Kolthos. To send an unranked guildsman, no matter what the guild, into his stronghold was an act of suicide.

"Kolthos? Is there something a matter?"

The shriveled necromancer glanced up from the board and spent a pleasurable moment appraising the blonde beauty that stood next to him. She was dressed in a sheer gown, silver bracelets tinkling on long sun-darkened limbs. She smiled infectiously as she caught up her long hair and, with long steel needles, deftly pinned it into place in a pile atop her perfectly formed head.

"No, nothing a matter. Just a small situation that must be dealt with."

"Then you won't be coming to bed, soon?"

"No," answered Kolthos. "Perhaps you could fetch me a snifter of brandy in the mean time."

Once again, the courtesan smiled. "As you wish." She turned heel and strode to a cabinet in the adjoining chamber.

Curious where the impending attack might be coming from, Kolthos moved to a silver basin filled with liquid. Stirring the dark waters, he intoned ancient incantations and peered into its depths. Gradually the swirling vortex settled and a murky image began to form.

"Very clever," muttered Kolthos. "He's coming in through the well room."

* * * *

The aqueduct was running high and swift. The storm had swollen the reservoirs and the water gushed through the stone channels with horrible fury. Kelvin Iron Gaunt pulled himself from the low well and rolled onto the stone flooring of the room.

Though he had only been in the waters for a few minutes, he shivered and rubbed briskly at his cold limbs. By anchoring his rope at the open well in Devil's Square, Kelvin had let the current of the aqueduct carry him several hundred yards beneath the city streets and buildings until he reached Kolthos' own private well. His employer, Antoni the Bloated One, had informed him of exactly how many well openings he must count before anchoring himself and climbing into the room above.

Except for a sheath of leather wrapped around his waist and the iron gauntlet on his left hand, Kelvin was naked. To avoid sinking to the bottom of the aqueduct he had foregone any armour. The glove, he never removed. He had lost his fourth and fifth fingers in an incident many years ago and the glove disguised this fact. The last two fingers of the glove were merely hollow. For weapons, Kelvin wore a bandoleer studded with rows of razor tipped throwing darts. Securely tied over his shoulder, a long blade was sheathed in oiled black leather.

Kelvin was apprehensive. Assassinating a sorcerer was a dangerous proposition. Several of the Guild's most skilled assassins had balked at the assignment, but Kelvin had jumped at the chance. In his own land, he had been a social outcast. Born into the lowest social strata, and it seemed that no matter how great the accomplishment he laid at the feet of the upper castes, he was still reviled. When he could stand no more, he decided to seek his fortune in the city of Bathos. His risky sword style and lightening speed earned some measure of respect in this new city, but he craved more. If he could succeed in assassinating Kolthos no one would dare show him disrespect and the fee for his job would make him a rich man...and rich men demanded respect.

Creeping on bare feet, Kelvin cracked open the door to the well chamber and moved stealthily through a maze of darkened antechambers. Thick tapestries of strange design hung across walls and doorways in shadowed folds. Carefully, he made his way past the ancient urns smelling of unholy content, the silver chalices and crystal beakers bubbling with potions culled from demonic lore, and piled tomes bound with human skin and containing the blackest of magics.

Ascending the levels of the tower, he slipped through musty chambers and entered a spacious hallway. The polished stone was smooth and cold on his bare feet. Light glowed from open braziers of red-hot coals, illuminating the pedestaled figures that lined the hall on either side. They stood still as statues, armoured in boiled leather cuirass, and each holding a pike so that they crossed overhead creating a tunnel of oak shafts and steel tips.

Warily, Kelvin moved forward. Antoni had warned him to be ready for deception. Perhaps these were warriors, not statues that waited for him to enter their trap. The hellish light cast a ruddy glow on their pallid, waxen features. Their open eyes were blank and glassy. No breath crossed their lips or nostrils.

These were men that had once lived, decided Kelvin. It was as though some insane taxidermist had stuffed and mounted them in their lifelike repose. That Kolthos desired such a display only testified that he was a sick individual, but Bathos was full of such perversions. On Hang Street, Kelvin had seen enemies of Emperor Vlad the Dark exhibited, by the hundreds, in this grisly manner.

Kelvin hastily moved down the hall toward the iron-banded door at the opposite end. As he reached the door a sickening stench assailed him. Looking behind him, he saw the dead men stepping silently from their pedestals. Hollow-cheeked and gaunt, they approached him on dead legs, clutching their pikes in ivory-fingered grips; dust swirling from their bodies as they moved.

As he lifted the door latch, Kelvin turned and faced the approaching supernatural warriors. With a practiced motion he reached over his shoulder and did so with such a speed that his blade appeared to jump, bared, into his hand. He gave the door a backward push with his heel and then dodged the thrusting pikes. Now, inside the outer reach of the spear tips, he had his undead opponents at a severe disadvantage. They were unable to bring their weapons into play and within moments, Kelvin was in the forefront of them. His sword blade licked out like lightening, slicing through bone and dry flesh and releasing putrid gouts of black gas.

The cuts were deep and Kelvin had already counted three dead, when he realized that his blows, although lethal to a living human being, were having little effect on his foes. A snow-white hand reached out and clamped, vise-like, on his throat. Kelvin gasped for air but none would come. As he struggled against the infernal grip, he felt other hands reach out to hold him. They clenched him with such fury that he feared he would be ripped limb from limb.

Only his sword arm was left free now, every other limb being held. With an awkward and desperate swing upward, the honed blade sliced through the wrist of the hand that choked him and passed a hair away from Kelvin's face. Devoid, now, of the corpse that was feeding it, the fingers loosened and the hand fell away.

With precision that was sharpened by fear, Kelvin cut to his left and right severing groping limbs with each stroke. In moments he was again free of the undead fingers, but still mired in the morass of speechless soldiers. Even those warriors whose limbs he'd cut from them still advanced, attempting to rend him with their gnashing teeth.

Kelvin sent several heads rolling and fought his way to a dais also occupied by a massive brass brazier. He was momentarily clear of the throng, but the respite was brief and they turned their vacant stare on him, pikes lowering to skewer him where he stood.

A drop of sweat rolled from Kelvin's brow and dropped into the brazier where it sizzled and died on the radiant coals. At this same moment, an idea sprang to life in Kelvin's head. Strength was not his best attribute. Of any hundred men he met on the street half of them could probably best him in a straight ahead match of force. Kelvin hoped that he would have enough to topple the brazier.

Wedging himself between the wall and the brass bowl, he pushed on the huge brazier with his feet. In a moment of searing pain and extreme effort, he leveraged the bowl over. Coals lapped over the feet of the foremost warriors and their dry flesh went up like tinder. Flames leaped hungrily, enveloping the warriors and leaping from soldier to soldier as it fed upon the noxious black gasses that hung in the air.

Leaping amongst the fiery chaos on blistered feet, Kelvin ran through the open portal and slammed the door shut behind him. He dropped an iron bar into the tarnished brass retainer brackets mounted chest high on each side of the door. He hoped this would prevent any survivors from trailing him.

His feet hurt badly, but he had been spared any permanently debilitating damage by the thick calluses on the soles of his feet. Limping along, Kelvin continued his search for the next flight of stairs. He was only, he figured, a few levels away from Kolthos' sanctum. Antoni the Bloated had said that Kelvin would find him there.

* * * *

olthos peered into the dark waters of his seeing bowl and intently watched Kelvin's progress. "Very clever, little man. Antoni did well in picking you. Not that you really have a chance."

The sorcerer watched as Kelvin climbed a level and entered a small chamber that was bare except for a strangely engraved ball suspended near the dome of the room's arch. Kolthos smiled and rose from his seat. He took several steps and pulled a velvet rope that hung from the ceiling.

The blonde courtesan came to his side, her skin smelling faintly of an exotic perfume. She handed him another goblet of deep red drink.

"I shan't be long, my honey suckle," Kolthos rasped. "The trap is sprung."

* * * *

The room was bare except for the gold ball that hung above. It was segmented, like an orange, and each panel was painted a different hue. Kelvin hadn't given it much attention, thinking it was nothing but an eccentric decoration, until the ball burst open spilling hundreds of sticks to the rough stone floor. They clattered around him, some striking him on the back and shoulders before bouncing to the floor.

Kelvin couldn't comprehend the reason the sticks had fallen until he saw, with growing horror, that the sticks were moving. They squirmed sinuously and in an instant became a swarm of deadly adders. With a deft sweep of his sword Kelvin cleared a circle around himself, hurling several snakes away. Completely surrounded, he watched as his small piece of floor slowly shrank; the sea of adders encroaching on him in an undulating, reptilian mass.

He was twenty feet from the exit door, but each step was littered with venomous serpents. He could probably clear a path with his sword were he given enough time, but the snakes were creeping up from behind him as well.

Kelvin sheathed his sword and, with his left hand, withdrew a handful of darts from his bandolier. With his right hand he threw with deadly accuracy, picking off the adders nearest the door and then working his way back toward himself. Each throw struck home, pinning an adder through the skull.

There was none better than Kelvin at the art of the throwing dart. He had won accolades and coin in many cities and rum-soaked taverns. From the time he was a child he had hunted bird and rabbit with the dart. That skill was put to the test now.

He had cleared maybe ten feet of path when the adders behind crawled up to his heels. Rocking forward on the balls of his seared feet, he launched himself into the air, over the striking heads of the adders and onto the flaggings he had cleared. From here, he scuttled forward on hands and feet until he reached the door.

Snatching up a dead adder, he dipped several darts in the venom of the snake and carefully replaced them in his bandoleer. Then he slid through the doorway and closed it securely behind him.

Several minutes later Kelvin came upon the blue cherry wood door for which Antoni the Bloated had told him to search. Kelvin took a deep breath to steady his shaky nerves. He'd come too far to fail now. Thrusting his hand into a leather pouch at his belt, he withdrew a skeleton key. The ring was brass, as was the long, narrow cylinder and studs that protruded. Antoni had told him that this would open the blue door.

He slipped the key into the lock and, ever so slowly, turned it until he felt the lock click into its open position. Carefully, he withdrew two of the venom-tipped darts. He would throw them both at once, aiming for the eyes when the wizard looked up to see what was the intrusion. As he let go, he would tweak the left dart with his thumb just enough so it would separate from the other, and they would both strike their target, blinding the wizard in both eyes -so that as he died from the venom he could not see to take vengeance.

Kelvin threw open the door and stepped in, throwing arm raised and darts ready to fly. The warmth of the warm marble floor hurt the burns on his feet.

Kolthos had watched Kelvin approach the door in his vision waters. Next to the chessboard, he was already standing, an imposing figure in his crimson robe. He made a small gesture with his left hand, and another with his right. Kelvin cried out once. The darts fell from his hand as his body disintegrated into ash.

Shaking his head, Kolthos smiled wanly. He shook his head. "A guildsman…when will Antoni ever learn." He glanced down at his chessboard. Already, the guildsman piece that represented Kelvin had also disintegrated into a fine dust that mounded the square where it had rested, but the Wizard's mouth dropped open when he saw the mystical cloaking fall from one of his own guildsman pieces; the one that sat next to his Mage. Revealed beneath the black exterior that was falling away was the figure of a woman.

"Surprised?" asked the courtesan as she withdrew the two needles from her piled hair and thrust them through Kolthos' back. They pierced his lungs, the sharp points protruding through his chest.

"Sedrah?" he gasped. "Antoni bought you?"

She twisted the needles, eliciting another gasp of pain. "No. This one I'm doing for free. You probably don't remember her, but I had a little sister. My Father couldn't make payment on his loan, and you forcefully took her instead. She wasn't like me. She was an innocent soul…not learned in the ways of the world. You sacrificed her for one of your foul experiments in sorcery!"

Kolthos sank to his knees, and Sedrah stood over him, blonde hair wreathing wildly about her like some flaming halo of a vengeance angel.

"But why send the other guildsman if it was to be you that did the job?"

"Simple, at full strength your magics are much too powerful. If you hadn't just expended much of your energies disintegrating that brave fool, you could easily have healed this wound I inflicted and killed me, too."

A fit of coughing racked Kolthos' body and crimson came in rivulets across his lips. He fell to the floor, clawing at Sedrah's gown. "You're right," he croaked. "I don't remember her."

Sedrah stabbed him again, once through the icy heart, and the ragged breathing came to a sputtering halt.

"You don't have to remember her," answered Sedrah finally. "There are six girls penned up in your dungeon below that will revere her name for the rest of their long lives. Because of her death, they will live to be free."

On her way out of the room, Sedrah picked up the iron gauntlet that was all that remained of Kelvin and, clutching it to her breast, went to release the girls below.

Part Six:
The Clock of Pentaz

In the chill air, thin wisps of fog hung above the cobbled streets of Bathos. It lent a deathly stillness to the dark and deserted streets and thoroughfares of the Mid-City. To Tschan, each step he took seemed to reverberate against the plastered walls of the buildings that grew up around Merchants Alley.

The hustle and clamor of the daytime market were nowhere to be seen now. Booths were closed up tightly, and all their goods removed to safer places. Colorful tents and bright awnings had been collapsed and taken home, the glittering jewels and gaudy pendants hidden away in locked boxes bound with iron. All that was left behind now was the detritus and refuse that marked another day of business as usual.

Tschan wrapped his dull gray cloak around his thin frame to ward off the chill of the night. As he turned onto the narrow and uneven Squander Street, the squall of a cat sounded in the dead night air; how far away, he could not tell, but the sound set him on edge. To walk the back alleys of Bathos was, always, to risk one's life, but tonight he was on dangerous business. He was paying a trip to the Boneyard.

There were half a dozen entrances to the Boneyard, but Emperor Vlad's patrolmen guarded each. For many centuries the city's dead had been buried in the catacombs of the Boneyard, until the very walls and tunnels were composed of the bones of the dead. This was a sacred place, and to be safeguarded against desecration. The Emperor allowed only select few to enter, and an unknown apprentice scholar, who had yet to make a reputation for himself, was certainly not going to be on that short list. Tschan's studies of the works of the ancient historians had uncovered that perhaps something of far more historical value than just bones was hidden in those catacombs, and going against the stern admonitions of Wilhelm, his tutor and overseer, Tschan had decided to take a look for himself.

First, he had unearthed ancient maps of the city from the archives of the planners, and discovered that there were easier ways into the Boneyard than passing by a watchman. The old parchment had called Squander Street by another name, but Tschan was sure that he had matched up the streets correctly. He came to a cankered metal grate set into the cobblestones of the street, and crouched down beside it. Grabbing a hold of the bars he attempted to lift it. His breath hissed out with the effort, but the metal had rusted it firmly into place, and his strength wasn't enough to overcome the gum of the rotted iron.

He had hoped it would be easier than this, and didn't relish the idea of standing out in the openness of the street while he worked the grate loose. Still, if he wanted to find the Blaspheme Chalice, he would have to take risks. He removed a burlap nap sack from his shoulders and opened up the mouth of the bag. Reaching in, he extricated a corked glass vial wrapped with rags. Carefully, he worked the cork loose from the mouth of the bottle. An acrid scent floated into the air, and Tschan began to pour the nasty smelling acid down the outside seam of the grate.

The alchemist's concoction foamed as it began to eat away the brown canker. After giving the acid several minutes to work, Tschan gave the grate another tug, but found that it still resisted his efforts.

He withdrew a chisel and a large mallet with a metal head from his nap sack. Inserting the thin blade of the chisel into the seam, he began to pound the tool with his mallet, until, with a final clank, the grate broke free, and he was able to heave it out and onto the damp cobbles.

The entrance to the grate was narrow, but so was Tschan's build, and after he gathered his tools he was able to slip into the darkness beneath the street, dragging his knapsack behind him. For a startling moment he fell free through the thick black air, the dank scent of mold in his nostrils; then he struck bottom, a sharp pain shooting through his right ankle as he slipped on the slimy surface below, and went sprawling on his posterior in ankle deep drainage water.

He had lost his nap sack in the fall, and he cast about blindly with his hands- splashing amid the chilly waters as he searched for it. Finally, his left hand closed upon the familiar roughness of the bag, and he lifted it from its damp resting place, listening as the water drained out into the puddle below. The young scholar winced as he stood, gingerly testing out his ankle, and finding that the dull throb increased to a sharp pain each time that he put weight on his right foot. He cursed his luck as he fumbled in his nap sack, it was a little early in his adventure to injure himself. Briefly, he considered turning back, but the lure of uncovering a lost ancient artifact goaded him on. What price was a sprained ankle compared to making the greatest archeological discovery of the century? If he could pull this expedition off, apprentice scholars would be coming to ask him for advice.

Eventually Tschan found the oiled leather packet that contained a score of matches. The packet had effectively resisted its brief exposure to the water, and the matches remained dry. After a few tries Tschan was able to strike a match on his teeth, and he managed to light a wax taper. When it began to burn evenly, the explorer raised the flame aloft. He sucked his breath in sharply as the light revealed the broken shards of bone, and the mounds of grinning skulls that surrounded him.

His candle illuminated walls that were built from the ribs of the dead and calcified into a horrific tableau that was slick with a sheen of dampness. Here and there, a skeletal hand reached out from the wall, or a crushed skull peered out myopically. Even the mortar of the floor was mixed with the bones of the dead, and Tschan could see the irregularities of a slime-coated shin or leg bone protruding above the stagnant pools of water.

Dripping some wax onto an outstretched and fleshless palm, Tschan pressed his candle into its dead grip and pulled a shellacked tube from his nap sack. Unfurling a parchment from within, he held it open to best take advantage of the light the taper shed, and began to examine the map he had combined from various fragments that had been laboriously copied from the ancient scrolls.

According to the map, the tunnel where he stood was part of a small section of crypts, which were separated from the main catacombs by a long subterranean hall. After imprinting on his memory as much of the map as he could, he tucked it safely back in his pack, retrieved his candle and began splashing through a series of small chambers. His ankle hurt him with each damp step that he took, but the grisly horrors that encompassed him kept his mind from considering his pain too closely.

The sheer volume of the bones astounded him. These skeletons represented the long history of the city of Bathos. These were forgotten ancestors whose stories and achievements had been lost in the inevitable march of the centuries. What tales did they have to tell? If only these bones could speak of the wars they had witnessed, the calamities that they had seen. Tschan could only imagine what information and wisdom that they might share with their descendants.

Thus far, Tschan's maps had guided him accurately, and he found a rotting door hanging on its hinges. Sliding past this, he entered the long tunnel that connected with the main Boneyards. The ceiling hung claustrophobically low over his head, flames from the taper licking at creosote-encrusted skulls. Fleshless fingers tugged at his cloak, reaching out from the walls as though to capture him and drag the scholar down to join them in their dead realm.

Tschan would have shivered in fear if he were a different man, but he was far too entranced by the historical significance of the chambers that he tread. The dead of the past held little fear for him, only fascination and curiosity. The hall gave way to massive vaults, where the dead were piled in mounds of lichen-covered earth, and the very arches above hung with the limbs of the deceased. The feeble light that Tschan held only illuminated portions of these giant caverns, and the nethermost reaches held their contents in the mysteries of darkness. The still air was thick with must and decay. The charnel house scent of death had subsided over the centuries, but still left a subtle and ominous bite to the atmosphere.

Halting, Tschan crouched down and consulted his map again, wincing as his ankle sent a sharp lance of pain up his leg. A moist earth covered the floor of the chamber, and the thin young man scraped it away, revealing a circular design carved into the stone of the floor. Ancient runes adorned the elaborate design.

"It's true," muttered Tschan. "The writings of Skelos spoke truly. The key is here, as he suggested. Now only if it truly leads to the Chalice of Blaspheme."

Tschan had spent his formative years studying the ancient languages, and he had excelled beyond the other students, but all that was in a controlled environment, moderated by the professors and master scholars. Here he could truly put his knowledge to the test. He carefully examined the runes, taking in the nuance of every character's curve, and the context in which they were used- and finally the meaning became apparent.

To go where only the damned have been
seek that which should ever be lost
Let the unholy number of Pentaz lead the way

Tschan smiled. Perhaps when the catacombs had been built twelve centuries ago the calculations of Pentaz had been obscure, known only in scholarly circles that debated the meaning and the finite qualities of time; but seven centuries ago the clock of Pentaz had been constructed to track time to its theoretical and logical conclusion, which was nigh approaching. The thirteenth century was the mark when time would cease to exist, and this, in the ancient records, had been referred to as the unholy number of the scholar, Pentaz.

Now the question remained, what did that number refer to, and was it to be taken literally as 1,300, or was it the number 13? Tschan wracked his brain, as he considered the possibilities, but in finality the only directional navigation of which he could think referred to the degrees on the compass. Fortunately, he had considered the possibility that he might need a compass to navigate through the subterranean channels, and he had come prepared.

The young scholar spread out his parchment on the damp earth, tacking down the edges with his knapsack, the shellacked tube, and a loose thigh and arm bone. He extracted an elaborately worked compass from a pouch at his side. The magnetized needle in the dial face spun erratically for a moment, then settled to a stop. Tschan adjusted the dial, and then compared the reading he took to the coordinates on the map.

A sudden skitter of tiny footsteps made Tschan start, and he wheeled. As he brought the candle around, the flame went out, plunging him into musty darkness. He cursed himself for not bringing a lantern. He had decided against it due to the amount of other tools that he had brought along, and the concern that he might break it crawling around in the Boneyard tunnels. Still, right now, he wished that he had a dependable light.

Fumbling around in his nap sack, he finally located the matches he had purchased from the alchemist and managed to strike another on his teeth. He coughed out a cloud of phosphorous smoke, as the match ignited. A half dozen mud-splattered rats the size of tomcats were exposed in the sudden burst of illumination, but they scattered as Tschan re-lit his taper. The sudden appearance of the rats had the scholar a bit unnerved, tales from his memory filtering back to him about giant rats cornering and devouring solitary victims who had wandered into the subterranean tunnels beneath the city of Bathos. These stories suddenly gained some credence as Tschan realized that once his candle had gone out, these rats had made a beeline for him, hoping to take him unawares.

Shaking from adrenaline rush, Tschan stood and shouldered his gear. He shoved the mallet with the metal head through his belt so it was within easy reach in case the rats were so bold as to make another attack on him. In his left hand he held his compass, and he made sure the needle was lined up as he walked toward the 13th degree. He crossed precariously over mounds of jutting bone, and across stone jetties that led through seas of bones. His compass led him across arched stone bridges that were constructed with mortar and the skeletons of the dead; beneath lay chasms, which yawning depths had been filled with former residents of the city of Bathos.

Keeping the needle steady, Tschan followed its lead through narrow caverns that crawled with vermin, and through mazes of jagged, dripping stalagmites. He began to question his conclusion that the riddle's answer had been the 13th degree, but still the path opened up before him, and he followed. Behind he could hear the patter of rodent's feet, and he knew that the rats were following him. His insatiable curiosity drove him on, despite the throb in his ankle, and the dangers that lurked ahead and behind.

With deliberate steps he crossed a narrow stone ridge; on either side slopes of sharp rock yawned and plunged into pools of darkness. He had no idea where the slopes ended; the frail light he held in his hand not able to penetrate the tarry shadows. Perhaps the chasm continued indefinitely on into the bowels of the earth, he could not say.

As he reached the opposite side of the stone bridge he looked perplexedly into the hanging darkness of the cavern's wall. It seemed as though his path had suddenly ended in a sheer cliff side. He stepped painfully across the uneven, but wide ledge, holding his candle forward so he might examine the pitted stone wall. As he stepped closer to the 13th degree, his candle pierced the wall of darkness, and he discovered a small niche below a mossy overhang. He ducked down and slowly eased himself inside the closed spaces of the niche, and found that it retreated further into the core of the granite wall.

Making slow progress, he worked his way to the end of the tunnel, and confronted a stone slab that barred any further progress. Its face was inscribed with ancient runes that were partially concealed by a slick moss that had invested itself in the face of the slab. Tschan took a chisel and carefully scraped away the growth so that he could clearly see the ciphers.

Now the thought of his grim surroundings were pushed away as Tschan giddily considered the possibility of finding the Chalice of Blaspheme. Some scholars considered the chalice merely a legend invented to solidify Emperor Vlad the 1st's claim of living god hood, but if he could find the artifact, proof that it existed would be indisputable. History read that when Emperor Vlad materialized from the ethos, he held the Chalice of Blaspheme in his hands, and said that one day it would bring another that would make him whole. However, the chalice was stolen- and hence, the blaspheme was committed against Emperor Vlad the Dark. Though no record of any marriage had been inscribed, the Emperor must have taken time to procreate, because Vlad the 7th ruled the throne now. Though far from immortal, the line of Emperors proved miraculously long-lived during the nine hundred years that they had ruled the ancient city of Bathos.

Tschan had finished clearing away the mold and growth, and he fell to translating the symbols. Using his chisel, he scraped notes in the layer of dirt that covered the stone floor so that he could better track his deciphering efforts. His candle burned low, dripping trails of crimson wax down and over the small rocky outcropping on which he had planted the taper.

The young scholar lost track of time as he became absorbed in his efforts. A rumbling in his stomach briefly snapped him out of his study trance, and he dug into his bag and found an apple, which he quickly devoured. Taking a few steps back to the curve in the tunnel, he tossed the apple core out onto the ledge. A score of beady eyes stared inward at him. The yellow orbs disappeared from view as the core skipped in among them, and the rats scattered, chittering excitedly.

With a frown, Tschan returned to his translation efforts. As long as the rats didn't grow too bold he would be safe, he hoped. He found another candle and lit it from the dying flame of the other, then pressed the new taper into the still-warm wax of the old.

> *Blackened, shriveled heart of the Emperor*
> *Soulless, existing in a weakened state*
> *Hide the Chalice forever*
> *Lest the full power of his evil be awakened*
> *Hammer nor anvil can destroy this cup- only time*
> *So turn and leave this curse buried forever*
> *Or when darkness sweeps the earth in the blistering,*
> *scathing cold of unending torment, Mahmackrah will rule again*
> *And you shall rue the day you set eyes upon this stone*

The inscription fascinated Tschan. The superstitions of the ancients had been strong. This warning was an important reflection of the historical politics of that time, decided Tschan, and he carefully committed the script to his memory. Apparently, some political foe of the Emperor had attributed some power to the chalice, either superstitious or psychological, and they had stolen the cup away and hid it here in the catacombs.

The reference to Mahmackrah was a bit perplexing to Tschan. He didn't know how this connected to Emperor Vlad, or the chalice. He had heard of an obscure cult that was centered in Old Bathos and was dedicated to the summoning of this god, Mahmackrah, although through what means or to what purpose, Tschan did not know. Several lines of the ridiculous warning, thought Tschan, had hinted that he should turn away from the stone, so perhaps this very slab was where the chalice lay hidden.

Inserting a chisel behind the flat stone, Tschan carefully hammered the blade in deeper, so that a dark crack appeared around the edges. The scholar's efforts to pry the stone loose were having little effect, however, so he began to furiously pound the handle of his chisel, until his arm felt weak, and his brow was soaked with perspiration. Finally, the stone broke away from its seat against the wall, and slid down so that its bottom edge rested against the floor, revealing a hole in the wall that was about a cubit square.

With bated breath Tschan held the candle up to the darkness, its flickering light playing along the rough edges of the niche carved out of stone. Finally, its yellow rays reached inside, reflecting from the surface of a golden chalice that was cankered with green. Tschan let the pent-up air hiss from his lungs. He wanted to reach in and snatch the thing up, but he restrained himself, and took time to admire the artifact. The bowl of the chalice was broad and deep, large enough to hold nearly half a bucket's worth of liquid, he estimated. On either side, were two ornate handles that curved from the upper lip of the bowl to the underside of the chalice near the thick cylindrical stem, which attached to a broad base inscribed with images of dripping drink.

Replacing the candle on its ledge, Tschan carefully reached in and grabbed hold of the Chalice of Blaspheme. As he withdrew the weighty cup, a sudden wave of nausea and revulsion pushed through him, causing him to drop the chalice to the floor where it struck with a dull thud. Tschan went down to the ground also, doubled over and convulsing, as though he might empty the contents of his stomach onto the floor. Finally the nausea passed, and the scholar shook his head. Had some sorcery been cast upon the chalice, so that it wouldn't be removed from the chamber?

Using the edges of his cloak, so that he made no direct contact with the metal of the chalice, he once again essayed to hold the cup. The feeling was there again, but not so strong as before, and he was able to slip the chalice into his knapsack without being overcome with sickness. Once it was packed away, he felt a bit better, and slipped the bag over his shoulders, before retrieving his candle and retreating back out toward the ledge.

The rats were reluctant to back away from his approach, but finally their nerve broke and they scattered just before Tschan reached the ledge. The scholar breathed a sigh of relief. He wasn't anxious to get chewed on by a pack of giant rats. True enough, he could probably beat them off with the mallet he had tucked back into his belt, but the lousy things often carried a variety of diseases- all of which were unpleasant, and some of them deadly. If the rats got hungry enough to jump him, he was unlikely to come out of the mess unscathed.

He inched his way back across the stone bridge, and happy to have the yawning chasm behind him, began to retrace his steps through the Boneyards. The pattering of stealthy feet continued to follow him and Tschan knew that the rats were still pursuing their prey, hoping that he would take a crippling fall or make a wrong turn and become hopelessly lost. Then when he died of starvation, the rats would feast on his lean frame. These comforting thoughts accompanied Tschan as the whisper of feet pursued him, and the drip of perspiration falling from stalactites echoed a hollow accompaniment.

Tschan's ankle still provided a nasty jolt of pain each time that he put weight on it, but he managed to keep up a moderate pace despite the discomfort. Eventually he returned through the low-ceilinged tunnel that hung with the bones of the dead, and splashed back into the dank chamber that he had dropped into when he had entered the Boneyards.

Overhead, a square patch of moonlight shone through the open grate, casting a square beam of pale yellow illumination down upon the bone-strewn floors. The exit was about ten feet over Tschan's head, and this was not a contingency that he had been prepared for. He hated to think that he had come this far only to die in the sewer ten feet from freedom. Daylight, he figured, was only a few hours away, and soon there would be hundreds of Bathos' citizens using Squander Street. Surely he could holler for help, attract someone's attention, and elicit their aid in crawling from the sewer. Though Bathos was not renowned for its compassionate citizenry, he could likely bribe someone to help him. Still, this tack would probably result in the notification of the city guard, and would end up with him rotting in jail.

The walls of brown encrusted bone might be climbable to someone agile, but Tschan was not known for his dexterity, and even if he managed to climb the wall, he would have to leap six or seven feet to the exit at the center of the ceiling. He doubted that he could pull it off with a bad ankle. He glanced around the room, trying to figure some other way he could escape, and he finally hit on a decent, but somewhat grim plan.

He began gathering the moldering bones, pushing the piles to the center of the chamber, gradually amassing a large mound of skeletal remains beneath the drain hole. When he had gathered a prodigious pile of the dead, he slowly mounted the tottering mound, bones snapping beneath his steps. Finally, he stood precariously atop the pile and reached upward, his fingertips still nearly a foot away from his goal. He carefully gathered his legs beneath him, and ignoring the jabbing pain in his ankle, leaped upward, his fingers catching on the damp cobblestones of the street overhead.

Using every bit of his available strength he wrestled his body upward so that his chest rested on the paving stones. Here he found that his nap sack had wedged between his body and the street, the small egress not allowing him to pull himself to safety. Awkwardly, he reached back and tried to slide the pack from his shoulders. With some amount of squirming, the thing finally came loose and the strap slid down his right arm, until he could grab it. With the pack removed from his back and firmly in his grip, Tschan was able to struggle out of the hole and pull the nap sack up behind him.

For a moment he lay face down on the slick pavings, the cold stone against his face, welcoming the air that was without the foul taint of death. A sudden cry forced him into action.

"There he is coming up out of the sewer!" shouted a mailed city guard at the intersection of Squander and Merchant Alley, his leather-gloved hand pointing at Tschan's prone figure.

Tschan galvanized his body into movement; leaping painfully to his feet, he turned and fled from the watchmen, who evidently had noticed the removed drain grate, and had been keeping an eye on the situation.

As the scholar came down upon his hurt ankle in full stride, it stiffened and he went tumbling head over heels, the chalice painfully gouging into his back as he rolled across it. This, however, was not time to indulge the pain, and he quickly regained his feet, and ducked down Severed Head Road, a street with an illustrious and gory past. Gray buildings were built in jumbles along the street, which uneven surface was cracked and terraced so that wheeled chariots were not able to safely pass this way. The homes tilted inward, some completely bridging the street below and meeting overhead.

Tschan frantically ran, passing beneath one of these conjoined buildings. As he stepped from its shadow, he heard a flapping above him and glanced toward the sky in time to see a half dozen black-clad figures leaping down upon him from a narrow ledge above. Their dark cloaks whipped behind them as they leaped, filling the moonlit sky with billowing black that accompanied them like satanic wings.

They landed around him, their feet striking the ground with nary a sound. None spoke as they closed in for the attack. These new assailants were certainly not of the city watch, perhaps he had the misfortune to blunder into a trap set by one of the hundreds of evil-worshipping cults that resided in the city of Bathos.

As they came forward, enveloping him with their dark cloaks, Tschan's hand went to his belt, and he lashed out with his mallet, striking bone and flesh beneath the shadowed hood of one unfortunate attacker. There was a groan, and the wounded assailant crumpled to the earth among the dark, bilious folds of his cloak.

There was no time for him to make a second attack, Tschan's assailants moved in with wraith-like silence, wavy daggers flashing in the moonlight, and the sickly scent of concentrated jasmine upon their breath. The scholar stepped aside, and a wicked looking blade cut a swath through the patch of space where he had been standing. One attacker swung a sword, and the flat of the blade struck Tschan in the back of the head, sending him reeling forward to the ground, where he went down upon his hands and knees. Someone kicked him in the stomach, and he coughed up bile. A knife descended, and severed the strap of his nap sack, other hands snatching away the weight of the bag and the chalice within. Tschan wanted to leap to his feet and take back the treasure that he had worked so hard to find, but a multitude of bony hands were holding him down.

One attacker grabbed hold of a handful of Tschan's short brown hair, and pulled his head back, exposing his bare throat. Another of the wraiths lowered a razor-edged dagger, preparing to draw the wave-shaped blade across Tschan's neck.

"For Mahmackrah!" spat his executioner.

The scholar gritted his teeth and prepared for the inevitable. How ironic, he thought, that his death would be just another in a long line of decapitations on Severed Head road.

Suddenly a cry went up from the mouth of the road. Footsteps slapped on the stones, and scale mail rattled with each step. The dark forms of his wraith-like attackers melted into the deep shadows at the roadside, taking the Chalice of Blaspheme with them. Foolishly, Tschan tried to gain his feet and chase after them, but a heavy forearm struck him in the back as he rose, pushing him to the ground. A heavy foot was placed upon the back of his neck.

"Don't move, or I'll snap your delicate little neck like a twig," growled the unseen watchmen. "You're going to regret the day that you tried to loot the Boneyards. The Emperor has a special prison for the likes of thieves like you."

"What about those men that attacked me?" gasped Tschan. "Are you going to catch them?"

"Nah. As far as we're concerned they were just helping us do our duty."

A couple voices joined the man in laughter, and Tschan felt a pair of heavy manacles being chained around his wrists. They snapped into place with a resounding thunk, and Tschan's heart sank as he felt the weight of his bonds upon his limbs. Surely, this could not be happening to him.

The watchmen removed his foot from Tschan's neck, and dragged him upward until he stood. The guard rubbed at his swarthy face, and licked thick lips as he examined the man that he caught. "You're a bit well-dressed to be a common thief, and a bit young to have moved up the ranks of the thieving guild far enough to afford those fancy vestments."

"I'm not a thief," insisted Tschan.

The guard laughed. "Yet, we caught you thieving in the Boneyard. That entrance is secret to the city folk, but not to the guards of the watch. You left the grate out of place so that we knew something was amiss. The Emperor has a very strict policy against people poking around down there, and even if, by some miracle, you get out of prison alive, the Thieves Guild has been known to do things to people that steal without their authority." He drew his thumb across his throat, and had a hardy laugh at Tschan's expense.

"Come along boy, I have a feeling the Emperor is going to invite you to go for a swim."

* * * *

The city of Bathos was in turmoil. Bands of drunkards roamed the streets with rum and whisky in broken-necked bottles; acolytes swarmed the roadways in violet robes, waving braziers that smoked with putrid smelling incense, dedicating the city streets to the embrace of eternal darkness and emptiness; children ran crying through the intersections, abandoned by parents who had given up their care, in order that they might indulge in drink and orgy for their final few days upon the Earth.

"Tomorrow we die," said the drunken reveler. "We must live for today, and take what little pleasure we can."

"Is that so?" growled Lothar. He motioned to the man's cart, and the shaggy brown pony that drew it. "Then you wouldn't mind lending me your transportation, I take it." He reached into his pouch and withdrew three gold crowns, minted with the sharp-nosed and thin-lipped features of the Emperor Vlad. He dropped these into the drunk's outstretched hand. "Perhaps these will enable you to make your last hours more enjoyable."

The drunk shrugged his shoulders and grinned widely, revealing a broken front tooth. "What good will a cart do me when the world ends? Take it, it's yours."

The pony was woefully undersized to be pulling a cart as large as this, so instead of riding Lothar took the pony by his bridle and led him along Cordon Road, until he came to Goods Street and turned onto it. This filthy avenue was frantically busy as last minute customers filled their bags with rice, wheat, and jerked beef- and paid exorbitant fees to the merchants who sold them. The demand was enormous, and the merchants were not about to pass up a chance to reap equally enormous profits by raising their prices accordingly- even though the end of the world might make all their earnings worth less than a tramp's spittle in the dust at the roadside.

Lothar stopped at the top of the street, halting in its center, letting the traffic flow around him. He stood a forbidding figure, his black cloak and raven hair floating out behind him, and his piercing gray eyes roving to the left and the right as if expecting danger to appear at any moment. Across his bare, and broad chest was a bandolier of throwing axes, and over his shoulder he carried a battle-axe with a spiked haft atop the blade. His waist was sheathed in thick leather, and his boots tipped with flat steel blades, which were a common climbing aid used by Thieves of the Guild.

Though also a member of the Warriors Guild, Lothar found himself in the same situation as the laborers and craftsmen that were desperately purchasing a store of food. Tomorrow, perhaps, there would be chaos upon the city, and there was no guarantee that food would be readily available on the merchant streets. The fees of both the Warrior's and Thieves Guild, not to mention the Emperor's taxation, had drained Lothar's pockets of coin, and only late last evening, at the expense of a child-slaver, had he been able to replenish the supply. The money certainly wasn't going to do the slaver any good now that he was missing his head.

A fortnight ago he had called it quits with both the Warrior and Thieves Guild, so he still had this new coin in his pocket, and hoped that it would be enough to get him clear of the stinking streets of Bathos once and for all. Of course, that was if the scientists, and scholars were wrong. If they were right, then time would be ending tomorrow, and it all wouldn't matter much anyhow.

Across the crenellated, sloping, and gilded rooftops of Mid-Bathos, Lothar could look into the streets of Old Bathos below, and see magnificent towers that had stood for many centuries and now tottered toward collapse, the bas relief of the subcity's walls, and the incredible artisanship that had gone into crafting the arching walkways and massive pillars. Among these wonders, were the most amazing of all, the pyramid of Lythos and the clock of Pentaz.

Lythos, the sorcerer king who had founded Bathos, had ordered the pyramid constructed according to the strictest of specifications. Built from granite, and covered with a thick veneer of black marble that was veined with purple, its slanting walls rose high above all else in Old Bathos. Its top did not come to a point, but rather, like a volcanic mountain, its upper reaches were a concave bowl. The reason behind this was to serve some mystical reason that Lothar didn't understand, but when the pyramid was finished, Lythos went to his construction and worked magics that he hoped would make him more powerful than any man. As the legend went, his spells went awry and he ended up summoning Vlad the 1st from some mystical dimension, who promptly overthrew Lythos, and 'liberated' Bathos.

If Vlad the 7th was indicative of the first Emperor's ruling style, Lythos couldn't have been much worse off under Lythos, decided Lothar.

Constructed centuries later, by the scholars of Pentaz, was the magnificent water clock that rose up in the shadow of the pyramid. Its massive gears were timed precisely, pushed by waters that fell into the bowl atop the pyramid, which were then stored in great tanks. This water was metered out in exacting measures, so that the clock would track time to its logical conclusion – which was tonight at the stroke of twelve.

Lothar watched the thin hand of the clock move rapidly around the massive dial, and saw the water gush out from channels below the clock, falling in misty torrents to frothing white pools many feet below. He shook his head. Could the scholars be right? Could all this end in the fleeting passing of a moment and become nothingness? He shrugged; best leave such deep thinking to the philosophers. He was going to make plans for tomorrow, just as he always did.

When Lothar left Goods Street several hours later, his wagon was considerably heavier and his purse considerably lighter. The pony struggled up Bathos' hilly streets, and Lothar walked alongside, not wanting to be an extra burden on the poor beast. Additionally, pedestrians tended to clear out of the way more readily, if they saw him at the forefront of the wagon.

As Lothar turned onto Crumble Street, he caught sight of a slight man, about a head shorter than he, that turned the corner with him. Lothar recognized the spiked brown hair, upturned nose, and smirk that the man habitually wore on his face. Although this fellow didn't seem capable of winning a fistfight with a ten-year-old street urchin, his appearance was a study in deception. Behind the child-like demeanor existed a lightening fast killer. Lothar knew the man as Balzac, a Thieves Guild enforcer. He tracked down people who had offended the guild somehow and usually killed them. Though Lothar hadn't seen him in action, Balzac had a reputation as being a deadly ambidextrous swordsman.

Lothar wasn't exactly on good terms with either the Thieves or Warriors Guild since he had forfeited his membership with them. He had a bad feeling that Balzac was coming after him. There was an old saying, 'The only way to quit a guild is to quit your life'. Lothar had seen the truth of this maxim demonstrated to him again and again. He doubted that Balzac was dropping by to break bread with him.

Still, Lothar had been in nastier situations. This wasn't the first time that someone had wanted him dead. He kept a cool head and pretended that he hadn't noticed the Thieves Guild's enforcer trailing him down the crowded city streets. Occasionally he would glance in Balzac's direction to track his location. The man was far too deadly a foe to allow him to sneak up from behind.

The dark-haired warrior scowled. He didn't like playing the waiting game. As it was, he was waiting for Balzac to make his move. Lothar decided that this was a bad tactic, and would probably result in his death. Besides, while Balzac followed he couldn't continue on home to the small loft that he and his wife, Sheesa, occupied. The Thieves Guild had been known to slaughter entire families in retribution for perceived slights against their authoritarian rule. Sheesa was pregnant with his child, and he didn't want to expose either of them to any unnecessary risk before he could smuggle them out of the city, and away from the infernal politics of the guilds.

Bringing the pony to a stop, Lothar set the wheel brake of the cart and made a show of adjusting the animal's harness. A crowd of the worshippers of Zig passed through the center of the street, shouting out a wild chant in which they welcomed the end of the world, and flailing their arms so that the tattered rags they wore whipped about like windmills.

Taking advantage of this diversion, Lothar slipped to the rear of the cart, and crouching low, walked alongside the parade of zealots, using them as cover. After making some backward progress, he deftly slipped through their ranks, crossing to the opposite side of the street upon which Balzac had been tailing him. The parade of Ziggites continued on down the road, and by the time they had passed, and Balzac discovered that Lothar was no where to be seen, the dark-haired warrior was behind the Thieves Guild enforcer, pulling back his head and putting the sharp blade of a throwing axe against his jugular.

"Did you come after me alone?" demanded Lothar.

"No indeed," answered the diminutive enforcer with a rather light tone, considering his dire situation. "I think you'll find my accomplices directly behind you."

Lothar shifted to one side, but it was too late. A club hit him in the shoulder, spinning him around. He lost his grip on his hand axe, and before he could bring it across Balzac's throat, it fell from numbed fingers to the cobblestones. Still on his feet, Lothar reached for his battleaxe, but before he could complete the draw, someone behind him swept his legs out from beneath him, and shoved him to the stones of the street.

As he came up to his hands and knees, someone straddled his back and put a knife to his neck.

Balzac's small feet carried him within sight of Lothar, who bared his teeth as someone pressed a knife into the flesh of his throat. "Hmm," said Balzac, putting a finger to his chin. "Wasn't this situation reversed only a few moments ago?"

With a small amount of satisfaction, Lothar saw that his axe blade had drawn a bit of blood at the side of the enforcer's neck.

"You see," continued Balzac. "I do a careful profile of all my victims, before I pay them a visit. I find out their strengths, their weaknesses, and their temperament. You, I discovered, are, what a more intelligent man than yourself might call, proactive. Let me explain it in a way that your feeble little brain can comprehend. You don't sit back and wait for things to happen, you force them to happen. So I merely used myself as bait, and waited until you came to me. Then we sprang the trap."

Without the luxury of being able to turn his head, Lothar did his best to see how many foes he was facing. Balzac was directly to his front, and he could see a man to each side of him. Another was on his back with a knife to his throat. That was at least four men, and there might be more behind him.

"Admit it," demanded Balzac. "I outfoxed you."

"I admit it," answered Lothar, chagrined more by his predicament than the fact that someone had proved smarter than he. He was well aware that the city was full of men cleverer and better schooled than himself.

"You are a popular man. There are representatives from the three guilds here to see you, and offer you the opportunity to live."

"I'm listening," answered Lothar.

"Of course, Tacher, who is holding the knife to your neck, and I represent the Thieves Guild. Jotham, to my right is an envoy from the Warriors Guild, and to my left is Zaydok- emissary for the Courtesan's Guild, who is evidently missing some of his property. Behind you are Karmel and Kayne, brothers, and childhood friends of mine, who so generously offered to help us out."

A couple of unfriendly chuckles erupted from behind him, and Lothar knew that Balzac had been telling the truth about the two men he hadn't been able to see. Jotham was a large man, bald except for a topknot. He held a club in hands the size of frying pans, and his arms were the girth of logs. Lothar had seen him around the guild house, and knew him to be a formidable opponent.

Zaydok, he had never laid eyes upon before. He was dressed in silk breeches and blouse, expensive jewelry adorning his fingers and wrists. At his waist, he wore a heavy dagger with a jewel-encrusted scabbard of brass.

All he could see of Tacher was the extremely hairy hand that gripped the blade beneath his chin, but he could certainly smell the foul-scented thief that straddled his back.

Together, he had six opponents, perhaps he'd best go along with them for the time being. As it was, any move he made now was likely to result in his death.

Balzac crouched down so that he could speak with Lothar face to face. "The only reason that we are offering you this second chance, is that in the past you have proven very profitable to both the Thieves and Warriors Guild. You also command a certain amount of respect among the younger members of the guild, though for the life of me I cannot see why."

Balzac continued. "The first thing you need to do is forfeit any monies that you obtained while you weren't officially working for the guilds. After that, you may continue to pay dues as is normally expected of upstanding guild members. The Courtesan Guild offers you the following options: Immediately pay them five hundred gold faces in exchange for Sheesa's freedom, or turn her back over to the guild, where they will terminate her pregnancy, and return her to work."

"How am I to pay five hundred pieces of gold to the Courtesan Guild, if I must forfeit all my earnings to the Thieves and Warriors Guild?" growled Lothar.

Balzac shrugged and opened up his hands in a comical gesture. "I suppose that isn't an option, after all. Just turn the scag over."

Lothar seethed with anger. He wanted to throttle the little thief, but the slightest move would spell death for him.

"Okay," said Lothar finally. "I'll start by taking you to my stash of earnings."

"Very well," answered Balzac. "I thought that maybe you would see the error of your ways. Of course, your realize that we must take the precaution of disarming you."

Karmel and Kayn came forward and removed Lothar's battle-axe and remaining throwing axes. When the two brothers had finished stripping his weapons from him, Tacher removed the knife from his throat and stepped off his back.

While the thief stood upright, he momentarily faced away from Lothar. This was the small opening that Lothar had been waiting for. He would die before he turned Sheesa and his baby over to the scum at the Courtesans Guild, and he might just as well do the dying now.

Lothar came into a crouch with his hand planted firmly on the ground, then he lashed out with his right leg, sweeping Tacher's feet from underneath him. As Tacher pitched backward, he threw his furry arms up into the air as if trying to catch hold of something to arrest his fall. His right hand still held his knife, and Lothar stood up and grabbed the thief's right arm with both of his hands, one above his elbow and one at his wrist. Using this leverage, Lothar twisted the arm hard, breaking Tacher's elbow joint as the thief hit the ground. Tacher screamed in pain, and Lothar slid his hands up to shrieking man's limp fingers, and pried loose the knife that they still, albeit weakly, gripped.

All this happened in the matter of two seconds, and Lothar leaped toward Karmel, who had prematurely turned to leave, thinking that their prisoner was safely disarmed. His eyes were fixed on Lothar's battleaxe, which he held up to examine the Smithy marks more closely. The initials HK were the last thing he saw before Lothar plunged a knife into his back, and through to his heart. He tried to yell, but only a whimper came out, accompanied by a stream of blood that drooled from his slack jaw.

Lothar let Karmel collapse, not bothering to pull the knife free from his back. Instead, he reached forward and plucked the battleaxe from the dying henchman's hands as the poor man crumpled into a heap.

Heavy footstep sounded behind, and Lothar ducked, simultaneously spinning, low on his heel. His axe snapped outward and chopped through Jotham's shin, just as the heavy club that the giant warrior wielded whipped over the top of his head. Blood spattered the street, and the emissary from the Warriors Guild went down with a horrible bellow. Though in extreme pain, the brave warrior took an awkward, but potentially devastating, swing at Lothar.

Barely sidestepping the attack, Lothar charged toward Balzac; who he knew to be the most dangerous of his remaining foes. But Balzac had fled, waiting for a more opportune time to fight, perhaps when the odds were more heavily in his favor. Kayn and the foppishly dressed Zaydok also took to the busy streets, leaping through gaps in the crowd that had gathered to watch the bloody spectacle, and fleeing as fast as their feet would take them.

A shuffle of leather alerted Lothar, and he turned to see Tacher launching himself into the air, a second dagger upraised, and held tightly in his right fist, while his left arm hung limply. There was no time for Lothar to swing his heavy weapon, so he merely thrust the axe, and the spike at the tip of the haft, forward. The henchman's momentum carried him onto the spike, which drove in under his ribcage and up into his heart. Lothar shook off the convulsing body, then used a snap of his wrist to clean the excess blood from the axe.

"Lothar," called Jotham weakly.

The dark-haired warrior looked at the wounded man skeptically, but saw that the giant club had rolled out of the man's reach. "What is it?" he answered.

"I know you to be an honorable man," said Jotham. "Though you no longer be a member of the Warriors Guild, I know that you would not let a fellow brother of the blade die a suffering death."

"You want me to kill you?" asked Lothar. Now that the heat of the battle was dying, he felt a twinge of regret at having to maim such a brave warrior.

"Yes," answered Jotham. "I will bleed to death soon, but save me these last moments of agony."

Lothar lifted his axe, and then hesitated. "You could still live."

Jotham shook his head. "I am a warrior. What good is a warrior with one foot?"

"I've heard of your exploits," answered Lothar. "Even with one foot, you would be more warrior than most." He tore loose a chunk of Jotham's cloak, and bound it into a tourniquet that effectively halted the issue of blood from the big man's leg. "A good leach will cauterize your wound with a torch to keep away the infection."

Lothar rose, shouldered his battleaxe and returned to his cart. He wasn't surprised when he found that some of the goods he had purchased, and so securely tied down were now missing. He was more surprised to find that a large portion of it was still intact, and resting in the cart. Thieves ran rampant in Bathos, and it was true that there was no honor among them. The only thing that had saved him from being picked clean while he was being detained by Balzac and his flunkies, was the fact that most of the goods were bagged or barreled by the double bushel. This made things a little too heavy for the average thief to shoulder and discreetly walk away with. A more enterprising robber might have jumped on the cart and rode off, but that would take a large measure of daring, and most thieves were, at heart, cowards. They took what they could by subterfuge and deceit, and the strong arm robbers and thugs waited until night, where they could work undercover of darkness; away from the prying eyes of the city watchmen, who might require bribes to overlook the crime, and away from the possibility of citizen interference- though this last obstacle was unlikely, for Bathos residents had grown accustomed to minding their own business, finding it much easier to look the other way than to get involved.

Lothar's shoulder was sore from the mashing that Jotham had given him with his club. An angry purple bruise was forming across his deltoid, and it throbbed fiercely. Still, his arm was functional, despite the pain, and Lothar knew that he had come out on the winning end of the battle. Jotham had not been so fortunate, and Karmel and Tacher hadn't lived to regret crossing him.

He hoped that this would be the last of the interference that he would see from the guilds, but he doubted it. The guilds were in turmoil, and they were anxious to show that, next to Emperor Vlad, they were still the absolute authority. When Lothar had sworn into the guilds, his oath had stated that he would remain a loyal member until 'the end of time'. Thousands of others had sworn by the same oath. Two weeks ago he had given notice, informing them that the 'end of time' was at hand. According to the scholars, it was, but the guild masters had felt differently, saying that time would exist until the day of Lothar's death. To spite them, he quit right at that moment, citing their refusal to release him as a breach of contract.

But the loss of one of their prize members made the guilds look as though they had lost face and power. They were out to make an example of him. He was sure that Balzac would be back, and probably with more men.

To ensure that he was not being trailed, Lothar took a variety of roads that were off the beaten track- away from Bathos' main thoroughfares. Finally confident that he was not being stalked, Lothar headed to Crawl Street, where he had rented a loft above an abandoned barn.

He picked the massive padlock on the dilapidated barn doors, and un-wound the rusty chain that tied the handles together. The huge doors creaked and wobbled as he opened them and led the pony into the dim interior of the barn. Several shafts of fading sunlight shone through small windows set high in the brick walls.

The air in the enclosed barn was musty, but the must was overpowered with a sickly sweet scent. A soft whinnying came to Lothar's ears, and he turned to see two muscular quarter horses stalled to his right. He had pur-chased them recently in order to facilitate an escape attempt from Bathos. After unhooking the pony from the cart he broke open a bag of grain and distributed some to the horses and the pony, which he secured in a third stall. The owner of the barn didn't realize that Lothar was making use of it, and af-ter breaking in, Lothar had realized why the owner had turned down his offer to rent it from him. The musty stalls were filled with opium bricks wrapped in waxed red paper marked with the golden lily seal of distant Cathay.

Though the sale of opium was not outlawed on the streets of Bathos, opium hailing from Cathay was forbidden by the Merchants Guild. The fragile purple poppy flowers of Cathay bore potent seeds, and the milky derivative, which was reduced in the sun to a brown paste, was far more potent than the opium grown within Bathos' domain. Sale of the foreign drug weakened the ability of local merchants to gouge their customers. If the Merchant's Guild knew of this stash of Cathay grown opium, they would see the place burned and razed to the ground.

Lothar had simply moved the bricks aside to make room for his horses. He had no use for the stuff himself. He had been to the smoky opium houses, and seen the addicted sluggards that whiled away their days, and even years, lounging on purple divans, while beautiful slave girls, scantily draped in red silks, brought them their victuals alongside gold inlaid water pipes- the bowls of which were packed with opium. It was a hobby that only the rich could afford, and yet he had seen wealthy merchants turned destitute by their enslavement to the stuff, and reduced to begging alongside the crippled and diseased.

After the horses and pony were fed, and their troughs filled with water from a cask, Lothar chained the barn doors shut, and locked the place up. He mounted a rickety wood stair at the side of the building. As he climbed the creaking wooden steps he looked out across the hard dirt road, speckled with imbedded stone, and at a few of the people drifting by in the hazy twilight. The sun was sinking below the sprawl of the city and Bathos' mighty towers and walls were darkened with deep shadows. Who knew what tomorrow would hold for them? The world would end at the stroke of twelve tonight.

As Lothar inserted a narrow brass key into the tarnished lock of the loft apartment, he caught a glint of steel from within the shadows of Barn Alley. Perhaps the guilds already knew of their whereabouts. No one with good intent lurked in alleyways.

Lothar pushed the door open behind him, and he backed into warm interior of the loft, eyes searching the roadways for signs of any other enemy. The shutters had been closed, and the room was black, but for the twilight shed by the opening of the door. A sudden rush of movement alerted Lothar, but it was too late. A dagger sliced through the air, striking Lothar between the shoulder blades.

"Die scum!" hissed the voice.

* * * *

Darkness settled over the city of Bathos, a blanket of chill and foreboding. Stannett uneasily shifted his plump form in the hard wooden chair, and finally got up to look out the narrow windows of the clock tower of Pentaz. Twilight sometimes plays tricks on a man's eyes, but the dark forms he saw lurking around the base of the pyramid of Lythos only added to the certainty in his heart that something was dreadfully wrong.

A chill came over him as he watched black-swathed figures detach from the shadows of the buildings flanking the broad-tiled courtyard that held both the pyramid of Lythos and clock of Pentaz. Swiftly, they raced across the open spaces, javelins held low at their sides. There were three ground-level entrances to the black-marbled pyramid, and one broad set of stairs that traveled up its face to the concave peak.

At each of the entrances, a pair of the Emperor's guards stood their dutiful watch. Stannett wanted to yell out from the clock tower, to warn them of the impending danger, but when he tried the cry caught in his throat and came out a muted gurgle. By then it was too late to attempt another warning, and he could do nothing but watch the horrible scene unfold.

The guardsmen crumpled to the ground as javelins burst through their bodies. Each entrance was swarmed by four and five figures cloaked in voluminous black robes that hid their faces from view. They quickly struck down the last resistance, and dragged the guards' bodies within the temple. Except for a tottering old drunk that obliviously zigzagged his way across the bare tiles, the courtyard was devoid of life.

Stannett peered down at the darkened halls that delved deep into the temple pyramid, and then he saw new guardsmen emerge from within the shadowed wells where the dead had been drawn. Though the clock keeper was too far away to recognize a face, he had an evil feeling that these were imposters, but on what sinister task were they set? As he watched, more of these robed robbers streamed from the shadows, filing into the depths of the pyramid- a line of ants upon some demonic mission.

All this Stannett could see from the west-facing window. He wondered if his very tower might be under attack from the south, and he rushed across the massive flagstones of which the tower of Pentaz was built, and peered out the south-facing window. He could hear the gigantic gears whirring and clicking as the water pushed them inexorably onward. After the water had done its job, it was channeled out massive funnels, and churned down the face of the tower in dual waterfalls that were nearly as spectacular as some nature had made, and dropped into foaming pools at the base of the clock tower.

Looking beyond the turbulent pools, he strained his eyesight, in the fading light, to search the outskirts of the spacious courtyard. There, from the bowels of the city, young and old filtered toward the clock. Some pushing their families and worldly belongings in small wooden carts; others boisterously tramping in with flagons held high while cohorts carried kegs of ale upon their shoulders; many came with fear in their eyes, uncertain of what the future might bring. They bore torches, a sea of glimmering light in the murky haze. At every stroke of the clock a great cry rose up from the gathering crowd. The tower of Pentaz was their god, and they worshipped each movement that it made. It marked each passing second of their lives, and now, perhaps, it would mark the end.

Stannett was mesmerized by the scene. What would they do? Finally, in a frantic realization that his safety might be at stake, the pudgy clock keeper ran to the water channel that crossed the courtyard between the tower and the pyramid. The channel was built on stone arches, across which an aqueduct carried a torrent of water from the massive tanks within the pyramid.

Walkways extended along either side of the waterway, giving the dark-cloaked assassins access to the clock, should they decide to cross from the pyramid.

The water poured through an open channel into the clock tower, where it gathered in a pool and immediately plunged down into the inner workings of the clock, driving the gears with incredible force. The water dropped so quickly that the basin where it gathered was a perpetual whir pool. Stannett remembered dropping a key, which fell into the pool, and how it was gone in a fraction of a second. He also recalled his relief when it hadn't gummed up the gears of the clock.

This all occurred to him in a fraction of a moment, and he didn't halt until he stood near the open doorway. The water gushed down the sloping aqueduct, throwing up a spray that wet the hem of his yellow robe. He reached up and grimaced as he pulled loose the heavy bolt that locked the portcullis' gears into place. Then he began turning the massive wheel, letting out chain into the gate's gears, until the iron bars had lowered across the walkways, and all the way down into the water below.

The waters hissed as they were split by the bars, but they rushed on unhindered. Stannett replaced the locking bolt, and felt a little bit safer, but he worried that the front door of the clock was unbarred. Though he knew that it was locked, he feared that would not be enough to detour a determined crowd. As the official clock keeper it was his duty to make sure that nothing interfered with the count of the clock. He pounded down long winding flights of circular stairs until he reached the ground level, winded, sweating and exhausted. That's when he heard angry cries rising from the crowd outside, and a pounding that shook the giant mahogany door. He could see the heavy timber beam, cut from ironwood, where it rested alongside the door, but always he had needed help when hoisting its massive girth. He doubted that he possessed the strength to lift it into place alone.

While he heard the discontent of the crowd outside grow louder and frantically considered his predicament, the door burst open.

* * * *

His hands were manacled together over his head, the rusted irons cutting into his wrists. The manacles were looped with a chain that ran upward to an iron spike that was driven deep into the bedrock stone of Drowning Man's prison. Cold water swirled around Tschan's calves, and the rats jabbered as they frantically rushed for higher ground.

Night was falling and the narrow shafts of light that shone through the crumbled slits, in the stone walls thirty feet above, began to dim. There had been no trial. Such conventions were only for the rich- if they hadn't yet bribed their way out of trouble. The Captain of the City Guard heard the crime which Tschan had been accused of and passed immediate sentence- life in Drowning Man's Prison.

Life in Drowning Man's Prison was generally very short. The Tiber River was notoriously mercurial, rising ten to twenty feet when heavy tides from the Black Sea washed back into the mouth of the river and backed up its flow into the salty waters beyond. A pair of grizzled guardsmen had escorted him in a battered skiff. Two hundred yards of hemp stretched from a massive iron hook imbedded in granite, to a like hook on Drowning Man's Island, which sat midstream, a forsaken rock upon which loomed a decaying gray building. The guardsmen used the massive strength of their upper bodies to pull the boat across the swift river currents until the skiff bumped its way into a hand hewn alcove, where the boat was moored to a rust-flecked rail.

"The sailor scum are predicting high sea tides for this evening," said one of his escorts. A worn leather tunic stretched across his barrel chest as he took a deep breath of the tangy air. "And I can smell the salt on the wind. It means that the seas are sweeping inland. It's likely this will be your one and only night in Drowning Man's Prison." He said this last with a hint of sympathy creeping into his voice.

"It may be the last night for all of us," said the second, tugging at a cauliflower ear that hinted at past brawls and fisticuffs. "That is, if the scholars are right about the clock of Pentaz."

They finished climbing the river worn steps carved into the face of the rock island, and Tschan's guards escorted him into the dank jail atop the desolate rock. As they shoved aside a water-swollen door that was threatening to burst its iron bands, the groan of the hinges brought cries from the forsaken souls who were imprisoned below.

"The waters are rising," yelled one. "Unshackle us before we drown!"

"The rats are eating my legs," cried another voice, more weakly than the bellicose holler of the first.

Tschan shot a glance at his captors, wondering if he could expect any mercy from them. Their rough exterior suggested that he could expect no compassion, but he saw a weariness in their eyes that was brought on by too many brutalities seen, experienced, and administered.

"Is there any hope of escape for me?" asked Tschan quietly.

The two men looked at each other. "Aye," said the pugilist. "It has been done before."

"Once," clarified Tschan's barrel-chested escort. "Evidently the manacles had nearly rusted through." His voice echoed hollowly as they descended a slippery stair within the decaying prison.

The jail was carved into the stone of the island itself and the cells below ground level. The walls were slimed with moss and the rush of the river was dampened and distorted as they descended into the insulation of the granite island.

"Maybe it could happen again," continued his jailer, "but our concern is not those who escape. Our duty is to see you manacled below."

A guttering torch lit their way into a dank cavern below. Tschan's jailers filed him past rows of manacles that were linked to pitons driven deep into the rock. Some still bound rotting corpses with gnawed flesh, and others skeletons had been picked clean. Their feet splashed through cold, ankle deep water that spilled in through cracks and channels that had been carved into the island bedrock over the past centuries.

The guardsmen with the mangled ears carefully examined several sets of manacles, and then chose a set for Tschan. "Hands above your head," he said.

Any last vestiges of hope remaining within his breast was extinguished now. This was the end of the line for him. The stench of the dead that filled this place proved it beyond any doubt. Tschan complied with the jailer's order, and he felt the rough oxidation of the pitted iron manacles press against his wrists.

The two men hoisted their prisoner by a long chain that ran from the manacles and to the piton above. Once Tschan hung several feet above the floor they secured the chain, and bid the young scholar adieu.

"It's best to be chained higher," one explained. "The rats are less likely to gnaw on your bones, and the water is less likely to drown you should it rise."

"I suppose I should thank you," said Tschan, though he was not really sure of it at all.

"If you should slip your manacles, there is a drainage sump halfway up the stairs. Good luck to you."

"And good luck to us all," muttered the broad-chested jailer as they splashed through the waters, leaving Tschan swinging in the dim light of the failing day. Around the jagged corners of the cavern he could hear other captives cry out to him, asking for news of the outside. He ignored their pleas, and watched as the swirling waters rose higher and higher, until the muddy liquid lapped up over his feet, and sucked at his ankles.

Desperately Tschan kicked his feet back to the rough stone wall behind him, seeking for some purchase on which he might support his weight, and relieve the pain in his wrists. Finally his feet found a small ledge on which he could balance.

His manacles were far too tightly drawn for him to slip his hands free as the guard had suggested when he left. The small amount of light that had shone through the slits far above waned as the sun fell, and now there was nothing more than the mere suggestion of illumination. Damp fur brushed past him as the rats paddled through the water, swimming to higher ground and easier ways to fill their stomachs.

Tschan also recalled the jailer's stories of the one man who had escaped because his manacles were corroded. Could it be possible? From his precarious perch, he slammed the manacles against the wall. He lost his balance and tumbled off the ledge, the manacles jerking him to a halt. It seemed a futile exercise, but Tschan considered the alternative. He had nothing to lose.

Time and again he climbed up on his narrow roost and used whatever strength and leverage he could muster to hammer his cuffs against the solid rock that was his prison. Flecks of rust rained down in his face, but he couldn't see the manacles to know if his efforts were having any affect. Still, he persisted and he finally heard a snap as the corroded cuff on his right wrist cracked open and fell away, releasing his hand.

Tschan's left hand was still locked, but as he hung forward supported by this hand, his toes still touching the ledge, he could scarcely believe that he had been successful. His excitement grew, and he drew himself back to a standing position upon the outcropping, and reached up to remove the pin that kept his left hand still enclosed in the cuff. It was but a moment's work to remove the pin. Slipping off the ledge he plunged into the frigid water below, and found that he was up to his neck in the swirling muck.

Though he could see little, he had taken stock of his surroundings during his descent into the prison, and struck out in the direction that he knew the stairs to be. He found that he made much quicker progress if he swam, and though he was no expert swimmer he was proficient enough, and after bumping into several walls, and skinning his knuckles, he found the steps which led upward to, what he hoped would be, freedom.

His sprained ankle stung as he smacked it against an irregular step and stumbled forward. More carefully, he mounted the stairs in the inky blackness, feeling ahead with his hands so he would not make a dangerous misstep. He felt his way to the top of the stairs, groping across time-worn steps slimed with growth. When he realized that he had made it to the top, he shuffled his way forward until his hands came into contact with the damp wood of the jail door. Tschan found the handle and gave it a tug, but the door resisted his pull. With both hands, this time, he took hold of the handle and pulled, but the portal would not give an inch. He braced both feet against the decaying brick wall at the side of the door and strained at the door handle, but it would not move, and finally he sank down to the floor in frustration.

He sat in the inky darkness for some time, listening to the sound of the river as it roared by the island. Gurgling cries echoed upward from the cells below, and Tschan wondered if they marked the drowning of the other prisoners that were still trapped below. A sudden burst of sick shame spread from the pit of his stomach, outward into his chest and face. He hadn't even considered trying to save the others who were trapped below. Instead, he had swum straight for the stairs, and for escape from the immediate danger of drowning. He thought about what he might have done to save the other prisoners, and then he realized that his efforts would have been futile anyway. His escape had been possible only because the guardsmen had been kind enough to use rust-weakened shackles to bind him. In the darkness he would have surely been unable to remove the shackles of the other prisoners and doubtless would have become lost in the unfamiliar corridors. His efforts to the residents of Drowning Man Prison would doubtlessly have proved futile.

This assuaged his guilt somewhat, and then his mind returned to the words of the guards. His attention had been diverted by the gravity of his situation, but now he remembered what the guard with the cauliflower ears had told him about a drainage sump being halfway up the stairs.

Slowly, Tschan began to retrace his escape from below. After descending each step, he would stop and run his hands across the rough wall, searching for some sort of drainage hole. Twenty-seven steps down, he found a barred grate set into a recess in the wall. By touch, he deduced that the hole was about three feet in diameter, large enough to crawl through if the grate could be removed. This was doubtful in Tschan's mind. He hadn't been able to open the locked door above, and he had no reason to believe that he might be able to pull a grating loose from its moorings in a stone wall.

As his fingers closed around the bars, Tschan heard the lap of water as it rolled up over his boots. Maybe, he thought, if he returned to the top of the steps, he could ride out the high tides, and wait until some other day when the guards returned with fresh prisoners. Still, he had himself seen times when the river would completely engulf the little island and the prison, submerging everything. At lower tides this drain would be a safeguard that might stave off the rise of water within the prison, but Tschan dared not predict the level that the river might reach tonight. Now might be his only window of opportunity to try to escape by way of this drainage channel. If he waited much longer it would be submerged.

Tschan gripped the bars tightly and began to pull. He was gratified and surprised when he heard the grate moan, and he felt it began to pull loose beneath his grasp. The grate had not been moored as tightly as he had expected. Finally, the thing wrenched free, and Tschan tumbled backward, splashing into the water that had, now, completely submerged the step upon which he stood.

Elated at his success, Tschan stood and crawled headfirst into the narrow recesses of the drainage tunnel. The sound of his own breathing was magnified in the confines of the passage, and he felt a wave of claustrophobia pass over him. It passed as quickly as it came, though, and he scraped and grunted his way through the ragged orifice, coating himself in the sickly smelling sediment that caked the walls. The darkness dragged on interminably, and soon water began to trickle by his legs and across his hands, the flow soon growing to a torrent. He worried that he might become engulfed in the flow before he could find his way clear of the drain. Increasing his efforts to a frantic pace, he struggled through the pipe. Water surged and sprayed around him; he took sputtering breaths and inhaled some of the run-off.

In a coughing fit, he finally pulled himself out of the drain, and found himself hanging several feet over the swollen river. Fortunately, a ledge of rocky stone was within reach. He pulled himself onto it, and viewed the shrinking island upon which he was trapped. A good fifteen feet of the rocky promontory still rose above the black current, but Tschan doubted that it would last the night uncovered. A full moon emerged from beyond a dark cloud, and the young scholar could see the city of Bathos bathed in its soft light- an illumination that washed away the harsh edges of the gritty reality, and bathed it in a fairy tale glow. This illusion was quickly dashed as Tschan discerned shadowy figures along Bathos' river walls. Jagged spear heads pushed up from long shafts held in mailed hands. These men were part of the Sea Patrol, watchful guards against enemy encroachment. The Emperor was fanatical about his military's constant vigilance and tonight would be no exception.

Tschan's eyes fell upon the hook that was driven into the stone of the island. Attached was the hempen rope, which ran for two hundred yards across the river, and to the shore of the city. However, the rising river had submerged most of the line, and it drifted loosely in the river, the current tugging at it, but unable to dislodge it from its sturdy fastenings.

The scholar knew that this rope might prove his only chance at crossing the raging river. To jump in and attempt to swim would result in him being swept down stream, and maybe drowned in the process. He could hang onto the rope as he crossed, but he doubted that he had the strength to resist the constant pull of the river, and not be torn away from his lifeline.

Fate seemed to be conspiring against him, and Tschan wrestled with the ideas of either staying put on the island and hoping it did not submerge, or leaping into the river and attempting to pull himself across by the rope. The last option seemed like a suicidal act of desperation, and the first a fatalistic approach that would result in either his death, or his re-imprisonment after the light of day once again shone. If he were thrown back in Drowning Man Prison again, it would be unlikely that he might escape a second time.

A shadow on the river caught Tschan's attention, and he peered through the gathering murk. He realized that what he was seeing was a rowboat that had thrown its tether and was loose upon the waters. It was careening toward the island and Tschan clambered wildly in the direction that it came. He reached the head of the rock promontory as the weather-beaten boat came within five yards of the island, and became momentarily engaged with a submerged boulder. Slowly, the boat began to rotate, swinging back into the current, where it would be swept away.

"No!" cried Tschan, and he splashed out into the waters that covered the edges of the island. Strong cross currents battled, ripping and pulling at him so that he almost lost his balance a half dozen times. The pain in his ankle was of little help, but Tschan found that the chill of the water helped numb the hurt, and made it easier to ignore.

He stumbled out and made a grab for the prow of the boat just before it slipped away. For a moment he battled the river, and nearly lost, slipping on a piece of loose rock. Then regaining his leverage, he was able to drag the boat into shore.

Water sloshed over the soggy floorboards of the boat, and a broken oar floated among the ribs of the craft. Tschan realized that he had captured a less than seaworthy boat, but he hoped that it would prove adequate for a short trip to Bathos. With a grunt he heaved the boat over, and the water drained out, scurrying back to the river in pulp-flecked rivulets.

Emptied of its slopping contents, the boat was much easier to move, and Tschan dragged it across the island, setting it next the hook and rope. Here, he hunkered down out of the slight breeze that came in from the Black Sea, and tried to stay warm while he waited.

It didn't take long before dark clouds once again drifted in front of the gibbous moon, and Tschan launched his craft upon the wild waters. He held the wet rope firmly in his grip, pulling himself across the greedy currents. He worked quickly, hoping to traverse the Tiber before the orange light of the moon could reveal his position to the guards along the river wall. Though he was light, and the craft, at first, easily rode the waters, he did not have the upper-body strength that his escorts to the island had possessed. For someone who was accustomed to mental, not physical exertion, this was strenuous, back breaking work. No amount of paper shuffling, and language study could have prepared him for this night.

Midway between the island and the shore Tschan had to stop in order to recoup his strength. He bent over, his arms overlapping the wet hemp of the rope, and regained his breath while the river seeped in between the floorboards of the dilapidated craft, and grabbed at the shell, attempting to pull it down river. Tshan's grip on the rope kept the boat from straying far, and finally the young man rose and forced his aching muscles to a second effort.

He was nearing shore when the moon broke free of the clouds and shed its light on the river. Tschan sucked in his breath and frantically heaved his slowly sinking craft across the flowing waters. It was becoming harder and harder to pull as he neared shore, the boat filling with more and more of the

Tiber River.

The moment that Tschan was dreading happened sooner than later. A shout went up from the guard, and hard leather boots pounded the stonework of the river wall as the watch rushed forward to intercept the boat. The scholar could see them gathering at the river's edge near the rope's knot. He heard a rush of air and a javelin imbedded in the boat about a foot from his leg.

Tschan was making little progress now. The boat was mired in water and sinking beneath his feet. He reached down with his right hand, plucked the javelin's point from the spongy wood of the water craft, and lifted it against the massive hemp rope. The strands parted easily against the sharp edge, and Tschan cast away the javelin, wrapped the rope around his left wrist, and plunged into the roaring river.

The river swallowed him up, the water boiling around his ears as it sucked him downstream in a current running strong beneath the surface. Tschan held tightly to the rope. Beneath the water he was blind, and each moment seemed eternal, his lifeline spooling out endlessly.

Suddenly Tschan was jerked to a stop. His head pushed above the surface of the Tiber, and he took a deep breath and shook the water from his eyes. At first, everything was black, but he could hear the shouting of the guardsmen. They were coming to get him, he was sure. A shift in the current flipped him over and banged him up against the river wall. Instinctively Tschan reached out, his fingers dragging along the wet brick and catching on the rim of some iron pipe that jutted outward. Effluvia spilled over his fingers, but Tschan was long past the point of being squeamish. He unwrapped his wrist, and climbed up into the pipe.

In the periphery of his vision he saw the flare of a torch, and he heard angry voices overhead. Without further delay, he turned and squirmed deeper into the pipe, blindly following its twists and turns as it delved deep under the city, and the upheaval that was fomenting above.

* * * *

The knife struck the hard wood of Lothar's battle axe and turned aside, slitting his skin and leaving a stinging, crimson thread. A shadowed figure burst forward from the dark folds of the dimmed room, and came upon Lothar, an upraised dagger catching a dim seam of light as it descended.

Lothar fell backward as his assailant came upon him, but as he turned aside the blade his nostrils filled with a familiar scent, and he embraced the form of the woman he loved.

"Sheesa. It's me, Lothar!"

Her frantic struggles to slay him halted, and she slowly raised herself from him, her foamy black hair spilling across her face and hanging in long lustrous locks that brushed Lothar's face. A sprinkle of freckles lay across the bridge of her nose, her dark eyes glittering fiercely, and her satin lips parted as she gasped.

"I'm sorry," her words tumbled out on top of each other, "I thought that you were somebody else. They've been watching the room all day, ever since you left. I'm so sorry. I could have accidentally killed you!"

"You're not the first to try, today," answered Lothar. "But you've got a decent throwing arm. You came as close as anyone to doing the job." He ran his fingers lightly across her cheek, and was amazed how well the sores from the quick leper death had healed.

"They've been hanging about outside. I've seen at least three different people. I've been watching through the shutters."

"I didn't see three," said Lothar, "but I think that you're right. I saw someone hiding in the alley."

"When it started to get dark I turned down the lantern so they couldn't see the shadow of my movement against the shutters and so they would be at a disadvantage when they entered. I thought that they had finally decided to make their move and kill me, so I was waiting with the knives."

"And you nearly got me, too," smiled Lothar. "You may get a chance to practice your knife throwing again before the night is out."

"When are we leaving Bathos?" asked Sheesa.

"Now," answered Lothar. "I've had enough of this stinking town." He came to his feet and closed the door, shooting a massive bolt to lock it securely.

"Gather your things," he said. "We're going to make a run for the city gate."

"My things are packed," she said. "Any idea where we'll go when we're out of Bathos?"

"I think we'll look up an old friend of mine. I saved his life once, and I have a standing invitation to help him with his farm."

Sheesa smiled. "What do you know of farm work?"

"Nothing," answered Lothar, "but I've always been a quick study."

His wife put a long finger against her exquisite lips, and examined him thoughtfully. "You say you actually know a farmer? And you're good friends with him?"

"I know it sounds unlikely. Thieves and farmers don't generally run in the same circles, but I managed to convince Milos to go back to farming before he got caught up in the Bathos rat race, and I sent him off with a nice bit of venture capital."

Lothar withdrew his battleaxe. "If we both leave through the front door at the same time our stalkers are probably going to take the opportunity to kill us before we can even get to our horses. The head of his axe bit into the wooden planks of the floor, and soon Lothar had chopped a gap between beams, and could look down into the barn below.

He crossed the room and rummaged among a rucksack, eventually producing a coil of rope. He secured this to a floor joist, and began lowering their few bags of belongings to the floor of the barn beneath.

"We can do this a couple of ways," said Lothar to Sheesa. "I can lower you down, or you can slide down yourself."

"I'm not so far along that I can't handle it myself," she answered. Midway into her pregnancy there was only a slight swelling to her belly, and her health had generally been very good. She wore a low cut blouse that hung loosely at her waist, and a pair of blue silk pantaloons. The casual observer would be unlikely to notice that she was pregnant.

Lothar hesitantly agreed to let her shinny down the rope by herself. She flashed a reassuring smile at him, and carefully lowered herself over the edge. Moments later she was safe amid the loose straw and opium bricks below.

After calling for her to move aside, Lothar dropped the few remaining bags that contained their worldly belongings. Then he slung his axe over his back, and quickly made the descent.

The shaggy brown pony, Lothar decided, would have to stay. He would only slow their escape. It would be fastest if they took just the horses, but Lothar was loath to leave the city without the supplies that he had purchased earlier that day. Though Sheesa certainly gave the appearance of being able to take care of herself, he didn't want to leave the city without having enough food and drink to last them for a long journey. Foraging for food didn't always put immediate nourishment in one's mouth, and Lothar didn't want to take the chance that she might have to go without nutrition for a day or two.

He hitched up the horses to the cart that he had purchased earlier that day. They whinnied and snorted as he strapped them into place. They could sense the tension in Lothar's demeanor. Sheesa directed her husband as he hooked up the straps and halters. She had more experience with horses than he.

Lothar checked the supplies in the cart to make sure they were all tightly tied. As an afterthought, he loaded a dozen bricks of opium into the back of the cart and threw a horse blanket over them. He figured they might be useful in bribing the city guard, should they prove reluctant to let them out of the city.

Sheesa climbed easily into the cart's front seat, and grabbed hold of the reins. "We're ready to go," she said softly.

"Not quite," answered Lothar, his gray eyes narrowed grimly. "The barn is locked from the outside. I've got to go open it."

Without saying another word he turned, his dark cloak floating behind. He scaled the rope in a matter of moments, gathering the line with his legs as he climbed, and then he disappeared into the dark apartment above. His questing fingers found the latch for the shutters of the north-facing windows, and he quietly pushed them open. The scent of the fish monger four streets down, drifted to his nostrils. Lothar crouched in the window sill, and then leaped outward, over the empty dirt alley forty feet below. Before gravity could rip him to the earth, Lothar reached out and grabbed hold of the joist that ran along the edge of the overhanging eave. The roof was constructed of copper, beaten into thin plates that served as shingles, so the supporting beams were built with strength in mind.

Legs dangling, Lothar turned himself around and hauled himself onto the roof. The copper shingles had long ago turned a dusty green color, and he quietly clambered across them on all fours, the blades built into his shoes giving him greater purchase. A slight breeze grabbed at his cloak, and wisps of charcoal clouds grazed the porous surface of the bright moon. Once he reached the peak of the roof he tied his rope to the protruding center beam and slid down, dropping silently onto the cobbles in front of the barn's door.

It appeared that he had, as of yet, gone undiscovered, and he quickly picked the lock on the door, and began removing the chain that ran through the double handles.

"Haven't you learned that messing with the Thieves Guild only gets you dead?" demanded a voice.

Lothar cursed himself. This was the second time that he had been taken by surprise that day. Without waiting to see who or why, he wheeled, swinging the chain that he still held in his hands. The rusted links snaked out, and wrapped around one of the two short swords that Balzac held in his hands. Lothar jerked, and the blade came free of the small man's grip, still entangled in the chain.

As Lothar got a view of his surroundings, he saw a half dozen assailants melt from the dark places; the thick door frame of the crumbling building next door; the stripes of black at the entrance to the alley; from behind the crumbled chimney of the old smithy across the street.

Balzak and Zaydok, still dressed in the pompous finery of earlier that day, were the nearest to him. Kayne was closing in, his flat skull lowered, and murder in his bloodshot eyes. Behind came three street thugs, the type of men who were, if the odds were heavily in their favor, happy to hire on to a gang killing for a few silver heads. What they lacked for in skill, they made up for in brutality and strength of numbers.

The small Thieves Guild enforcer fell back from Lothar's sudden onslaught, but Zaydok, not realizing his tenuous position, pressed forward with outstretched dagger. Lothar let loose some slack from his chain and swung it in a sparkling arc over his head, Balzac's short sword still attached, and scything outward. The flailing sword struck Zaydok in the neck, severing his head from his body, and pushing it tumbling through the crimson-flecked air.

The chain shuddered at the impact, losing its momentum as the sword broke free and clattered across the stones of the street. Lothar abandoned the heavy links, and in one practiced movement unlimbered his axe, holding it out before him. For the moment his foes did not press the attack. Most of them had given the spinning chain some distance.

"Sheesa," cried Lothar. "Let's go!"

She had heard the clash of iron and steel from her seat within the barn, and had been tensely awaiting the results. At Lothar's call, Sheesa snapped the reins, and the horses surged forward. The barn doors burst open, and Lothar narrowly stepped aside of the horses' slashing hooves.

The thugs scattered, not foolish enough to hurl themselves in front of several tons of horse flesh, and the cart that careened behind. As the cart passed Lothar he leaped upward onto its step, and grabbed hold as it jounced across the uneven stones of the street.

Balzac took this opportunity to speed forward, and take a shot at Lothar's exposed back. As he came Lothar twisted, bringing his axe down toward the Thieves Guild enforcer, but Balzac shifted his attack and brought his blade up to intercept the axe. The two weapons reverberated in a brief embrace, and then the cart hurtled through the ragged line of enforcers, rattling into the gloomy tenebre of the city beyond, the shouts of their pursuers echoing behind.

Sheesa let out a triumphant cry that rebounded from the soot-stained city walls. When they had put some distance between they and their attackers, she turned to Lothar, who had climbed into the cart and sat beside her, his battle axe resting across his lap. "Who was that who attacked us? Was it the Thieves Guild or the Courtesan's Guild?"

"It was both, with the Warriors Guild to boot" answered Lothar. "They pooled their resources."

"What is it?" she asked, "that makes them so concerned with us. Why do they want us dead so badly?"

"It's all about greed," said Lothar. It was a sentiment that he could relate to, a thief was nothing without greed- but only a foolish thief let avarice control him. Greed had a way of destroying all reasoning and common sense.

Sheesa guided the horses through a bewildering maze of streets. They passed under the massive gargoyle-flanked arches that split the walls between Mid-City and Old Bathos. They hoped to cut across Old Bathos and leave by the Northern Gate Road, which wound through the grave fields- so called, because they were the site of many an ancient battle, and the dead were buried in mounds, which to this day rose up against the sky, elliptical markings that witnessed of gargantuan slaughters, and titanic struggles of the past.

As they first entered Old Bathos, the streets were bare and empty. Occasionally they would see a peasant scuttling across the roadway and into the safety of a building, but the way was clear. Many eyes peered at them from behind closed shutters, dusty panes of warped glass, or barred windows, but it seemed that few dared venture outside as the end of time drew near. Perhaps they knew something that Sheesa and Lothar did not, or maybe they were just wiser than the fleeing pair.

They crossed streets of tottering towers etched with ancient glyphs, and rode by massive structures with carven facades that writhed with angels and demons. Domed minarets gilded with gold and silver glinted in the orange moonlight, hinting of strange mysteries contained in their smoky inner reaches. Sheesa urged the horses past abandoned courtyards tangled with gardens of waving yellow opium blossoms, and past ancient tunnels that plumbed the depths of the city, and the foul, haunted temples that were long buried beneath.

As they plunged deeper into Old Bathos, the streets became alive with wavering torchlight. With fire borne aloft, shapes coalesced from the hazy darkness, their numbers increasing until the streets became crowded and glutted with the citizens of Bathos. It was as if they were of one purpose. All were drawn forward to the Clock of Pentaz to watch the final stroke of the clock as it heralded the ending of all time.

Initially, Lothar and Sheesa had planned to cut through the heart of the city, through the courtyard of Pentaz, and past the temple pyramid of Lythos, but as they reached the courtyard and saw the choke of humanity, they wondered if they would ever be able to cross the blazing sea of tumult that lay ahead.

"What do we do now?" asked Sheesa.

Casting his sight to the rear, Lothar realized that they were hemmed in. "There's no going back, now," he said. "We can only go straight ahead."

The horses were jumpy. They disliked the mire of human-kind that pushed in on their flanks. Sheesa did her best to calm them and guided them slowly forward through the shouting masses. Their progress was agonizingly slow as they pushed their way through drunken revelers and robed cultists who watched, waited, and prayed for the finish of life, gasping at each tick of the Pentaz clock. The clock worshippers kept their gaze forward, neither looking to one side or the other, acting as though the horse and carriage in their midst did not even exist. They moved only when the horse jostled them aside, and Lothar and Sheesa gradually passed through their ranks and into a mob of intoxicated celebration beyond.

As they neared the clock tower their forward progress came to a halt, and their cart was transfixed as though a fly in a spider's web. Once their motion was halted, the mob became bolder, several unsteady men climbing aboard the rear of the cart to loot it of its contents.

"Off the cart!" ordered Lothar.

They looked at him with bleary, uncomprehending eyes. "Why should we?" answered the larger one belligerently.

Lothar raised his axe so the man could plainly see it. "Because I'll separate your head from your shoulders if you don't."

The man was too drunk to be impressed. "I don't think you even know how to use that thing. You look like one of those Warrior Guild rejects that is too weak to actually use a weapon, but carries one around to look like a big man."

A crowd of jeering ruffians had pressed closely around the cart now, shouting their assent at the big man's insults. Lothar knew that if he didn't cut this man down to size right now, the drunk would rile up the crowd, and he and Sheesa would be ripped to pieces.

"Trust me," answered Lothar. "You don't want a demonstration. Get down now."

The man let loose a belly laugh and pulled a fishing knife from his belt. He began to clamber across the barrels. "You got a mighty fine looking woman there," he said. "I think I might just help myself."

Lothar's attack came so swiftly that the man never saw it coming. The troublemaker looked down, bewildered at the throwing axe that had suddenly sprouted in the center of his chest. Then he gave out a horrible shriek and toppled backward into the crowd. The mob roared at this affront, and they took hold of the cart, shaking it so fiercely that pieces came off in their hands.

Sheesa slashed at a rough hand that reached up to grab her from her seat. She stood, pressing toward the center of the cart as a half dozen arms replaced the one that she had cut. Lothar kept them at bay with his axe, but they had little chance against the crazed mob. Sheer numbers would drag them down, and they would be at the mercy of these lunatics.

"Cut a horse free," said Lothar as he took a swing at a skinny young man who had ventured too close, a machete in his bony grip.

Sheesa turned and cut the horses loose. The first panicked and bolted, rearing up and striking down the nearest of the crowd that had pressed in too tightly. With a wild whinny he galloped over the prostrate bodies of those he had struck down, and much of the crowd cleared the way for its flight.

Managing to rein in the other horse, Sheesa leaped to its back. A dozen hands reached up to pull her down, but Lothar jumped to the horse, and landed on its dark back behind his wife, slapping the flank of the beast with the flat of his axe. The horse surged forward with a start, bowling over human beings like dominos. For a second the beast faltered as it slipped on the uneven footing below, and Lothar thought the horse would surely pitch over and roll on top of them, but the black equine kept his hooves under him, and galloped forward.

Angry faces flashed by, some with questing arms that held clubs or even swords. To discourage anyone from venturing too close, Lothar lashed out to the left and right with his battleaxe. Sheesa desperately tried to guide the horse away from the mob, but the square was full, and there was nowhere to go. Finally the horse leaped high over a line of craning spectators, and came down in the frothy white of the pools beneath the water clock. The edge of the tiled pond was shallow and the horse threw up gouts of water as it sped along the edge.

Lothar leaned forward, pointing out a door in the base of the tower. "Take us there," he said.

Sheesa dug her heels into the horse, and urged him, splashing, out of the water and up a narrow stone ramp to the iron wood door at the top. They both slid off the dripping horse, and with another slap, Lothar sent it on its way. A crowd of drunken revelers surged up the bottom of the ramp. Lothar couldn't understand their anger, and many in the crowd didn't either. A mob mentality had taken hold, and it was all about passion, and not about reason.

Lothar tried the door. He put his shoulder into it when it didn't give, but it stayed firm. He withdrew his lock picks, and inserted them into the key hole. Time was of the utmost importance here. He didn't have the luxury of leisurely unlocking the door. If they were to survive, he needed to open it in the next few seconds.

Fortunately, Lothar had many years of experience with locks. He had apprenticed with the best thieves in the business, and there were few locks that could resist his skill. His nerves screamed at him, and his fingers wanted to fumble with the picks, but he calmed himself, and carefully quested the lock, until it gave to his gentle enticements.

The crowd was near; men and women brandishing clubs and knives. Lothar again threw his shoulder against the door, and this time it came open. He pulled Sheesa inside, and slammed the door, catching and crushing outstretched fingers between the door's heavy wood and its steel frame. Screams and curses of pain sounded from the outside.

"Lock the door! Lock the door!" urged a pudgy man attired in a yellow robe.

In his fear, the man had neglected to specify just how, but Lothar spied a heavy timber leaning nearby. He dared not abandon his post at the door and lift it into place. One moment of weakness at the door, and the crowd would shove it wide open.

"Take my axe," grunted Lothar, "and push it under the door. Wedge it shut."

Sheesa lifted her dagger and cut the strap that kept the axe in place on Lothar's shoulder. Dropping her knife, she crouched down with the massive axe blade, and shoved the point of its haft underneath the door as far as she could.

The clock keeper hurried over, and used his weight to tighten the makeshift wedge. Sheesa backed off as Lothar left the door, and put his shoulder to the massive timber. Grunting and straining, he lowered the thing into the gigantic brackets that framed the door. With a resounding clang he let the timber fall into the brackets.

The door stood firm, bodies pelting against its outer surface, sounding like hail stones on a copper roof.

* * * *

Tschan wandered for miles in the dark sewers of the city. Long ago he had lost track of any and all direction. He traveled by sense of touch, the darkness closing around him like a cold, slimy blanket. He wished now that he hadn't been so eager to plunge into the depths of these tunnels, but at the time he figured it preferable to being caught by the city guard, weighted down, and thrown back into the Tiber River.

He slowly rounded a turn in the shaft, and a glimmer of light appeared before him. At first he thought it was just the white spots that he had been seeing before his eyes, some sort of biological reaction to the complete darkness in which he was immersed. But as he drew closer he became more and more convinced that the illumination was real and not some trick of the optic nerve.

The light fluttered before him, disappearing at times, and then reappearing, accompanied by a steady clapping noise that would fade away as the light did. Finally, as he approached the wavering yellow illumination that appeared on the floor in front of him, his mental faculties were able to put two and two together. It was torch light that he was seeing, somewhere above him someone was carrying torches, and the fire light was reflecting down an angled metal pipe, and shining out onto the floor in front of him.

Carefully Tschan traced the glow of light, and discovered a loose fitting wire grate in the darkness to his left. The lines of it were barely discernable, a hazy gray in a background of black. The grate was easily removed, and Tschan managed to contort his long frame into the narrow confines of a shaft that climbed upward.

He painfully wormed his way higher, emerging twenty feet above from a floor-level duct that emptied into a hall tiled with black obsidian. Tschan could no longer hear the footsteps of the group that had passed by earlier, yet he could see a flickering light issuing from a niche far down the pentagon shaped hall. Painfully, Tschan got up to his feet and crept across the cold tiles. He was covered in dirt and grime from head to toe, and his clothes were still soaking wet from his swim in the river. When he reached the niche he found it empty, but for the cresset that illuminated a series of skillfully carved pictographs that dated back centuries.

As the scholar lifted his hands to warm them in the radiant heat of the torch's flame he examined the carvings. This was a type of pictograph, which he was quite familiar with, and though he did not know where he was, or what kind of danger that he might be in, his curiosity over rode those concerns, and he began to translate the writings in his head.

And when the Dark One shall come down from Lythos' mountain
From which thou standeth Beneath

He shall be but just half a man
To summon his mordant soul and feed his failing strength
Lythos' Bane must be Taken by Force
The chalice must once again drink of victims' blood
An Hour until the End of Time
And Evil will become one with Earth
The Demon King made Whole, and its name is Mahmackrah

Tschan finished translating this and a horrific vision filled his head as the nightmare pieces juxtaposed with those already in his head. Could this chalice be the same as the Blaspheme Chalice that he had uncovered in the Bone Yards? From the inscription he knew that he stood beneath the pyramid of Lythos, for it was occasionally referred to as the mountain of Lythos in the ancient papers and histories. But the Emperor strictly forbade entrance to the pyramid, and Tschan wondered why he had heard so much activity within these very halls.

From somewhere above he heard a scream filtering down to him, and he wondered if indeed the sacrifices had begun, which would fill the Blaspheme chalice with the blood that might bring forth the greatest evil that mankind had ever known. His scholarly skepticism had been swept away, and he had become a believer in the cryptic writings of the ancients. Perhaps Wilhem had been right when he advised Tschan to steer clear of the chalice, and that certain historical relics were better left alone.

Someone had known of his plans to search out the chalice, and they had been waiting for him. They had hidden from him on the Road of the Severed Head, knowing that he would be chased by the city watch, and disguised in flowing black robes, they had beaten him, and stolen the chalice to use for their own infernal purposes.

Tschan wondered who it was that might have betrayed his confidence, because whoever it was that ambushed him had known all along when he was going into the Boneyard and what he was coming out with. The young scholar felt a horrible guilt flowing through him, and he dropped his head. It was his fault. If he had not uncovered the whereabouts of the chalice, none of this would have happened.

Footsteps sounded in the hallway, and fear galvanized Tschan to action. He took the torch from its cresset, and raced down the hall, plunging into a south-running corridor that slanted downward. His lungs breathed in the stagnant air as he ran, but this was like fresh air compared to the stench-fouled atmosphere that had enveloped him when he had crawled through the sewers from the river.

He didn't know where he was going as he raced away and left all but his own echoing footsteps far behind. They did not pursue him, but Tschan did not stop his flight. A horrible dread had come over him, and he feared that if he slowed he would succumb to its evil presence. Still, the pain in his ankle was constantly with him, reminding him that he was still alive.

Finally the corridor ceased dropping, and it closed to a narrow slit that smelled of grease. Tschan could hear a grinding and clicking that grew louder and louder. With great effort the young man steeled himself, and slowed his pace as he emerged into a great underground chamber clogged with gears and cogs.

Resting his hands upon his thighs, Tschan leaned over and made an effort to regain his wind. Evidently, he had passed through some corridor that ran beneath the courtyard, and led to this chamber of inner workings for the Clock of Pentaz. Once his breathing had normalized, he slowly began to work his way between the huge brass gears that were enmeshed in a precise mechanism that would allow the clock to keep its perfect time. It was truly an engineering feet, but Tschan did not admire the gears too closely. Many of them were titanic affairs that turned with enough power to catch an unwary man and effortlessly crush him in their unthinking grip.

He gave the machinery a wide as berth as possible while squeezing his way to a series of narrow iron ladders that pushed upward through the foundation of the clock tower, and on between raging torrents of water, that drove massive paddles, whirling manically in the white-capped jets. These paddles pushed the gears that counted the seconds toward oblivion, marking each moment with another tick on the broad face of the gold-scrolled clock far above.

A mist sheened Tschan's mud-encrusted cloak as he passed through the hazy innards of the tower, and ascended to a narrow catwalk behind the clock's glowing face. Tapers from oil lamps burned long, undulating orange flames on the ledges that encompassed the circle of the clock. These were connected by a series of stairs so that the oil reservoirs could be filled regularly, ensuring that the flames would last throughout the dark of the night. But tonight, thought Tschan, the lamps would expire well before daylight came- if it came at all.

The cogs were eerily lit by the lamps' illuminations, and the flickering flames cast strange shadows that moved and changed shapes as the gears inexorably turned. In some inexplicable way, the shadows were more terrifying to Tschan than the utter blackness from which he had crawled beneath the city, and he didn't tarry long behind the clock face, finding a series of metal ramp ways that led into the rear portion of the tower.

He slipped out of a narrow passageway into a long, well lit hall constructed with meticulously chiseled stones perfectly matched in size and in color. A window let in a draught of fresh air, and from below he could hear the rumble of the mob, and see the profusion of flaring torchlight that intermingled in the square like a swarm of fire flies.

Flat footsteps slapped on the floor, and Tschan turned to see Stannett the clock keeper standing at a bend in the hall, arrayed in his yellow robe. Beyond him stood a striking woman with raven hair that fell to her waist. She was taller than the keeper, and wore a series of throwing knives thrust through the loops on her belt, which was draped over one hip and hung loosely, serving no function other than to hold the weapons. Her blue pantaloons were torn, revealing the smooth skin, and taut muscles beneath. She held a knife, which was drawn back past her ear, ready to be hurled.

"Move and I'll stick this in your gullet," she said.

Tschan weighed his chances of being able to dive back through the door that he had come. A moving target was difficult to hit with a knife, and it would take him just one quick movement to get behind the cover of the stone archway, and back into the maze of walkways and gears. There, he might be able to hide himself, or at least present a less-ready target.

This moment of hesitation allowed Lothar to move up behind him, and as Tschan leaped, the warrior swept the scholar's feet from beneath him, and shoved him, hard, to the stone floor. Tschan bit his lip as he felt the point of the dour-faced warrior's axe thrust against his neck.

"A good assassin should be alert for diversions," said Lothar, wryly remembering how Balzac had lured him into a trap earlier that very day.

"I'm not an assassin," choked out Tschan. "I'm a scholar."

"Perhaps you think I'm a fool?" said Lothar, pressing a bit harder with the spike of his axe. "You think I don't know that assassins use mud to cover the whiteness of their skin so that they can better blend in with the darkness?"

Sheesa had come up alongside Lothar now, and looked down at the man who claimed to be a scholar. She still held her throwing knife between her thumb and forefinger. "He's either an assassin, or a hog farmer," she said. "And there is no reason for a hog farmer to be skulking about in the tower of Pentaz tonight."

"I'm a scholar," insisted Tschan. "And I can prove it."

Stannett looked on the confrontation uncomfortably, rubbing his hands together in nervous agitation. "Maybe he is what he says," he offered weakly.

"I am. I am!" agreed Tschan.

Lothar eased off the pressure of his axe. "I'm waiting," he said, cold skepticism in his gaze.

"Have any of you noticed strange goings on in the pyramid of Lythos?"

Lothar and Sheesa shook their heads.

"Besides the masses of people here to view the ending of time?" asked Sheesa.

"I have noticed something strange," interrupted Stannett excitedly with waving arms. "The guards at the gates of the temple were killed by assassins. I watched it happen."

Sheesa looked out the window and she could see men in the emperor's uniform standing watch at the entrances of the looming monolith. "It seems that they've been resurrected."

Stannett shook his head. "Those aren't real guards. The assassins replaced them with their own men."

The Clock of Pentaz began to chime, striking eleven times. A hush fell upon the mob outside. Only one hour remained before time completed its course.

Sheesa turned to Stannett. "Do you really think that when the clock strikes twelve, demons will come up from the earth and consume every living thing?"

Stannett soberly pondered the question. "Perhaps," he answered. "The ancient scholars were endowed with such a great wisdom that they were able to predict when time would end. Obviously, something world-changing, and of great gravity will come to pass, but even Pentaz did not dare predict what exactly might happen."

"We'll find out in an hour," said Lothar. He picked up Tschan from the floor and shoved him against the wall while he searched for weapons. He was puzzled when he found none. "The most dangerous thing that you carry, is the stench of the sewers," concluded Lothar.

"I escaped from Drowning Man Prison," explained Tschan. "And I crawled through the sewers, emerging beneath the pyramid."

"Then how was it that we found you in the clock?" asked Lothar.

"There is a passage beneath the courtyard."

A flash of lightening lit up the room, followed by a deep rumble that belched from the sky. Dour clouds rolled in at supernatural speeds, gathering above the concave upper reaches of the pyramid, their bellies lighting up as white lightening forked out, striking the surface of the pyramid, and searing its marble face. Thunder belched in rapid succession, shaking the tower of Pentaz. The crowds below began to howl in fear. They could see that their doom was at hand, and its visage was horrible.

Stannett stood open-mouthed, gazing at the awesome sight.

"What is going on?" asked Sheesa, though the words were purely rhetorical.

Satisfied that Tschan wasn't an immediate threat, Lothar let him go, and the mud-caked scholar staggered over to the window. "It's the dark ones, he said finally. They have the Chalice of Blaspheme, and they are, even now, making sacrifice to the evil god Mahmackrah." He ended in a mutter. "They are summoning the second half of the Emperor's soul."

Lothar narrowed his eyes, his hands busy as he retied the strap to his battle axe, which his wife had earlier cut. "I wish we were about a hundred leagues away from here, but if we have to be near the pyramid, the clock tower is certainly safer than being with the rabble below."

Tschan's eyes were glazed. "It's my fault," he said.

"How is it your fault?" asked Sheesa.

"I found the chalice, where it had been hidden away for centuries. I should have left it alone."

Dark figures moved atop the pyramid, faint screams echoed down during lulls in the thunderous storm. The crowd waited in awestruck silence.

"So where is this Chalice of Blaspheme?" asked Lothar.

"They have it." Tschan motioned to the dim forms streaming into the convex bowl of the pyramid. "They stole it from me, and now they will summon an evil that will suck the earth of all its life."

"So the legends of demon's rising from the earth may be true after all?" asked Sheesa.

Tschan nodded. "Except that this demon will materialize from a dark dimension- the same dimension from which our Emperor came. I didn't believe it, though, until now. Until I saw this."

The black billows in the sky lit up again, and flaming hail pelted the pyramid, hissing from the clouds, and ricocheting off into the masses below.

"I've seen demons," said Lothar. "And they scare me, but I think we'll be safe in the tower."

Shaking his head, Tschan looked down at the floor, and recited the words from the tablet that he had found deep in the Boneyards. "Or when darkness sweeps the earth in the blistering, scathing cold of unending torment , You shall rue the day you set eyes upon this stone."

Lothar looked up into the sky, and saw a malignant shape forming in the sky, bilious black flesh that took on no specific form, but spread its flabby weight, blotting out the moon with its gargantuan mass. Hundreds of inky tentacles undulated from the beast in obscene harmony, and thirteen mouths opened and shut in unchecked hunger- wide gashes, lined with yellow fangs dripping bile.

Tschan had been required to study all religion and cults, and he recognized the dark god, from illustrations in the ancient texts. "It's Mahmackrah," he hissed, and he once again recalled the translations he had made in the Boneyards, and the Temple of Lythos. "Mahmackrah is the Emperor's soul."

Stannett sank to the floor, overcome with shock, and for minutes the others were too stunned to move or speak. They simply stared, mesmerized by the thing, which had crawled forth from some netherworld's abyss, foolishly summoned by ignorant zealots on an unholy mission.

Finally Tschan spoke. "The goblet must feed on the blood of victim's until the stroke of twelve. If I can take the goblet back, and keep him from feeding, I can send Mahmackrah back to whatever unholy hell that he came from." With determination on his face he sprang from the window, and moved back the way he came."

"Stop, you fool," said Lothar reticently. "You don't even have a weapon, how are you going to take a goblet from armed foes?"

"I don't know," admitted Tschan. "But I have to do something. I'm the reason that evil thing is hanging in the sky!"

Normally Lothar would have let the fool run off to his death, but there seemed to be a germ of truth to what the young scholar was saying. More than that, Lothar realized that nothing was safe from Mahmackrah's tentacled grasp. If this evil god was not stopped, Sheesa and their unborn child were unlikely to live out the night. Even if it meant his own death, he would have to become a part of this insane crusade.

Lothar handed Tschan one of his throwing axes. "Use this as a hand-axe, the haft is shortened, so you need to catch your enemy by surprise, or close in before they can lower a longer weapon and have you at a disadvantage."

"Thank you," said Tschan.

The dark-haired warrior caught him by the shoulder as the scholar tried to leave. "And I'm going with you. There is no way that someone unskilled in weapons could hope to succeed at this venture."

"No!" yelled Sheesa as she realized Lothar's intentions. "I won't let you do this. You can't leave me here alone."

Lothar looked at Sheesa, and answered without raising his voice. "You know that if I don't do this, none of us will ever live to see the outside of Bathos' city walls."

Sheesa hung her head. "I know it, but do come back to me." She stepped forward and embraced her husband's hard frame.

"I'll do my best," he answered.

Stannett struggled to his feet, not daring to let his gaze wander out the window, and to the caliginous behemoth that blocked out the firmament. "I'll protect her with my life," he said.

Lothar grasped his wrist. "I appreciate that, but you may find that Sheesa is a very capable woman."

Without further goodbyes Lothar followed the scholar into the spinning innards of the clock. They descended long ladders, through misty clouds that threatened to extinguish the flame of their lantern, and passed through tunnels beneath the city square in which the mob cried aloud in a frenzied terror.

Emerging in the shadow-shrouded depths of the pyramid, they began to ascend long stone ramps that carried them upward to the sacrifices at the peak of the structure.

"So if this is the soul of the Emperor come to join him, why is it that the Emperor's guards who were at the entrances to the temple were killed?"

Tschan had pondered some of these questions as they had passed beneath the city square, and so the theories were quick to jump to his lips. "One of the ancient writings I discovered said, that in order for the ritual of summoning to be effective the pyramid-temple must be taken by force. Our Emperor has never been one to value human life overly much. Surely he would sacrifice a few of his own men's lives in order to accomplish his goals?"

"Do these followers of Mahmackrah know that they are doing the Emperor's work?"

Tschan shrugged. "I do not know. But Emperor Vlad has shown time and again that he is adept at manipulating political and religious forces when he desires to do so. Perhaps they do his will without knowledge of it."

By using the underground passage they bypassed the guards at the outer entrance, and they had gone unmolested, but as they neared the top Lothar knew that things were about to change. He admired the scholar's bravery, and sense of duty, but he doubted that the young man would live beyond the first conflict. If they were fortunate they would find that the followers of Mahmackrah were also novices in the arts of war, but Lothar knew that it was dangerous to underestimate any opponent. Even the greenest of warriors could prove a deadly foe; often the erratic and unmeasured nature of their attacks were difficult to predict and therefore difficult to counter.

Inside the pyramid's walls all noise from the outside had been shut off. They heard only the sound of their own footsteps echoing ominously, and the sound of their voices as they echoed back with strangely sibilant overtones. Now as they climbed to the upper reaches of the pyramid the roar of thunder came to their ears, and beneath that they heard the horrible screams of dying men and women, their cries nearly drowned by the pounding of fiery hail as it squelched itself against the pyramid.

They reached a narrow hall with an arching ceiling that broke from the main passage. A line of chained men and women extended from the hall. These stood wide-eyed, listening to the horrible deaths of their fellow prisoners, knowing that soon it would be their turn to die. As they saw the two intruders they looked on with hope.

"Save us!" pleaded a woman with disheveled brown hair. She reached her shaking, and manacled hands out from the tattered sleeves of her gown in a gesture of forlorn appeal. Lothar put his finger to his lips, to urge her to silence. He took the lead and slid past the row of prisoners that were chained on the right of the narrow hallway, holding his battle axe at the ready.

The prisoners regarded the two interlopers with a variety of emotions. Anger and hatred registered on some of their faces, as they assumed that these two men were also followers of Mahmackrah. Others looked at them with bewilderment, and yet others with a hopeful glint in their eyes. But in all of their faces there was dread. They knew that something beyond the wretched evil, that they daily experienced, had come to Bathos.

The mouth of the tunnel opened up onto a ledge that ran around the inner circle of the bowl. On this ledge crouched three figures dressed in charcoal robes. They bent over a prostrate man, who they manacled to two eye-bolts, one at his head and one at his feet. The ledge was drenched with the blood of previous victims, but because of the knife edge held to his throat the man gave no struggle. His only hope for life lay in two men whom he had no idea existed.

Overhead the bile-drenched form of Mahmackrah was becoming more solid. His long tentacles lashed out and snatched victims from the square, feeding them, one after the other, into his thirteen gnashing mouths; each death giving him sustenance to survive on the earthly plane for just a few moments longer.

From thirteen different doors inside the bowl of the Pyramid of Lythos, the followers of the dark god were slaughtering innocents, the blood draining from runnels on the ledge, and down the concave surface until it reached the center of the bowl. An intricate diagram was etched deep into the stone- a thirteen-pointed star, etched with ancient symbols and runes, the meaning of which, if fully comprehended, would blast a man's mind.

Above the bowl, twenty feet higher than the ledge, hundreds of robed-figures completely surrounded the concavity. Their hands were linked, and their midnight robes flapped in the unnatural winds. They seemed impervious to the hail and lightening as they sang out a chant of summoning in some alien tongue.

In the center of the bowl rested the Chalice of Blaspheme. It lay in a depression so that the crimson waters that issued from the dead poured into its open mouth, where it was mystically consumed, and the energy imparted to Mahmackrah, who hovered directly above.

This horrific scene greeted Lothar and Tschan. It was too much for the feeble mortal mind to digest, but Lothar knew that inaction meant death, so he leaped forward past the last of the victims, and split open the skull of nearest worshipper of Mahmackrah.

To his credit, Tschan came close behind him, catching the second cultist by surprise, and sending him flailing over the side of the ledge with a split collar bone. His conquered foe mouthed a horrible scream as he tumbled downward, like a rag doll, to join the limp bodies of already discarded sacrifices, which had fallen into gory heaps as they were pushed over the ledge.

The third worshipper backed off, his hood falling away and revealing an intelligent face seamed with age and wisdom. A full head of white hair strung out in the wind, as did the long white mustache that fell down past the edges of his cleft chin.

Lothar checked his blow as Tschan cried out.

"Wilhelm!?"

"You wouldn't listen to me, would you son?" said the old man. "Once you had discovered the whereabouts of the chalice, we tried to keep you away. We had planned to go into the Boneyards and retrieve it ourselves."

"I'd been telling myself that I was a fool to ignore your advice," said Tschan. "I thought maybe you had been trying to save the world from a horrible tragedy…not instigate one."

"It's not too late to join us, son. Imagine being among an elite group of rulers, backed by the power of Mahmackrah!"

"Imagine this," answered Tschan. His axe smashed through his mentor's skull and brain. The student had become the master.

Twenty feet above, the chanting worshipers had noticed the fall of three of their men. Like a murky wave they leaped down to the lower ledge. Behind them, other black robes came forward, linking hands, and taking up the chant without missing a syllable.

Some of the jumpers twisted their ankles, and lurched from the ledge, falling down into the bowl, and others crumpled with shattered legs. Many, though, came on unhurt, unsheathing long daggers with wavy blades, and hilts made from green bone. Their screams resounded in Lothar's ears, and the unmistakable scent of jasmine permeated the air.

* * * *

Sheesa searched the top of the pyramid hoping to see some sign of Lothar, but all she could see were the hazy forms that circled the concavity of the structure as they chanted out multi-syllabic dirges to the obscene god that dominated the sky; a horrid and evil god, feasting on bodies plucked from the fleeing crowds below. They trampled each other in their frantic haste to escape, but the exits from the square were blocked off by soldiers with linked shields and lowered spears. To Sheesa, this confirmed Tschan's suspicions that the Emperor was somehow linked to the summoning of Mahmackrah.

At the sound of Stannett's voice, Sheesa turned away from the dreadful carnage.

"Come quickly! They're scaling the walls of the clock."

Sheesa followed Stannett into his sanctum of churning gears and cogs. They negotiated a series of iron walkways, and he pointed out a window. Above the frightened churning of the crowd, several figures clung to the side of the tower, their fingers holding to mortared seams in the tower's face. They were dressed entirely in black, sheathed short swords slung across their backs, and their faces smeared with soot.

"Assassins," hissed Sheesa. "The guilds have sent them to kill Lothar and I. Even now they'll stop at nothing to maintain their power."

Stannett blanched. "Assassins?" he gulped. "That's even worse than I thought."

Sheesa took stock of the situation. She could see three of them, staggered across the front of the tower, clinging like flies. They still had a good seventy or eighty feet to climb, and it was possible that they might slip and fall.

"Check all the other windows of the tower, and make sure that there are no more," she said to Stannett.

The clock keeper nodded his head and began making rounds from window to window, quickly disappearing from view behind a large gear on the opposite side of the clock's face.

Sheesa watched the thick flames that back lit the glass face of the Pentaz water clock and got an idea. She went to the nearest and snuffed the flame. Carefully, she began rolling the clay reservoir to the window where she had first seen the assassins. One of them was almost directly below her. He was closer now, having climbed about fifteen feet in Sheesa's absence.

With a grunt she hoisted the heavy reservoir to the window sill and let its contents gush from the jar, and over the outer wall. Moments later it had sluiced over and between the fingers of the climber below her. He said nothing as the oil dripped past him, but attempted to move out of the slick to a drier portion of wall. His grip failed and he plunged silently to the pools below. Sheesa did not see him rise from his fall, and the waters rolled over the body in a crimson wash.

She turned her attention to the assassin on the right, and saw that he held a long and narrow tube to his lips with one hand, while holding to the tower with the other. Sheesa started as something moved across her line of sight, mere inches from her face. Pulling back, she saw a needle-tipped dart imbedded in the mortar, close to where her head had been positioned. A red smear on the tip of the dart told her that it was poisoned.

She didn't dare put her head out of the window again, lest she actually be hit. Assassins were feared because of their efficiency. She knew that they would take turns climbing now, while the other waited with a blowgun at his lips.

Stannett came huffing and puffing to Sheesa's side. He noticed the broken shards of the oil reservoir where it had fallen and cracked during her sudden retreat from the window.

"What happened here?" he asked.

"I got one of them," she answered.

Stannett raised his eyebrows, and made a move to look out the window and see the results of Sheesa's efforts.

Sheesa grabbed him by the back of his robe. "Don't. They'll put a poison dart in you. They almost got me with one." She pointed to the dart that was still imbedded in the window frame.

"I didn't see any other climbers," said Stannett. "So it's just the two that are out there." He motioned to the front of the tower, with a short jab of his forefinger.

Casting about for something that might give her an idea or a plan, Sheesa noticed a long wooden staff with a hook planted on its tip. "Take off your robe," she said.

"What?" exclaimed Stannett.

A few moments later, Stannett stood in long tunic and breech cloth, shivering in the breeze that whispered through the window. His yellow robe was arrayed on the end of the hook, which he held in his hand.

Sheesa stationed herself at a window about thirty feet to the east. She held a knife in her right hand, and raised it high as a signal to Stannett, who saw her across the expanse of turning machinery. He thrust the top of the robe through his window. A faint compression of air could be heard, and a dart imbedded itself in a fold of the yellow cloth.

While Stannett worked his distraction, Sheesa leaned out her own window and peered through the dimness to locate the camouflaged figures in the night. Fortunately, this was the leeward side of the tower, facing away from the Temple of Lythos, and though the affects of the carnage could be seen, as witnessed by the panicking populace, they were, as of yet, in no danger of being set upon by Mamackrah, who had plenty of food trapped between he and the clock tower.

For the first few moments Sheesa couldn't find the assassins on the wall face, and then a bulky shadow lunged toward her from the side of the window. Somehow one of the assassins had managed to climb the intervening space while she had been preparing the diversion. She let out a startled yell, and fell backward, thrusting her knife outward as a climbing claw raked the air in front of her face. As the assassin fell through the window on top of her, Sheesa felt her knife bite through the dark clothing, and she was glad that she had transferred the poison from the dart to the tip of the blade.

The assassin went into a sudden paroxysm, and Sheesa rolled from beneath him. Moments later the man stiffened and died, a rattle dwindling in his throat. Sheesa had seen too many horrible things in her lifetime to be squeamish now. She didn't trust assassins, and wondered if he might be playing possum. Crimson leaked out onto the gray stones of the floor as Sheesa slit her assailant's throat. There would be no nagging questions now.

She searched the corpse and found a blowgun in the belt at his waist. Next to this was a leather case in which a dozen poisoned darts were precisely packed. She had never used a blowgun before, but decided now would be a good time to learn. Deliberately, she loaded a dart in through the mouth piece, careful that the poisoned tip would never touch anywhere that her lips might. Her nostrils flared as she took air into her lungs, and poked her head out the window.

Stannett's diversionary robe still hung out the window, serving little purpose now, other than to serve as a sign post for the location of the window. The glow from the clock face illuminated the climbing form of the third assassin. He was a few feet below Stannett's window, and reaching up to grab hold of the sill. Sheesa took a few moments to aim, then let the air burst from her cheeks. The dart sped toward her target, but a gust of wind altered its flight and it skimmed off the tower's face, missing the climber.

The assassin heard the sound of the attack, and had already deduced the location from which the dart had come. Without wasting precious seconds in confirming his suspicions, he grabbed hold of the window sill, and vaulted into the interior of the clock tower. As his feet touched the sill, a double tipped dagger leaped into his hand.

Stannett cried out in surprise and attempted to shove the assassin from the window with the pole he still held in his hands. His assailant, however, was too fast, and Stannett merely succeeded in knocking the assassin upside the head; a stinging blow, but buying the clock keeper only a fraction of a second.

Within three seconds more the assassin knocked Stannett to the floor, and was astride him, dagger raised high over his head for the stroke that would finish the clock keeper. A sudden sting in his side snapped the assassin's concentration, and he looked down to see a dart protruding from his ribs. Within moments the poison took hold of him, his muscles seizing and his brain numbing. Stannett reached up and pried the dagger from the man's fingers, before the assassin fell back in a fit of spasms that ended his life with merciful quickness.

Stannett came to his feet, and watched the beautiful Sheesa approach him across the catwalks, the blowgun still in her hand. "Your husband was right. You can take care of yourself."

"Sometimes," said Sheesa. "But in this city, sometimes is not enough."

* * * *

Lothar fought off the first wave of robed worshippers. They swept upon him in a berserk frenzy, but his battle axe gave him an advantage over his knife-wielding attackers. Their knives were long, about a foot-and-a-half , but his battle-axe stood nearly to his waist, and with that extra length he was able to sweep Mahmackrah's worshippers before him, knocking many of them from the ledge as he wounded or killed them.

Above them, the hideous god had not sated his appetite. Hundreds upon hundreds were shoveled into the demonic beast's gelatinous belly to be digested alive. Lothar pushed forward and momentarily swept the ledge clean of his assailants. He shook the crimson gore from his blade.

He turned to Tschan. "We're never going to get out of here alive if we go back the way we came. You make a run for the aqueduct, and I'll catch up with you."

Lothar gave Tschan a push to get the scholar moving and then leaped from the ledge. He landed in a crouch, on the uneven flagstones of the down-ward arching bowl, and ran past the heaps of dead and dying until he reached the lowest part of the bowl. Here he leaned down and plunged his hand into the central pool where the crimson rivers met. He wrenched the submerged Chalice of Blaspheme free from the socket where it had been planted by the cultists of Mahmackrah. A wave of revulsion swept through him as the sensation of pure, unadulterated evil threatened to overcome him. Lothar struggled to retain control over his mind and body, resisting the urge to throw himself on the ground and cover his head with his hands.

A horrible cry split the heavens. Mahmackrah's deafening call erupted, shaking Lothar to his very soul. Unimaginable fear and pain coursed through him while its piercing call persisted. Lothar feared that his presence was no longer ignored by the beastly demon god above; he had interfered with the flow of life to the demon, and now he was going to pay.

Lothar placed the chalice against a stone and he drew back his axe. If he could destroy this thing, maybe he could halt this living nightmare. He brought his axe down against the chalice with enough force to bend and mangle steel, but only succeeded in chipping the edge of his blade. He tried twice more, but nary a scratch appeared on the goblet, and the edge of his axe blade became a crumbled ruin. He cursed as he looked up and saw the flapping figures of robed cultists descending to kill him.

In one deft movement Lothar shouldered his axe, and began sprinting across the bowl, upward toward its edge. His battle axe slapped against his backside as his powerful legs propelled him, leaping over rivers of blood, and past the horrible slaughter of sacrifice. He outdistanced his pursuers. In one hand he held the chalice.

Ahead, he could see Tschan escaping the bowl, only to meet with the ring of worshippers surrounding the top. He saw Tschan make a limping charge at the line, not waiting for them to surround and overcome him. The scholar leaped high and broke through their ranks, tumbling and sliding down the slanted exterior of the purple-veined pyramid.

Lothar was faster than Tschan, and he was mounting the edge of the bowl only a few moments after the boy. Swathed in flowing black, his enemies came to meet him, but he drove them back with the blunted edge of his axe. Hope began to surge through him, suddenly dashed when a thick tentacle wrapped around his waist and jerked him into the air.

"Tschan!" bellowed Lothar.

The young scholar checked his sliding flight down the smooth surface of the pyramid, and turned to see Lothar being drawn up toward Mahmackrah. Clutching his axe firmly in his left hand, Lothar drew back with his right and hurtled the goblet.

It soared through the air, past lashing tentacles and into Tschan's outstretched hands. He fumbled with the chalice, but then grasped it firmly, tucking it in against his body.

"Go!" yelled Lothar. He raised his axe and severed a tentacle, black ichor splattering across his face. Gravity sucked him down toward the pyramid, but before he could strike the hard stone below, another of Mahmackrah's tentacles slapped his leg, winding tightly around it, and jerking Lothar upside down.

Stubbornly, Lothar clung to his axe. The air was thick with black strands that grabbed, ripped, and pulled at him. He lashed out with the axe, ripping through the web of tentacles that had taken hold and threatened to tear him apart. Black ichor hazed the air, chunks of gelatinous flesh flew thickly as Lothar flailed in desperation at the appendages that gripped him. But for every black rope that he cut away, three more would take its place, and he was drawn relentlessly up toward the reeking orifice into which he would be fed.

Lothar would not easily give up his life, though, and even as he was shoved within the gaping, fetid maw, he sawed at the strands that bound him with the ragged edge of his battle axe. As the mouth closed over him and the last tentacles withdrew from between Mahmackrah's shapeless lips, Lothar could be seen hacking at the gelatinous innards of his enemy, and then his battle cries were muted.

The end of time was rapidly approaching as Tschan stepped onto the aqueduct. He fled along the causeway, with his stolen prize clutched firmly in his right hand. Water roared down the channel below the path he ran. His ankle had swollen to twice its normal size, but he ignored the pain. He knew that slowing his pace would surely mean death.

Glancing up over his right shoulder, he realized that he had not escaped Mahmackrah's discerning eye. Black ribbons snaked after him, and he knew that he would soon follow Lothar to his doom unless he could somehow move faster.

He hurled himself into the water. Its raging torrents swept him toward the clock tower at a greater velocity than he ever could have achieved on his own two feet. He struggled to keep above the waters, but never relinquished his grip on the chalice.

Maybe it was too late to vanquish the demon god. Perhaps he had already taken on enough sustenance, either from the blood of the sacrifices, or from the flesh of the victims that he was consuming from the vast crowds who had witnessed his appearance. Or maybe there was still a way to send this demon back to whatever hellish dimension from which he came. If only there was some way to destroy this cursed chalice.

Dark appendages spanked the fast-flowing waters as they searched for Tschan amid the swift currents. Still, he was able to stay ahead of the questing tentacles, and he thought his escape might successfully be made, until he slammed into the lowered iron bars that filtered the waters before they plunged through into the tower, and whirlpool beyond.

He grabbed hold of a crossbar with his left hand, and held himself above the current as he shouted into the tower for help. Soon he heard footsteps and responding voices. A half-naked Stannett ran to the gate in a breech cloth and tunic, holding a pole upon which his flapping golden robe was hooked. Sheesa was on his heels.

"Take this," shouted Tschan. He reached out his hand, extending the chalice.

Careful not to touch the poison dart, Sheesa removed the robe from the pole and hook. Stannett reached out with his pole and carefully hooked the handle of the chalice before drawing it back to the stones upon which he stood.

As they watched they saw tentacles snaking up the aqueduct.

"Open up the gate!" urged Tschan.

Stannett needed no further spurring, and he began to crank the gate open as fast as he could move his thick arms.

"Where is Lothar?" asked Sheesa. She dreaded the answer she expected to hear.

For all his education, Tschan could not verbalize his answer. He merely shook his head.

Sheesa sank to the ground sobbing, thinking of the father that her child would never have.

As the gate rose Tschan climbed down the crossbars, staying mostly submerged, as the tentacles combed through the waters, searching for the one who had stolen the chalice. Finally Tschan slipped beneath the gate, and Stannett extended the pole to him, dragging him against the sucking whirl-pool, and to relative safety on dry ground.

In the hopes that he might remember something that could help save them from their plight, Tschan began to run through the ancient texts that he had translated beneath the Boneyard. As he did, tentacles began to slip through the gate and windows of the tower, sliding across the waters and then the floors, using their tactile nerves to search for living prey.

Sheesa had her head buried in her hands, oblivious to the probing appendages that snaked toward her. Like dark jelly it slipped across her boot and over her leg. Her sobbing ceased and rage took over. She reached down to her waist and pulled loose a throwing knife. With startlingly quick movement, she brought the knife down, and skewered the tentacle. As it pulled away, the knife slit it down the middle, ribboning it into two oozing halves that flailed ineffectually about the room.

Tschan ran the line over and over in his mind, 'Hammer nor anvil can destroy this cup- only time'. He turned and ran deeper into the clock, where the smell of grease permeated the air, and the lamps that lit the clock-face burned high. He took the water-cleansed chalice and shoved it into place between the teeth of two massive gears.

Maybe, just maybe, time could destroy the chalice. Slowly the gears ground together, and the chalice began to cave beneath the powerful cogs until it became a shapeless lump of metal that extruded and leaked from between its gnashing teeth.

A terrible cry went up from Mahmackrah, and the glass face of the clock of Pentaz shattered, its shards raining down into the pools below as its hand moved to strike twelve, and the massive machinery of the clock ground to a stop. The sound of its gong died as quickly as it started, ending in a sickening squelch.

The probing tentacles retreated from the tower like snapped whips. Mahmackrah did not have enough energy to remain upon the earthly plane, and converging dimensions battled for superiority, lighting the sky like an aurora borealis. Vortices formed in the heavens, ripping the shapeless god apart, and emptying its half-digested contents onto the gore-splattered pyramid below.

Then the dark god was gone, leaving behind only death, carnage, and terrified survivors; the aftermath of time followed to its mathematical conclusion. But still, life went on, and the citizens of Bathos learned, loved, and felt pain and sorrow.

Sheesa rose up and crossed the aqueduct to the pyramid, the tears still flowing and wet on her face. The followers of Mahmackrah had fled the destruction of their god, only to be torn apart by the angry mob below. There among the gory scraps, Sheesa searched for a sign of her husband, and when finally she was about to give up on the futility of the task, a man rose from the carnage with a groan. Bloody hands still clutched the shattered remnants of a battleaxe, the haft of which had been snapped. His tattered cloak had been eaten away by the digestive juices of the beast, and his skin was burned with lesions, his eyes glazed over and unseeing.

"Lothar!" cried Sheesa.

The warrior-thief finally let the broken haft of his weapon fall from his numbed fingers, and he opened his arms to his wife's embrace. Dark clouds drifted away from the moon's pocked face, and likewise, the mob drifted to their respective homes, to start another day in a new epoch.

Part Seven:
The Sharven Conspiracy

Darkness had long since settled over the Mid-City, and beneath the black velvet skyscape the denizens of Bathos came out to play. The young and beautiful sons and daughters of barons and baronesses came to join the raucous festivities along Peacock Street. They came, flaunting the traces of nobility in their veins and their inherited wealth, to mingle with rich guildsmen, fat off the taxation of their underlings, and to rub shoulders with the thugs, cutthroats, and thieves that populated the silver-gilded tavern halls.

They loved to soak in the excitement of the gaming parlors, and reveled in the danger that the less-than-respectable patrons brought to their lives. The gaming halls and taverns, themselves, cared not whence the gold came. It only mattered that their patrons arrived with gold lining their pockets, and left with their coin purses lighter.

Jotham strode unevenly down the green stone that was set with a close-knit precision unfamiliar to many of Bathos' city streets. His stride, however, would be uneven no matter the smoothness of the surface he traveled. His left leg below the knee was gone, and he wore a hard oak peg in its place.

Carriages and chariots of wealthy revelers lined the streets in front of various establishments, their haughtily dressed occupants disgorging into red velvet-draped doorways, near which stood burly guards whose purpose was to filter out those who did not carry enough coin to make their visit profitable enough. Courtiers stood by attending to the horses, awaiting the eventual return of their masters, when they would bear them back to their marble mansions in a state of drugged stupor.

Drunken cries came the street side, and Jotham swiveled his tree-trunk neck to see a group of inebriated men and women laughing hysterically at the sight of his wooden leg, and some joke uttered at his expense. Jotham let the laughs roll off his broad shoulders and lowered his bald pate, letting his single top-knot fall over his shoulder. Even crippled, he was a formidable sight.

He towered over even the stout doormen that guarded the entrances to the private pubs and casinos. His arms were meaty limbs that ended with massive hands that were cris-crossed with pale scars.

Broad chest straining the seams of his earth-colored tunic, he took in a breath of the feculent-tainted air, and he passed next to a slow moving phalanx of leather-clad ruffians. The scent of alcohol carried along in their wake, and they eyed the crippled warrior with rum-abetted bravado, giving little heed to the broad-sword that hung at his side, sheathed in worn leather. At the center of this circle of six ruffians, an obviously drunken dignitary made his staggering way down the street, accompanied by two gorgeous women, whose scanty silks suggested that they belonged to the Courtesans Guild.

The dignitary's pudgy face split into a grin as the raven-haired beauty on his right whispered something into his ear. The voluptuous blonde reached beneath her patron's crimson cape of silk, and put her sun-darkened arm around the man's waist. For one moment, Jotham's gaze met hers and he thought he detected a glitter of malice in her eyes that belied her jovial outer countenance.

Before the warrior could give much thought to the courtesan, the night came alive with the whoosh of displaced air. The missiles came from the tenebre-darkened corners of the street, and from the night-shrouded building tops. Javelins rained down on the procession, and Jotham ducked as a glittering spear tip cut toward him, and passed over his lowered shoulder, glancing off the stones of the street.

Others were not so lucky; three of the six ruffians cried out as the javelins pierced their leather garments, and they went down, leaking their crimson blood on the dark green stones of Peacock Street. Scarcely did Jotham have time to react to the sudden rain of javelins when he heard brisk footsteps pounding the street. Black-cloaked assassins emerged from the alleyways before and behind them, wielding curved blades that flashed dully, reflecting the meager light of the oil lamps that hung in profusion from the building-fixed cressets.

Jotham heard the soft pad of footsteps on his right and he drew his broadsword forth in one smooth movement. He could smell the oil that he had used on his sheath as his thick arm drove the blade outward and toward the incoming sound. The razor edge of the broadsword cut through cloak, and the unarmoured flesh beneath. Out of the corner of his eye Jotham saw the assassin's torso split asunder from his waist, the two halves falling apart as a frightful scream gurgled from the dying man's lips.

Confusion reigned as the cloaked figures leaped in and cut down their surprised foes. The raven-haired courtesan screamed as the shorter man she escorted pushed her away and reached for his short sword. His action came far too late, for his blonde escort had already plucked his blade from his gemmed scabbard, and with little compunction she took a handful of the dignitary's hair and pulled his head back so that his throat was exposed. In one moment she had drawn the blade across the dignitary's neck, and as crimson began to rivulet from the wound she let the man fall to the ground and leaped for the shadows at the roadside.

Immediately Jotham could see that her flight was going to take her right past the spot in which he stood. For an instant their blades came together, the metal ringing as it shivered from the impact, then she flashed by him, her bronzed flesh disappearing into the cloak of the alley's darkness.

Even if Jotham had been so inclined, it would be fruitless for him to pursue the assassin. His peg leg wouldn't carry him half as fast as the female could run- and this certainly wasn't his battle to fight. Even as he watched, the dark clad ambushers disappeared into the night, leaving the crimson-drenched street in their corpse-strewn wake. Their target had been assassinated, and their mission was complete.

Of the six ruffians who had been parading down the street, only one still stood; the others lay dead and dying. The living ruffian stood next to Jotham, scarcely believing the events of the last few moments. He put a dirty hand to his protruding jaw, while still clenching his sword blade firmly in the other.

"They killed Rufus!" he exclaimed in shock. He stepped over and knelt next to the fallen body of the man whose safety he had been charged with, and realized that there was no hope of saving his fallen cohort. Already the eyes were glazing over and the blood ceased to flow from the lethal wound.

Jotham stood over the two men and examined the expensive finery, and gold chains that the dead man wore. "Who was he?"

Fear entered the ruffian's eyes when he spoke. "Rufus Astor, the Prince of Thieves."

"The name's not familiar," grunted Jotham.

"Not to a warrior," admitted the man, "but he was second in command for the Thieves Guild, and my job was to protect him. I heard rumors that the Thieves and Warriors Guilds might be conspiring to cut the Assassins Guild out of the picture, but I didn't think the assassins would be so bold in their retaliation."

Now Jotham could understand the fear that he read in the man's face. It was unlikely that things would go well with this young ruffian when he returned to report his failure to the Guild.

"You had best get yourself to the Under City and hide yourself from the Guild," said Jotham. "That's about the only place in Bathos where you might hope to lose yourself from the eyes of the guildmasters."

The ruffian was trembling when he stood up, and motioned to the body Jotham had cleft in twain. "You saved my life," he said to Jotham. "That assassin was cutting toward me. If you hadn't been standing there, and intercepted him, he probably would have killed me. I've been drinking," he admitted. "I never even heard him coming."

Jotham's eyes turned from the man's frightened face to the Prince of Thieves at their feet. Amid the crimson puddles, Rufus' right forearm lay so that the inside was facing upward, and a geometrical tattoo, inscribed with numerals around the circumference, was etched in the skin.

The big warrior shrugged. "Maybe some day you'll have the opportunity to return the favor. In the meantime, you'd better get lost. If this Rufus was a prominent guildsman, you can bet that the city guard will be here to round up the suspects- and you or I are as likely to take the blame as anyone else."

In moments Jotham and Arus parted ways. While Arus fled to the Under City Jotham moved as rapidly as his leg would allow, and cut through Stack Alley, hoping to put as much distance between himself and the scene of the crime before the city guard came upon the carnage. It was always a dangerous proposition to travel the back alleys of Bathos, but traversing them at night was tantamount to suicide.

This night, however, good fortune smiled upon Jotham, and the cut-throats steered clear of the big warrior, deciding to wait for less dangerous, and more vulnerable victims to prey upon.

* * * *

Vastak rubbed absently at the scar that crossed the bridge of his mashed nose. "Give the cripple an assignment and get him out of here," he bellowed, "something easy that he won't mess up."

Jotham had once been considered a formidable warrior, and not long ago, before he had lost his right leg below the knee, no one, even if they were second in command of the Warriors Guild, would dare to have mocked him to his very face. The massive warrior silently took the abuse, shifting his wooden peg leg on the polished stone within the high-walled sanctum of the Warriors Guild, while he awaited his assignment for the coming week.

The dispatch general was no warrior, himself little more than a scrawny, and aging book keeper with white-shot hair, and he moved uncomfortably in his hard oak seat while flipping through the yellow parchment pages of the massive ledger that stood open before him. Finally his wrinkled finger fell upon a listing, which he deemed suitable.

"Perhaps this will do," he said.

Vastak bent his thick bull-neck, and leaned over the back of the dispatch general to read the description of the job, which was inscribed in a cramped, and mannered handwriting. "An old warehouse in Wharf Town," muttered the Warriors Guild's second in command. "That should be a nice out of the way assignment for you."

"It's a simple guard duty job," elaborated the dispatch general. "The place warehouses mortar and general lapidary tools. It's unlikely to be the target of a Thieves Guild looting party."

Jotham shrugged his broad shoulders, but a vein throbbed above his temple, belying his more apparent nonchalance. "What time do I report?"

"Before sunset. You're taking the night watch."

The giant warrior nodded, his nearly bald pate reflecting the gleam of a nearby oil lamp. The top knot on his head swayed sinuously as he turned and walked unevenly toward the archway, his peg leg resounding hollowly in the chamber each time that he stepped with his left.

"He's of no use to us," growled Vastak, loudly enough for the dozen warriors within the hall to hear. "He should get himself a membership to the Beggars Guild. They've got plenty of room for invalids on their membership rolls."

A couple of the younger guild member laughed uproariously at this comment, and Jotham was not oblivious to their jeers. He swiveled his craggy skull on his tree-stump neck and marked the men who had laughed at his misfortune, storing their names in his memory. It wasn't revenge that he sought, but in the city of Bathos it was wise to remember who was your friend and who was your enemy. These, Jotham realized, were two men whom he could not count on for support in the future.

With one thick forearm Jotham pushed aside the heavy oak door, and stepped from the chamber's dim interior into the bright sunshine of Sell-Sword Street. The street was alive with the flash of bright blades, and the gleam of burnished armour. This was the central hub for the Warriors Guild, and the awning-covered booths of weapons and armour merchants lined the streets- the clanking of the blacksmith's hammer ringing against the stone walls of the guild halls, barracks, and gaming rooms that grew up alongside the black-paved streets of stone.

Even now, the sight of brave men at arms jesting and fencing raised a thrill in Jotham's soul. He loved the heft of the sword in his hand, and the scent of molten steel brought back nostalgia for the time he had purchased his first sword. Ruefully, Jotham rubbed at a knob atop his thick skull, and remembered that the day he had lost his leg below the knee, he had been carrying a club and not a sword.

He had been under the impression that he going to be part of a group that would rough up a fellow warrior who was considering taking leave of the Guild. He hadn't realized that the weapon play would turn deadly so quickly. It had all happened in a matter of moments, two of his cohorts were dead and he permanently maimed and bleeding to death. Only the intervention of the man who had stolen his leg, kept him from dying from blood loss. At first he had cursed the man as a villain, but regardless of the despiteful treatment of his fellow warriors, Jotham was grateful to be alive.

He had a long walk in front of him, and his mobility was not as good as it once was. Cutting through the crowded streets of the MidCity, he passed through the grim soot-stained archway of its dividing wall, into the steep and winding streets of Hill Town. Bright pennants fluttered from sky-impaling towers that flanked the impenetrable walls of the governor's keep. Even now, Jotham could see sailors patrolling the crenellated walls, armed with bows of yew, and manning massive ballistaes.

Opulent mansions built by unimaginable wealth, sprang from the hilly slopes, surrounded by manicured gardens and spiked stone walls. Below, Jotham could see Wharf Town spreading its less-luxuriant streets and tenements, its streets crawling like dirty tendrils toward the banks of the vast Tiber River, which cut between stone-built banks on its way to the Black Sea.

Jotham's pace slowed in Hill Town in order to take greater care on the downward slopes, which were treacherous for one who had lost the use of a foot. He passed several city patrols that were arrayed in boiled leather cuirasses, and armed with scimitar and broad sword. These were patrols arranged by Icarod, governor of Hill Town, and were reputed to have a higher degree of honesty than those of the troops employed by the Emperor- which wasn't much of a feat, reflected Jotham.

The patrols took note of Jotham, but did not question or harass him. The Guilds were not openly embraced in Hill Town, but were allowed to operate as long as they didn't interfere with the governor or his plans.

Jotham turned on Painter Street and followed its torturous and winding route down to the rusting gates of Wharf Town. He took this route, not because it was the quickest path, but because, beside Sell-Sword Street, this was his favorite part of Bathos. Due to slightly less burdensome taxes and several other considerations Icarod was considered a patron of the arts. Sculptors, painters, and performers often migrated to this part of the city. They set up their wares alongside the curving walls of stone-carved building facades, painting and sculptures crowding the streets, and vying for attention of the passerby. The smell of roasting pork, and chicken wafted through the salt-tinged air, and Jotham paused and purchased a few skewers of chicken from a vendor who was roasting the meats over a stone fire pit constructed above the cobbles at the street's edge.

He gave the sun-burned vendor four copper crowns from the small pouch at his belt, and paused to listen to a frail-looking man who sat on the curb playing a pear-shaped lute with bent neck. As he listened, his eyes wandered through the crowds, and he noticed a familiar figure in serious conference with a short rat-faced man dressed in a black tunic and pants. Jotham saw the jutting pommel of a dagger appear from beneath the sweep of the little man's dark cloak, and wondered if the rodent might not be connected with either the Thieves or Assassins Guild.

The man whom he recognized was a muscular fellow with short brown hair and square jaw. His noble visage, and bold acts had inspired the confidence of the Guild Master, and he had rapidly been promoted up through the ranks of the Warriors Guild to hold the position of Third General, just under Vastak.

The small man slipped through a crevice between a tent awning and the stone facing of a building, and Travis turned his attention to the crowds around him. Almost immediately he spotted Jotham's huge frame towering above the rest of the crowd. Jotham's distinctive top-knot further set him apart from the common-folk that perused the booths and who watched the musicians and acrobats performing on the winding street.

Travis brushed away some imaginary dirt from the leather cuirass that he wore, and waved to Jotham as he intersected the milling populace. Jotham was surprised that Travis had taken notice of him. In the past Travis had made no effort to be on friendly terms with him, and now that he had lost a portion of his leg, Jotham was even more surprised that such a powerful person would take notice, let alone seek him out.

"What brings you to this part of Bathos?" asked Travis as he drew near, his brown hair rippling back from its center part as a light wind traveled the alley of the street up from the Tiber River.

"For this next month I'm on assignment for warehouse night watch in Wharf Town."

"Why do they have you watching the Sharven warehouse?" asked Travis. "There are higher profile and better paying assignments, for which you would be much more suitable."

Jotham nodded in agreement. "Ever since I lost my leg, Vastak and the Dispatch General won't put me on anything that might see any action. Maybe I'm not as mobile as I used to be, but I can still swing a mean sword."

"I tell you what," said Travis. "I'm going to have a talk with Vastak tomorrow, and see if I can't get you assigned to something better. Work the Sharven warehouse tonight, and I'll have a plum assignment for you tomorrow."

Jotham raised his eyebrows, surprised to be receiving such direct intervention by someone with so much authority in the Warriors Guild. "I'd appreciate it," he said. "It's tough to put food in the belly when you're guarding bags of mortar."

Travis laughed. "I'm not even sure why Sharven bothers hiring a guard. What little stone that is worth stealing from his warehouse is in hundred pound blocks. How many thieves do you know that would throw one of those things on their back and run down the alley?"

"Indeed! Most thieves are much too lazy to steal something so heavy."

Travis clapped Jotham on his broad back. "Well, I must be going- guild business you know."

"Thanks for putting in a good word for me," said Jotham as Travis retreated up the street.

"Consider it done," answered Travis, then he disappeared into the crowds.

Jotham's ebullient mood had fallen by the time that he reached the Sharven warehouse. The sun was sinking below the horizon, and long shadows spread their sticky tendrils across the litter-strewn roads that merged along Stone Cutter Street. Only a few blocks away from the rotting wharves that lined the river bank, the scent of the water was thick in the air, and the light breeze helped carry away the stench of the nearby fish houses.

Between the dim gray bulks of the warehouses and cantinas that grew up along the river bank, Jotham could see the furled masts of a thousand sailing ships- many from the far corners of the known lands, whose captains had guided them, their holds full of goods, to Bathos, the most powerful city in the world.

As a young warrior Jotham had done hundreds of assignments like the Sharven Warehouse. There was little danger, and consequently there was little pay to be had. He spotted the stone walls of the Sharven Warehouse up ahead. To either side of it rested similar warehouses, the narrow alleys between darkening as the daylight died in the sky.

The warehouse reached three stories high, and Jotham knew that much of the building's interior was open space in which burlap bags of mortar powder were stacked to staggering heights. The roof of the building was built with a low wall around the top, in which periodic fist-sized holes had been drilled so that rainwater could drain off the slightly slanted surface.

From the street Jotham could see a few windows that circled that bottom floor. They were each barred with three rods of iron, each the diameter of Jotham's thumb. Milky glass panes were set in the frames to keep any wet from seeping into the warehouse and hardening the carefully stored mortar.

Jotham gave the warehouse this cursory examination as a matter of habit and professional pride. Though he expected no trouble, he liked to know of the possible entry ways of which thieves might avail themselves.

As the warrior entered the dusty interior of the grime-covered building, the warehouse boys were departing for home, weary after their long day of manual labor. He signed in with Sharven at his office in the back of the warehouse. Sharven was a stout merchant with large forearms built from heaving the very stone that he sold. Emblazoned on his left forearm was a geometrical sigil that was marked with a series of numbers at each point of the design. Jotham immediately recognized the marking as the one that he had seen on the corpse of Rufus several nights earlier.

In general, it was good policy to keep one's mouth shut and not ask too many questions. Questions make people who have something to hide nervous, and nervous people will often take steps to do away with those that are too inquisitive. Thus, Jotham chose not to inquire about the meaning of the tattoo, despite the strange circumstances during which he had first seen the marking.

"I'm bringing a few business associates in for a late night meeting," said Sharven in a high voice. "We'll be coming in through the back entrance so don't be alarmed when you hear us come in. I don't want you accidentally killing us all as intruders."

Jotham smiled. "No, Sir."

Sharven departed and before long the warehouse became entombed in silence, only the flickering oil lamps that Jotham tended keeping the night at bay. The one-legged warrior made regular rounds through the maze of towering burlap bags, and past the pyramids of granite and marble blocks, checking the barred windows around the perimeter, the three locked doorways, and even climbing the thick wooden ladder to a loft filled with broken and discarded stone cutting equipment, and cracked sledges which had yet to be repaired.

Jotham peered through a dusty pane of glass set in a window of the loft. Craning his neck he could make out the slivered moon reaching its apex in the sky. He could hear the sinister reverberation of bells as the clock of Pentaz rang out its midnight chimes. The guilds had insisted that it be repaired as quickly as possible so that their members would have less claim on having fulfilled their contracts by serving until the 'end of time' as their oaths unequivocally stated. Even as the sound of the bells died, Jotham heard the creak of a door toward the rear of the warehouse.

He made his way to the wooden ladder and quickly descended to the cold stone floor of the warehouse. To mute the sound of his wooden leg against the stone, he had tied an old rag around the tip of it, so now his steps were nearly silent as he crept toward the back door.

The big warrior rounded a sledge of stone in time to see five cloaked figures entering the warehouse through the back door. The foremost of these threw back his hood, and Jotham recognized Sharven's ruddy visage. Without making his presence known, Jotham stood in the shadows and watched the assemblage as they drew back their hoods, their faces becoming visible in the wavering oil light of Sharven's lamp.

"Where's the cripple?" asked the second man. He threw back the concealing cloak and Jotham blinked as he recognized the handsome features of Travis. Immediately Jotham recalled his conversation with the man, and realized that the kind words that had been spoken to him were merely lip service.

"Probably got tired of hobbling around, and curled up to take a nap with his peg leg!" roared the largest of the men. His face was turned, but Jotham recognized the same voice that had cruelly taunted him earlier that day in the hall of the Warriors Guild. The voice belonged to Vastak.

The fourth man possessed sharp features and beady eyes that darted to and fro as if searching the darkness for enemies. Despite his vigilance he did not pierce the blackness that concealed Jotham from sight. "Is this place safe?" he hissed.

Sharven nodded. "Every window is barred, and every door is locked with three deadbolts."

The man took these assertions dubiously. "You are talking to the King of Thieves, here. Those are but pitiful deterrents for a well-trained, and determined thief."

"I realize that," answered Sharven. "Our real safety lies in our cloak of secrecy. If no man beside ourselves knows of our secret meeting, then we can be assured a measure of safety."

"Yes," assented the man, "but even the walls have ears. Nothing can be truly sure."

The fifth man removed his hood now, and as he turned Jotham saw the same rodent face that he had seen in covert conversation with Travis earlier that day. The man removed his cloak in silence, making no comment as he paused to take in the overshadowing towers of cut stone that were stored within the cold warehouse walls.

Still Jotham made no move to make his presence known to the others. He watched as Sharven led the clandestine group to a small storage room on the east side of the warehouse and shut the brass-bound cedar door behind them. When the last reverberation of the closing door had subsided, Jotham checked the outer door and found that each of the three dead bolts were again firmly in place. To add to this protection Jotham heaved a heavy cross-beam into place across the back door, dropping it into thick steel brackets set in the stone wall on either side of the portal. Jotham had not placed the beam earlier, only because of Sharven's warning that he would be coming in for a late night rendezvous.

From the caliber of his company, Jotham could tell that the merchant's meeting had to do with more than just the business of stone cutting. Sharven, apparently, kept powerful company, for his meeting involved both the second and third in command of the Warriors Guild, and no one but the Guild Master of Thieves could make claim to being the King of Thieves. There was a conspiracy afoot. What this conspiracy was, Jotham wasn't sure that he cared, but one didn't last long in the City of Bathos without a healthy sense of paranoia, and so Jotham went, once again, to check the doors and windows of the warehouse- to ensure that no enemy had tried to creep into the building while he had been watching the co-conspirators entering through the back.

As he checked the still firmly locked front door, and the barred windows along ground level, Jotham wondered what connection the tattoo played in this evening's events. The imprint had been a geometry of overlapping triangles that formed a disjointed jumble peppered with numerals. Both Rufus, the dead second in command of the Thieves Guild, and Sharven bore the marking. Perhaps others of the night's conspirators wore the marking, too. What their aims might be, Jotham couldn't say.

The warrior was jarred from his thoughts by a faint squeak from the roof of the loft far overhead. Another, less wary, person might have passed the noise off as the sound of the warehouse settling, or perhaps a tree branch scraping against the building, but Jotham knew that both were unlikely answers. No tree stood near to the warehouse, and the stone structure had stood here since before his birth, constructed on the bedrock pan through which the Tiber River flowed.

Warily, Jotham began to climb the huge wooden ladder to the loft. He moved quietly and deliberately, listening for further noises. As he crouched amid the jumbled chaos of the loft he held his breath, his ears searching the darkness. The noises came more clearly now; the soft squeak of timber as footsteps crossed the roof above. None of these noises were as loud as the first that had snapped him from his reverie below, and if he weren't sitting quietly in the loft, Jotham doubted that he would have heard these steps at all, so careful were the footfalls of those above.

Jotham slid the shutter of his oil lamp wider until its light flooded the loft. Holding the lamp over his head he examined the ceiling, and discovered a trap door some ten feet over his head. A thick metal hasp was bolted to the inside of the door, and a heavy paddle lock secured it.

As Jotham watched, a narrow spike of glass was thrust through the seam of the trap door, and it came to a stop just above the lock. Immediately crystal drops of liquid began to roll down the shard of glass dripping on the U-shaped arm of the lock. The moment that the liquid came into contact with the metal it began to sizzle and fume- eating at the lock.

The big warrior had seen padlocks eaten away by acid before. It was a method that the Thieves and Assassins Guilds used when they wanted to gain silent entry, and weren't able to pick the lock. The acid was a highly corrosive concoction that was available from only a few alchemists in the City of Bathos, and Jotham had heard that it didn't come cheaply.

With two high-ranking members of the Thieves Guild meeting below, Jotham guessed that these were members of the Assassins Guild that were doing the breaking and entering. This surmise was based on the fact that it had been assassins who attacked and killed Rufus, Prince of Thieves on Peacock Street several nights passed. Jotham assumed that whatever guild war had been started, was yet to be concluded. Probably the Assassins Guild figured they could knock off of the headman of the Thieves Guild here tonight, and put a finish to things once and for all. Sharven's secret meeting had turned out not be all that secret after all.

Jotham smiled wryly. Now he, a crippled warrior- of all people- was caught up in the middle of a guild war. What cruel twist of fate had dropped him in the middle of this maelstrom? Or was it a twist of fate, wondered Jotham. Travis had known that he was going to be doing duty at the Sharven warehouse, without Jotham informing him specifically where he was going to be performing his night watch. Maybe Travis had deliberately conspired with the dispatch general at guild headquarters to have him assigned to this job. Maybe Travis wanted a cripple to be on watch tonight, someone who wouldn't have the physical ability to stop the double cross that he had set up with the Assassins Guild.

As this suspicion sank in, Jotham set his jaw with resolve. He would show Travis how a crippled warrior could handle himself!

* * * *

On the roof of the warehouse five figures cloaked in black huddled around a sixth who carefully dripped acid from an unstopped jar marked with arcane writings. A trail of smoke rose up through the seam of the trap door as the metal of the padlock below was gradually eaten away by the corrosive substance.

A chill wind whipped off the river, flapping their dark capes, and blowing back their cowlings, revealing the sinister, hollow-eyed visages of the conscience-bereft assassins beneath. With white-knuckled grips they held their poison-tipped blades, hopeful that their deadly points would soon draw blood.

"That should be enough," croaked a flat-faced assassin with greasy hair that spidered across his parchment white features.

The assassin performing the task glanced up in annoyance, his voice grating like steel against stone. "I've done this a hundred times. It can't be rushed."

Once again he bent down over his task, but as he did the trap door flew unexpectedly open, catching him on the point of his chin. Acid splattered from the tumbling jar, eating through dark cloth, and then burrowing into the chest of the assassin who had been carefully dripping it moments before. He screamed horribly, clawing at his own flesh as if to rip it away before the acid could inflict further pain.

Leaping from a tower of stone that he had quietly stacked beneath the trap door, Jotham burst from the opening and landed heavily on the black tar roof, his oak leg digging into the tar. As soon as he stood firmly on the warehouse's windswept surface he lashed out at the surprised assassins, severing an upraised hand still clutching a ruby-pommeled dagger, and slicing through an exposed neck that rolled from its dark cowl in a gout of black blood.

In scant moments Jotham had cut his opponents' numbers in half. Perhaps with full use of his legs he might have been able to press the attack and finish his opponents in one surprising flurry of swordsmanship, but he was only able to take several steps forward. Yet, with the minimal movement that he was capable of, he brought down one more enemy beneath his dripping broadsword.

Now two assassins faced him. They split, circling toward opposite sides, their swords erect and wary, sticky venom coating the razor tips. The groans of the dying suddenly ceased, and the only sound that remained was the flapping of dark cloaks in the invisible wind. The sliver of moonlight above showed Jotham the poison-tipped blades, and he knew that if he allowed the assassins to outflank him, it would only be moments before one of them nicked him, and the venom began working its way through his blood stream.

In old times he would have charged toward the nearest and spun around him, so that he was again facing both foes. Because of his limited mobility this was no longer a feat he was capable of performing, which meant that he had to adjust his tactics.

As he stood, his back was to the open trap door, and any attack that pressed him might push him backward onto the precarious pile of stone that he had barely managed to climb, and probably result in a twenty foot fall to the loft on which the stone was stacked. Jotham decided to move into a more advantageous position. As the assassin to his right crept toward him, Jotham snapped out with his sword and struck the outstretched weapon of his enemy. For a moment, the sword rebounded away and Jotham took the opportunity to pivot on his right leg. As he turned and planted his wooden leg, the second assassin lunged, but Jotham was prepared for this attack. He swung simultaneously, striking the hilt of the assassin's sword before the venomous tip could reach him, and bending in the hand guard so that it cut into the assassin's knuckles.

The assassin hissed in pain, momentarily withdrawing from the fray as his compatriot launched an assault on Jotham's left side. Blade clattered against blade, and Jotham used the awesome strength of his torso to drive the attacker back, pushing him through the open hatch. The assassin was not prepared for the fall, and he teetered on the pile of stone before it gave way, collapsing on itself. The assassin was carried downward by gravity, and finally pinned by several hundred-pound blocks of granite, which crushed his legs beneath their pitiless weight.

Jotham didn't allow the scream of agony to distract him as his final opponent had hoped. Ignoring the pain of his caved hand guard, the assassin slipped forward with deceptive speed; speed that Jotham could not hope to match. The warrior fought a desperate battle against the flurry of blows that plied the dark air, moving on a treacherous blood-slicked roof as much as his legs would allow him.

The onslaught continued in an unceasing barrage of potentially deadly blows, most which Jotham barely warded away. The poisonous blade licked out again and again, questing for an opening- hungry for the touch of Jotham's skin. The assassin was not trying for a decapitating or disemboweling blow, he merely desired to break the skin, and let the venom of his blade seep into the giant warrior's blood stream.

Jotham was sweating hard, his nerves sharpened to the ultimate edge of awareness, his heart pumping adrenaline to every muscle. Neither man spoke, each intent on the movement of his enemy, and letting the clash of their blades do the speaking for them. The rasp of steel on steel was their dialogue, and the clamor of their swords echoed out across the barren rooftops and the empty streets.

For long minutes they battled, neither giving more than a few steps to the other, before regaining it. Finally, it was Jotham's lack of mobility that decided the battle. Each step he took was with deliberate concentration, and he planted firmly after each move he made. The assassin would glide in to his left and right, probing for some weakness in his defense, slipping the tip of the blade toward any of the warrior's flesh that lay exposed.

With grim realization Jotham continued the fight. He knew that he faced a seasoned killer, and wondered if he had the skill to overcome and gain victory. In times past he would have overwhelmed his opponent, striking powerful blows that would drive his enemy back. He would follow up, never giving his foe the opportunity to recover, keeping him off balance until he could strike the fatal blow. No longer, though, did he have the ability to quickly follow his opponent- and he wasn't sure if he could match this man on sheer skill alone.

The assassin sped forward again, grim determination sparking in his steely eyes, and a fierce broken-toothed scowl on his face. As the tip of his sword flicked toward Jotham's neck, his nimble feet slipped on the pooled blood that lay on the roof. Pitching forward, his momentum carried him onto the tip of Jotham's broadsword, the point ripping through his sternum and out through his back. Crimson waves crossed over his vision, and the assassin's full weight fell upon Jotham's sword.

The massive warrior twisted his blade until he was sure that his enemy was dead, taking care that the curved blade of the assassin fell from the slackening grip, and that the toxic point did not come near. Finally he shook the spasming body from his gory blade.

Jotham surveyed the carnage that he had wrought, checking to see if any of his foes still might pose a danger to him. Bodies were twisted in death throes, a decapitated corpse lay drenched in blood, and huddled at the corner of the roof, the only living assassin groaned as he clenched at the stump of his wrist in pain.

For one brief moment Jotham felt a twinge of regret at the death and destruction that he had dealt. It hadn't been so long ago that he had been in the assassin's position-and the renegade warrior, Lothar, had spared his life. As Jotham slowly approached his last living opponent, the man whimpered out a futile defiance.

"Go ahead and kill me," he grimaced. "It won't help. The job has already been done while you wasted your time killing us on the roof top."

This revelation alarmed Jotham, but he didn't let it show on his face. "Bind your wound and get lost. If I find you here when you get back I won't be giving you another chance to live."

The assassin nodded, his face wracked in a grimace of pain. Jotham saw dark cords twisted to sharp grappling hooks, and realized how the assassins had gained the roof top. He limped over to the nearest of these and reversed the grapple so that it hooked on the outside of the rooftop wall. Stringing the hemp cord out between both his massive hands, he tested his weight against the line to assure it held securely, than he leaped backward through the open hatchway, and into the interior of the loft.

Using the strength of his upper body, he lowered himself the twenty intervening feet to the cascade of stone that still held one of the assassins pinned beneath their prodigious weight. The cloaked killer kept silent as Jotham stumbled over the tumult of stone to the flat boards of the loft, hoping that the warrior wouldn't see him lying in the pool of yellow light shed by Jotham's still burning lantern. But as Jotham came near, the assassin's hand crept within the dark folds of his robe, and clutched the hilt of an envenomed dagger hidden beneath.

Jotham caught the movement from the corner of his eye and before the assassin could reach out and slice him with the concealed knife, he brought his sword from his sheath and hacked through the assassin's neck. Crimson splayed across the granite, and mingled with the dust on the floor, but the warrior had no time to linger over the result of his handiwork.

The assassin above had hinted that his cohorts were killing Jotham's charges while the battle had raged above. Jotham wanted to find if there was any truth to the words the assassin had spoken, or if they were just vain bravado to spite him in his victory. He descended the ladder and crept along the wall, a cold breeze alerting him to a broken pane of glass.

Jotham paused briefly and saw that the glass had been removed and the bars had been cut away with a hacksaw. He raised his lantern and the thin rays revealed a sheet of sap paper laying in the alley outside, pieces of broken glass still attached to it. Jotham had heard enough tales to know that the sap paper was attached to a window pane before the glass was broken. The sticky sap from a cedar tree adhered to the glass, silencing the sound of the break-in. The paper was then pulled away with the shattered glass of the window pane still attached.

This had been the method used to enter the warehouse while the battle had been raging above. Jotham doubted that he would have noticed the sound of a breaking window above the din of the fight, even if the sap paper hadn't been used. Doubtless, his opponents hadn't expected him to put up as much resistance as he had. Probably they had expected a crippled night guard to be easy prey- and had hoped to surprise him while he slumbered at his post.

In the dust of the dry mortar that had seeped from burlap bags, Jotham could make out the overlapping imprints of the soft shoes that assassins often wore to abet their silence and climbing. The marks were split between the big toe and the rest of the feet, leaving cloven marks. Jotham was no expert tracker, but from the jumble of footprints he guessed that at least two or three assassins had entered through the window.

Jotham followed the marks toward the back door of the warehouse where they veered off to the left, running between pyramids of stacked stone toward Sharven's office where the warrior presumed that the secret meeting was taking place.

Indeed, the warrior found the stout door to Sharven's office wide open, but the room was dark and devoid of life. Holding his broadsword firmly in his right hand he lifted the oil lantern in his left and let its rays illuminate the stone room. Behind the broad desk, a bookcase piled high with dusty account ledgers lined the back wall.

Though the floor of the office was much neater than the warehouse, and had been swept free of mortar dust, Jotham's brief examination showed that the assassins had tracked in powder on their shoes and a cloven-foot trail led to the rear of the office, and then disappeared into thin air at the book case.

It wasn't uncommon for buildings in Bathos to be constructed with some kind of storage cellar, and often the well-to-do of Bathos would hide the room, and refit it as a secret chamber for storing valuables. Little was safe from the Thieves Guild, and the citizens of Bathos often went to extreme measures to thwart the burglars, and pilferers that seemed endemic on the night time streets.

Jotham's examination took little time to uncover the secret passage behind the shelves. The assassins had not entirely replaced the bookcase, and a ragged black hole beckoned behind. Jotham roughly shoved the bookcase aside, and entered the gaping maw, descending into the womb of the earth. Roughly hewn stairs led down perspiring walls that grew thick with moss. Silence closed in on him, the claustrophobic confines of the walls grating on Jotham's nerves. Finally sound filtered up, bouncing against the wet walls of the tunnel; it was the clamor of combat, and Jotham heard the all too familiar screams of the dying.

Increasing his pace as much as he could without risking a tumble down the stairs, Jotham came to the bottom of the steps and followed a twist in the tunnel that emerged upon a small room. The door of the room was thrown open, and the still body of the rat-faced thief lay twisted across the threshold. Jotham's cursory glance revealed no mortal wound, so he suspected that it was a poisoned dart that had induced the death.

One of the assassins lay dead, a few feet into the tapestry hung room, and beyond that an intruder dressed in the dark crimson robes of the grand-master assassin lifted his hand and Jotham saw the bristling tips of those poison darts protruding from the leather-gloved palm. At the rear of the grand-master, an assassin cloaked in billowing folds of midnight crouched with curved blade drawn, guarding the back of his lord. The rear-guard caught sight of Jotham, black eyes glittering as a malicious grin flashed from the deep shadows beneath the concealing hood.

As the rear guard sped forward to meet Jotham, the grandmaster assassin cast the darts from his hand. The motion was made with a deceptive ease, which belied the years of practice that had gone into developing the infernal skill that would allow such a difficult throw. The barbs spread from his palm, speeding forth and each striking their target. The King of Thieves fell against the wall, two black-vaned darts protruding from his neck. He clutched futilely at the pin pricks of pain as the diabolical poison raced through his blood stream. With the same cast the third dart had flown forth, and Vastak warded it from his neck only by lifting his right arm, and having the missile ricochet from the metal-studded bracer that he wore on his thick forearm.

Of the group who had entered the warehouse at midnight, only Travis and Vastak remained standing, but Jotham's attention was turned away by the assassin who lunged at him with speed that was nearly supernatural. In his confidence that he could make a quick killing, Jotham's opponent over extended himself. The big warrior twisted as the assassin's blade passed by him. Jotham blocked the assassin's curved sword with his own straight broadsword, and with his left hand he hurled the lantern that he still held high.

The lantern's glass shattered upon impact and oil splattered across the midnight folds of the assassin's cloak, instantly igniting them in an orgy of licking flame. As the flaming killer leaped away from Jotham, he threw himself to the floor, rolling along the finely woven carpets in an attempt to extinguish the enfolding fingers of fire that consumed him.

Several uneven steps took Jotham forward, and he brought his blade down upon the prostrate form of the man, feeling the ribs cave in under his blow. Only now did the assassin cry out, but the outburst was feeble and his life was extinguished even as the scream died on his crimson-flecked lips.

This victory took Jotham only moments to achieve and he stepped over the still flaming body of his foe, swinging his broadsword at the exposed scarlet-swathed back of the grandmaster assassin. This master of all assassins had made a fatal miscalculation, depending upon his cohort to successfully keep the rear clear from any danger. Even so, he whirled as he heard his fellow assassin cry out in pain. Droplets of venom flew from his thin blade as he spun, but Jotham's broadsword had already cut deep, slicing through a thin mesh of chain mail that was concealed beneath the scarlet robes. The grandmaster fell and they watched as he spasmed and died.

His face and forearms splattered with red droplets, Jotham looked up at Travis and Vastak, the only two men, beside himself, who remained alive in the room. "Not bad work…for a cripple," he growled.

Vastak stuttered out an embarrassed response. "It's not bad work for any warrior," he admitted.

"Here's my question to you," said Jotham to Vastak. "If you knew that you were going to have an important meeting here tonight at the Sharven warehouse, why would you allow the assignment general to post a cripple on night watch duty?"

"But I didn't know where the meeting was to be held," answered Vastak. "Only Travis did, and he was as surprised as I was when Sharven informed us that you were the one on duty here tonight."

Travis nodded in agreement.

Jotham shook his head. "Travis wasn't surprised. In fact, he had an agreement with the dispatch general to assign me here. He met me in Hill Town and knew my assignment before I could tell him where it was. There was no way he could have known unless he had instructed the dispatch general to assign me to this warehouse."

Vastak squinted and turned his attention to Travis, his right hand went down to the pommel of his dagger. "Did you have some reason why you wanted a cripple posted on guard duty tonight?"

Travis smiled suavely, not showing slightest perturbation at the suspicion that had been thrown upon him. "The man has a reputation as a liar. I'm not even sure why you would give his word the slightest bit of credence."

"I've never heard anyone say Jotham was a liar," repudiated Vastak. "In fact, he has a reputation for honesty. Not once has he been accused of holding out on guild dues."

"My safety was at risk here tonight, also," answered Travis. "Are you forgetting that? Why would I put my own life on the line by posting anybody on night watch that I thought might be less than capable?"

"I don't think your life was ever at risk," answered Vastak. "Not once did an assassin's poisoned dart come flying in your direction. What kind of deal did you have with Assassins Guild? How much were they paying you to betray your own guild?"

"Now you're just jumping to conclusions," answered Travis with a disarming smile. "I told no one of our meeting here tonight. If word leaked out, it did so on the side of the Thieves Guild."

"Word did leak out," interjected Jotham. "I don't think there is any question about that."

With one quick movement, Vastak withdrew his dagger and sliced open the bulging pouch that Travis wore at his waist. Sparkling gems spilled out and bounded along the carpet, coming to rest in a riot of overlapping colors that rivaled that of the rainbow.

"There's the blood money!" said Vastak. "I know that the Warriors Guild pays in gold, not gems. Those jewels were your payment for betraying us."

Now Travis' glacial exterior was cracking. He blanched and realized that no excuse was going to satisfy either Jotham or Vastak.

"Take it," he mumbled. "Take it all. Not one word will pass my lips."

"Of that I am certain," answered Vastak as he lunged toward Travis with the point of his dagger.

Though Travis had made his way in the world by use of his charm and wits, he was also an accomplished fighter, and now he fell back on that skill as his last resort. The monks of the goddess Sharn, who lived in elaborate caves burrowed into the Slopes outside the walls of the Upper City practiced a peculiar form of weaponless combat. Travis had fooled one of the young monks into showing him some of the forbidden arts of this weaponless combat, and now he used one of the katas that he had learned.

He twisted to the side while simultaneously stepping toward Vastak. This gave Vastak no room to wield his weapon, and Travis locked his arms around Vastak's knife arm, in a move that produced enough pressure to break the arms of most men.

Vastak's arm held enough muscle mass that it did not snap under the vice-like pressure, but his fingers went numb and the knife slipped from his grip. Travis was about to let loose with a kick that would snap Vastak's knee, when the point of Jotham's blade drove up beneath his chin and into his brain.

Gushing black blood Travis fell instantly limp, and his body slumped to the floor.

Standing over Travis' body; the man who would have killed him if not for Jotham, Vastak was still too proud to offer an apology to the crippled warrior for misjudging his worth to the Warriors Guild. Instead, he offered something else.

"I owe you my life," he said. "What can I do to repay you?"

Jotham looked down at Travis' inert body. "I believe there is a command position open. I'd like to fill it."

"You'll have my recommendation," answered Vastak.

Part Eight:
Last Stand in Bathos

Black blood spilled from the gnashing maw of the infernal hounds, steam blowing from the slitted nostrils above their crimson-flecked muzzles and billowing into the cold night air. They dipped their sleek heads, growling and tearing at the struggling form, which they had run down in the fetid confines of Butchers Alley- their master's doing nothing to discourage them from tearing their prey limb from limb, and slackening the leashes of the beasts so that they could have at their downed quarry.

The dark-cloaked beggar let out a horrible cry as the midnight black beasts tore at him, the dirt-encrusted cobblestones running crimson as the beasts devoured his flesh. Finally, the emaciated man fell still, his soul parting his lips and slipping into the ether.

As the man fell dead, a smile crossed Balzac's lips and he plucked at his spiked brown hair, his small feet shifting on the cobblestones as he edged closer to the dogs' feeding frenzy to peer at the victim. He frowned when he could get no clear view through the turmoil of black-fur and blood drenched maws.

Balzac turned to the dog handler, who towered over him, his face set with a grim smile of satisfaction, and his heavy brow furrowed over cold eyes that glowed with sinister appreciation for the carnage that the dogs had wrought that night. "Procktar," he ordered," Clear the beasts away so that I can make sure it was Lothar that we got."

Procktar swiveled his lumpy head on a neck the size of a tree-trunk. "There is no calling off the infernal hounds once they've began to feed. If you come too close you'll join their dinner party, whether you like it or not."

"I've got to be sure that we've killed Lothar."

"Are you sure that scrap of cloth that you gave me was worn by Lothar?"

"Sure as I'm standing here," said Balzac with a supercilious sneer. "I tore the scrap from his cloak with my own sword-blade."

Balzac had a reputation as a deadly killer, and many swore that his blade was the fastest that they had ever seen. Few had crossed swords with him and lived to tell about it. Still, the Thieves Guild enforcer was scarcely more than five foot tall and he looked as though a ten year-old street urchin would be more than a match for him. Procktar had difficulties bringing himself to fear someone so small and slight.

"Maybe if you would have aimed your sword more carefully you wouldn't have needed to go to the trouble to hire the services of the infernal hounds. The Sorcerer's Guild is sure to be charging you a pretty coin for the use of their dogs."

Balzac's child-like visage transformed into something horrible to behold as anger took hold of him. "Are you questioning my sword skills?"

It was difficult for Procktar to hold in a laugh. His barrel chest exhaled and his snug leather tunic loosened. "I'm just thinking that the Thieves Guild wanted Lothar dead quite badly."

"That's right," answered Balzac, his anger easing slightly, but his manner still confrontational. "I need to be sure that this is Lothar."

Procktar shrugged his broad shoulders. "It's doubtful that there will be enough of him left to identify."

Now the third man inserted himself into the conversation. He was much bigger than Balzac, nearly as wide, but not as tall as the dog handler. He wobbled his bullet head and gripped a jagged long-knife in his scarred right hand. "Lothar killed my brother, I need to know that this is him the dogs are eating."

"The two of you can rest easy," said Procktar. "These hounds are mystically bred- once they catch a scent they don't mistake it. They've never been wrong. This very group of dogs has hunted down escapees from the Emperor's own dungeons- all the way across the tortured peaks, and they never once lost the scent."

Kayne licked his thick lips with a dry tongue, and a hideous chuckle escaped him- carrying with it all the anxiety and pent-up desire for revenge that he had harbored in his breast since Lothar had plunged the point of a battle axe through his brother's chest.

* * * *

Jotham scratched at his bald pate with a hand that was hatched with the scars of old battles. He shook back his single top-knot and shoved aside the stacks of parchments that held provisioning and recruitment requests from a hundred different merchants, guilds, and organizations around the city that needed the strong arm of the Warriors Guild to protect them from harm.

His rise from disgrace had been abrupt, and he hadn't been prepared for the deluge of paperwork that was included with taking over the position of third in command at the Warriors Guild. He glanced around at his room of operations, and sighed wistfully as his eyes fell upon the glittering array of sword, spear, and knife that were mounted on his walls. He was getting restless; he wasn't sure just how much more of this paper pushing he could take, but at least he knew he was integral to the organization. No longer was he considered a useless cripple that couldn't hold his own in battle; he was treated with respect and accorded all the privileges of his position.

He reached out with thick arms and hoisted himself from his oak chair, standing on his good right leg, and the hard peg that replaced the lower part of his left leg. As he shrugged his massive shoulders, his door flew open and he saw the familiar sight of Vastak's smashed nose and scowling face. "I've got a job for you," said the Warrior Guild's second in command.

Jotham's face brightened. "Will it pull me away from this cursed paper shuffling?"

Vastak grinned evilly. "Aye, that it will. And this is a job which will be of personal interest to you."

"I'm listening," said Jotham as he eased out from behind his broad, polished desk, and began cutting a hunk of cheese with an implement more suited for gut-stabbing than cheese-carving.

"I've received several reports that Lothar has been seen around the city."

Jotham immediately stopped what he was doing and dropped his dagger next to the cheese on the silver platter. "I thought the Thieves Guild claimed to have tracked him down with infernal hounds."

"I have reliable reports otherwise."

"Do you think that the Thieves Guild is feeding us false reports for some reason?"

Vastak shrugged and flicked at the broken bridge of his nose. "I smell something fishy. Maybe they just want to save face by killing him themselves, but the fact is that Lothar broke his charter with the Warriors Guild, also- and we owe him death. Already we've lost half a dozen other fighters who have followed his example. We need to end this thing before we lose a grip on the Guild."

"You want me to assign some people to track him down?" asked Jotham.

Vastak shook his head. "I want you to personally take charge of this one. He took your leg. You've got some extra incentive to see that this deserter gets what's coming to him. I want you to put together some men and hit the streets."

Jotham reached up and plucked his broadsword from the wall, fondly feeling the heft of the weapon in his massive hands. "I'll take care of him," he said.

* * * *

Lothar walked Iron Street slowly. The bright light stung his eyes and he could see little more than a myriad of shadows moving around him on the crowded street. He was unable to make out the detail of the faces passing by, or of the brightly colored signs that hung swinging in a chill wind that filtered up the maze of Bathos' streets from the broad, dark ribbon of the Tiber river far below.

The warrior-thief wrapped his dark, ragged cloak tightly around his lean, muscular frame- concealing the array of throwing axes, which crossed his chest, and lending him some protection against the breeze that cooled the otherwise warm day. Once Lothar drew his cloak tight he shifted his battle axe; the haft the weapon was shattered just below the steel of the blade, which held the HK imprint of the blacksmith who had forged the weapon.

Even in broad daylight it was dangerous to walk the city streets of Bathos, but a blind or crippled man could find safety only if it appeared that he had nothing worth stealing. Even legless mendicants had been found slain for the meager collection of copper coins they had amassed during a day of begging. Though Lothar held himself erect and walked with a confident carriage, his steps were slow and sometimes faltered as he tried to pierce the veil of darkness that covered his eyes, and make out the dim outline of the street's cobbles below his black-booted feet.

Swallowed by the demon Mahmackrah who had been summoned by his dread followers to the Pyramid of Lythos, Lothar had been lucky to escape with his life- but the acids in the foul beasts innards had made him blind for weeks, and only now had his vision healed to the point that he could venture out onto the streets without his pregnant wife, Sheesa, leading the way. Without his full eyesight he felt vulnerable to attack, and this was compounded by the fact that his battleaxe had been ruined in his battle against Mahmackrah.

Blurs of color passed by him in an unceasing stream, interrupted only when someone bumped into him. Though, with broad chest, muscular arms, and raven locks that streamed boldly behind him, Lothar looked more like warrior than thief, he had once been a member of both guilds, and was familiar with at least a hundred different methods of picking a man's pocket. Even now he could feel fingers reaching, and plucking at his belt pouch. Properly executed, the bump and the grab would occur simultaneously so that the victim would notice only that he had been bumped- not that his pouch had been stolen.

This thief's timing, however, was off, and the questing fingers came a fraction of a second too late. Perhaps someone who wasn't as well versed in the arts of thievery as Lothar might not have noticed the lapse in execution, but the difference was night and day to Lothar. His right hand shot out and grabbed hold of the thief's wrist, while his other hand came out and found the elbow of the same arm.

Holding the elbow and the wrist, Lothar could control the movement of the unfortunate thief's arm, and in a moment he had wrenched the arm around the man's back and shoved his face into the stone wall of the building at the edge of the road.

The thief cried out as blood burst from broken vessels in his nose, accompanied by a sharp pain as his right arm snapped.

Lothar hissed through gritted teeth. "Scum! What's wrong, is a blind man too much of a challenge for you? Maybe you're too used to robbing amputees…"

He kicked the legs of the thief out from beneath him and let him collapse in a pile at the roadside. Unless this cutpurse was working alone, he would have two accomplices lurking nearby, pretending to be part of the crowd, but ready to insert themselves between the fleeing thief and his victim, should the victim notice the theft and take up pursuit. They would slow pursuit enough that their friend could get away, and then melt back into the crowd.

Lothar crouched down and felt along the cobbles until he found the splintered handle of his battle axe, and then he stood. Perhaps his sudden attack had cowed the backup thieves from taking any action. By nature, thieves were a cowardly lot, and avoided putting themselves in any situation that might get them maimed or killed. After continuing down the street for another ten minutes, Lothar became satisfied that the back up thieves had decided on the most prudent course of action, and wouldn't be harassing him.

Finally Lothar was able to make out a street sign hanging from a rusting iron stanchion hammered into the side of a building. The sign was in the shape of a battleaxe and though Lothar couldn't read the sign now, he knew that it was inscribed with the words HK Armoury. Even now he could hear the sound of the blacksmith's hammer ringing out, and the scent of brimstone filled the air.

He turned into the blackness of the doorway, and found that the warmth of the forge was a welcome respite from the bite of the breeze outside. His eyes took some time to adjust to the dim interior, but in a few moments he was able to make out the burly form of Henri Koulotte wielding a hammer, and his less-burly apprentice working the bellows around the red-yellow glow of the forge.

Lothar waited while Henri turned a blade with tongs and pounded the thing into shape, when finally he reached a stopping point, he threw aside his thick leather gloves and left the intense heat of the furnace, his hairy chest wet with the sweat of his exertions.

"I'm surprised to see you still in town...or alive, for that matter," said Henri. "I've already had several inquiries about you."

"Guild enforcers?" asked Lothar.

"No doubt they were," answered the blacksmith. He wiped away the bits of white ash from his thick brown beard, his huge forearms writhing with the slight bit of exertion. His face was heavily lined, betraying the age that his thick and powerful torso did not show.

"A small man that looks like a child?"

Henri nodded. "Accompanied by a brawler whose head was shaped like a lead pellet for a sling."

"I've had the displeasure of running into them before," said Lothar.

"They offered me one hundred pieces of gold if I informed them next time you came in."

Lothar reached into his pouch, and produced a purple amethyst the size of a dagger's pommel. "I'll do his offer one better if you keep your mouth shut," said Lothar. "This should be worth twice what he's offering."

"Keep it," said Henri. "Thief or no, you've always been honest with me, and I'll not turn in a friend to the guilds."

"And your apprentice?" asked Lothar, turning his attention toward the thin figure that was stoking the fires.

"Charl will keep silent if he knows what's good for him. I've used my smith's hammer to pound more than metal, and if I need to pound the skull of an apprentice with an imprudent mouth I will."

"I do appreciate it," said Lothar sternly. He lifted the broken battle axe and presented it to Henri. "I also need your services to repair my axe."

Henri clucked disparagingly as he examined the weapon. "What have you been hewing? Stone? Beside the new handle, the edge of the blade needs to be ground and sharpened. It also appears to be pocked as if it were etched with some sort of acid, but I should be able to have Charl polish that out for you. I'd offer to forge a new axe for you, but I suspect you're in a hurry."

"I'm afraid so. Any number of people may have recognized me on the street, and be making their way to the guild offices right now to collect on the reward."

Henri reached for his hammer and quickly chiseled the shattered haft out of the eye of the axe head. "I'll get started on it right now. Do you have other business or would you like to wait here? You were always fast on your feet, if the guild enforcers show up you can always duck out the back way."

"I'm not as fast as I used to be," said Lothar as he squinted hard, trying to clear his impaired vision. "I got some of the same acid that etched my axe in my eyes."

"And on your skin, too," said Henri critically. "It still looks a bit red in patches. You've been messing with the wrong people."

"I'll say," answered the warrior-thief.

It was almost two hours later by the time Henri and his apprentice had finished sharpening and polishing his axe, and installed a new haft. Lothar profusely thanked the blacksmith and paid him in gold before slipping out the back, and traveling down several twisting alleys, finally emerging on Hack Street. The breeze had died now, but Lothar passed a shivering mendicant crouched in a urine-stained alcove.

"A copper coin so that I can buy a cloak?" shivered the man, his voice coming rough and aged through his chattering teeth.

Though normally any citizen of Bathos would turn a deaf ear to a beggar's pleas, Lothar's heart was occasionally softened by a plaintiff cry, and he turned and gazed at the dim shape of the beggar crouched against the wall, shaking from ague.

"I'll do better than that," said Lothar as he unstrung his cloak and handed it to the beggar. "It's a little ragged, but it's still thick enough to give some warmth."

The mendicant showered profuse thanks on the warrior, and Lothar dropped a gold coin in his hand. "Visit the apothecary, mayhap it is not just the cold that makes you shake."

Before the beggar could shower another heaping of praise upon the warrior, Lothar slipped down Hack Street, turning right on Master Street when he recognized the tarnished brass gargoyle that jutted from the corner of a dilapidated building which housed a tailor's shop at street level. Even as he passed Lothar could smell the scent of musty cloth wafting from the dim doorway.

Lothar strode purposefully, his footsteps surer, and the weight of his slung battleaxe reassuring on his back. Though he could read no signs and barely make out the shape of the faces around him, he was able to negotiate the treacherous cobblestones with only a few minor missteps and no major mishaps.

The muscular fugitive followed Master Street, past long rows of shops and towering tenements scrolled with eroding carvings of beast and demon that hinted at Bathos' sinister past. He passed beneath the obsidian archway, which crossed through the crumbling wall that separated the Mid-City from Old Bathos, and here dark towers rose against the cerulean skies, notched with arrow slits and jagged crenellations, and dripping with crusted blood that the centuries of rain had yet to wash away.

Ominous copper domes rose, cankered green by time; some of these looming structures were abandoned in fear of the ancient evils that crept from subterranean tunnels carved beneath, and yet others housed the richest of the ancient bloodlines- pale slaves waiting on every whim while their masters hoarded their gold and gems in twilight-lit caverns, which were protected by devious traps and unspeakable horrors summoned and bound by the darkest of sorceries.

Some of this was rumor; some of this Lothar had himself learned by hard experience. He left the main thoroughfare and passed by high walls topped with poison-smeared spikes. Though he could not see the poison upon the jagged spikes, he could see that the foliage, which had in places sprung up from between the cracks of the cobblestones at the roads edge, had withered into a dry, brittle brown. The rains had washed the poison from the spikes, and down the wall to choke out the life of the plants beneath.

He traversed a winding stair and crossed through a series of over-arching bridges, and through a dark tunnel that flamed with torchlight set in sconces along the stonework beneath. When he emerged he found himself surrounded by buildings that towered up around him, the crumbling foundations thrusting upward to meet a maze of bridges and streets that had been built over this portion of city that had once been ravaged by earthquake. They called this the Underground- not to be confused with the Under City, which lay adjacent to Old Bathos, cut out from the hilly climes upon which the sprawling city of Bathos was built.

The Underground was a place that attracted those who didn't wish to be found, or those who wished to ply their trades without the interference of the Guilds who controlled the rest of the city. Here a blacksmith, a fletcher, or a prostitute could toil in anonymity, and reap the rewards of their labors without paying the taxations of the Guilds and the Emperor.

Occasionally, the Emperor would bring his troops into the Underground and attempt to clean it out, but the residents would slink back into alley's that riddled the Underground like a maze, and hide in their holes until the storm had passed- only to return later and resume their activities as if nothing had happened.

Very little light seeped through the cracks overhead, and torch smoke rose thick in the air, while the flickering flames cast sinuous illumination across the narrow roadways. Here the streets were lined with scags and courtesans- some hideous and some beautiful- offering fleeting pleasures at a cost. Lothar ignored their entreaties, and when they saw it was he that passed, several of them quieted.

"How are the eyes?" asked a woman with sharp features, and a gorgeous mane of straw-colored hair that fell to her silk-entwined buttocks.

"Well enough to walk without assistance, Renna," answered Lothar who was able to recognize her voice, but wouldn't have been able to distinguish her otherwise. "Have you seen Sheesa pass this way?"

"Not less than ten minutes ago."

Lothar nodded. "Any trouble today?"

Renna shook her head. "All's quiet."

Down a twisting alley Lothar came to a wooden door at the bottom of a small flight of worn steps. He knocked thrice at the door and a woman's voice answered. "Who is it?"

Lothar didn't answer, but knocked three more times. He heard the bolt slide open and the door opened to let him in. He stepped through into the brilliant lantern light and locked the door behind.

Sheesa threw herself at him and he caught her in his strong arms as she kissed him with satin lips, her foamy black hair spilling across his face. From this short distance he could see her dark eyes glittering, and the sprinkle of freckles that lay across the bridge of her nose. He recognized the subtle scent that she wore at the hollow of her neck.

"I do hope that it's Sheesa I'm kissing," he said as they broke off momentarily. "In my blindness, I could be kissing the wrong girl."

"You've gone to far too much trouble for me, to make such a potentially fatal mistake," she said, her voice bright with merriment.

"I smell some food. Did you round up something to eat?"

"I did," said Sheesa. "There is a roasting pit not far from here, and I purchased a brace of roasted hens. They should still be warm if you hurry."

As soon as he had laid aside his battleaxe and removed his bandolier of axes, Lothar hungrily tore into one of the hens. Despite their exile into the Underground, he and Sheesa were laughing and talking merrily when they were interrupted by the scrape of the door upon the lintel and threshold.

Lothar leaped to his feet and grabbed for a throwing axe as a dim figure threw open the door and stepped inside the small chamber, hand on the hilt of the sword that hung at her side.

Sheesa's vision was clearer than Lothar's and she saw the woman in the doorway. Her hair was spun the color of gold and it fell across her bare shoulders and halfway down her back. Her eyes were cold blue, and the nose slightly upturned, her philtrum sloping into a full upper lip, which was slightly larger than her lower. Her form was voluptuous, her breasts confined in a close-fitting tunic of hardened leather, yet striations of muscle could be seen working in her shoulders and arms. At her leather bound waist she wore a sheathed blade, and her legs were booted to her thighs. Lothar could smell the subtle and beguiling scent of the crimson lotus; a blossom that was used to create the deadliest of poisons, but in small amounts, and mixed properly, created a potion that was said to charm and bewitch men.

"Sedrah?" breathed Sheesa. "What are you doing here?"

Lothar paused with his arm cocked back, ready to throw the single-bladed hatchet he held in his hand- even the handle of which might punch through a piece of oak half an inch thick.

"Speak up woman!" he said to the blonde in the doorway. "Why are you here?"

"I've been hired to kill you," she said. "And I'm here to give you fair warning."

Sheesa's voice was cold and bitter. "I thought that you were one of the few people I could trust. I guess that I was wrong. You're like every other back-stabbing, lying, cheating, piece of scum in this city."

Sedrah cast her eyes down at the floor as she shut the door behind her. "I know," she said, "but I don't have any choice. I failed to kill Lothar once already, and the Assassins Guild will have my hide if I don't make the kill this time."

The corner of Lothar's lips curled up, baring the teeth beneath. "I had hoped that we would meet again as friends, but if you want death then come and get it."

A subterranean wind pushed from a narrow hallway at the back of the room and flared Lothar's black hair into a dark halo around his grim visage. He stood like a statue, his axe drawn back, his wounded eyes tracking the hazy figure of Sedrah- each movement that she made.

"I'm not here to kill you- not now," she said sullenly. She untied her sheath and let her sword drop to the stones of the floor. "Sheesa's been the only true friend that I've ever had. I'm here to warn you that I'm going to have to kill you if you don't get out of the city. I have no choice." She pulled a stool up to the rough-hewn wooden table around which Lothar and Sheesa had been eating, and removed a roll of parchment from a pouch at her waist.

"You've traded one devil for another," said Sheesa. "The Assassins Guild is no better than the Courtesans Guild. You're still forced to do things you shouldn't have to do."

Sedrah didn't respond. She rolled out the parchment, and with a swift movement she pinned it to the table with a skewer. "That's the order of assassination," she said. "If I don't do it, the Assassins Guild is full of people that will, without feeling the need to give you any warning at all. I hope that you understand, I'm doing everything that I can to help you."

"Well I hope you'll excuse me if I don't fall over myself to thank you for your generosity," spat Sheesa.

Sedrah rose, stooping to pick up her blade before opening the door. She spoke with her back turned, as if she didn't dare look them in the eye. "I'm sorry," she said, and the door closed behind her.

Sheesa tore the piece of paper from the skewer and examined it in the lantern light. "The Thieves Guild is paying five hundred pieces of gold for your assassination," she said.

"I've had people try to kill me for a handful of copper coin," said Lothar. "The difference now is that this bounty won't go away. If Sedrah doesn't kill me then the Assassins Guild will assign the contract to someone else. I'd have to kill every last assassin in Bathos to get clear of this bounty."

"Maybe that won't be necessary," said Sheesa. "We can flee the city."

Lothar shook his head. "It's just as dangerous outside of Bathos. Bandits are thick outside the city walls, and if I haven't got my eyesight we're not going to be able to defend ourselves."

"Maybe we should just take our chances," suggested Sheesa, her dark eyes flashing with sudden intensity. "But if Sedrah shows up again, I want you to kill her. If you don't, I will."

"The only way that she'll kill me is if she catches me by surprise- and she tried that before at Devil's Head."

"Don't underestimate her," said Sheesa. "She's dangerous. Not only is she lethal with her blade, but she can beguile a man in seconds."

Lothar laughed. "No need to worry about me on that account. Not only am I hopelessly in love with you, but I can't even see Sedrah well enough for her to beguile me with her beauty. Her powers of seduction are wasted on me."

"We're not safe here anymore," said Sheesa. "How do you think Sedrah found us?"

"The Underground is swarming with former courtesans who want to ply their trade without paying guild dues. Probably you have a mutual acquaintance that remembers that you and Sedrah were friends, and didn't think it would do any harm to tell her where we were hiding."

"Renna?"

"Maybe," said Lothar. "It doesn't much matter now. We've got to get out. Perhaps you're right, maybe we should take a chance at leaving the city, but we need to purchase some provisions before we go. It may take several days to get things together so we can leave. Maybe by that time my vision will have improved."

"Where can we stay in the meantime?"

Lothar considered this for a time. "There's an abandoned tower in the Mid-City that should provide us plenty of space. It shouldn't take much for me to break in."

"Why is it abandoned?" asked Sheesa skeptically.

"It used to belong to a wizard named Kolthos. He's dead now, but they say that his ghost still haunts the tower."

"And does it?"

Lothar shrugged. "I broke into the tower after his death looking for anything valuable that I might be able to carry off. I certainly didn't see his ghost."

Sheesa still wasn't entirely convinced, and this was reflected in the tone of her voice. "I suppose we'd better get moving then."

* * * *

A hard rain began to fall, spattering down the chasm of the dark alley and pelting the two figures that stood at the weathered wooden double doors that barred entrance to the bowels of Kolthos' looming tower.

Lothar crouched, working at the massive padlock that held the thick links of chain wrapped tightly around the heavy iron handles. His dark mane was plastered to his neck, and rain water poured down his scalp and across his face as he gave his lock picks a final twist. The padlock clicked and he pulled the hasp loose and began unwinding the heavy links of chain.

Sheesa was wrapped tightly in an oilskin jacket that shed the rains, dark drops rolling from it as she pressed the swell in her stomach and felt the kick of the child, that she and Lothar had created, within. She forced her eyes upward and to the ominous spire that needled into the cloud-darkened skies. Its dark windows stared down like soulless eyes, and made her shiver in spite of herself.

Lothar pushed the tower doors and the portal yawned, exposing the rank darkness that lay beyond. A foul stench swept out of its mouth causing Lothar to grit his teeth, and Sheesa to fight back the impulse to retch.

"It smells like a slaughterhouse," she said.

"The scent sticks in the basement," said Lothar. "Up above, there is fresh air circulating through vents."

Sheesa reached beneath her jacket and unsheathed a throwing knife. Her fingers nervously rubbed the leather wrapped hilt as she followed Lothar into the darkness. Only after they entered the room, and Lothar chained and locked the doors from the inside, did he strike the flint on the lantern, and shed light on the cavernous room that they had entered. Empty cages lined the concave walls and the place reeked of refuse.

"What sort of animals did Kolthos keep here?" asked Sheesa.

"No animals- humans," answered Lothar. "He sacrificed them to gain favor with the nether-demons."

"The favor of the nether-demons didn't keep him from dying."

"No it didn't," replied Lothar. "It seems that the devils are little concerned for the welfare of even their patrons."

Lothar led the way to a set of stone stairs set at the edge of the wall.

These circled upward past the wide arches that supported the stone ceiling, and they soon they were slipping through musty chambers and down hallways lined with empty pedestals, their footsteps disturbing the layers of ash that lay on the marble laid floor, and creating swirling eddies.

They stepped across broken hafts and carelessly strewn spears and halberds that littered the floor as though they had been discarded by some fleeing army. The room beyond was bare except for a segmented golden ball that hung like a chandelier overhead, its lower segments hanging open and revealing the emptiness within.

"Did you find anything here worth looting?" asked Sheesa.

"A few odds and ends," said Lothar, "but surprisingly little for a man of such reputed wealth and power."

"Do you think someone beat you to it?"

"No," said Lothar. "Most thieves are looking for some easy loot. They're not interested in raiding a wizard's lair, be he alive…or dead."

They followed the stairs upward until they reached the pinnacle of the tower, and trod the marble-tiled floors beyond an open iron door. A thin residue of ash lay on the floor, with chess pieces scattered from a shattered stone board.

Sheesa's face tightened as she examined the wreckage. "There are footprints in the ash," she said. "Someone has been here recently."

Lothar's poor vision had made him oblivious to the tracks on the floor. "Is there anybody here now?"

Sheesa cast about the room, peering into the recesses of the vast fireplace carven with massive and small sigils the shapes of keys, through the veils of hanging and torn tapestries, and past the ash-strewn divans that still were piled with silken cushions, and pine tables with open decanters of wine still resting on their polished surfaces. "I don't see anyone," she whispered.

Lothar crouched down to study the tracks from a close distance, but he could make out nothing.

Sheesa bent down alongside of Lothar and examined the imprints in the ash. "This person has been here more than once, or he stayed here for a long while. The tracks overlap."

An eerie warble came to their ears- a call inimitable by human tongue-

and then a brief fluttering of wings. A narrow balcony jutted out from the tower, the stained glass door broken, panes of multi-colored glass lying in shards beneath the billowing curtain.

Lothar stepped quietly to the curtain, his booted feet crushing the glass beneath as he stepped and pushed aside the light drapery with the tip of his battle axe. Rain spattered against him, hurled from the turbulent skies above. The balcony was empty, water pooling on its floor as it spattered from the waist-high wall that enclosed it.

A stairwell railed with wrought iron curved around the side of the tower, built into its grim walls, and ascending to the crenellated reaches of the structure's open top. Once again, Lothar heard the perturbed warble they had heard moments before.

"You stay here," Lothar told Sheesa. "I'm going up to see what's going on."

Sheesa's satin lips turned up in a wry smile. "You need a pair of eyes to go with you," she said. "You can't see much of anything."

Lothar was loath to admit this truth. "I'll be fine," he said. "I'm not completely blind. You stay here and keep a look out."

Sheesa brandished a throwing knife, and her eyes sparkled with mischief. "I'll skewer anything that I see."

Lothar's faced took on a quizzical expression, and finally it resolved into a grin. "I'll be sure to give you some warning before I come back."

"You've seen what I can do with one of these things."

"And it nearly cost me my life," he said shaking his head. He turned and crept up the wet stone steps, the wind and rain beating at him as he climbed. Bathos spread out below him, a twisting maze of corruption and hate; gaunt towers, twisting alleys, grand palaces, and guttering torchlight shining through barred windows- even here at the tower top, and with unimpaired vision he could scarcely have seen the edges of this hive of evil and despair. It seemed to stretch on indefinitely- unending misery- millions of souls looking out for themselves, with no compunction about stabbing their best friend in the back for a few copper pieces, or a couple shots of whiskey.

Lothar stepped onto the tower top, into the circle of jagged crenel teeth, and a bolt of lightening hissed in the distance, casting a brief flash of illumination so bright that it hurt Lothar's eyes, but still revealed the buck-toothed figure that crouched next to a covered cage, his eyes wide with fear and his wet fingers trembling with anxiety.

"D-d-don't kill me," he stuttered out. The tail end of his words were swallowed in the deafening roar of thunder that rolled over the tower.

Lothar waited for the ringing in his ears to subside, cradling the battleaxe in his arms, and letting the elements rip at his flesh. He took several steps forward toward the lumpy shadow where he had previously seen a man. He tried to make his steps bold, so as not to let on that he could scarcely see his quarry. "Who are you?"

"My name is Vanose," answered the man, his coarse, sand-colored hair plastered to the side of his face in dripping ropes.

"And what are you doing here?" Lothar stepped close enough now so that if he desired, he was in striking distance with his battle axe- or so he guessed, he couldn't be entirely sure.

Vanose answered through chattering teeth. "I'm sorry. I didn't know this was your tower. Please let me live."

"It's not my tower, but I want to know what you're doing here all the same."

"Covering my pigeons, so that they are safe from the storm."

With his left hand Lothar reached out and lifted the oiled tarp that lay over the top of the cage. Within he could hear the fluttering of wings, and caught a glimpse of feathers as the anxious birds attempted to fly, perturbed by the storm.

"Have you been keeping these birds here long?"

"About a month," answered Vanose, "but I meant no harm. They're messenger birds. It's just that I had no place to keep them, and I thought that this tower was unused."

"I plan on using this tower for a few days," said Lothar. "After that, you can have it back- all to yourself."

"Just me and the ghost?" asked Vanose.

"Ghost? What ghost is that?"

"Why, the shade of Kolthos. I've seen him myself!"

Within a few minutes Lothar, aided considerably by the forks of lightening that painted the boiling sky, persuaded Vanose to leave the tower top. After satisfying himself that Vanose was unarmed, Lothar led the way down the steep, slick steps, calling out to Sheesa before he brushed aside the drapery and entered the room.

She refrained from hurling her blade, and looked at the stooped and bedraggled form of Vanose who followed Lothar through the opening. "Is this the visitor whose been making our mysterious footprints?"

"It is," said Lothar. "This is Vanose. He's been using the top of the tower as a roost for his carrier pigeons."

Vanose looked up shyly at Sheesa through a veil of tangled and wet hair. When he saw her beauty, he quickly averted his eyes. "M…madame," he stuttered as he bobbed his head deferentially.

"That's probably the first time I've ever been addressed as such," she laughed. "You can call me Sheesa."

"Vanose claims that he's seen the ghost of the wizard Kolthos roaming the tower."

Sheesa's dark eyes narrowed. "Has he ever harmed you?"

Vanose shook his head. "He shakes his fist, and makes angry faces, and once he touched me."

"Did anything happen to you?"

Vanose lifted his head some, and shook his head again. "He gave me a chill, but nothing more."

"He's dead. An assassin named Kelvin killed him," said Lothar. "He can't harm us now."

Sheesa shook her head. "It wasn't Kelvin that administered the final blow. It was Sedrah."

Lothar's brow furrowed. "The same woman who's after me now. I didn't realize she was so accomplished. It's an impressive thing to kill a wizard and live to tell about it."

Vanose listened to this intently. "You're not going to kill me are you?"

Lothar looked hard at the young man who stood before him. His better judgment told him that no one could be trusted and that the safest thing to do would be to hew him down and throw his body into the basement of the tower- but he couldn't bring himself to do the deed.

"Can you keep your mouth shut?"

Vanose nodded seriously, his lips pressed tightly together as if to illustrate his ability.

"I'll make you a deal. You keep your mouth shut about us being here, and I won't kill you. Do we have an understanding?"

"Yes, sir." Vanose face relaxed visibly with the prospect that he might be allowed to live.

"How did you get into the tower?"

"There's a refuse pit at the back of the tower. I sawed the bars and climbed in through the hatch, bringing my birds in one at a time."

"And the cage?"

"I built it myself from things I found in the tower."

"And these pigeons of yours are trained to carry messages?"

"They are," said Vanos scratching the side of his jutting nose.

"If you can get a message to a friend of mine in Greenshire, there's a gold in it for you. He's been expecting us, but I need to tell him that we've been delayed."

Vanos face brightened considerably. He had gone from thinking himself dead, to being paid a considerable sum for his services in the matter of a few minutes. "I can do it," he said eagerly.

"Good. Sheesa will write out a message for you to send tomorrow." Lothar turned and stumbled over a chair that he hadn't seen. He cursed as he located the dim form of the seat, and scooted it into a position where he could sit.

Vanose watched him with curiosity. Finally he couldn't contain himself. "Is he blind?" he whispered to Sheesa.

"Blind, but not deaf," answered Lothar with a growl. "But not so blind that I couldn't find you with the edge of my axe should you fail to keep your mouth shut."

Vanose glanced from the glowering face of the warrior to the fair-skinned Sheesa.

"He speaks true," said Sheesa, without a smile touching her lips. "There is no better friend to have than Lothar...and there is no worse enemy."

* * * *

The next few days Lothar and Sheesa spent their time purchasing supplies for their flight from Bathos. Lothar was able to grope his way around the city, but he was increasingly marked by sharp-eyed thieves and ruffians who realized that his vision was impaired, and thought him an easy target. At least twice he fought off attempts to pick his pouch, and another time split a ruffian's skull open when the mugger tried to waylay him in an alleyway.

Though their store of supplies beneath the tower of Kolthos were growing, sadly, Lothar's eyesight had improved little during the intervening days. Still, Lothar and Sheesa resolved to go ahead with their plan to slip out of Bathos and seek-out Milos, a farmer whose life Lothar had once saved deep in the tombs of the ancient kings. Though they had been fortunate enough to avoid detection by the squads of guild enforcers that swept the city streets, they realized that their luck would not hold out indefinitely, and that if they stayed in the tower for too long they would eventually be discovered.

Vanose crept in and out of the tower to feed his birds, and sometimes to send a message away or receive one from a returning pigeon. The Emperor had banned carrier pigeons so that he was the only source of information going in or out of the city, and so Vanose did a brisk black market business sending messages without the consent of Emperor Vlad. If he were discovered, of course, the penalty would be death by drawing and quartering.

The ghost of Kolthos had not shown himself during Lothar and Sheesa's stay, and they both began to wonder if maybe the overactive imagination of Vanose had been responsible for the sighting, and Sheesa began to tease Vanose- who, no matter what imprecations she might tease him with, soberly shook his head, and attested to the fact that he had seen the wizard's shade within the very room they sat.

All that remained to be purchased for their impending departure was a good pair of draft horses, and confident that his eyesight was at least good enough to lead them back to the tower, Lothar set out down Brack Street, striding between rows of stone buildings, their jutting garrets crawling with ivy, as the brilliant red sun sank, painting the sky with gold and pink.

He reached the five-way intersection at Equine Crossing, where green-cankered roofs of copper gave way to stone stables roofed with slate hewn from the quarries across the Tiber River. Now the sun sank behind the distant horizon, long fingers of roseate light clawing futilely at the sky.

Lothar halted at a wedge-shaped stable, which was closed up tightly against the impending night, and the robbers and killers that would soon be openly roaming the streets. He rapped sharply on the metal-wrapped door, and finally a small hatch the size of a fist opened up at about eye level. Because of the shadows within, Lothar couldn't see the face of the man who peered out the hatch, but he had done business here before.

"Elgin, I need to buy a pair of draft horses."

Elgin grunted incomprehensibly. "It's getting late. Come back tomorrow. Besides, didn't I just sell you two draft horses not more than three weeks ago?"

"I was robbed," said Lothar. "Let me in and I'll make it worth your while."

Elgin groaned his acquiescence and his thick fingers fumbled with the bolt at the door. "If I'm not careful, I'll end up being robbed, too."

Elgin opened up the door and let Lothar slip inside. While he did he glanced out at the shadow-eclipsed streets, the umbra of night slowly creeping, and lengthening its dark fingers as the sun sank. A frown creased Elgin's thick, ruddy face, and his jowls drooped, then he shut the door tightly and shot the bolt.

"Did you know that you're being followed?"

Lothar spat a curse. "How many?"

"Two. They're hanging around in Stink Alley, about a block back from here. I'm surprised you didn't notice them."

Lothar looked at Elgin's blurry visage. "Unfortunately, my eye sight isn't what it used to be."

"How's that?" asked Elgin.

"I got some acid in my eyes."

"An Assassins Guild concoction?" asked Elgin, referring to one of the Guild's tactics of blinding their opponent with acid before going in for an easy kill.

"No, digestive acid," said Lothar without further explanation. "Show me your best draft horses, and don't try to take advantage of my condition. I know where you live."

Elgin clapped a hand to his chest. "Me?" he said, pretending to be hurt by the comment.

"Do you see anybody else here?"

In ten minutes, Lothar had picked out a pair of horses. He used his hands to check the muscle tone of the animals. Admittedly, he was not an expert with horses, but he could tell a sick or unfit animal when he saw one- or in this case, felt one. He paid Elgin ten pieces of gold for the privilege and slipped out the narrow gap in the stable door, which the horse trader quickly closed and locked. "Good luck," he said. "And if you ever get robbed again, you know where to come."

"Right," answered Lothar sourly. He was down to a half dozen pieces of gold, and that wasn't much to be starting a new life with- not after all the money that he had seen slip through his hands over the years- most of it taxed away by the guilds and by the Emperor, and some of it lost in dice games, or spent on women who loved him until his money ran out.

He casually glanced at the road behind him, but in the deepening gloom he could see nothing but empty street, and the glowering windows of over-hanging garrets that flickered with newly lit lanterns and candles. Still, he knew they were there. Perhaps he could outrun them on horseback. Both of the horses were caparisoned with reins, and harnesses, but his plan had been to use them to pull a cart, so they wore no saddles.

Lothar was no horseman, but he managed to grab a handful of mane and pull himself onto the back of the largest horse. The beast moved uneasily beneath the warrior thief, and snorted apprehensively. Lothar leaned forward and patted the beast on its corded neck, and muttered a few words in a reas-suring tone.

The horse ceased its nervous shuffle on the cobblestones, and Lothar glanced behind. The second horse stood a few feet off, Lothar still holding the reins to this equine in his hand. Beyond that, down the darkening streets and somber gray walls thick with shadows, he could see no sign of his pursuers, but as he caught his breath he could hear the shuffle of footsteps coming up the road, and heard the muffled slap of a scabbard against leather breeches, and heard the growl of a hound.

There were hounds with the men in the shadows! He couldn't see them, but he knew that they were coming for him. As he was about to spur the horses forward, an unearthly howl rebounded from the stone walls of the ancient buildings that lined the street. The howl chilled Lothar to the bone, its keen note cutting at his eardrums and making him grit his teeth in pain. This was not the howl of a normal hound. Only once before had Lothar heard such a howling- the night that he and three fellow thieves had raided the gold-limned mansions of Koard Quatl, and unearthed his treasure hoards from the coffers within. Surely, this was the howl of the Infernal Hounds; sorcerously imbued with supernatural scent and speed, equipped with razor talons, and teeth that could tear a man limb from limb. That night in the courtyards of Koard Quatl they had ripped apart his three brave comrades, and only he had escaped with his life. Since that fateful evening he had managed to avoid another encounter with the beasts, but now he had provoked the wrath of the Guilds by breaking the contracts and oaths that bound him until the end of time, and declaring them null and void because time had indeed ended when the Clock of Pentaz had struck its final and deadly notes the night he had been blinded by the demon Mahmackrah.

 Sharp fear stabbed at Lothar's chest as he dug his heels into the flank of his steed and urged the animal on. It leaped forward and began to gallop down Onwall Street. Pulled by its lead, the second horse followed along, its iron shod hooves throwing a sharp clatter against the steep walls around.

Behind him he could hear the cries of the dog handler as he loosed the Infernal Hounds. "Kill!"

The pair of hounds unleashed yet another horrible chorus of howls as they burst down the streets, their sleek black forms streaking through the falling shadows like fleeting nightmares.

Lothar didn't know how long the horses could stay ahead of their supernatural pursuers, but the chilling howls of the beasts drove them into a frenzy of fear, and they began to gallop wildly down the street. Lothar was forced to let go the lead of the second draft horse as the steed jerked and tugged at the line, his nostrils flaring, and his eyes wide with abject terror, his mane tossing behind him as he sped crazed down the narrow road.

To stay astride of his own horse, Lothar leaned low over the beast's neck and held on with all of his strength. Several times the horse's wild flight lifted Lothar from the beast's back, and only his tight grip on the harness of the steed kept him from flying off and tumbling down the cobblestones. Already the horse was beginning to lather, its side heaving as much in fear as from the exertions of its flight.

Ahead, Lothar could make out a stone arch that crossed over Onwall Street, and beyond that the bright glow of lantern light, through which shifted the dark masses of the crowds of Bathos' citizens going about their evening business in Market Square.

Heedless of any human impediment, his horse plunged onward, snorting and heaving as it broke through the ranks of the Square's crowds, scattering merchant and patron before his frothing bulk. The horse carried away tent poles, and crushed displays, sending miniature pears rolling before it, and dragging a rainbow colored awning behind.

In hot pursuit, the snarling pair of infernal hounds bounded through the crowds, leaping across fallen bodies and snapping at man, woman, or child who unintentionally wandered into their path. They wound through the crowd with supernatural speed, ever closing the distance between they and their quarry.

Lothar hazarded a glance backward and saw that in moments the beasts would be upon the horse. He didn't know whether the infernal hounds were on the scent of the horse or on his own scent, but he decided to take a gamble in the hopes that the hounds would continue to pursue his horse. In the chaos of the crowd, he slipped from the back of his steed, and to the cobbles of Merchants Square, immediately sliding into the panicking crowd in an attempt to put some distance between his horse and himself.

A few moments later the infernal hounds came skidding to a halt at the same spot where Lothar had left his horse's back, and they turned, their baleful eyes flashing, and knife-like incisors gnashing as they slavered in anticipation of their kill. They caught the divergent scents, and turned to plunge into the crowd after the fleeing warrior.

Lothar turned and could see the sleek black heads bobbing among the parting crowd as the hounds leaped after him, drool splaying from their dark lips. Women screamed, some fainting away, others scooping up their children out of harm's way, yet others abandoning their progeny to the infernal hounds, which ignored them, blind to all but their prey.

Fighting his way through the crowds, Lothar realized that his flight would prove hopeless. There was little reason to believe that he could outrun the hounds even if his eyesight were working at full capacity. He crossed beneath the red awning of a basket maker, whose booth was flanked by two glass-paneled lanterns of brass. As he passed by, Lothar snatched up one of these lanterns, the oil in the brass cistern sloshing and the flame rising higher. He found his flight suddenly halted by a stone wall carved with somber figures of horned gods, which loomed over him, maliciously staring down with dead stone eyes. Given some time, perhaps he might have been able to scale the statues, but the infernal hounds were gnashing at his heels, and he knew that time was something of which he didn't have the luxury.

Lothar turned and put his back against one of the titanic sculptures of Dagon and made his stand in front of the temple. He remembered how these hounds had ripped apart his friends; moving with deceptive speed they had lunged at their throats and tore them out in the blink of an eye. Even now, Lothar could see the dark blurs of the dogs as they streaked through the crowds. The speed with which they moved was supernatural, and he realized that if he moved to block the hounds' attacks he would need to strike abnormally early.

He hurled the oil lamp as the first dog approached and it arced through the air, striking the paving stones of the street immediately ahead of the racing dog. The glass shattered and flaming oil spilled and splattered. Lothar had been hoping to hit the dog directly, but his aim had been poor.

The dog leaped through the yellow tongues of flame, scarcely noticing them as they licked at his gleaming black fur. Before Lothar thought the first dog was possibly within leaping range he lifted his battle axe and swung- even then his attack was nearly too late. At the moment his axe struck, he could feel the foul breath of the infernal hound hot against his throat, and the flecks of saliva as they splattered on his face. The keen blade of the axe bit into the hindquarters of the infernal beast, and knocked it away before the razor incisors could clamp shut on Lothar's throat.

The infernal hound howled as it went to the ground, dark, bubbling blood spreading in thick pools across the dirty cobblestones. The dog snapped viciously at Lothar's booted ankles, but Lothar stepped away as he launched an attack at the second hound, which was already coiling its wiry thews beneath it to spring at the warrior's neck.

Still recovering his ready stance from the first blow, Lothar was unable to fully bring the axe into position. Instead he raised the pointed spike mounted atop the axe's haft, in an attempt to fend of the hound. The point plunged into the chest of the dog as it sprang, and Lothar used his strength to hurl the beast to the ground. Even then, the wound was not enough to keep the dog down, and as soon as it struck the cobblestones it scrabbled to its feet, razor claws clicking on the street.

Lothar didn't give the beast any time to launch another attack, he immediately brought his axe down on the dog, splitting its narrow skull to the vicious teeth set inside the slavering mouth. Dark blood spattered, and Lothar cursed as he felt sharp teeth rip through the thick leather of his boot.

He turned and saw that the first dog had dragged itself up behind him by its forelegs and clamped its teeth into his ankle. Lothar plunged the point of his axe down into the body three times, until the grinding of teeth ceased, and still he had to lean down and pry the vice-like jaws away from his boots.

Once the jaws of the beast had been pulled away Lothar examined his tattered boot, and saw where the teeth had sunk into his flesh. He was bleeding, but not profusely, and he realized that his thick boots had saved him from having his foot torn completely away from his leg.

Around him, Lothar could hear the crowd's exclamations.

"Those be infernal hounds," exclaimed a cracked an aging voice. "No one has ever slain an infernal hound, let alone two of them!"

Many hustled away from the gory scene, not wanting to become involved in what they feared was a feud between wizard and warrior, but others pressed forward to take their place, anxious to see history being made in front of their very own eyes. Lothar couldn't see the expressions on their faces, and he feared that the dog handlers might be coming shortly. In the crowd, Lothar wouldn't be able to tell the difference between foe and bystander. He would be at the mercy of his enemies.

Using climbing skills honed by a hundred different burglaries, Lothar turned and began to climb the statue of Dagon, his dripping axe now sheathed safely across his back. He was having some difficulty picking out handholds by sight, so his progress was slowed as he ran his free hand across the face of the carving until he could find a grip to pull himself upward.

Climbing the tangled beard of Dagon, he reached the shoulder, and now found the going a bit easier. He reached up and took hold of the god's horn and pulled himself onto the curving stone saddle. Above him was the awning of the temple, which protruded to form a roof over the carven gods. The stone of the awning was ornate with symbols and effigies, and Lothar found easy hand holds as he reached up to pull himself onto the roof.

Thirty feet below him, he heard the rattle of armour and the tremor of sword blades as they were pulled from their sheaths. A deep voice boomed up toward him.

"In the name of the Warriors Guild, I demand that you descend and surrender your blade!"

As Lothar tightened his grip on the awning, he turned his head and found that a squad of warriors had gathered beneath, lamp light reflecting from their burnished cuirasses. At the head of them was a burly man who towered over the rest, and he called up to Lothar again and repeated his demand.

Lothar couldn't see well enough to make out the warrior's features, but he could see the top knot, and the shape of the peg that replaced the man's missing left leg below the knee. Now Lothar realized who was addressing him- none other than the third in command of the Warriors Guild, Jotham. The man whose leg he had, himself, taken in a bloody encounter with enforcers from both the Thieves and Warriors Guilds.

Lothar had shown Jotham mercy that fateful afternoon, and had bound the warrior's severed leg to keep him from bleeding to death, but he knew that he could not expect such mercy in return. Jotham had since risen in the ranks of the Warriors Guild, and had oaths to uphold.

"I'm no longer beholden to the Warriors Guild," shouted Lothar. "I've fulfilled my oath; the Clock of Pentaz has witnessed to that."

A sprinkling of cheers rose from among the spectators in Market Square.

Jotham frowned as his squadron of warriors lifted their spears and cocked their arms back, awaiting for the command to strike. "Come down now, and perhaps we can find a peaceful resolution to our differences."

"The Guild has ordered me dead," said Lothar. "You know that."

"I do," said Jotham, "but if you'll renew your oath to the Guild I may be able to persuade them to countermand that order."

Lothar shook his head, long raven hair stringing out around his chiseled features. "I appreciate what you're doing," said Lothar, "but I'm afraid we may be forced to cross swords yet again. I'm not going back to the Guild!"

So saying, Lothar swung his body upward and hooked his legs over the top of the stone awning.

Jotham's brow furrowed deep, and torchlight reflected from his shining bald pate. He had attempted to be merciful, but Lothar left him with little choice. "Spears!" he ordered.

Immediately ten spears went into the air, but only a few were thrown with enough force to reach Lothar high overhead, and those that did, glanced away from the awning- missing the escaping warrior as he rolled onto the roof top and leaped through the gaps in the crenels above.

At each corner of the temple, the female avatars of Dagon stood watch, their stone wings furled around their voluptuously carved bodies, and each holding a stone scimitar at the ready. Though of marvelous artisanship, Lothar didn't have the time or eyesight to appreciate the intricacies of the stone statues. The roof top was set up with defense in mind, and he didn't figure that it would be long before the priests of Dagon heard about the commotion outside their temple and let Jotham and the Warriors Guild through the temple and up to the roof where they could eliminate the intruder.

Peering through the haze of his wounded eyes Lothar studied the roof top, pacing across it until he found a stone slab set with a large iron ring. Lothar figured that the slab must weigh at least a ton. Probably within the temple there was a counterweight mechanism, which would allow them to move the stone aside and give them easy access to the roof.

It was important that Lothar find someway to keep his enemies from gaining access to the roof. Jotham wasn't stupid, and Lothar was sure that, even now, the Warriors Guild commander was having his men surround the temple. He would send a runner to get reinforcements from the Warriors Guild, and then they would try to gain the roof through the temple of Dagon.

For a counterweight system to work, Lothar knew that the stone had to have somewhere to slide. He knelt down and thrust his fingers into the gap around the edges of the slab. On the long sides of the stone the fit was nearly flush, but on the short sides there was a sizeable gap, and a cavernous space. By shoving something between the slab and the channels where it was supposed to slide, Lothar figured that he might be able to jam the mechanism and effectively lock the slab in place. He plucked two hand axes from his bandolier and thrust them into the gaps along the short sides of the slab. They didn't entirely fit, so Lothar used the flat of his battle axe to pound them home, firmly entrenching them in the gap.

Satisfied with his handiwork, he stood and walked to the perimeter of the building. He looked down among the gathering crowds, and upon Merchant's Square, which was aflood with torchlight. Overhead, a half moon rose in the misty sky, and Lothar felt a surge of fatalism pass through him. He was going to sell his life dearly tonight.

The temple of Dagon stood separated from all other buildings by a space of at least twenty yards, but as he looked at the sloped rooftops of the structures around he thought that he saw furtive figures moving about in the turrets and gable windows. His enemies were gathering. If they couldn't meet him face to face, they would be more than happy to shoot him down from afar.

Lothar could see the glitter of armour worn by sentries posted around the temple, yet he could not pick Jotham out of the crowd. His eyes were only good for recognizing shapes, and not distinguishing details. From a distance there would be no way for him to make out Jotham's top knot and peg leg.

Lothar settled with his back against the avatar in the northeast corner of the building, cradling his battleaxe in front of him. The night air was brisk, and he thought of the ragged cloak, which he had given away to a beggar. It had been obvious that the hounds had his scent this evening, and he wondered what had become of the beggar who had been wrapped in a cloak that carried a scent, which was being hunted by infernal hounds. His act of kindness, might have inadvertently resulted in a man's death.

Lothar closed his straining eyes, and reached out with his other senses. He listened to the rumble of the crowd below, and to the sound of Dagon's priests as they attempted to use their ropes and pulleys to open the jammed slab. He smelled the scent of cooked pork drifting up from the square. It wasn't enough to mask the underlying stench of Bathos- an odor so pervasive that he rarely noticed it any longer. The scent of the crimson lotus wafted to his nostrils, subtle but unmistakable.

His eyes blinked wide open, and his body tensed for action- his knuckles white upon the haft of his bloodied axe.

"Sedrah!" he hissed.

She approached across the roof top, veiled in darkness, her hair trailing behind her in gossamer confusion. Her long stiletto blade was unsheathed.

"Quiet!" she whispered.

"You want to kill me silently?" growled Lothar.

"Are we friends?" she asked as she drew nearer.

"I once thought so," answered Lothar, a sneer forming on his full lips.

"I'm not here to slay you, I'm here to help you."

Lothar's brow furrowed. "Then I'm afraid that my friendship will be something that you take to your grave. I'm guessing that there are two score men waiting out there to take me down."

"Closer to a hundred," answered Sedrah. "With more on their way."

"Thieves and warriors?"

"And assassins. I'm not the only one that they've sent."

"This is a bad time for you to have a change of heart," said Lothar. "Mayhap you should reconsider."

She shook her head and licked her crimson lips. "If I can climb up here so can others. How did you manage to kill two infernal hounds while you're half blind?"

"Sheer luck," said Lothar. "Did you see Jotham in the crowd?"

Sedrah shrugged. "I don't know who you mean."

"He's the headman for the Warriors Guild- top knot, peg leg."

Recognition sparked in Sedrah's dusky blue eyes. "He's ordered archers into the gables around the temple."

"Have you got anything that we can use against them?"

"You really are blind, aren't you?"

Sedrah removed a crossbow from her back and placed it on the rooftop between them, then she unwrapped a cloth and revealed a quiver that held forty double-headed bolts.

"How is your aim?" asked Lothar.

"I've been practicing," she said.

Lothar smoothly drew back the cable of the crossbow and laid a bolt in the groove. He handed the crossbow to Sedrah and motioned behind him, past the avatar and at the windowed gable of a nearby tannery. "I thought I saw something moving about in there earlier. You want to take a shot?"

Sedrah squeezed up alongside of Lothar behind the stone avatar and carefully sighted the crossbow at the center of the window, which shutters were now wide open. She aimed low so that the bolt would slice through the window just above the sill. The blonde assassin eased back the trigger, and the cable snapped forward, pushing the bolt through the air faster than the eye could follow.

There was a short cry from the dark interior as a crossbowmen pitched backward with a bolt in his skull.

"Did you get him?" asked Lothar.

"I hit something," she said grimly. "And if it was just a wounding I think we'd still be hearing the screams."

"Sedrah," said Lothar. "We're going to make them rue the day they ever heard of us."

As though his words were a signal for their enemy to attack, a chorus of shouts went up, and a dozen dark figures slipped over the edge of the eaves. Preceding their charge came a hail storm of arrows. Bow strings snapped in turreted rooms and windowed gables. Shafts snapped against the gracefully arched spine of the avatar by which Lothar and Sedrah crouched, and a half dozen other shafts flew thick but missed their shadowy targets.

"They're shooting blind!" criticized Sedrah.

"Just the same way that I'll be fighting," shouted Lothar. "Get in among them so they can't use their archers without hitting their own men!"

A couple arrow shafts drove through the air, one tugging at his pants as Lothar charged across the stone rooftop of Dagon's temple. Then, in an instant, he was at the opposite edge of the roof, where a host of thief enforcers were scrambling over the edge of the overhang- some of them pausing to affix rope lines and grapples to ease the climb of the next wave, while others leaped to meet their prey.

Sedrah did not join Lothar in his headlong charge. She paused at the avatar, putting her back to it as she put her foot in the stirrup of the crossbow and cocked the cable back. Lothar had drawn the cable back with only the strength of his arms, but she didn't have that kind of power in her torso, and resorted to the more standard way of cocking the weapon.

As Lothar ran across the top of the building she watched the crossfire of arrows and bolts with great interest, picking out the spots where many of the missiles had originated. Now she took careful aim and began to pick off the archers and crossbowmen that had carelessly cast aside their concealment once their target had exposed himself. They stood in dark garrets with arms quivering, their bowstrings drawn back waiting for an open shot at the dark figure that plunged into the line of thief enforcers and began hacking them to pieces. The axe blade dipped up and down, hewing through the enforcer ranks.

Sedrah carefully aimed and sent a bolt plunging through the side of a gnarled archer standing in a shadowed garret. His arrow loosed, breaking against a stone crenel atop the temple of Dagon, and his stout body pitched from the window and down the green copper leaves that roofed the steep pitch of the building.

Immediately Sedrah lowered the crossbow and put her left foot in the stirrup as she arched her back to pull back the cable.

Meanwhile, Lothar found himself in the thick of things. His charge had kept the thief enforcers from forming a solid line, and he hewed into them before they were ready, cutting down a half dozen of them in the space of seconds. There was little subtlety to his attack. He could not see them well enough to interpret the subtle hints that indicated from which direction an attack might come. He watched the posture of their shapes, and the gleam of reflected moonlight from their weapons- shifting his stance to avoid their attacks, or attacking first.

In a moment he was through the ragged line, and chopped down two thieves attempting to pass through the gapped teeth of the temple's crenels and onto the roof. As he stepped on to the stone eaves, an arrow whisked past him and struck a thief who was bent over, affixing a grappling hook. The thief toppled from the eaves and plummeted thirty feet to the cobblestones below, landing on his skull with a sickening thud.

Lothar didn't know whether the shaft had been aimed by Sedrah or by a misguided foe, but he didn't pause to find out. He worked his way along the eaves, cutting down the thieves that clung there, burdens of coiled rope weighing them down as they attempted to pull themselves onto the roof.

A wiry thief attached a grappling hook, and as he tightened the rope Lothar sliced through his arm at the shoulder, and kicked him, flailing, to Merchant's Square below. The crowd below was in a frenzy, cheering and cursing at the turn the fight had taken. They were hungry for blood, and

Lothar was merely whetting their appetite for the slaughter to come.

The final enforcer didn't bother fastening his grapple, and instead whirled the three-pronged hook around his head, swinging it on the rope line to which it was attached. Lothar didn't see it coming out of the corner of his eye, and the claws raked him across the cheek leaving three bloody lines.

The warrior-thief grimaced, but the wound was minor, and he couldn't complain. He had mowed through eleven foes armed with swords and knives, and came through without a scratch. Things were bound to get worse.

The enforcer was emboldened by his success, and thought to repeat the same tactic that had drawn blood from his foe. Lothar raised his axe as the grappling line swung around again, interposing it between himself and the rope. The line wrapped around the head and shaft of the axe, and Lothar yanked the rope free of the thief's grip. As the enforcer reached for his short sword, Lothar leaped across the intervening gap and skewered the man on the spiked haft of his axe.

He lifted the thief into the air as though he were a wriggling worm, and then cast him from the spike of his axe to the square below. Even as the body left his axe, two shafts slipped from a nearby cupola with narrow windows cut into its onyx-tiled walls. One arrow broke against the blade of his axe, and the second slipped by him, scoring his shoulder with a crimson cut.

Lothar quickly leaped behind the nearest crenel, dragging the rope and grapple with him. He crouched down behind the stonework, and began to unwrap the line that tangled his axe. He knew that half dozen ropes had been secured to the roof's edge, and that even as he crouched here under cover that more Thieves Guild enforcers were swarming up the lines.

If he leaped out and began cutting the ropes he would likely be skewered by arrows from the cupola. If he stayed put, he would soon be surrounded by another wave of enforcers. This time he wouldn't have surprise on his side; with the cover of the archers the thieves could easily outflank and cut him to bits.

Lothar had nearly resolved to rush out and try to cut the lines, when he heard the snap of a crossbow. Sedrah was crouched on the rooftop, her crossbow still steady as a bolt left it and streaked through the right window of the cupola, and cut through the archer hiding behind.

There was a horrible groan, and Lothar saw a bloody hand suddenly protruding from the window, an unfired arrow hanging in the limp, dying grip.

Immediately the second archer in the cupola returned fire, his hastily fired arrow narrowly missing Sedrah, and skimming along the stone-laid roof top.

Lothar had one final throwing axe in his harness and he slipped it out of its leather loop. He could see the shadowy bulk of the cupola, and that an arrow had been fired from a dark crevice within that bulk; that crevice was his target. The throw was nearly thirty yards long, and Lothar would be attempting the cast with three pounds worth of axe; but he attempted it just the same.

The double-bladed hatchet arced into the air, and spinning, it descended through the dark crevice of the cupola's window. Lothar heard a meaty thud and the bellow of pain that followed.

Sedrah raised herself from behind the adjacent crenel, her narrow blade rasping as she summoned it from its sheath. "Nice throw for a blind man!"

Lothar grinned maliciously as he threw himself out on the eaves. He stooped and withdrew a long knife from his tattered and bloody boot, and peered over the edge of the ornate roof. A half dozen lines each held two or three thief enforcers who hauled themselves up the rope hand over hand, grabbing the rope between their feet so they wouldn't slip back down.

The blinded warrior didn't wait until the thieves were close enough for him to make out the features of their faces. He assumed that their intentions were malign, and put the sharp edge of his knife to the first rope. It cut through the hemp strands as if they were gossamer cobwebs, and though he couldn't see the fear in their eyes, he could hear the fear in their cries as they plummeted to the square, careening from the one of the idols of Dagon that decorated the temple walls.

Without waiting to see the final results, Lothar leaped to a second line and cut it loose. Already, Sedrah had moved to the opposite end of the roof and was making her way down the line, cutting the ropes with the tip of her stiletto blade as she strode cat-like along the eaves.

They met in the middle, a line of carnage spreading out below them on the cobbles of Merchant's Square; broken bones and necks, twisted limbs, shattered skulls, and if a thief were lucky only a sprained ankle or a few bruises.

An arrow shaft passed through Sedrah's flowing blonde hair, just missing her neck as it plunged on into the darkness.

"We've still got snipers in the lofts!" called Lothar. As he ducked down an arrow shattered against a nearby crenel and several splinters struck Lothar in his blood-splattered hand.

Sedrah ran low after Lothar and took the outside of the adjacent crenel. "Our luck isn't going to hold out forever," she said. "Look!"

Below in the courtyard a mass of warrior's had gathered. Many of them carried bows, and even now they raised them, sighting in on the two figures crouched on the eaves.

Lothar couldn't actually see what Sedrah was gesturing at, but he guessed by the tone of her voice, and ducked to the other side of his crenel even as Sedrah slipped to the other side of one. Immediately an archer on the west side of the temple fired from the dark window of a storehouse, and the shaft passed completely through Lothar's left forearm.

Sedrah laid another bolt in her crossbow and fired back, the bolt ripping through the gut of the archer who had fired on Lothar, collapsing him into a writhing, screaming heap.

Lothar gasped and grabbed at his arm in attempt to staunch the free flowing blood. A hail of arrows arched up over them like birds in flight, then came down, scattering themselves across the hard rooftop of Dagon's temple. The avatars of Dagon still stood proud and impassive, splintered arrows hanging from their stone wings.

Sedrah came to Lothar's side and applied pressure to his wound until the bleeding slowed. "They'll be coming up the other side now," she said. "First the assassins, and then the warriors."

As Sedrah bound his wound with a handkerchief, Lothar shook his head. "You're still unwounded, why don't you see if you can make an escape?"

The assassin smiled wryly. "It's a little late for that now. We're completely surrounded."

Lothar grabbed the assassin's wrist in his bloody hand. "I want to thank you while I still can. What better friend can their be than someone that will give their life for another?"

Sedrah smiled softly. "At least I die with honor."

She glanced to the west edge of the temple roof, and saw dark forms emerging over the eaves. "It looks like we have more visitors."

Lothar's dark eyes flashed. "Let's give them something to remember."

They ran low across the building top, unwilling to present a target to the archers who remained below. Fortunately, it appeared as though they had been ordered to cease fire because of their allies who had climbed the opposite end of the building.

Lothar grimaced as he wrapped his left hand around the haft of his battle axe. Intense pain shot through his arm every time he tried to manipulate his fingers. He was blind and wounded, but he was determined to go down swinging.

Balzac stood casually awaiting them, swinging two swords in front of him as though he were cutting at imaginary blades of grass growing from the temple roof. His nose was upturned and his mouth turned in a perpetual smirk. He was little larger than a ten-year-old boy, but he had a reputation for lightening quickness, fighting with a blade in each hand, and delivering deadly accurate strokes all the same. Sedrah did not dare ignore dismiss these stories out of hand.

Flanking Balzac to the right, just a few paces behind was the flat, stubbled head of Kayne, who tested the edge of his scimitar with a callused thumb while watching Lothar with hate-inflamed eyes, slowly licking his dry, thick lips.

To the left was a large man wearing the heavy leather gloves of a dog handler. His craggy skull was lowered, sinister light gleaming from red-rimmed eyes beneath his heavy brow. In his glove he held a whip braided into nine tentacles, each laced with bits of glass and metal to make its bite more painful.

Lothar did not recognize the men that stood before them, and Sedrah whispered a few words to him, and he nodded as she informed him whom they faced, and what weapons they bore.

"So," said Balzac. "I see that you've taken up with yet another courtesan. You're appetites are astounding!"

Lothar's left arm throbbed with intense pain, but he bit it back and concentrated on the enemy at hand. He had no idea how he was going to compensate for Balzac's amazing speed and ambidexterity when he could scarcely see his outline on the rooftop. He knew that Sedrah was good with her blade, but he wondered if she would prove fast enough against such a skilled and unscrupulous foe.

"Are you here to talk, or are you here to fight, whelp?"

Still gripping a straight blade, Balzac raised a slender hand to his chest in mock indignation. "Why your words wound me! Of course, I'm here to fight- but before we kill you both I want you to be informed of the indignities, which your corpses will suffer after your death."

Lothar strode steadily forward as Balzac launched into a perverse tirade. Balzac loved to talk, but there was an ulterior motive- he was trying to delay he and Sedrah long enough for reinforcements to arrive. For all his brash talk Balzac didn't want to go up against the two of them until he had the clear advantage- in numbers and overwhelming force.

Sedrah broke off to the left as Lothar moved to the right. Balzac immediately saw that they were attempting to outflank his trio, and he side-stepped so that he and Kayne were moving directly toward Sedrah. This left Lothar facing the dog-trainer, Procktar, alone. Either Kayne figured that Procktar could hold his own, or he didn't care and planned to double team Sedrah, and take her down quickly enough that he and Kayne might turn and slay Lothar.

Without breaking stride, Sedrah slipped her narrow blade back into the scabbard at her side and reached over her shoulder, leveling an already cocked and loaded crossbow at Kayne who had moved ahead of Balzac to within a couple paces of sword reach. The crossbow vibrated in her hands as the bolt left its runnel and tore through Kayne's heart.

Suddenly the hatred left Kayne's eyes, changing to blank dismay as he sank to his knees, clutching at the spurting hole in his chest.

With quickness so incredible that it was difficult for the eye to follow, Balzac slipped forward to press his attack and take advantage of Sedrah's weaponless state. Sedrah thrust her empty crossbow outward, pushing the oak bow of the weapon against the outstretched blades of her diminutive foe. This bought her a fraction of a second, and even as she abandoned the crossbow her sword licked out to ward off the flurry of attacks, which Balzac made against her.

Lothar hadn't seen Kayne's unexpectedly quick death, and he figured that he needed to take out the dog handler quickly in order to even the odds and help Sedrah ward off her multiple attackers. He realized that, as painful as the dog-handler's cat of nine tails might be, the whip was not a lethal weapon unless he was lashed a few dozen times. Lothar resolved to rush the large man and put him out of his misery before he could get off more than a few lashes with his whip.

Procktar, however, seemed blinded to the deficiencies of his weapon. Tears rolled down his cheek as he raised his whip with one mighty arm. "You killed my hounds!" he bellowed out in rage.

Lothar lashed out with his axe and took off Procktar's descending arm at the elbow- before the metal-braided lashes could even touch him.

"Join them in hell," muttered Lothar as the second stroke of his axe sheered through the dog-handler's ribs and slew Procktar.

The dark-haired warrior wrenched his axe-blade free with his right hand, his injured left arm momentarily spasming in pain as it recovered from the shock of the two blows. Lifting his weapon before him, Lothar crossed the roof top to where Balzac and Sedrah were engaged in frantic swordplay. Their blades rang against each other with fierce abandon, and Sedrah appeared to be holding her own, but her tanned flesh already showed crimson where Balzac's deadly blades had scored hits.

Lothar tried to move silently up behind Balzac, but as if the agile killer possessed some sort of sixth sense he glanced back in time to see the raven-haired warrior towering over him, axe raised. He swung around to meet this new attack, but faltered when Sedrah drove her blade through his side. Lothar finished the job by splitting Balzac's skull.

The warrior shook the gray and crimson gore from his axe, while the blonde assassin wiped the blood from her narrow blade on Balzac's corpse.

"I'd say that Bathos is a better place for being rid of this scum," decided Sedrah out loud, but Lothar was not there to hear her. He slipped to the edge of the temple behind the avatar at the northwest corner and saw that a long ladder had been placed against the cornice of the fluted column at the roof's edge. Already a half dozen warriors were scrambling up the ladder, and along the edge of the building, Lothar could make out the vague outlines of at least three more ladders, swarming with the bulky forms of members of the Warriors Guild. Even now, a scarred hand was pulling at the highest rung.

Lothar threw himself against the stone avatar that rose at the building's corner. Exerting all his strength he pushed at the statue's curved backside, his powerful legs shoving until the winged messenger of Dagon toppled suddenly, crushing the top most warrior, and breaking into three sections, that carried away a string of climbers, and snapped the ladder in half as though it were a twig.

The screams and cries of the fallen warriors echoed up to him as Lothar sprinted along the eaves, the adrenaline of battle easing the twinge in his calf where the infernal hound had bitten him, and allowing him to function despite the agony in his left forearm. Before he could reach the next ladder warriors leaped onto the stone eaves.

There was a rushing like the wind, and quick footsteps to his left, and Lothar heard Sedrah's voice crying out to him that it was she and not an enemy approaching. Side by side they engaged the growing enemy phalanx. Employing every trick of the blade that she knew, Sedrah fought deadly and cool- her blade slipping in with subtle stealth, again and again, to run a warrior through at the arm, leg, throat, or breast.

Though lacking the subtlety of the sword, Lothar wielded his axe with a bloody finesse that the ancient streets of Bathos had seen only few times before. He fought against dark shapes illumined by the rising half-orb of the yellow moon, his blade cleaving limb and skull, breaking sword and shield before him, and driving screaming warriors back over the edge of the eaves to tumble to the sharp cobbles below. If his sight had been fully healed, he might have recognized the faces of many guild members that he had fought alongside in times past- brothers of the blade with whom he had once sworn his allegiance. Perhaps fate had spared him the sight of so many of his brethren falling beneath his axe.

Lothar and Sedrah worked their way down the edge of the overhang, slaying until they reached a ladder, which they hurled down before working their way to the next. Almost as quickly as the ladders were thrown down, they were again raised further down the eaves so that Lothar and Sedrah soon became surrounded by foes. They fought back to back, the stones wet with blood beneath their feet, and bodies of the dead and dying heaped around them as though they were some sort of breastwork.

Some of the warriors began dragging away the slain while others came forward with spears passed up to them from below; weapons that could strike from a distance without much risk to the wielder. It was obvious to both Sedrah and Lothar that their stand was coming to an end. They would be taken down with lances, and finished off at close range after they were wounded too badly to resist.

Suddenly, when they thought that all hope was lost, a great commotion arose from the courtyard.

* * * *

Jotham watched the progress of his warriors with grim displeasure as they were hurtled from the roof top of Dagon's temple. Already he had sent close to a hundred men to the top of the temple, and at least half of those now lay in the courtyard- dead or injured. And who knew how many more of his men lay slaughtered on the temple roof? Even now he could see the heaps of bodies by the light of the moon, and the gruesome cries of the wounded and the clash of steel against steel rose a horrible clamor in the night.

He ordered a half dozen leeches to attend to the wounded that were strewn beneath the eaves of the temple, and ordered that long spears be handed up to the warriors above so that they could deal with their foes from a distance. The only archers that he had were on trade from the Archers Guild, and they had been chewed up by the return fire from the female assassin, which had somehow sneaked past their perimeter and joined Lothar on the roof.

According to the Interguild Agreement assassins weren't sanctioned to carry missile weapons within the city unless allowed to do so by special waiver from the Archers Guild- who, of course, never dispensed such a waiver in order that they might better control the price of hiring an archer or crossbow-man. It was far too difficult to get more archers on short notice, and after the Thieves Guild and their cronies had attempted and failed to finish off Lothar and his assassin ally, it had been up to the Warriors Guild.

A warrior on the roof called down to Jotham and reported that the warrior and assassin were surrounded, but not yet subdued. Tired of playing the general, and not being a part of the action, Jotham moved toward the nearest ladder, meaning to climb to the roof despite his peg leg and personally see that the situation was wrapped up as it should be.

It would be a great embarrassment to the Warriors Guild that so many had been killed and injured in the process of taking only a man and a woman, but it would be a greater embarrassment should they fail their com-mission. As Jotham was heading toward the ladder he heard the thunder of horse's hooves in the square behind him, and he spun on his wooden leg in time to see three broad-chested stallions bearing through the ranks of his warrior reserves. Each of the chestnut stallions bore a rider accoutered in black leather mail studded with iron rivets.

The great weight of the horses bore down the unprepared soldiers, trampling them beneath iron-shod hooves. The riders rode low on their horses, swinging bastard swords that cut down unprepared warriors as they turned to face this new enemy. For a moment the horses split, wading in among the ranks of warriors and driving them before the stomping feet. When the warriors had scattered into the far flung corners of Merchants Square the horses recombined and drove straight toward the ladder where Jotham stood.

Though of no great agility, Jotham moved to the outer flank of the leftmost horse, so as not to be subsumed by horse's flesh and trampled beneath the heavy hooves as had a half-dozen of his men. As the rider neared, Jotham went down to one knee and lashed out at the horse's legs with his broadsword.

A bastard sword whistled over his head, carrying a portion of his top knot away with the stroke of the blade, and then the horse stumbled as its forefeet were cut away from beneath him. The horse pitched to the cobbles, hurling its rider before him to be dashed senseless to the ground.

Jotham quickly rose and stepped unevenly across the cobbles. He struck quickly, beheading his fallen foe before his friends could come to his aid. The cries of the horse rose to a fevered pitch as the poor beast thrashed about on its side, stabbing its good hind legs in any direction.

The melee above halted for just a moment at the sound of the commotion below. Lothar took this moment to brush aside a questing spear head, and he leaped into the surrounding enemy, casting about with his axe, and driving them back for one brief moment.

Sedrah followed closely, her razor-honed blade licking out at anyone who tried to close ranks, and leaving them with a sliced forearm or thigh. In one harrowing instant they fought their way free and burst from the wall of warriors that contained them. They sprinted through the teeth of the crenels. Lothar and Sedrah each jumped onto one of the ladders that leaned against the temple eaves, and putting their feet and hands against the outer rails of the ladder, they slid downward, using the leather heels of their boots as brakes when they neared bottom mere seconds later.

No sooner had they reached the Courtyard when the ladders were belatedly thrown down from above; too late to do the climbers harm. They moved aside as the massive wood rails toppled and cracked. The horses whinnied as their riders jockeyed them away from the falling lumber, and Sedrah and Lothar found themselves standing only a few feet away from a pair of horseman, whose mounts stood among the litter of fallen and broken men.

The first of the horseman removed an iron helm revealing a field-darkened, and weather worn face. Sun streaked hair spilled across the rider's broad shoulders. The eyes were bold and frank, and the mouth above the square jaw honest but stern, and Sedrah couldn't help but thinking the man dashing despite the peril of their situation.

The rider examined Sedrah frankly, and he smiled when he saw Lothar standing beside her. "Both of you mount up!" he demanded.

Lothar could see the forms of the horses and riders, but had no idea who was addressing them. "Who are you?"

"Milos! Don't you recognize me, Lothar?"

"The voice sounds familiar," admitted the raven-haired warrior. "I'm not sure why you are here, farmboy, but I'm glad. Give me your hand!"

The slap of a footstep and sharp tap of wood against stone filtered through the mayhem, and Jotham approached through the carnage. "You're not going anywhere," said the one-legged warrior. "You've slain and routed my men, but you'll not leave until you've faced me again. Get your axe ready!"

Milos' face hardened as he saw Jotham. "You were the one that slew my retainer, and you'll face me before you face Lothar!"

Jotham swiveled his bald head on his bull neck, his brown eyes narrowing, and the tendons working beneath the scarred skin of his forearms. "You'll have to wait your turn, son. But once I've disposed of Lothar, I'll be happy to give you a shot."

Sedrah glanced apprehensively at the few remaining ladders. Already warriors were swarming down the rungs. "We don't have time to stay and chat."

Milos' second retainer, a pale-skinned man with pale blue eyes and a broad chest that tapered to a tiny waist leaned over and took Sedrah's hand. In a moment she had settled into the saddle behind the rider.

Jotham directed a sharp gaze toward Lothar. "Leave and I'll hack you down as you try to get on that horse."

Lothar chuckled, moving casually toward the black bulk that was Jotham. "You had to do it, didn't you?"

"What's that?"

"Make me regret the day that I saved your life."

"It was the same day that you nearly took it!" countered Jotham. His broadsword swung outward and caught in the haft of Lothar's upraised axe. He wrenched it out, pulling loose a finger size chip of the white oak from which the handle was constructed. But before he could completely free his sword, Lothar brought his axe blade down and twisted, momentarily tangling the two weapons. He was about to tear the broadsword free from Jotham's grasp when a spasm shook his left arm, and his numbed fingers were sapped of the strength necessary to perform the maneuver.

"Get back to the tower!" Milos ordered his pale-skinned retainer. "Tell Sheesa that I'll be bringing Lothar along shortly."

Sedrah leveled a cold gaze at Milos. "See that you bring him back alive." She made no threats as to what she would do if Milos failed to do just that. That much was implicitly clear.

The retainer and Sedrah rode off on horseback into the dark and narrow streets beyond as several fighters gave futile chase on foot. Milos circled his own steed, wary of the warriors who descended to the street and who slowly closed around him. Inside of this circle, Lothar and Jotham stood ready- each looking for an opening or weakness that might prove fatal to the other.

Then suddenly as if some silent signal had been given, they sprang forward and struck, both of them giving great groans and crumpling under the blows they administered to each other. Milos spurred his stallion forward, reaching down for the bloody body of Lothar, and barely grabbed hold of him by the empty leather bandolier that crossed his chest and shoulders.

His first visit to Bathos, Milos had been but a young farm boy anxious to try his mettle in the great city of Bathos. He had brought with him a strength bred by the rigors of farm life. Now, on his second visit to Bathos he brought a strength hardened by years of fighting to keep what he built, and a taciturn willpower that was fueled by cold pragmatism. He was no longer the naïve farm boy that he once was.

With amazing strength he hauled Lothar up to the stallion's back, even as he spurred his steed through a gap in the ever tightening circle that was forming around them. A javelin went whirring by their heads, and another broke against the arch of Floodfast Street as they crossed from the even flags of the square and onto the sunken and uneven stones of the crooked road that was lined with jagged steps leading to high doorways.

Milos felt Lothar stir.

"Curse Jotham," muttered the raven-haired warrior-thief.

"I'm glad you're still among the living," said Milos. "I had my doubts for a moment."

A continuous wave of vertigo passed over Lothar and he hung onto the horse for dear life. He glanced down at his side and saw a nasty sword wound that slashed across his left ribs. "I'm going to need to be stitched together," he said, "but I think it was the loss of blood from my wounded forearm, more than anything, that did me in."

"Hang in there. I'm going to get you back to the tower and we'll see if we can't patched."

"Where's my axe?" asked Lothar.

"Probably still stuck in Jotham."

"I remember hitting him above the eye. Did I kill him?"

"I didn't stick around to find out. He went down though; same as you."

"I'm not complaining," said Lothar, "You're timing was fortuitous, but why are you in Bathos? I thought we agreed that we would meet at Vesuvus?"

Milos nodded. "The last message Sheesa sent me via carrier pigeon indicated that you were having some difficulties with your eyesight, and it was keeping you from leaving town, so I came the rest of the way with two of my men to see if you needed some help. I found the tower alright, but Sheesa said that you had gone down to the stables on Equine Street, and hadn't yet returned."

"So you came looking," finished Lothar.

"What are friends for?" said Milos.

"How many years has it been since we tried to loot the emperor's tomb, farmboy?"

"It's been at least ten," said Milos.

They turned on Belfry Road and as the horse galloped down the empty streets a swarm of bats took to the sky nearly blotting out the face of the moon.

"I'm a lucky man to have a friend such as you."

"You earned my friendship. You could have easily left me to die in the tombs all those years ago, but you treated me better than one thief could ever expect from another."

"Maybe so," conceded Lothar, "but I never expected you to save my life in return."

"And what did you do to earn that woman's friendship who fought with you on Dagon's Temple?"

"Sedrah tried to kill me once," said Lothar, "but when we met again I didn't attempt to return the favor."

"From the bodies heaped below the temple, I'd say that she has more than repaid her debt."

"That she has."

They turned again on Congers Street. Even at this hour the windows along the road were brightly lit, and red-glassed lanterns hung out in front of many of the buildings.

"A few more minutes," said Milos. "A few more minutes and we'll be back at Kolthos's tower."

* * * *

Sheesa felt an unnatural chill pass through her body and she woke from a restless sleep. She sat up on the wizard's divan and brushed back the foamy black locks of hair that had fallen across her exquisite features. She gasped, sucking in air through her satin lips as she once again felt a chill pass through her- as though someone had slipped an icicle through her body.

She stood and looked around her, thinking that maybe Vanose had come to care for his pigeons, or that perhaps Milos or Lothar had returned, but she found the room empty and devoid of life. Absently, she stood and crossed to the chess board, examining the pieces of the game that she and Lothar had started earlier. For all of his understanding of guild politics, and the political strategies of the dozens of rival unions, he was remarkably easy to beat on the chess board.

Sheesa dragged a guildsman across the board, and noticed that one of the dark squares had separated from the other squares carved from stone. She pried at the gap and pulled the entire square loose, discovering a golden key lying inside the board beneath the playing surface. The key was inscribed with the symbols of a language with which Sheesa wasn't familiar, yet she thought she knew what to do. She crossed the room and stepped into the massive fireplace, wading through the ash until she reached the back wall, where the vast array of key-shaped designs were scrolled into the stonework. Over her head, the vast chimney yawned, and there was a slight moan as a breeze filtered down.

Finally she found a design that matched her small key, and she pressed it flat into the impression. For a moment nothing happened, then a deep rumble shook the room as though a mild tremor had passed through the earth's crust. The back wall of the fireplace opened up revealing a small chamber beyond.

Sheesa retrieved a lantern and passed through the fireplace and into the room. Lifting the light high, she stood in shock at the profusion of gold coins, and gems that sparkled from teakwood coffers and pearl-handled totes.

Then, as she thought that she could be surprised no further, a hazy form materialized before her; a withered face, with cold soulless eyes, a skeletal body wrapped in the robes of a sorcerer, and long tapered fingers that shook with rage as his shrunken lips mouthed soundless curses. She knew that she was staring into the face of Kolthos' shade; the ghost that Vanose claimed to have seen roaming the halls of the tower.

Sheesa's first instinct was to be afraid, to flee from this foul, haunted den of blackest magic, but then she paused. If this spirit could harm her, why hadn't it already done so? She stood her ground, staring into the eyes of the incorporeal thing until it faded from sight, only a whisper of drifting mist remaining.

"This place brings back bad memories," said a soft female voice from somewhere behind her.

Startled, Sheesa turned, grabbing up a throwing knife from the sheath at her side. She found the blonde assassin standing at the mouth of the fireplace, her leather tunic spattered with gore, and clotted furrows across her arms and shoulders.

Sheesa's first thought was that Sedrah had slain her husband. "Where's Lothar!"

"I left him with Milos," said Sedrah. Behind her, Milos' pale man-at-arms silently nodded his assent. "The guilds caught up with him in Merchant's Square and he took a stand on top of Dagon's temple."

"Is he alright?"

"He'll live," answered Sedrah. "But he was wounded in the arm."

"And what were you doing there?" asked Sheesa suspiciously. "The last time I saw you, you warned Lothar that you would kill him next time you met."

"I had a change of heart," answered Sedrah slowly. "I realized that a good friend is more valuable than a guild membership could ever be. Can you forgive me? I was blind."

Now Milos' pale-skinned retainer spoke. "She fought alongside of your husband. By all rights both of them should have been slain."

Sheesa sheathed her dagger, and heedless of the clotted gore that speckled Sedrah's clothing, she rushed to her and they embraced.

When they separated, Sheesa spoke. "I want to show you something that I found in a secret room beyond the fireplace."

When Sedrah had seen the treasure trove that lay beyond she breathed in awe. "Kolthos' treasure room! There's enough there to buy us all freedom from the guilds- or there would have been. Lothar and I killed so many that there isn't enough treasure in the Emperor's vaults to buy us immunity from their wrath."

Lothar limped into the room with Milos supporting him. "Then I suggest we pack up whatever it is that you've found, and get out of Bathos. We've got two horses, and a cart, and enough provisions to last us until we reach Vesuvus."

Milos turned to Sedrah. "What of you? Will you be coming with us? I've got a parcel of land and a small keep three days travel from Vesuvus. You're welcome to stay with us."

Sedrah nodded. "I've worn out my welcome in Bathos, you can count me in."

As the loaded cart left the dark mouth of the tower's portal carrying five passengers to the east gate of Bathos, a pale shade appeared on the balcony far above and shook a futile fist at the group that was escaping with his earthly treasures- but the mystical powers Kolthos once possessed had faded with death, and now he was left only with his own hollow hate to keep him chained to Bathos, the City of Corruption.

Books from Pulpwork Press Authors:

Joel Jenkins

Dire Planet Series:
Dire Planet
Exiles of the Dire Planet
Into the Dire Planet
Strange Gods of the Dire Planet
Lost Tribes of the Dire Planet

Tales from the City of Bathos Series:
Escape from Devil's Head
Through the Groaning Earth

The Gantlet Brother Series:
The Nuclear Suitcase
The Gantlet Brothers Greatest Hits
The Gantlet Brothers: Sold Out

Damage Incorporated Series:
The Sea Witch
The Sun Stealer

Denbrook Supernatural:
Devil Take the Hindmost

Children's Books:
The Pirates of Mirror Land

Arthurian Fantasy:
Island of Lost Souls

Collections:
Weird Worlds of Joel Jenkins
Weird Worlds of Joel Jenkins 2

Biography:
One Foot in My Grave

The Greattrix Chronicles:
Skull Crusher

Lone Crow:
The Coming of Crow

Barclay Salvage:
Off Season
One for the Dark and Shadowed Sky

Derrick Ferguson
Dillon Series:
Dillon and the Golden Bell
Four Bullets for Dillon
Dillon and the Pirates of Xonira
Dillon and the Voice of Odin
Young Dillon in the Halls of Shamballah
The Vril Agenda (with Josh Reynolds)

Joshua Reynolds
Dracula Lives!
The Vril Agenda (with Derrick Ferguson)

Russell Anderson, Jr
How the West was Weird
How the West was Weird 2
How the West was Weird 3
How the West was Weird: Campfire Tales
Myth World

Coming in 2015
The Specialists (Sly Gantlet & Dillon) by Joel Jenkins & Derrick Ferguson

For more information on these and other titles or for online ordering visit us at PulpWork.Com or find our titles at Amazon, and BarnesandNoble.com

For a free ebook or Kindle book visit the author's website at JoelJenkins.net

www.ingramcontent.com/pod-product-compliance
Lightning Source LLC
Chambersburg PA
CBHW070337260626
47160CB00003B/1072

* 9 7 8 0 6 1 5 4 9 7 9 4 5 *